ActivAmerica

ActivAmerica

BY MEAGAN CASS

2017 WINNER, KATHERINE ANNE PORTER PRIZE IN SHORT FICTION

University of North Texas Press
Denton, Texas

10 9 8 7 6 5 4 3 2 1

Permissions:
University of North Texas Press
1155 Union Circle #311336
Denton, Texas 76203-5017

∞The paper used in this book meets the minimum requirements of the American National Standard for Permanence of Paper for Printed Library Materials, z39.48.1984. Binding materials have been chosen for durability.

Library of Congress Cataloging-in-Publication Data

Names: Cass, Meagan, author.
Title: ActivAmerica / by Meagan Cass.
Other titles: Katherine Anne Porter Prize in Short Fiction series ; no. 16.
Description: First edition. | Denton, Texas : University of North Texas Press, [2017] | Series: Number 16 in the Katherine Anne Porter Prize in Short Fiction series | "2017 Winner, Katherine Anne Porter Prize in Short Fiction."
Identifiers: LCCN 2017032671| ISBN 9781574416947 (pbk. : alk. paper) | ISBN 9781574417050 (ebook)
Subjects: LCSH: Sports—United States—Fiction. | Sports for girls—United States—Fiction. | Sports for girls—Social aspects—United States—Fiction.
Classification: LCC PS3603.A867845 A6 2017 | DDC 813/.6—dc23
LC record available at https://lccn.loc.gov/2017032671

Cover and text design by Rose Design

ActivAmerica is Number 16 in the Katherine Anne Porter Prize in Short Fiction Series.

This is a work of fiction. Any resemblance to actual events or establishments or to persons living or dead is unintentional.

The electronic edition of this book was made possible by the support of the Vick Family Foundation.

For Judy, Alan, Betsy, and Isaac Cass

Contents

Acknowledgments   ix

The All-Mutant Soccer Team   1

ActivAmerica   14

Portrait of My Father as a Foosball Man, 1972–2012   29

America's Funniest Home Videos Episode 25,857:
   Helicopter Dad   32

Interview with the Ghost of Jaws' First Victim   38

Backyard Dreams   40

The Parents' Guide to UltraSport Children   48

Ping-Pong, 12 Loring Place   57

The Hawthorne Dynasty   62

Grayhound   73

Jews in Sports   76

Autumn Begins in Hawthorne, New York   92

Calling All Soloflex Men   99

Girlhunt, Spring 1999   112

The Body in Space   116

Egg Toss, August 1989   130

Night Games   132

How Mary Lou Retton Took Over Our Lives
   in the Summer of 1994   149

Love Song for Ellipticals After Divorce   168

Reverse Trampoline Fail   171

Tampax Pearl Active Soccer Girl   176

Notes   181

Acknowledgments

Thanks to Jacob Brower, Roxane Gay, Mike Young, Tawnysha Greene, Jac Jemc, Lania Knight, Tara Laskowski, Scott Peterson, Kate Lorenz, Ander Monson, Sean Bernard, and Emily Schultz, for first publishing some of these. Thanks also to the folks at Magic Helicopter Press.

Thank you to managing editor Karen DeVinney, who took such care with my work, to series editor Andrew Briseño, to marketing manager Bess Whitby, to judge Claire Vaye Watkins, and to the entire staff at University of North Texas Press.

Throughout the writing of these stories, Alan Cass and Judy Cass provided me with love, care, financial support, and a blue desk every time I came to New York. Betsy Cass and Isaac Cass are the kindest siblings I could ask for. Trish Camia-Cass and Jason McArthur, thank you for welcoming me into your warm homes and lives. Thanks to the Turners, and to my Cass aunts, uncles, and cousins. Shasta Grant, Anne Rasmussen, John Copenhaver, Lindsay Merbaum, Amy Sayre Baptista, and Anthony Abboreno gave me insightful and encouraging comments on drafts. My friends kept me healthy, loved, and eating good food through several interstate moves. Thanks especially to Connor Chauveaux, Mark Jenkins, Mike Walonen, Tina Mitchell, and Forrest Roth, to Adam Clay, Tessa Mellas, T.A. Noonan, Emily Capettini, Shanon Pepita O'Brien, Andrea Scarpino, and the Sundress Crew. Thank you Holly Kent for the necessary talks, thrifting, escapades, and deep care since I came to the prairie. Thank you Erin Elizabeth Smith, my poet twin, for your love, jokes, brilliance, and middle-of-the-night talks all these sixteen years.

I am grateful for my mentors at the University of Louisiana Lafayette, Rikki Ducornet, Kate Bernheimer, and Yung-Hsing Wu.

Josh Henkin and Brian Morton provided invaluable guidance and support at Sarah Lawrence College. Thanks also to my supportive colleagues at the University of Illinois Springfield, and to the UIS College of Liberal Arts and Sciences. Thanks to my students.

These stories first appeared, in slightly different form, in the following: "Pearl Active Tampax Soccer Girl" in *Parcel*, "The Parents' Guide to Ultrasport Children" in *Washington Square Review*, "ActivAmerica" in *Bluestem*, "The All-Mutant Soccer Team," in *Joyland Magazine*, "American's Home Video's Episode 25,857: Helicopter Dad" in *DIAGRAM*, "Interview with the Ghost of Jaws' First Victim" in *Mojo*, "Autumn Begins in Hawthorne, New York," in *Puerto del Sol*, "Portrait of My Father as Foosball Man, 1975–2012" in *Corium*, "Grayhound" in *NOÖ Journal*, "The Hawthorne Dynasty" in *PANK*, "Artesian Grand Bahama Hot Tub, Winter 2005" in *Ardor*, "Olympic Visitation: How Mary Lou Retton Took Over Our Lives in the Summer of 1994" in *Aethlon: The Journal of Sport Literature*, "Ping-Pong, 12 Loring Place" in *Hobart Web*, "Love Song For Ellipticals After Divorce" in *Stymie: a Journal of Sport and Literature: The Feminine Perspective Issue*, "Jews in Sports" in *Grist: A Journal for Writers*, "Egg Toss, August 1989" in *SmokeLong Quarterly*, "Calling All Soloflex Men" in *The Pinch*, "Girlhunt, Spring 1999" in *Devil's Lake*, "The Night Game" in *Prism Review*, "The Body in Space," in *ekleksographia*. "Calling All Soloflex Men," "Grayhound," "Egg Toss, August 1989," "Ping-Pong, 12 Loring Place," "Backyard Dreams," and "Portrait of My father as a Foosball Man" also appeared in my chapbook *Range of Motion* (Magic Helicopter Press).

The All-Mutant Soccer Team

The kids we play from downstate like to say it's inbreeding, the reason our skin is neon green, our teeth blue, our hands like flippers growing from the sides of our bodies, no arms to speak of.

"Have fun with your sisters tonight!" they'll shout after a game in Chappaqua or Bedford, watching us pile onto our team bus.

No one will play us at home. Who can blame them? Our field is next to the lake everyone in the tri-state area has heard about by now, the reason for all the birth defects and mutations and cancers like the kind that killed my mother last winter. Everyone knows about the accidental chemical relocation, the reason the water smelled vaguely of burnt plastic and car air freshener and stopped freezing in winter.

As compensation, the corporation pays half our medical bills. They say it's too expensive to clean up the lake, so they put a barbed wire fence around the shoreline, hung all these signs about liability and risk, how no one will pay if you go beyond this point. The surface glows green all day and all night. When an errant soccer ball lands on the surface, it sizzles before it sinks, like raw chicken thrown into a hot pan.

• • •

Back when my father and mother moved to Dover, the lake wasn't so bad. I've seen the pictures, my mother pregnant with me on the muddy beach, her striped bathing suit straining around her stomach, my father beside her in an ill-fitting Speed-o, behind them the water a crisp, travel brochure blue.

My father had just gotten his job as the district art teacher. They'd moved from Queens, where the rents were too high anyway, bought a dilapidated Victorian right on the lake, peeling paint and a turret with an oval shaped window. It looks like a kid's drawing of a haunted house, which my mother loved.

She worked as a freelance graphic designer, had her own studio on the edge of the property, a small barn that still smells like hay and cows. She was always trying to get me to draw in there while she sketched a new logo for a downstate ballet school or spa.

"Enough with the video games. Enough with the screens. Let's see what's in your head," she'd say and open a thick sketchbook.

At the end her eyes were huge and her skin was pale green and her arms were like insect arms and my head was far away. I drew aliens in space ships and aliens on distant planets. While my father drank whiskey and painted abstract shapes in the basement, I drew the Milky Way and aliens on Mars, laser beams streaking from their fingers. I drew like I was still eight years old, in love with Star Trek and Star Wars.

"Interesting concepts," my father said. "I like how you captured the surface of Mars."

He hung the drawings in the basement where my mother could no longer go. That spring, after she died, he came up with the idea for the soccer team.

"We both need to get healthy," he said, a drill book from Wal-Mart in his shaking hands. "Nothing wrong with your legs. No reason you can't excel. My great grandfather played back in Italy, you know. It's in the blood."

He was sober for the first time in weeks, his eyes rimmed red. "We'll call it 'the Dover Galaxy,' like that team from Los Angeles. Dark blue and silver uniforms. You can draw the logo. Sounds cool, right?"

"Cool!" I said, lilting my voice up like a younger, happier kid.

• • •

We're an all-mutant team, the normal kids long immersed in football and basketball. Guys came out of the woodwork, guys whose parents home schooled them because of the bullying and guys who'd been expelled years ago for fighting back too hard. They walked up to my father the first day of practice, new Wal-Mart soccer balls at their feet, their cleats the same neon green as our skin, their faces fixed in a hard expression like, "Try to fuck with me. Try it."

"Good to see you're ready to work," my father told them.

They had no skill—none of us did—but they played with an explosive rage, running full throttle at loose balls in the August heat, using their hips to push you out of the way, scratching at your side with their fin-hands, which was more annoying than painful, like getting sawed with a butter knife. When they headed the ball, they'd torque their whole bodies and grunt like they'd been stabbed in the gut.

Jackson, a guy expelled for bringing his grandfather's antique mace to school in the second grade, was my favorite. He'd show up to practice with an iPod and speakers, play death metal while we ran the ten laps my father required as a warm-up. I'd never heard music like this, bands with names like Cannibal Corpse or Skeleton Witch or GWAR, the singers growling through nettled hurricanes of sound. He sent me MP3s, which I played in my room with the door closed, the volume on my laptop turned as loud as I dared.

"I just wish I could understand them," my father would say, opening the door, squinting in a way I'd learned to hate. "That's what makes me nervous."

"You're not supposed to understand them. That's the point," I said and shut the door on him.

After practice, he'd take the whole team to the Pizza Hut in Carmel, put it on a credit card. We'd chow down, not caring how people stared at us while we ate, a loud process that involves leaning our heads close to the pizza and angling the slice toward our mouths, exposing our blue teeth.

It felt like we were a team in an old movie. We were the rag tag misfits who would sock it to the nasty, beautiful kids from the wealthy town, to their stern, Russian-sounding coach. Our coach was the crotchety alcoholic who could get competitive but really only wanted us to have fun, to believe in ourselves.

On Sunday nights, the one night we didn't have practice, my father would drink his whiskey and we'd flip through the manual, studying how the blond, tan boys in the pictures trapped the ball with the insides of their feet on pristine green fields, used their heads to arc the ball into a blue sky.

Just before dark, my father would lead me outside to try some new move out. "Look at us, a couple of aficionados," he would say, losing his balance now and then, the lake green and stinking behind us.

And for a whole hour we could forget that my mother was gone, that she wasn't in her barn working the way she usually did after dinner, that she wouldn't call us both to the television soon to watch something on the travel channel, that she wasn't planning our next trip.

• • •

Back before she got sick, my mother and I loved to play "Where will you live?" We'd sit at the kitchen table, a yellowed atlas spread out before us. "It could be any city," she'd say, the fifty states flying through her hands, her eyes closed. Wherever her index finger landed, that was where I'd live.

We'd imagine my life in Nashville, New Iberia, Scranton, Yellowstone, Chicago. We'd go online and look up the best restaurants, the weird foods, the local attractions, the odd historical museums.

I loved Denver the most. We'd been once on a cross-country trip, when I was eight, and I remembered the snow-capped mountains, the silver skyline, a restaurant where they served rattlesnake. I'd live in what my mother called a loft space, a whole wall made of glass looking out on the downtown. Maybe I'd design video games. She'd said I could go to school for that.

"You've got to make different kinds of games though," she'd told me. "I'm sick of all the violence, all the women with their boobs out getting murdered. Promise me that?"

I'd blush and promise and hope I'd live long enough to do something like that. No one knows what our life span will be. We go for cancer screenings three times a year, take iron pills, get the occasional blood transfusion. Sepia toned pamphlets tell us to "make the most of every day," and "be the healthiest you." Since we turned nine, we've been given a shifting cocktail of anti-depressants to prevent mass mutant suicide, which I guess is a thing where other accidental chemical relocations have occurred.

"Travel produces endorphins," my mother would say, convincing my father to put another set of hotel reservations on a credit card.

She loved to take trips, even if it was just down to Cold Spring to try a new restaurant. We were poor but we always had nice suitcases from the Macy's in the Chappaqua Mall, gold-zippered Samsonites shaped like bullets that could be dropped from 1,000 feet and suffer no damage, they'd done tests.

If we were going away—to Grandma's apartment in Queens, to a ten-dollar-a-night camp ground in the Catskills, cross-country that one time after Grandma died and we got some extra money—she'd always want to leave before sunrise. She'd shake me and my father awake in the dark and we'd bitch how it was inhumane to be in the world so early.

"Fuck you, mom," I might shout, and then she'd pull me out of bed, hard, her nails digging into my skin.

Once we got in the car, though, everything in me would relax. We were leaving Dover, leaving our house and our routines and everything that had gone wrong with us. She would drive faster than my father ever did, her windows cracked open in summer and winter, the air rushing around us, washing the sleep from our skin.

And it is this, this feeling of motion, of travel that we love about soccer, through September and into October, through all the ass kickings, through the taunts that we are sister-fuckers and horror movie extras and sewage rats. We love boarding our team bus, a rusted school bus my father fixed up and helped me paint to look like deep space, the Milky Way sprawled across the hood, the Millennium Falcon flying across the side. We love getting on the highway, our shit town, the lake that warped us, our everyday lives receding behind us, the hot air blowing through our windows, our water bottles still cool in our duffle bags.

The games themselves, we could skip. The boys downstate have been trained at elite camps since they were six, can move the ball faster than we can think. Their skin is clear, their teeth white, their arms normal. They play in climate-controlled domes designed to protect their bodies from pollutants. We step onto the fancy turf, beneath the fluorescent lights, and our bodies buzz with anger and fear. Waiting for the start, we tie and untie our cleats. We give each other wedgies. We crack awful jokes about the other team, how they look like a robot army, like a bunch of metrosexuals with their jerseys perfectly tucked in and their hair salon cut.

We've all had "the talk" with our parents by now, a stilted conversation on a couch with the TV turned off, about individuality and how it is good to be unique, how the world is lucky to have us, how grateful they are to have a mutant child, how they wouldn't trade us for normal looking boys. We never felt so loved and so alien, so grateful and embarrassed and full of hate.

We are relieved when the games are over, when we get to go to the Burger-hop in Scarsdale or Yorktown or Ardsley. It's always fancier than our Burger-hop, with fifties era records on the walls and Elvis posters and waitresses in poodle skirts and no signs in the bathroom saying there is a hidden video camera and that drug users will be prosecuted.

We always order more than we can eat. We get back on the bus full and tired, wishing we could keep going and never look back. We talk about the future. Jackson wants to run a medieval weaponry shop in Texas, or start a band. Two of the homeschoolers want to move to Hawaii and learn how to surf.

"You all pick up your game, we'll check out travel tournaments for this summer," my father promises. "They have ones by the beach and ones by the mountains."

• • •

And in the movies about kids' sports teams, this is when we get better. This is when we swallow our shame, our anger, our lethargy, our hate and pick up real skills. This is when we get a ringer—a Mexican kid, or a normal girl with a soft spot for mutants—then face off against the biggest shitheads in the league for the championship.

This is when we win and sneer in their faces. This is when the shithead Chappaqua coach breaks his clipboard over one knee and calls his own son, the star striker, an idiot. Or this is when we lose but it's the joy of playing that sustains us. This is when we shrug our shoulders and laugh and make vows about next season as we dump coolers of Gatorade over each other's heads.

What happens instead is that one by one, the other teams cancel on us. Ardsley says they have no time in their schedule. Bedford says they have a competitive tournament coming up and can only play teams who've been in the league a minimum three years. Apparently it's in the rules that they can do this. Teams with no United States Youth Soccer Federation ranking can be skipped at will.

Getting the ranking involves paying federation officials to come to your town to observe your practices, then paying the $10,000 ranking fee. In other words, we could never afford it.

On the days our games are cancelled, my father has us practice instead. We show up in the November heat—it won't cool until December, when it will drop into the negatives overnight—and runs us through drills that get increasingly harsh.

"We've got to stay ready," he says ominously, and assigns us a series of sprints instead of our usual laps, duck walks designed to rip the muscles in our legs so stronger ones can grow, heading drills that go on forever, ringing our skulls.

"Our chance will come. We don't need any ranking," my father says, as we struggle across our field, which is all dust and faded lines, drier than the surface of Mars.

"I think I need a break from soccer," I tell him one night.

"You need to keep playing for your mood," he says. "The experts agree. It's as good as taking Zoloft."

He is quoting the Wal-Mart manual, which also says that sports make you shoot higher in life, that while we can't all be Pelé, we can't all be Diego Maradona, we can experience our own small measure of glory. We can make our soccer dreams come true in our own small way.

"My mood is fine," I say and disappear into my monstrous new music.

The day before Halloween, Chappaqua calls: their field is no longer equipped to deal with our special needs. They do not specify what our special needs are.

My father makes a series of phone calls, sets up a last-minute scrimmage against LaGrange. They are from a shit town up north like us, but they've been doing this longer, will nonetheless kick our asses.

"Can't we just have a weekend off?" I ask. We are in the kitchen, a Rice-a-Roni dinner on the stove. "I want to draw, play some videogames. I have a life besides soccer."

"If that's what you want, be my guest," my father says. "I'll tell your teammates you had other plans."

And I do think of Jackson, still running his heart out even when we're down 7–0 against Bronxville, green sweat pouring down his face. "Fine," I say, my face turning the color of bread mold, I can feel it.

And we get our asses kicked, our worse loss yet. The classy teams hold off at 9–0, pass to each other instead of scoring, but LaGrange pushes into the double digits. Jackson and I get red cards for instigating a fight, for calling the LaGrange boys red neck sheep fuckers and for trying to claw at their eyes with our fin-hands.

"I don't know who that was out on the field today," my father says to me on the bus, barely looking at me. "Next time, just stay home."

"Maybe I will," I say, so tired and drained I can barely hold my head up.

Thanksgiving weekend and Edgemont cancels the night before. This is our furthest away game, two hours downstate. They have safety concerns. They want to wait until more studies have been done. They are looking out for our well-being as well as their own. They don't want anyone to get hurt. In the kitchen, I can hear the coach's sympathetic voice as my father nods his head, the phone loose in his hand.

"Studies my ass. They're not contagious," he says at last. "We're showing up Saturday. You better be there or you'll have my lawyer to deal with."

We both know, and the Edgemont coach knows, that no one in Dover could afford a lawyer. Still, my father tells everyone to plan to play, to be at the middle school parking lot at 6 a.m. the next morning.

"No one's going to be there," I tell him. "They won't play us."

My father sighs heavily. He's standing at the counter, his coach's bag packed with First Aid supplies and energy bars and extra waters and a flask of whiskey, his polo sagging on his thin shoulders

"We'll deal with that possibility as it occurs," he says. "I'm trying to teach you boys to follow through. I'm trying to teach you, you don't just go home and sit in your room when things get difficult. There's a whole world out there."

"Easy for you to say." I am tired of playing the teachable and coachable open-hearted son. I want to stop taking all the pills they give us. I want to feel the full bitterness and rage and sadness of everything in my head.

"Right. That's a productive response. I'm going for a drive," my father says.

As soon as he shuts the door, the house fills up with a murky dread and I wish he would come back. It is haunted in here, my mother at the kitchen table with her atlas, as if the whole thing is ours to traverse, my mother fighting with my father about whose turn it is to cook, my mother bald and with huge, alien eyes, drinking my father's whiskey alone at the counter. The sun is setting and the shadows are leaking from every doorway, every window. I head out into the back yard, juggle a ball up onto my thighs the way my father showed me.

• • •

No one talks the whole way to Edgemont, even the home school kids who usually can't shut up. We're sleepy and demoralized, our arms crossed over our space-themed jerseys, our heads tucked into our chests. My father takes the curves too fast, our bodies swaying back and forth through the Hudson Valley hills.

When we pull up to the dome, we know immediately something's wrong. There are no cars in the lot and the lights inside are off.

"Hello? Hello?" my father says, banging on the door.

We stare through the bus windows. The light is thick and warm, shining on the dome, heating us up. We could fall back into a deep, dark sleep and never wake up. We could melt into the rubbery seats.

"Mother fucker," Jackson says at last, and goes to join my father. We watch the two of them pull up the granite rocks that line the walkway, slam them through the glass door. Jackson reaches through the jagged hole and pulls the lock.

"What are you waiting for? Get your stuff," my father shouts at us.

We walk uncertainly toward him, our bags heavy on our shoulders. Inside, the lights are off and the turf field is a dark, quiet stage, a flat lake. There is only the hum of the vending machines and the climate control system. A janitor approaches, a tired looking man around my father's age, his shoulders hunched, a bandage around his head. His face is thin and pale green like my mother's once was.

"Whoah, whoah, whoah," he says, looking from the door to my father, to us. "What happened to that door? Who are you people?"

"We're looking for the Edgemont Hotspurs. We have an appointment," my father says, like the Edgemont Hotspurs are a doctor who's refused to treat us.

"Oh, they're out of town this weekend," the janitor says, looking down at his boots. "Some tournament in Connecticut."

"Must have been a miscommunication," my father says. "We have an appointment."

Jackson pushes past him, heads out onto the field to kick around. The other kids follow. I stand behind my father, my feet welded to the floor.

"I have it right here," my father says. He reaches into his pocket for the creased schedule.

And all at once I can't take it, how his hand will shake, how the schedule has every game time in bold, in Garamond font, my mother's favorite, and our team logo at the top, a tiny solar system he had me draw back in August. I want to kick him in the side, hard, to shout in a guttural voice that I'll never be happy and healthy the way he wants, that I'll never be healed, that I'll always be weird and shattered and poisoned.

"Dad, just give it up already," is what I say, and stalk back to the bus.

In his duffle bag, the flask is tucked behind the First Aid kit. The whiskey goes down harsh and toxic. When my father emerges from the dome, his bald head bent, the other boys with him, I slide it back into the bag.

"Can we go to the Burger-hop?" one of the home schoolers asks.

"We're going home," my father says, so quietly I can barely hear him. "I'm sorry about this, boys. Maybe it is time for a break. You all have done a great job this season."

I put on my headphones, turn up Cannibal Corpse, the music filling my whole body, the alien ogre monster growling through my bones. Back in Dover, my father doesn't ask me about the missing whiskey, or why I'm stumbling when I get off the bus.

"Go take a rest," he tells me, and lets me pass out for the rest of the day.

That night, after he goes to sleep, Jackson comes over. We sneak more whiskey and drink too fast out on the lawn, steal my father's hedge trimmers, cut a hole in the barbed wire surrounding the lake and walk down to the beach. The toxic sand is still warm from the day's heat, the water shrouded in a thick green fog.

"Paradise," Jackson says and I laugh.

On other nights, we will disappear into that fog. We will forget our fathers and our mothers and our coaches and our teachers and anyone who has ever cared about us. We will play with our own deaths, terrified for weeks after, waiting for the pain in our guts, for the new dizziness that means cancer. While we wait, we will write our own ugly, indecipherable songs.

Tonight, though, we are more exhausted than anything else. We lie on our backs, our bodies thrumming with alcohol, the stars vague blurs. A plane flies over us, two red dots, and I imagine all the beautiful suitcases packed into the cargo hold, imagine myself stowed inside one them, my eyes closed against the cold. Eventually, the lid opens. The owner of the suitcase screams and I step out into a brand new world.

ActivAmerica

The day they announced the new health plan at Village Mart, I called up my ex-husband, Peter, and told him to send the divorce papers, I was ready for that last formality, ready to start our lives apart.

"That's right, honey. You tell him," my best friend Connie said.

She works in the Home Goods section and I work in Fabrics & Crafts. We were in the break room, our new ActivAmerica running shoes in our hands, white faux leather with big, bubbly soles. "Old lady sneakers," my kids would call them. I didn't care how they looked if they meant my own health insurance.

"Hold on a sec. You know you have to exercise for that plan, right Sheila?" Peter said.

"Please. I think I can handle a little running."

It's true I've never been in shape. My weakness is Little Debbie Oatmeal Crème pies, which they sell a hundred for three dollars at Village Mart. It's what my father gave us as kids when our mother went for her cancer treatments, the first of us to get sick.

No one's little after eating a hundred of those things.

And I've never gone in for exercise. Who has the time or patience for that crap? When the kids hit high school, Peter had wanted us to join this fancy gym in Chappaqua. "We'll have more energy for each other, for our other interests," he'd say.

"You cut down on the Scotch, help out more around here, maybe I'll consider it," I'd snap, then stalk up to my craft room, browse patterns I was too exhausted and too terrified to try.

Still, I could move-it when I needed to. At Village Mart, I'm on my feet all day helping people pick the best fabric for a tablecloth, a wedding dress, bedroom curtains. It's quite busy. The economy's shit, so everyone's trying to cut back, learning the skills their grandmothers knew. I don't mind the work. I've sewn my own dresses for years, can look at a fabric and know how it will cling and move around the body, how it will feel on bare skin, how it will billow in a Hudson breeze.

"I've got this," I told Peter on the phone.

"Why don't we give it some time? Just to make sure you're safe. Let's give it three months. I'm glad you'll be taking better care of yourself."

In the background I could hear a folk rock band we saw at Jones Beach back before the kids. I dug my fingers into the fat of my thigh, tried not to remember his hand draped over my shoulders, the taste of fried dough and light beer, our bad habits still light on our bones.

"Fine. Three months. I hope you're having a good night," I said and hung up.

• • •

The next day, Village Mart was all a commotion. They'd bulldozed the sidewalks around the shopping center to put in a bright blue track, set up folding tables in front of the store with all the official paperwork.

At lunch, Connie and I stood in line, the noon sun burning the tops of our heads. It was hotter than any September we could remember, the hills a charred, brown color. "Climate intensification," my kids' teachers' had called it, like it was something good, something to get psyched up for rather than something to be afraid of.

"Welcome to ActivAmerica Health, where we put fitness first," the plan representative told us. He wore thin red jogging shorts and a matching polo. A badge clipped to his pocket said *Scott Watkins, Corporate Wellness Specialist and Tri-athlete.* "What questions can I answer for you ladies?"

We'd heard all the details on the six o'clock news. A bunch of corporate lobbyists and politicians had gotten together. We'd get coverage if we "demonstrated our commitment to health and fitness" through daily runs around the track. We could go as slow as we needed, but it had to be a run, not a walk. It had to be at least one mile, verified by an official ActivAmerica monitor on an official ActivAmerica track.

"We're sure there are thousands of Americans eager to make a change," our state representative had said in a press conference on the White House lawn. "All you have to do is decide to be healthy, then stick with it. That's the key."

So far, Village Mart was the only corporation to sign on. McDonalds and Dominos were in talks. A red banner strung across our store read, "Village Mart: First in Building a More Active America."

"You nervous at all?" Connie asked me as we walked to our cars that night, thick binders of paperwork we should have read more closely tucked under our arms. "You know, running in this heat? Running period? Every day?"

"We'll keep each other going," I said. "We'll drink lots of water like they say in the pamphlet. It's only a mile."

• • •

Twenty years ago, after my mother died and around when my father got sick, I worked at a specialty fabric store called Maxime's

Creations, where healthcare was included. "We want to reward our workers with experience and talent," said Maxime, a batty old woman in too much velour, impressed by my portfolio of play costumes and dresses from high school, bold yellows and oranges with fierce collars and wide belts.

I was nineteen, hadn't gone off to college like my friends. I figured the gig and some light costume work on the side would be enough, and I wanted to take care of my dad. Maybe, one day, I'd try costume design at one of the CUNYs.

Then I met Peter, with his steady high school English job, and people stopped asking me what I'd do with my life. You could say I stopped asking too. I was busy, part-time at the store, then at Village Mart when Maxime's closed, taking care of the kids in the afternoons and my father too. I missed doing my own sewing projects, a mosquito itch in the chest, but I was so tired at the end of the day I could barely think.

I can see now that I could have looked out more for myself. I tell my daughters, "Make your own way. Don't depend on anyone else."

A year ago, our youngest gone off to college, Peter announces he's met someone at the high school, a music teacher.

"She just puts me in motion. I can't explain," he said, his eyes all bright. He was wearing a work shirt I didn't recognize, this beautiful turquoise and white check pattern, 100% cotton. "We both know this isn't working. It'll be better for both of us."

"Fuck you," I told him, stunned. Everything had been, if not fine, settled into a pattern I thought would hold us into old age.

"I won't abandon you," he promised.

And we stayed married on paper until I found better work. We've had every kind of cancer in my family. Once, they did an investigation of the lake we all swam in, of the plastics company down the street from us. There was a settlement with which we bought a cabin up in the Adirondacks, which we then sold to cover my older sister's medical bills.

"You'll find something soon, I'm sure," Peter said.

He moved to Pelham, closer to the city, closer to his new woman, and I got rid of half my closet, bought new fabrics, everything heavier and in shades of dark brown and deep purple. I wanted to feel like a new person too. I found patterns with more structure, spent my late nights sewing and searching jobs on the Internet. None of it was anything I'd done—manager of a moving company, manager of a grocery store—but I was motivated, organized, basically friendly. It was like Peter said, something would bite.

I was doing okay, a whole week without crying, three oatmeal cream pies a night, when he came back home.

"Can we talk for awhile?" he asked, and then he fell apart on our couch.

The music teacher had left him. He was sorry about our marriage, he wished things were different, he missed me. He wasn't sure what he wanted.

It happened this way every three, four months. He'd try to date someone, it wouldn't work out, and then he'd come home lonely, regretful, confused, his hands covered in the rash he always gets when he's anxious, tiny red bumps all over his palms. We'd kill a bottle of Scotch, get sentimental. We'd remember the good times: the winter we fell in love, drove into Manhattan every weekend for an art film; the winter we dumped the kids at his parents' house, escaped to New Orleans, a whole week of powdered sugar and bourbon and used book stores.

I'd tell him funny stories about Village Mart, about the woman who'd demanded imported velvet for her daughter's figure skating dress, the family of five who wanted leather for matching motorcycle vests. He'd laugh, his shoulders brushing against mine.

Eventually we'd pass out, part of me wanting to stab him in the guts, part of me hoping he'd love me again. In the morning, after he left, I'd cut up whatever garment I'd been wearing when he came over. I'd slug through the workweek, snapping at customers and cursing him under my breath, a woman full of rage and cheap cream, a woman made of the stiffest tulle.

● ● ●

The day they finished the official ActivAmerica track they had an elaborate ribbon-cutting ceremony.

"Good luck!" Peter texted me that morning.

"Asshat," I thought, and turned off my phone.

They called us outside and lined us up at the start, everyone in the official polyester blend athletic shorts, oversize ActivAmerica T-shirts, and those cheesy sneakers. Connie and I, we'd tried to maintain certain fashionable touches: I wore silver bangles and a leopard print bandana and she wore her favorite earrings, black Lucite clip-ons that looked like insects crawling up her ears.

"Accessories are not recommended," Scott Watkins, *Corporate Wellness Specialist and Tri-athlete*, told us. "You want your body free of encumbrances."

"Sweetie, I haven't been free of encumbrances since I was eighteen," Connie told him.

He smiled hard at us, his teeth white and straight, and walked away.

At the front of the store, executives and politicians stepped up to a plywood podium, gave more speeches about accountability, about building a culture of wellness, about resisting temptation, saying no to pizza and donuts and sloth.

"I feel like we're in gym class," Connie said, staring down at her thin, veined legs. "Only then you'd get water breaks."

My T-shirt stuck to my back and the waist of my shorts felt tight. The news cameras flashed around us. "Let's just get this over with," I said, trying to forget my own thick, pale legs.

At last they turned the microphone over to the official ActivAmerica monitor. "Hello, ladies and gentleman! How you all doing today?"

His Village Mart polo strained around his gut and he wore a thick gold chain around his neck, his skin a leathery tan. He reminded me of my father if he'd lived this long, a man who biked fifteen miles a day but loved his bacon cheeseburger and fries on a Friday night.

"No slacking," he told us. "I wouldn't allow it with my track team back when, and I won't allow it here. Okay, let's get healthy."

He blew his whistle and we were off, the sun sinking behind the Village Mart buildings, the sky a toxic green-yellow-orange, the air pressing on our skin like Vermont flannel.

The former high school athletes from Sporting Goods, the twenty-something girls from Women's Clothes, and the middle-aged men who managed us raced ahead. We kept pace with the pregnant cashiers and the geeks from electronics. Only the greeters were slower, seniors who could barely walk, sweat dripping down their lined faces.

"It's not right, making the grandmas and grandpas do this," Connie whispered to me and then slowed to a walk.

"Keep your feet in running mode, Ms. Huff," the monitor said over his megaphone.

We slipped into the slowest jog we could muster, a kind of stilted moonwalk. I tried not to think how we must look on the cameras, a fat middle-aged lady and a thin, older lady in ill-fitting shorts, sweat stains blooming all over our shirts.

The former athletes finished fast. We gasped past them as they gave interviews about how much they liked the new plan, how it would benefit them and their young families, how they could feel that runner's high already, their minds and bodies stronger and happier and more alive.

The managers stood bent, large stomachs heaving, hands on their knees, their pale faces red. The greeters were shuffled off to the side, away from the cameras, given thick packets with instructions in proper running form, nutrition, training exercises to do at home.

"You get three free days a year," Scott Watkins reminded them. "Think of this as a free day. A practice day."

"They need about 365 of those free days," Connie said when we were done, pulling her thinning hair up into a tight bun and then letting it go. "Hell, I might need that many."

Then she coughed her painful, smoker's cough, her whole body shaking.

She was like me, a newly separated woman, only she was the one who'd left. "He wanted us to move to this Disney town for old people. Clubs and group dinners and pre-furnished houses. I'd have shot myself in some generic recliner."

She moved to Hawthorne's only apartment complex, made her place up like a sixties office, all spacey Saarinen chairs and sleek coffee tables. Her husband, a bank loan officer, made the divorce official right away, kicked her off his plan and remarried.

"We've got this," I told her now. "It'll get easier."

"What I've got is a back ache."

We hugged, fell into our dented minivans.

• • •

For the first month it only got harder. Our bodies ached all day and all night, no matter how much Ibuprofen we took. There was no Hollywood soundtrack, no movie montage pulling us through. We did not get sexier or happier. My inner thighs chaffed, red rashes that made the softest khakis painful. Connie developed huge blisters on her heels and what the monitor called shin splints. Every step made her wince.

We ran as slow as we could, talked until we lost our breath. Then we put our heads down and pushed to the finish, our chests burning, our legs leaden with pain, the car fumes from the parking lot hot as a dumpster fire around us.

"You can do this. Keep breathing, ladies," the monitor told us. "Open up. Nice big strides."

"If he tells us to open up one more time, I swear I'll deck him," Connie said, her voice crackling. Then she fell into a coughing fit.

"Screw this whole runner's high thing," I put in. "You only feel good because you're not running anymore. That's not a fucking high. That's relief."

By week five, though, we had made some improvement. We could jog a lap without moon-walking.

"Looking better, ladies. You keep at it," the monitor told us.

I thought how he must have been a good coach back when, how the students must have appreciated his toughish-love style.

And we both started making what ActivAmerica calls "Intake Changes." Might as well make this easier, we told each other. I bought frozen vegetables for stir-frying, stuck to the cans of Light Broth soup instead of the thick clam chowders I preferred. I threw out all my Oatmeal Cream pies, reasoning they wouldn't do anyone any good. For lunch, I brought sandwiches with that brown bread they say is better for you.

Connie took this medication to quit smoking. "I'm pretty depressed, but the dreams, Sheila," she told me. "Last night I ballroom danced with the entire cast of *Mad Men*."

On my shifts in the store, I could feel the new muscles in my legs, every movement a sweet twinge of pain. I started thinking about dating, about sex with someone who loved me.

There was a guy from Sporting Goods I'd had my eye on, a former marine who'd hoped to design video games after the war.

"Those interviews," he'd told me once in the break room. "They looked at me like I was an animal, like any moment I might smash their computers, pull out a sniper rifle."

Village Mart was impressed by his physique, stuck him by the weight-lifting systems and ellipticals, an example of what a middle-aged man could accomplish.

"How's it going, muscle man? What you bench these days?" Connie asked him now, out on the track, elbowing me in the side.

"Really, it's just a lot of lifting my own body," he said. "Don't tell anyone, but those machines will warp your muscles all out of proportion."

"Mine were warped to begin with," I said and he laughed.

His name was Rick and he ran with us after that. Some nights, after we logged our run, the three of us would go for beers at the Village Mart Grill on the far side of the parking lot. His hand would fall on my shoulder while he told some story about debauchery overseas, or the kinds of video games he'd wanted to make, war re-enactments to help veterans work through their PTSD.

"We could help guys face what they've been avoiding," he said. "It's not like what you saw over there just goes away if you tell yourself it's over."

He was nothing like Peter. He kept his hair in a military buzz cut, wore his old combat boots and cheap button downs, loved sci-fi and Star Trek and comic books. Come November, I let him take me home. His house was small and sparse but he had an impressive collection of gourmet cheeses and hams imported from Spain.

"How do you afford all this?" I asked him.

"When I want something, I save up for it. I don't settle for something half-good. That's no way to live."

For a moment, I was scared to take off my clothes. Sure I'd been running, eating better, but my body didn't look much different, the body of a woman with low energy.

I pulled my T-shirt and bra over my head in one ungainly motion, braced myself.

"Damn," Rick said, taking his shirt off. "Just, damn."

When it was over, I wanted to make myself a whole new wardrobe, everything tight over my hips and thighs, low cut down my chest, a fine layer of vicuna wool.

• • •

The next night, out on the track, Connie found us and made a point to ask, "I'm not cutting in, am I? I don't want to be the third running wheel."

"Fuck you. Since when are we wheels?" Rick said.

The track was nearly empty, the buildings buzzing like distant chainsaws in the quiet. By then, lots of people had dropped off the plan. The geeks got bored and frustrated with running, fell into deep, frozen pizza depressions. The pregnant cashiers gave birth, needed more than the three free days, of course. Fatigue took out the single parents and anyone with an illness and anyone who worked double shifts for the extra dough.

The greeters got injured or sick, and then they couldn't find an official ActivAmerica doctor to verify they were "100% immobile," a requirement no one noticed when the reporters were still around.

"Look at my ankle," a thin, hunched woman shouted at the monitor one hot November night, pulling up her pant leg, pointing to her black and blue, twisted joint. "Does it look like I can run to you? Does it?"

"I'm sorry, hon," the monitor said. "I believe you. You know I do."

"That's going to be us one day," Connie whispered to me. "100% immobile? It's ridiculous. This whole thing. They want us to fail. You run until you fall into your death bed."

"What else can we do? You've got another job lined up for us?" I snapped.

All week I'd been favoring my left calf, a nettled shock every time I stepped down.

"You know, if you needed a break, we could always get a quick and dirty Vegas marriage," Rick said one night after sex. "We could take off a Saturday, drive out there. I've been meaning to look for other work. Then you could—"

I stopped him right there. "I'll marry you because I want to, not because I have to. And I don't even know if I want to."

He got serious after that. He hadn't meant to insult me. He liked being with me, whether we were married or not.

"Good," I told him. "That's good to hear."

I bought ice packs and hot packs, kept at my cut vegetables, my Light Broth soups. I filled out more applications for jobs online, ones with better benefits. School secretary. Dental receptionist.

"Send the papers, please," I texted Peter, a week before Thanksgiving. "I'm doing fine."

The packet arrived three weeks later, the first real day of winter.

"Fucker," I thought, knowing it was another test.

Winters these days come suddenly and like a metal door slamming shut. In three days the temperature had dropped forty degrees and a foot of snow had fallen. I felt a new wave of fear as I drove to work, the world icy and silent around me, the trees sagging under their new weight.

At Village Mart, they were plowing the parking lot, the track still covered in white.

"No way we're running in this," Connie said in the break room.

But that afternoon they distributed blue thermal underwear, polyester ski hats, and those thin, polyester-blend gloves they sell five pairs for a dollar at Village Mart. Out on the track, the cold settled over our bodies like wet cement.

"Seriously?" said Rick.

"No weather exceptions for non-management," the monitor told us, his face shining with Vaseline, heavy lines around his mouth, dark shadows under his eyes. "It's in your binders. I'm sorry. I wish I could cut you all a break. If this were my team, we'd be running inside."

"Who pays if I slip and break my neck?" Connie asked.

"You'd have to check the binder," the monitor said, shaking his head. "I think there's a liability clause."

I didn't want to know his story, what they were paying him and who was sick in his family and why he needed the money. I only wanted to kick him in the shins.

"Let's hope no one freezes to death," Rick said loudly. "That would be bad for business, wouldn't it? A more hypothermic America?"

We set off around the icy oval, our feet going numb in our sneakers, our lungs stinging. It was only us and the former athletes from Sporting Goods. Some of them had specialized gear: masks for their faces, brightly colored shells, thick gloves meant for skiing.

"My mother might have some extra pairs, if you guys need," a high-school girl offered us, slowing to our pace. "She gets me and my brother a pair every winter. We ski up in Vermont for Christmas."

"That's very kind of you," I said, my voice like curdled milk. "We'd appreciate that."

How nice, to grow up taking such vacations, to grow up healthy and strong and protected from the elements, to be able, at seventeen, to offer full grown adults your charity. I felt my whole body tense, my stride turn to mincing steps that felt nothing like dancing.

"She's a good kid," Rick said, giving my shoulder a squeeze. "She's trying to help."

"I know. I know she is," I said, and put my head down.

We ran without speaking, the air hitting our chests like smashed picture-frame glass. Coming around the curves we leaned into each other, steadying each other as the sun went down and the temperature dropped, our faces cold, hard masks.

At the edge of the shopping center, the Village Bar and Grill glowed. We were sure the managers and the executives and Scott Watkins were inside eating Kobe beef burgers, watching us through the windows, laughing as we staggered like drunks, laughing as we blew on our hands, laughing as Connie fell on her ass, bruising her tailbone and losing one of her Lucite earrings, laughing as she searched the snow for it on her hands and knees, laughing as she gave up and limped off to her car.

Back at my house, Rick and I sat on my couch sipping hot toddies, waiting for our bodies to thaw. I stared at the thin packet of papers Peter had sent, in the center of the coffee table. It struck me how little paper it took to dissolve a marriage, less than it took to get a free mammogram.

"Listen," Rick said after awhile. "No one would blame you if you threw those things away. This plan, it's irresponsible, unethical. They didn't give us any training for this. They'd never do this even in the Marines."

I took a long drink of my toddy, the lemon and honey and whiskey coating my chest. The cells in my breasts or pancreas or cervix might already be mutating, multiplying into masses. I would fail the mile tomorrow, or the next day, or five years from now. My flawed, overworked, poisoned body would drop out of the Culture of Wellness. Connie was right. It was rigged and it was only a matter of time.

"Fuck, I don't know," I said, pushing the papers further away. "I'm starving."

I went to the fridge, pulled out the fancy ham Rick had brought over a few nights before, put it on my best ceramic platter. Serrano ham, produced in the Sierra Mountains of Spain, made from the landrace white pig, he had told me.

"Shit, it's beautiful," he said now.

And it was, the thin, purple pink slices arranged in a fan the way he'd shown me, streaked with fat, shining in the light of my lamps. We ate it slow, savoring the salty, bitter richness. We joked about moving to Spain, about farming the white landrace pig, about dedicating our lives to the Serrano ham.

I thought of Peter, alone at his computer all those nights of our marriage, drinking and watching art films I'd refused to see with him. I remembered tunneling into sleep at eight p.m., heavy with fast food and an anger I could not name, tunneling away from him. I wished we'd been kinder to each other. I hoped he felt less alone.

And then I made a decision that was terrifying and stupid and that nonetheless filled me with joy. After Rick conked out, I went on the computer, looked up ski clothing, learned about the Three Layer System—base, insulation, outer layer—and which fabrics worked best. There was a company in Taiwan that sold Gore-tex and polyester diamond knit, but it wasn't cheap. Maybe I'd find old children's suits and jackets at the Goodwill, could patch them together?

"We look like the brute squad," I knew Connie would say.

A pattern formed in the air above me, a bulky armor, a phantom woman, a prayer for safety I whispered to myself later, in the dark, the ham still rich and bitter on my tongue.

Portrait of My Father as a Foosball Man, 1972–2012

Born with a hole punched through his chest, born to be skewered and spun, legs fused, armless, how could he hope to be agile? How could he hope to turn maradonas, to bicycle kick, to stepover, to Cruyff, to slide tackle in the rain in the manner of Manchester footballers? How could he strut pubs after games, raise a beer stein to his lips, dance to Diana Ross and David Bowie, fuck models?

Yet he was not unhappy. This was never real soccer, his grass always plastic, his ball taffy yellow, his game more like the buzzing collisions of pinball machines than the solemn geometries of the Dutch futbol system. He liked the syncopated grace of the pull shot, the solid bang of the bank shot, the gunshot zing of the snake shot fired from the three bar. His early self was apple cheeked, fixed with an amused expression, his body a V-necked uniform that gestured toward a human chest, thighs. His hair was dark and perfect. His foot was clubbed but at least it was a foot, painted cleat black.

And while he never touched those other men strung beside him, never that, you could say he was in love with them, with their nightly dance together in those smoky, wood-paneled saloons in Buffalo, in Elmira, in Binghamton, with the long-haired, cowboy-booted women and the bell-bottomed men who played for cash, who carried the table on national tours, the foosball men's bodies sliding back and forth in flatbed trucks speeding all across their thick, rambling country.

Born stuck in green and white, he'd always wanted to travel, loved the fresh accents of Ohio, Wyoming, and Louisiana, loved it when the night ended and they all lay together, the foosball men, tilted at odd angles. They did impressions of the attempts at love and fucking they'd witnessed, dissected the regional juke, reiterated their love of the Rolling Stones, of "Satisfaction," for what foosball man does not know the futility of coming close and missing over and over, of being flung toward the object of desire and flying through empty air? What foosball man has not wanted, just once, to punch a wall, to gyrate his hips to "Night Fever" or Chuck Berry, to hold a woman against his chest, to pull her hair, hard. "I can't get no," they'd sing to each other, half drunk on human beer-breath and longing.

Back then he could not have imagined the silicone plenty of the nineties, the weak-wristed competitions on the set of *Friends*, the long hours of gentrified flirtation. He could not have imagined the college bars with names like Marley's or J.P. Kelley's or Catch 22, where the coeds' slams and 360 spins nearly killed him, the frat boys lifting the table by the rod handles when they started to lose and letting it fall, shouting, "Dude, this shit is rigged."

He could not have imagined the suburbs, the dim middle-class dens with the dog piss stained carpeting, the sticky fingered children who would leave him still for months on end to play *Mortal Kombat, NBA Jam Extreme, Madden*. He could not conjure the anger and loneliness that would make him over in those years, how his face would disappear, his body turned to a streamlined, robot soldier body hovering above a table named "Tornado" or "Dynamo," his clubfoot smoothed to a spike. He could not know it would end like this, in a row house basement in White Plains, his field filled with dusty African Violets and yellowed tax files.

Don't get him wrong—he does not want to move like you or I, does not share the Little Mermaid's naïve desire to be transformed, to have his single leg split, to dance a ballroom waltz with a gowned bride, to be part of our world and all that crap. It's just that it's been so long since anyone turned his metal spoke heart with purpose, so long since he's shone his twitchy, hummingbird grace, so long since he's listened to human players laugh and talk smack and howl in victory and defeat, the way real players on real, muddy fields must howl, he used to figure, like it mattered more than anything else, more than having parents who loved each other and loved you, more than beauty and being cool, more than high cholesterol, more than looming dementia, howls so loud and so deep they reverberated through the whole table, seemed to come from him.

America's Funniest Home Videos
Episode 25,857: Helicopter Dad

April, a Tuesday, and we were all at home. They'd closed Penny's school again because of the cold, there was no contract work in Hawthorne, and Cara's X-rays had come back bad, silver spiders spreading in each breast.

We hadn't told Penny yet. Cara's librarian job was part-time, no insurance, and I'd gotten us the cheap kind that only covers X-rays and check-ups. I'd meant to upgrade but then the cold kept deepening—four years since the last thaw—and the work slowed and our heat bill kept rising no matter how low we kept it.

I was looking for a new job, anything with benefits: a janitor, a manager at a fast food restaurant, a filer in a cold, gray room. I'd already put in some applications. No one was hiring but I'd done a lot of work for influential people in town, had refinished the basements of doctors and lawyers and engineers, made-over their kitchens with marble counter tops and state-of-the-art appliances, crafted additions to their subdivision houses, tiny apartments for their dogs and out-of-town guests.

Every year, the clients gave us expensive, thoughtful Christmas gifts: Broadway show tickets—I was a theatre kid in high school—so we could sit in a plush, toasty theatre for hours and imagine ourselves in Saigon or the South Pacific; gift cards to the luxury mall in White Plains, where we bought long underwear meant for skiing to wear around the house; rare bourbons that Cara and I would give to Penny in tiny spoonfuls with her after-dinner tea, the liquid warming all our bodies.

I had all these connections. A call would come through soon and then we could tell Penny. We'd present a calm, united front, and she would have hope.

"Stop teasing the dog," Cara shouted at her now.

She was filming another one of her shorts with her camera phone. The dog was supposed to be a zombie-werewolf and Penny had slid a Halloween mask over her head, causing the animal to howl in anguish and confusion.

"Let's all get some air. Get the stink off us," I said.

"Please," Cara said, smiling at me like I'd suggested Disneyland.

I went into the closet, pushed aside the cans of bulk chili and extra blankets and grabbed the remote control helicopter, still in its red, white, and blue Toys R' Us box.

I'd gotten it for Penny that Christmas.

"What do you even *do* with it," she'd asked.

"Next thaw, I'll show you," I'd told her, and then, of course, the thaw never came and Penny forgot and it was kind of old fashioned anyway, Cara, said.

Of course she was right. We all love video games now, love playing out the different plots in Quarantine and Diseased Dead, love roaming cities we've never been to, cities with green palms and hot beaches and plenty of sun, cities where it is warm enough to wear short sleeves and dungarees as you shoot diseased zombies, raze crumbling hospitals, board sleek, private jets to Costa Rica or Brazil to find the hidden cures inside insect abdomens.

And maybe part of me was dreaming of heat and jungles and intrigue when I bought the dumb thing. Royal blue with silver stripes up and down the sides, it looked like something out of the nineties sci-fi thrillers my father loved as a kid, like the corporate craft the scientists would take to the island inhabited by mutant reptiles. At the end of the movie it would lift into the sky just in time, a pack of genetically engineered raptors clawing at the propeller.

It looked like a joke and it looked like a cartoon. It looked, when I was honest with myself, like something my father would have bought me as a kid, something meant to make me interested in physics instead of drama, a toy I would have broken on purpose.

Now I carefully installed the tiny motor, popped in the batteries, attached the propeller, wedged the stern looking pilot into the black leather cockpit.

"She's ready to rip," I told Penny.

"Can we get hot chocolate afterwards?"

"We're cutting back. Austerity budget. We're saving for a special vacation."

"We're wasting gas by going out."

"That's right. Why don't we stay home and we can work on your math."

"Okay, geez," she said and ran up the stairs.

All year she'd been stuck on fractions. When I tried to help her, she'd get red in the face and flee the kitchen table, disappear into her room to watch a horror movie, or to work on some new script with a monster who sounded like me, used all my same catch phrases.

"You're going to learn something new for once," I shouted up the stairs, then burst out of the house and into my truck.

The cold felt like swallowing drill bits. I cranked up the heat, sat with my hands balled in my gloves. The neighborhood was quiet, everyone's drapes taped tightly over their windows, the lawns white and empty and blank, not even sledding tracks. The driveway basketball hoops and lacrosse goals waited for shots that would not come, the nets frozen stiff, gilded in ice, catching the noon sun. The sky was blue and the light was bright, streaming through the windshield. By the time Penny and Cara came out-side in their fleece masks, I was sweating in my parka.

"Nice of you to join me," I said.

"Relax, Nick," Cara said, her hand on my shoulder. "We need a good day."

"I'm looking forward to this, dad," Penny put in, trying to be the good only child.

I drove us away from our run-down neighborhood, away from our streets lined with broken down cars and uncollected garbage, past the shuttered school which used to be my school, past the glassy corporations with their heated artisanal fountains, dream worlds of light and water rising and falling behind artesian brick walls, across the interstate and into the gated streets of the rich. My construction truck always had clearance.

"Where are you taking us?" Cara wanted to know. "Do you have a job today?"

"Look at that," I told Penny, pointing to the greenhouses steamed with heat, the indoor pools domed in blue glass, the sauna perched beside a man-made pond. You were supposed to sit in the sauna until you overheated, then jump into the cold pond.

"It cleanses your pores," the client, the founder of an online auction you've never heard of, had told me.

Now I explained it to my daughter.

"Cool. I want to try," Penny said,

"An engineer lives there," I heard myself say. "Maybe one day you can build yourself one. A little less with the camera, a little more with the fractions."

"I'm trying as hard as I can," Penny said, her voice breaking. "Leave me alone."

"Yes, leave her alone please," said Cara.

"I'm sorry," I said, my gloved hands graceful as paws on the wheel. "It wasn't my best subject either."

I'd lasted two years in engineering at State, the only classes my father would pay for. I had trouble sitting still in the underground computer lab, trouble concentrating on the four-hour engineering tests. I'd finish an hour early, then go to the movies.

"Short sighted," my father said when I came back to Hawthorne. "Throwing your education away."

I worked under him for the next ten years, the two of us trading mean-spirited remarks during jobs, all *if you hadn't* or *if you would have*. When Penny was born, I wouldn't let him around her alone, hired distracted teenagers instead. I worried he'd say something cruel to her, make a crack about her mini-plays, her story boards, something like *Good luck getting a producer*.

Also, part of me blamed him for the turn my life had taken. A larger part than I like to admit now. I wanted to get even.

"A kid should be allowed to be creative," I'd say pointedly during Penny's Thanksgiving screenings, when we showed her movies on the big-screen TV for the whole family. "We want her to have options."

"That's great," my father would say, and go for more beer.

"I grew up in a different kind of world," he told me before he died on a bitter day in September, the beginning of another nine-month winter. "I wanted you to be safe."

"I appreciate that," I'd said with all the kindness of a bill collector.

Now I couldn't say what I wanted for my daughter. I only knew that I was scared. I drove us to the outskirts of town, out to the abandoned Loews where my father had watched movies as a kid, where I'd watched them too.

"Why are we here?" Penny said, looking up at the busted glass, the faded, faux-gold columns, the blank marquee.

I wanted to tell her: this is where we used to go back when it was warm enough to dream the craziest dreams, back when winter was a season we kept boxed in our attics. I wanted to tell her that she infuriated me and that she also gave me hope. I wanted to say, remember me, remember us, as people who struggled but still enjoyed life. Remember us as people who loved you.

I said, "This is the flattest place in town. Let's rock and roll."

And the parking lot was a perfect field of white, so bright it hurt my eyes. I popped on my sunglasses, walked to the center, my body all stiff and lumbering. I placed the helicopter on the snow pack, took off a glove, started her up. There was a congested, whirring sound, somewhere between a mosquito and a broken snow blower.

"It's not working," Penny said. "Can we go get hot chocolate now?"

"Hold on," I heard myself snap, my fingers going numb. I pulled up on the joystick, hit the blue button, and the thing rose heavily into the air.

"Wow," Penny said with exaggerated enthusiasm. Then she took out her phone, trained the camera on me.

And as you know, *Funniest Home Video* fans of America, I zoned out before long, piloted the thing directly into my own head, my clumsiness and stupidity captured for all eternity by my daughter, who will go on to live her own moments of clumsiness and stupidity regardless of what my wife and I tell her.

What you don't know is I was thinking of those nineties sci-fi thrillers, of how baffled the genetically engineered dinosaurs must have felt when they woke up on earth again. They must have thought they'd tricked extinction, or that the drought and cold and death they remembered was only a dream. Here they were in this warm, green place, everything the same, everything they loved all here except there was this strange new buzzing sound, getting closer, getting closer now.

Interview with the Ghost of Jaws' First Victim

What I wanted was to get laid. We had pot, a bonfire, cable knit sweaters. The night was scalloped with acoustic guitar. He was on vacation from a Greenwich prep, tan with butter-blond hair, a member of the rowing team. I knew to make myself mysterious, to weave the dunes on the balls of my feet, to trail garments, to play at Little Mermaid years before the Disney version.

Like the sound of a drunk driving crash on the L.I.E. Like a hundred cosmetic scissors stabbing my legs. It took forever.

He'd fallen asleep.

After: men ball-pointing my name on reporter pads, on autopsy reports; men in badges hammering warnings to telephone poles; men netting their wives' roasts for bait; men in small boats wielding long harpoons; men with cold fathers, war stories, advanced degrees, a love of whiskey; men eager to hunt their jerry-rigged Moby Dick. Also boys swimming for merit badges, boys sailing play crafts, boys pretending to be sharks, fins strapped to their backs. The wives and mothers lay on Macy's towels, adjusted straw hats, watched the sea.

What can I say about what I dreamed, what I would have become? They wrote me flat as a girl on a beach town billboard, bikinied, hip cocked, welcoming men to forget their wives' stretch marks and winter tweed, their kids' test scores and fall allergies, their station wagon commutes, their happy hour guts, their weaknesses, their own monstrousness. I was the siren they had to kill off to begin their quest.

Should I tell you I loved archaeology? Would you like to picture me on a plane to Peru, my perfect hair tucked beneath a bucket hat, my purse filled with bone brushes and trowels? Archaeology Barbie?

Call my family in North Hempstead. Tell my mother I was beautiful before the end, my body backlit with moonlight, my long hair waving. Tell my father I actually liked cribbage. Tell my sister to stop plucking above her eyebrows, to be wary of boys from Connecticut.

Backyard Dreams

"Problem with jets or poltergeist?"

—*Hot Tub Forum, Whatsthebest-hottub.com*

H er husband put it on the credit card without asking her, like the big screen TV in '89, that huge, dark mirror, like the foosball table for the kids in '96 that now sits unused in their basement, rows of still, faceless men, their children moved to other states. He bought it even though they are selling the house this coming summer, moving away, separately or together, she can't say yet.

"Remember that trip to Killington? The hot tub?" he asked when the construction crew showed up back in September, in a truck that said "Backyard Dreams" on it, the words fringed in cartoon palms. "Negative twenty and we're out in that water. It's so cold our hair is freezing, but we're burning up."

She nodded, though these days she can barely recall those nineties ski trips, the five of them locking into quick release bindings, their middle boy, Ari, always going too fast, wrecking, so that Max had to help him collect his strewn gear, find the missing poles, the gloves, the expensive Sports Barn hat. It must have moved her to see him do this, in the parka and faded ski-pants he bought back in Buffalo, in college, when it was enough for them to cross-country flat fields, come home and make love in their rented bungalow, when they didn't know about Killington or Mt. Snow or Jay Peak, didn't know how lift tickets could be a kind of pretentious jewelry, displayed on jacket zippers all season long, didn't know the ways marriage would make them unrecognizable to themselves, the ways they would betray each other, would feel like they were walking in ski boots in their own house, their movements alien, hulking, dangerous to every small, bare thing.

What she remembers is watching the *X-Files* in high-ceilinged, vacation condos, their faces bathed in neon green light, her body sore, her tongue thick with cabernet. She remembers the blue trails in the blue mornings, moving cautiously down hill in what the instructors called the pie shape, unable to parallel the way her husband and children could. She remembers being the rickety boat they were pulling, or struggling to free themselves from. They would look back at her now and then to make sure she was still there, waving, then turning forward again, their lithe, athletic bodies getting further and further away.

Now here she is, her kids gone to other time zones, a barn of a house in a Northern suburb, a bad real estate market, this husband who eats fast food on his way home from work, Doritos in bed, refuses to exercise, to take care of himself, even though her younger brother died of a heart attack last June. This husband who fell in love with that woman at his job, the one with good taste in music and a sense of humor, who loves Woody Allen, who could take a joke, or so he told her the first time he left, five years ago. He's been gone, and back, and gone, back six months now.

And yes, he says he loves her, that he made a mistake. Yes, she's said she's trying to forgive him, has said *return*, has asked for the warm bread of him in her bed again, but now she's not sure, the years of her marriage gathered around her like stray cats. She looks at him and tries to see his hands tracing the line of her back, tender the way he was at the beginning on a single bed in a Binghamton dorm. How can she let him near her body again? *You fucked someone else* was all she could shout for months after, her own skin on fire. No, she doesn't want a soak with him in this over-priced, excessive thing.

Also, it's haunted. Since November's hard gray she's heard it turn on in the middle of the night on its own, has seen the glowing cauldron of it out their bedroom window, all four turbo jets firing, making a sound like a dishwasher breaking heirloom china, or like a crashed spaceship struggling to take off, to rise from the icy grass of their lawn.

"Hey, get up, look," she tells him, poking him in the stomach.

"What?" he says, stumbling out of bed, staring out the window. "What's wrong?" It always stops when he's awake.

"I'll fix it myself," she says at last, pushes out into the cold, unplugs the damn thing.

Still, it happens again the next night, and the night after that. The women in her new hiking group look at her strangely, ask her if she's tried meditating. "Yeah, yeah, yeah," she says, knowing she's seen what she's seen.

She knows the same way she knew something was wrong before the affair. There were his late nights at school, writing report cards weeks before they were due. There was the new music he'd play in the car—Thelonious Monk, some Swedish rock band she can't remember the name of—the distant look he'd get while he listened.

"What are you thinking?" she'd ask him.

"Nothing much. Just trying to listen," he'd say and turn up the volume.

She decides to ignore the hot tub—she has her own life, her own obsessions to think about, he's already taken too much from her—but still it's hard to sleep. She watches late night TV on the living room couch, dozes to exercise infomercials, men and women dancing in rows in leotards and tight shorts, or riding stationary bikes, or lifting Nautilus weights, the world behind them turquoise and sunny and tropical and fake. During the day she moves in a haze, her body slow and heavy, as if she's underwater.

"We could bring our books out there, turn the porch light on," he says when she comes home late from her AA meeting at the Methodist church, her head ringing with everyone else's promises to change. "It might help with your back. We could put your bath salts in. You're not supposed to—water quality—but we could."

It has to do with anxiety, her doctor has told her, the tightness that wraps around her shoulders at night, a raccoon settled there, digging in its claws. He's suggested medications with names like health clubs, like glossy, water front apartments in failing cities: Zoloft, Solaris, Paxil, Polaris, Clearview.

No thank you, she isn't going to quit one drug only to take another. She isn't going to dull the way she feels, even if Max tells her it doesn't work that way, that depression isn't like a headache of the heart, it's more like an alien stuck inside your body, or a black, oily muck in place of your guts, pressing at your skin, threatening to spill out, to destroy everyone you love.

"Come on, sweetie. Just give it a shot," he is saying, coming up behind her as she wipes the kitchen counters down, his small hands on her shoulders, kneading the tight muscles there.

She thinks of her mother in the years when her father's drinking was the worst, when he'd walk to the Seven Eleven down the block, buy whiskey, drink the whole bottle in the parking lot, then call from the pay phone saying he didn't want a ride, he could move fine, he just wanted some company on the walk home. They'd appear on the shaded, Long Island street, her mother tall, broad shouldered, in boots from Hellers, her father thin in corduroy living room slippers, leaning into her so that you could see how much stronger she was, could guess that when he went five years later—heart attack, the way they all go in her family—she would have something of herself left, would get a job at the Port Washington Beach Club teaching kids the backstroke, would visit Ireland where her grandparents were from, would sell the house and move into her own condo in Cutchogue, would take the valuable furniture and leave his prized, unread copy of *Ulysses* behind.

"There's something not right about it," she is telling Max in the kitchen, "Just watch it a minute. It's like a horror movie."

They stare out the window, but the hot tub is quiet and they can't see it anyway, get only their own reflections, her face long and pale and worried, his laughter-lined, heavier in the chin.

"It's probably the automatic filter cycle," he says. "*I'm* going in. It's a waste to not use it." And he leaves her there. She hears his heavy step on the stairs, then his sigh.

And he is trying. He's gone to therapy with her, came to her four-year anniversary with yellow tea roses, her favorite, didn't make fun of the key chains, the other tchotchkes. They have their routines. On Friday nights they go to the art theatre in Chappaqua, then to the diner for dessert and to talk about the movie. On Saturdays they hike Turkey Mountain, that gradual, half-mile hill. They make fun of the young couples with their expensive anoraks, their hiking poles, their heavy packs. She identifies the plants, tells him the names, and he listens. He does not rush her.

Before the affair, they'd talked about moving to White Plains when the youngest left, a real city with restaurants they could walk to, live music on the weekends, streets with sidewalks and historic buildings and bookstores and legitimate bustle. They'd talked about a life with more than lacrosse fields and team dinners and trips to the mall, more than lawn mowing and garden weeding and gutter cleaning.

She presses her face against the window glass, looks out at their yard, wonders if she'll miss it. There's the rusted skeleton of the Sears playground he installed back in the eighties, the monkey bars he helped the children weave through, holding their flailing bodies in his arms in the afternoons when she couldn't handle the sound of their voices, the swirling mess of them trailing glitter and scraps of colored construction paper through the house, when all she wanted was to sip a glass of red wine on the couch and read a mystery.

There are the tiny cages of the lacrosse goals. She remembers how he'd play with them in the after-dinner hour, the child-sized stick ridiculous in his hands, his motions clumsy and exaggerated, all to give her more of that blurred, merlot calm she was craving.

There's the spiked pen of her vegetable garden, her flower beds like freshly dug graves. There are the trees that held the dead dog's lead. There's the rotting hutch that held the rabbit that ran away. There's the new machine, stuck in the deck, sheathed in its turquoise "Backyard Dreams" cover. "An Artesian Grand Bahama," he's told her it's called, like the name of a vacation cruise they might take. She never has been on a cruise.

And there he is sliding through the porch doors in the L.L. Bean robe he bought for himself the Christmas of '94, that year she hadn't gotten it together to buy presents, that year she crashed their Quest on the Taconic, drunk, their youngest in the back. He is walking across the icy deck, tottering like he's in ski boots, lifting the cover, plugging it in, starting it up, stepping away like it's a toy he's frightened of.

She thinks of him as a boy, left alone for whole Saturdays while his parents bowled and his sisters shopped the Miracle Mile, how he'd play in his father's workshop, how once he tried the table saw, nearly sawed a finger off.

"Child services almost took us away, after that," he'd told her one night, their first year living together. He was teaching second grade in Elmira and she was still looking for an occupational therapy gig. Her own father had called her a hausfrau, a girl who'd given up, a lost cause.

"Maybe they should have taken us," he said. "Or at least given us some safety goggles. A first aid kit. Some back up."

They had laughed. She put her hand on his hand across their garage sale Formica, thought, *I am going to love this man until he forgets, until we forget, love could ever be like that.*

Out on the deck the Grand Bahama heats, the steam rising around him. He stands for one long, awful moment under the sharp, winter stars, barefoot, half-naked in his Caldor bathing suit, his belly drooping over the waist, the gray hair on his shoulders like stunted wings and she knows what he is doing, making himself vulnerable like this in front of her, making her want to put her knowing hands on those shoulders, work out his knots but still she can't look away from him, sliding one leg, then the other, into that unearthly, neon green.

And maybe she is stiff, is chilled in a way that only hot tub water can sooth. She is leaving the window, pushing out into the cold, is standing in front of him, rolling out her shoulders, taking everything off: the Espirt shoes he has mocked for their burnished copper color, the jeans her daughters call "mom jeans" for how they come in at the ankle, the old turtle neck sweater he said makes her head look stuck on.

And for once he is not laughing. He is looking at her, at her stretch-marked stomach, at her flat, flat ass—the ass of all the women in her family—at the inky shadow of her cunt, almost like the first time, like he's grateful but he's not sure what to do, like he's amazed and terrified. She slips in across from him, gasps at the thick heat. The haunted jets turn on, then off, then on.

"This is unacceptable. I'll call the company tomorrow," he says.

"It's fine," she says, her hand moving to his thigh. "It adds an element of surprise."

The yard is white and frozen and lunar around them, her perennial bulbs buried beneath, cold and hard as fists, persistent as grudges. They stare at each other, the porch light like a search light, their bodies turning hot, their faces reddening, their hair, flecked with chlorinated water, beginning to freeze, to shine.

The Parents' Guide to UltraSport Children

Stage I

Prepare to be frustrated with your UltraSport child. Your son will seem to simply be taller, not faster or stronger or more skilled, his shots careening over the backyard lacrosse goal into the pachysandra. Your daughter will continue to miss her tennis serve, only now her J.Crew wardrobe no longer fits. Her cardigans bare her bony wrists. Her corduroys leave her ankles—small and prone to spraining like your ankles—exposed to the October cold. All that money you spent at the factory outlet in Monroe down the drain.

And how they eat! The brined Thanksgiving turkey you learned to make from the Food Network, the garlic mashed potatoes, the maple pecan pie baked from scratch, all of it shoveled down their gullets in five minutes flat. No leftovers. Then, late at night, you catch them at the freezer pawing at a box of Hot Pockets.

"No more food. Kitchen's closed!" you announce and they freeze, guilty and ghostlike in the half-light and then you feel bad.

"Okay, but put your plates in the dishwasher."

December and their feet hang off their Pottery Barn beds. Their desks are too short so they complain of cricks in their necks. You can't buy new furniture—you're a dental hygienist and your husband is a teacher, you can barely afford the UltraSport treatments—so you break out the yellowed Reader's Digest carpentry guide you got for your wedding, elongate each piece yourself. Up and down the block, wealthier neighbors add special, high-ceilinged additions, their houses swelling into McMansions. The fall air fills with drywall powder and sawdust, the bite of chainsaws.

You may have doubts during this stage. Your daughter's gold necklace with the star pendant, the one that belonged to your mother, may rip from her thickened neck during a practice, lost forever. Your daughter may say she hated it anyway: too delicate for her new, athletic tastes. Your son may punch your husband in the shoulder during a shitty Jets game, as per usual, but now the bruise spreads wide as a basketball and throbs for weeks. Both children are on edge, a dropped water glass, a stubbed toe, a head bumped on a doorway causing hysterics.

Continue with the regimen: three blue pills a night, washed down with Arctic Spring water. Remember that the treatment comes recommended from the US Olympic Development Commission. Think of the competition, of the other enhanced children your son and daughter will face come spring. Don't you want them to be prepared?

Do you want to be like your parents, your silent, Catholic, alcoholic parents who sent you hurtling, bewildered into every new thing: junior high and the terrifying transformations of your body, high school teachers who touched your knee, called you darling, boys who pushed your head down in the Port Washington yacht club boathouse, the alien horror of childbirth, how you thought your body would split down the middle?

We recommend you show your children our fun, informative video, entitled "Play Ball!: Your Athletically Enhanced

Body and You," available in the UltraSport catalogue. It features professional actors from shows your children will be familiar with: *The Disappeared. Lost. Hostage. Revenge.* It will help your children know the kinds of changes to expect, with special sections on clothing, nutrition, personal hygiene, rage, and sex with the non-enhanced. Turn it on for them in the basement den, shut off the lights, and run upstairs, your face going red despite yourself.

Stage II

On the field, on the court, you will barely recognize them. Marvel at their new confidence, their new reflexes, their sudden success. Your son has moved from third to first string attack. He comes home from an away game on Long Island flushed and happy, devours his meal and chats about crease rolls and dodges instead of disappearing into his room to play Diseased Zombies 5. He gives you the play-by-play, then busts out his math homework right there at the kitchen table. You don't have to stand over him while he does it, don't have to threaten to call the tutor he insists smells like soup.

And your daughter no longer walks with her head down. She has stopped picking at her lips and missing showers. On Friday nights, she goes out to parties with her teammates instead of reading your old Kerouacs, listening to your old Joni Mitchells. Come April she has a boyfriend, an athletically enhanced kid on the lacrosse team with your son. He buys her a necklace from the UltraSport catalogue, a golden tennis racket the size of your hand on a sturdy chain.

And now and then, on the sidelines or the bleachers, watching your son perform an especially savage series of checks, or watching your daughter hit a shot aimed like a bullet at her opponent's head, you may feel a flicker of fear. You may think: who are these graceful, ruthless competitors? Is this the same boy who is afraid of birds and once tried to play Bob Dylan on the acoustic guitar? Is this the same girl who used to write nature poems in fancy Barnes and Noble journals and strung hundreds of tiny beads into necklaces?

Your UltraSport children are now part of an elite tribe. You are a part of that tribe, too. Clap your hands, and shout their names. Order larger plates and cutlery from the Ultrasport catalogue, designed to match your Macy's. Order our special line of enhanced athletic drinks, available in cherry and lemon flavors. Admire the plastic bottles when they arrive, how they shine like gemstones in a children's cartoon. Place them in the new fridge you've purchased just for your children.

Go to Costco on Sunday and load your cart with gallons of tomato sauce and mayonnaise, enough ground beef to feed a classroom of non-enhanced children, five flats of canned tuna. When you pass your neighbor, whose children are in band, nod at your cart and say, "Varsity kids. What can you do?"

"A small country could eat that," your neighbor will say.

Ignore the judgment in her voice. Laugh and shake your head, then casually mention the upcoming state tournament, the calls from college recruiters you've been getting. You can't get through a meal. You barely sit down before the phone rings again. Maryland, Syracuse, Johns Hopkins. Enjoy this stage. It goes so fast.

Stage III

Results vary wildly at this point. We ask you to read with caution, to act with caution, but not just because your UltraSport children are now so strong they pose a real physical threat to those around them. This is not a definitive guide, and it does not speak for everyone's experience. We cannot account for every variable.

Your daughter may, upon being refused an item from the UltraSports catalogue, kick a hole straight through the living room wall. This is normal. She may push past you to her room, sending you flying against the doorframe, causing you to chip your front tooth.

Afterward, she will weep and rake her giant hands through your hair and say, "I'm so sorry mom. I didn't mean to do that. I feel like the Hulk."

She'll spend the night on your bedroom floor like a younger child who's had a nightmare. You will not be able to sleep, her breath a hot wind that ruffles the curtains, makes you and your husband sweat through the sheets.

"Maybe we should take a break from the treatments," you'll tell her in the morning.

"I promise I'll be better," she'll say, her face going pale. "Don't take that away from me."

Your son may have a party while you are away with your husband for the weekend, a mini-vacation during which you were supposed to have sex. The drunk UltraSport children may climb up onto the roof and dance to the Grateful Dead, denting the house like a half-crushed soda can. Your son will try to fix the dents with his fist. When you get home, you will Neosporin the cuts on his knuckles while he clamps his eyes shut. The air will smell of beer and a sweat as strong as cow manure.

"We need a new roof," you will tell your husband.

"Can't afford it until fall," he will say, glaring at the new refrigerator.

For the rest of spring, the entire family will walk around with bent backs and twisted necks, every room a cave. You and your husband will lose each other in these cave-rooms, the effort to search too much. You'll lose the sound of each other's voices, unable to pick them out over the percussive sounds of your children forking and chewing their platters of food.

The hole your daughter kicked into the wall will grow larger, despite your slap dash Sheetrock job, will let in the spring rain, mildew creeping up the walls. One night, in the kitchen for a glass of whiskey, you find a bat perched on top of the refrigerator, his rat face scrunched up, his leathery black wings folded behind him. It will take you and your husband five hours to chase him out of the house, terrified, armed with your children's UltraSports gear.

"Hahaha, you look like gladiators from that show," your children will say as you struggle to wield the giant tennis racket, the massive lacrosse stick, your faces floating in your son's outgrown lacrosse helmets.

"Go back to bed," you will tell them, but they will only stand there staring at you, vaguely amused, like you're that show they're watching.

As their seasons wind down, you will stay later and later after work, enjoying the neat, pastel calm of an empty dentist's office, the scent of fear gone, the closet of free toothbrushes and medical smocks in order, the files updated, the instruments soaking in blue sterilizing liquid. You may disappear under a nitrous oxide ocean, just for an hour or two.

At this stage we recommend you grant your children's request to move to our state-of-the-art athletic facility on the edge of town. It is just until they leave for college—a year or two—at a reasonable price as far as these facilities go. Take out a second mortgage. Help them pack their many suitcases. They will live with other enhanced children and a staff trained to anticipate their needs. The ceilings are high, the rec room a dome the size of a minor league hockey rink.

"We'll be right at home, if you need us," you tell your children, rocking up onto your toes to touch the distant moons of their faces.

Out on your back deck, sipping leftover athletic drinks with your husband, you can see the dome glow through the trees, the neon green of fireflies and expensive cleats. You may feel your heart break. Go back inside, into the new quiet. Work to repair your house. Re-patch the hole and, come fall, hire contractors to re-align the foundations and fix the roof. Cut up the credit cards. Throw away the economy foods. Purchase tiny Greek yogurts from the organic store, farm fresh eggs by the half-dozen, baby carrots, quarter-pound portions of beef. You may feel an intense relief in the latter part of stage III.

And look at how your children thrive, packed off to gleaming dorms at D1 universities, to complimentary wardrobes of the finest sports brands, to silver stadiums with enough luxury boxes for all the parents. It will almost feel like watching a professional game on television, there in the plush leather recliner, your child so huge and so small and so far away.

If a certain hit seems too hard, if your child takes a minute too long to get up, if you hear certain stories in the news—Ultrasport children with brain damage, Ultrasport children, newly married, beating each other up, Ultrasport children, cut from their team, committing suicide, a heart bursting in a body grown too fast—if you fear you have made a mistake, remember: we were not born to sit on couches, content. To be human is to test your limits, to push yourself, to move beyond the body and the heart you were given.

Your children, they are mostly fine. They have learned skills that will serve them the rest of their lives: initiative, leadership, and perseverance. After their moments of unspeakable beauty, so rare on this earth, they will go on to law school, to business school, will thrive in corporate jobs in mid-sized cities.

And they will not forget you. They will arrive every few months, then every few years, to celebrate the holidays of their childhoods. You'll wake to a huge, half-familiar face in your bedroom window, or a knocking that rattles the heirloom china they're too big to use. You will think of that comedy they loved when they were young, before the treatments and the recruiters and the scholarships, the one with the quirky mad scientist who shrinks his teenage kids. They run in a pack, lost in the suburban lawns, dwarfed by blades of grass.

You will wonder, if you were shrunk to the size of an ant, would your kids find you, scoop you up and hold you tenderly in their palms? Would they stay up all night searching for a cure? Or would they squint down at you from far away, hand you a giant slice of bread, a grape the size of a bowling ball, then resume their lives in perfect ratio?

Some days you will call them inside, help them slide back through the doorways, clear out the furniture in the living room so they have a place to recline. You will love how their bodies fill up every room again, how you cannot take a step without hitting an orthopedic shoe, a greasy strand of hair, a knee lined with ACL scars, ankles that are still like your ankles, only larger and braced.

You will make rushed trips to Costco, serve great vats of spaghetti, administer gallons of Tiger Balm, their aching backs like alien planets you're exploring, here and there a chicken pox scar or a birthmark that sends splinters through your chest. You will listen to them complain about the muzaked hours at their desks, the painkilling pills large as eggs they need to get through their days, the way their once tremendous muscles sag like sacks of wet dirt, the way that life hasn't been as enhanced, as outsized, as ultra as they thought it would be.

"You're just going through another transition," you will tell them, hoping it's the truth. "Change is hard for everyone. It will be all right. You'll find a new way. You always do."

Other nights, your fear and exhaustion will be too much. You will dread the chemical smell of their department store scents, the loud cracks of their joints, the heavy way they walk now, scuffing the floors, kicking over vases, breaking the new teak furniture, their athletic prowess fading. You and your spouse will hide in the bedroom with the lights off, will nestle into each other beneath the quilt your mother made you for your wedding, the quilt you keep meaning to give to your daughter though it would barely cover one leg. You hold each other and wait for the knocking to stop, for the beautiful stillness to return.

Ping-Pong, 12 Loring Place

I t was the day after Christmas when our parents began to argue and we went down to the basement, to our new Titan 360 Pro ping-pong table, my brother Ari and I. We were unsure about the game itself. We'd never had any use for actual tennis, for the precision of serving, the expensive rackets, the white shorts and sneakers the tennis players wore at the snooty club across town. We were soccer kids, preferred our games messy and earthy and fluid, our black cleats worn and cracked with age, our fields all mud and divots and geese shit, our polyester jerseys stained with dirt, streaked with blood.

But the argument upstairs was painful—another woman, the bottles of wine our mother kept hidden in her rock garden, tucked inside the holly—and we were restless. It had already been a bad winter, the snow piled high on either side of our driveway like bunkers for an arctic, suburban war. We'd spent too many days sitting in our own stink watching *The Price Is Right*, guessing the cost of blenders and entertainment centers while our mother read novels about the Holocaust and our father went to work in his Highlander, extolling the benefits of four-wheel drive.

Underground, we picked up the wooden paddles, ran our fingers across their red, stippled faces, served our first, awkward serves, volleyed. It felt silly at first, the ball light as a hollowed-out Easter egg, its bounce a cartoonish click. We were trained to do so much more with our bodies, to Cruyff and scissor and corner kick, our arms and legs muscled from dribbling through strings of cones, from weaving up and down sidelines, from countless suicides. We laughed, shrugged our shoulders. We used too much force, the ball careening against the gray walls or hitting the ceiling, flying away from us to die on the industrial carpet.

Slowly, though, we developed what our soccer coaches called "touch." We studied the surprisingly serious manual that came with the table, learned the nuances of top spin and back spin, experimented with the flick, the block. We watched McEnroe, Connors, and Borg on the television, laughed at their tantrums, practiced their footwork. Our rallies grew longer, more heated, our bodies slamming into the gray walls as we struggled to return the push, the loop, the lob, the chop shot.

We played best out of three, best out of five, best out of seven, the sun shining cold and hard outside the tiny basement windows. When we were hungry, we snuck upstairs for turkey and Doritos sandwiches. Or we microwaved deli cheese on Ritz crackers, or chicken nuggets, the pale centers burning our tongues. Soon our paddle handles shown with sweat and grease.

Best of twenty-one, best of thirty-nine, the light out the windows gone blue-gray, and we decided to create our own honorary paddles, crept into the unfinished side of the basement. Our father had used the space as an art studio before we were born. We took out his old tempera, revived his stiffened brushes with warm water, painted the wooden sides red and gold, wrote our ping-pong nicknames in black sharpie.

"Sarah Ballerina," my brother wrote on mine, for the way I sometimes spun when I served, leapt gracefully for returns, my girlhood dance training seeping into my game.

"The Fireball," I wrote on my brother's, for his temper, our mother's Irish temper, everyone said. The year before, when a teacher accused him of cheating on a spelling test, he had overturned his desk, ran away, had to be coaxed out of the crook of the playground's curly slide.

"Control yourself," our parents were always telling him, handing him his Ritalin.

Though in other ways, he seemed more comfortable in the world above the basement than I ever was, with his pack of soccer-playing boys, his confident slouch, his button-down shirts from American Condor in the Hawthorne Mall. Up there, I was a pale, thin-voiced girl dressed in boy's clothing, a girl who read horror novels in the band practice room during lunch, a girl who looked at her feet when she walked, who already had her mother's hunch.

Down here, I looked for any advantage, took pleasure in goading my brother into actual fits, singing "We Are the Champions" when I won, which was rare; he was the better athlete. His face would turn red. He would hit the ball across the room, then throw his paddle so that it became chipped at the edges. He would demand another game—best out of sixty-three, best out of seventy-seven, best out of eighty-nine—and if I didn't agree, I was a quitter and thus automatically forfeited the championship.

"Okay, okay, okay," I would say, smiling, collecting the ball from behind the water heater.

And I wish I could tell you that as the games went on, I grew more empathetic. I wish I could say that as the argument upstairs intensified and outside the neighbors took down their Christmas lights, dumped their bare pines at the bottoms of their driveways to shiver in the wind, I became a better sister, that when, at best of four-hundred and fifty-three, my first boyfriend appeared on the basement steps, I didn't leave Ari mid-volley to make out with him in the art studio, didn't lose track of how much time I spent there in the fetid dark, tunneling into my own heat, my own blood roaring in my ears.

I wish I could say that at best out of seven-hundred and one, when the sun set and the windows went dark and my brother's face flushed with acne and the words upstairs changed to the sound of objects being thrown, I knew the value of our ritual, knew to protect it from my own selfishness.

Instead, I disappeared again and again, emerging tired and hickied and eventually, sore, to find Ari fallen asleep watching the Knicks, a plate of cracker crumbs on the coffee table in front of him. Or he and his friends would be playing Madden NFL and drinking Red Bulls.

"Hey," I would say, while they virtually tackled each other.

He'll feel that one tomorrow, John Madden would proclaim.

"We're playing," Ari would answer, refusing to look at me.

Other times, though, I'd come back and it would be just us again, a brother and sister alone in a quiet basement in the middle of a winter that would not end. We'd listen to the crashes upstairs, guess at which objects were being thrown: Our father's paintings from the seventies? Our mother's Fiesta Ware? The expensive paperweights she got as teacher's gifts, golden apples shining in watery glass, prehistoric insects we didn't know the names of stuck in amber?

Better not to listen too hard. Better to take up our paddles, to begin again, then again, our intricate, rhythmic song, to play until our wrists ached and our bodies thrummed while outside the sun rose and the air warmed and the snow, at last, melted, spilled down the driveways in dirty rivers. Better to master our regulation 9 foot by 5 foot, black-top surface, to angle our shots to nick that pro-quality edge banding and striping, to brush against the padded corners while our mother threw away the bottles hidden in the holly and our father threw his clothes into garbage bags, got into his Highlander, and moved out.

It was summer, the basement windows full of black-eyed Susans, when our mother stood at the top of the stairs and told us to come on up, it was time to quit playing, time to pack our things, I was going to college and she was selling the house, buying a smaller one without a basement, without room for a ping-pong table. By then our paddles were barely functional, the stippled rubber worn away from the faces, the red and gold paint dulled. Before we left, Ari put them in one of our grandfather's old cigar boxes, buried them in the backyard. A time capsule, we called it, as if some distant, future family would know to dig it up, would decipher the hieroglyphics of our nicknames, long blurred with sweat. As if nothing was passing away.

The Hawthorne Dynasty

We were the Hawthorne Dynasty girls' U-14 soccer team and damn we were bad. We kicked with our toes and we couldn't trap, the ball knocking off our shins, hurtling out of bounds or to the other team. Our coach, Kitty Huff, was infamous for her racy clothing and misguided rants. During games she would pace the sidelines in a miniskirt, high heels, and an animal patterned blouse that showed the tops of her tremendous breasts, the same outfit she wore to the anesthesiology filing office where she was a secretary, a job that required her to come in on Saturday mornings before our games.

Come on girls, boot it! Will you get it out of there already? Kick it! You're not even trying. You think I'm playing around? she would shout, her voice rising in volume and intensity when we started to lose, which was often, usually to some team from Chappaqua or Fox Lane with a coach who knew more about the game than Kitty did, some stern father in an Adidas track suit and Sambas who stood with his arms crossed, thinking, no doubt, about a complicated drill from a European manual he was going to try at his next practice.

Our practices were disorganized, leisurely affairs, held Monday and Wednesday nights on a scraggly field behind the abandoned elementary school. For an hour we fumbled in pairs with throws-ins and inside ankle passes, then played a version of sharks and minnows adapted for soccer, one of us the shark, the rest of us laughing minnows. *You think this is funny girls? Just go home then, will you please?*

Then we'd scrimmage until the sun went down. For that last long hour and a half, Kitty would go quiet, yelling only when one of us became obviously distracted, stopping to fix her scrunchie or to stare out at the darkening trees or to talk to another girl about the upcoming Dave Matthews Band concert at Madison Square Garden. *Come on, girls.*

Most of her ire those nights was reserved for her daughter Alana, our fidgety striker, faster and more talented than any of us, a legend in the batman leagues, the reason for the three-goals-per-player maximum rule. She had what people called a nose for the goal, knew how to find that magical, empty lane in the center and streak through it, away from the pack, how to fake out defenders, though no one had ever formally taught her the Maradona, the stepover, or the Croiyff, her mother couldn't afford to send her to those expensive soccer camps out on Long Island.

"Come on, Alana, get with it," Kitty would say during a practice, when her daughter abandoned one of our repetitive drills, stood juggling the ball on her insteps.

During games, though, Alana was different. She never lost her focus, worked herself into a trance that scared even her. While the rest of us warmed up, talked *My So Called Life* and the upcoming English essay on *The Catcher in the Rye* and the new flannel they were selling at the GAP in the Hawthorne Mall, she spoke to no one, kept her Walkman on, scraps of AC/DC or Metallica leaking through the yellow ear buds. She pushed the ball back and forth between the insides of her feet, faster and faster, her eyes closed, as if she was engaged in some kind of sacred ritual, working to conjure a hurricane or praying for luck, which maybe she was. When the starting whistle blew, she snapped her fingers, rocked onto the balls of her feet and didn't stop moving until it was over, growling *here* when she wanted the ball, or *move* when we got in her way. She wore her blond hair loose, and on break-aways it would stream back behind her, catching the afternoon sun so it looked like her whole head was on fire.

Do it, Alana! Boot it!, her mother would shout.

When the eighty minutes had passed, when we'd shaken the opposing teams' hands and dispersed to take off our cleats and shin guards and chat some more, she would sit alone in the center circle, her head in her arms, breathing hard, sweat shining on the back of her neck, too keyed up to drink water or eat the oranges someone else's mother had brought in a Tupperware.

"Sometimes I feel like my heart is going to rip through my chest," she told me once at her house.

Before high school began we were friends, played one-on-one in her weedy backyard, then made boxed mac and cheese in her kitchen, letting her four cats lick the bowls when we were done.

"Sometimes I don't remember the games at all. Like they're these dreams, or black holes I fall through," she said.

"Maybe take it easier then," I told her, jealous of her talent. I was a tentative left wing, unable to hold the ball for long, always passing it to someone else as soon as I got it. It was years before I understood this as a variation on cowardice, a kind of emotional flinch.

"I don't know how," Alana said, reaching down to pet one of the cats, a tuft of fur rising into the dusty air.

Her house, a two bedroom behind Caldor, was never clean, always smelled of cat piss and dirt and old meat. I remember how surprised I was, the first time I came over, to discover she lived there, this muscled, wild girl who could, on her good days, turn a soccer field to a tinder box beneath her feet.

"She's just so intense. I worry about her," Kitty would say proudly after a game, if Alana had scored and was crouched and heaving that way.

If Alana had failed, Kitty's reaction was another story. After we'd shaken hands with the victors—if Alana didn't score, we never won—she would grab her daughter by the elbow and say, "Get up. Enough of that."

"Thank you all for coming," she would tell the parents, and lead Alana to the parking lot, to their rusted Astro van with the piece of cardboard stuck in place of the front passenger side window because Alana's father had bashed it in with a baseball bat the summer before, when Kitty wouldn't let him into their house drunk.

"Take care, you all," Kitty would shout from inside, then crank her engine and peel away, gravel and dust shooting from beneath the tires, something by Diana Ross or Mariah Carey blasting from the stereo.

Our parents—teachers, dentists, doctors, architects, computer programmers at IBM, real estate and insurance agents—would shake their heads, vow to volunteer to coach next season, muttering, *I should have this year, it's just with that damn commute, there's barely any daylight left when I get home. And they only have one year until they play varsity.*

Us girls would shrug, go back to our conversations about music and clothes, not thinking too hard about the fate of our star, who we'd already started to think of as different from us in a way that had nothing to do with soccer, involved her eighties haircut, her giant sweatshirts from Caldor, the cheap lunches she brought to school: Wonder Bread sandwiches filled with marshmallow fluff, cans of off-brand soda.

White trash, we began to whisper behind her back, in the cafeteria, eating our Boars Head turkey on brown bread. Our first year of high school, we ignored her when we saw her at the mall with her high-school dropout boyfriend who sold pot in FDR Park after school.

And we were sad, but not overly surprised, when Alana didn't get along with our new coach, a man who'd read multiple books detailing the Dutch futbol system, who came to us with instructions on how to cut, how to move up and down the field in triangles, how to practice our touch at home, in our pink-walled bedrooms, with tennis balls. Alana resisted his set plays, saying, *Don't tell me where to run*, bristled at riding the bench, quit a month into the season, throwing off her jersey and walking off mid-game.

When she started cutting her classes, switched to the alternative high school in Lakeland and then dropped out of that, too, we figured it made a kind of sense. That was what girls *like that* did, girls who blew their older boyfriends in crap ass cars in the FDR parking lot, girls who smoked cigarettes in front of their part-time jobs at the A&P—we had gigs at Fit Club, coaching rich kids in our game—girls whose mothers worked for an hourly wage, girls whose fathers could be seen stumbling out of the Coach Light Inn pub next to Camel Video in the Hawthorne Heights shopping center at all hours of the day and night.

"We've lost touch," I told my parents, when they asked about her.

"That girl was always bad news," my parents said, glad I was no longer going to the dinky house across town with the paint peeling and the soccer goal with the rotting net and the weedy backyard and the parents who were never home.

This even though my parents had their own, ugly problems, their own loud, bitter fights—my father had a mistress, my mother was often wine drunk—fights which raged regularly in the after-dinner hours, ringing through the quiet suburban nights, causing our neighbor's springer spaniel to bark spasmodically on his lead. Our white columned colonial was cleaned once a week by a Nicaraguan cleaning lady, the black and white tiled vestibule mopped, the heirloom, mahogany furniture polished. Saturdays my father mowed the lawn, pruned our pine hedges, washed our leased cars, which always looked new and had no broken windows.

In college at NYU, in philosophy and feminist theory classes, I learned to hate these images of middle class quietude, came back angry, having learned words like patriarchy and repression and materialism, came back ranting about the generic provincialism of the suburbs, the fact that my mother did all the cooking and my father planned all our family trips. I switched my GAP cardigans and jeans for Goodwill dresses, my loafers for combat boots, cropped my hair into a pixie cut, convinced I was becoming a new and better person, that this is how you escape where you are from.

"We tried our best," my parents would say, when I called the town where they raised me a Play Mobile town, the house I grew up in a Play Mobile house, like the kind my sister and I had as girls and that came with a dog that looked like our dog, a balcony that looked like our balcony, and a plastic barbeque to put on the plastic patio, where our actual patio sat.

I rarely rode the Metro North home during those years, except to see my childhood dentist, or to pluck a book from my solid oak shelves, or for holiday vacations, when I'd watch the reality television I claimed to hate for its caricatures of the working class, and let my mother do my laundry and change my sheets. *I just need a break*, I told myself.

It was during one of these vacations, the winter of my senior year, that I got the latest news about Alana.

"I fear for that girl," my mother said, the two of us sitting at the antique dining room table sipping chamomile tea. "I ran into Kitty at the A&P. She says Alana's mixed up with some guy who's into drugs. They drink at the Coach Light on the weeknights. Sometimes even in the afternoons."

"I hope she's okay," I told my mother.

I'd never been in a bar on a weekday before, never mind in the afternoon, and so this behavior seemed dire to me. It would be five years before, through my divorce and the loss of my first teaching job, I would discover my own talent for mid-day drinking, my penchant for creating my own, convenient black holes for blaming any number of things—my infidelities, my ungraded papers, my empty bank account—on alcohol.

That night, though, lying awake, I was scandalized and saddened by Alana's supposed downward spiral. Clearly, she was becoming a drunk. I thought of all the cracks I'd made at her expense, all the ways my friends and I had tacitly cut her out of our lives because she couldn't afford the right clothes, couldn't afford to see Dave Matthews Band for ninety dollars at the Garden, couldn't handle the criticism of our tough, old man coach. I remembered how, at my high school graduation party, buzzed on strawberry daiquiris, we paged through the leather bound photo albums my parents kept of my life, found a group shot of the old team, did our best impressions of Kitty.

Boot it, girls! Get it out of there already, will you? Kick it! Jesus, Mary and Saint Joseph.

Mine was the best by far; I've always been good at impressions. I made my voice high and airy the way Kitty's was, shook my head in the same desultory manner, ran my hands through my hair the way she would after a loss. I did not bother to inhabit her beyond that hour and a half on the sideline, though, did not bother to think of how the cold would have seeped through the cardboard Astro van window in October and November, or of how bone tired she must have been after spending the morning typing the Latinate names of surgeries into Excel spreadsheets for hours, then attempting to direct twelve ungrateful girls in a sport she barely knew herself, had only seen in brief snatches on ESPN in the middle of the night when she couldn't sleep.

How weary she must have felt when it hadn't gone well, when it seemed like her daughter, more wily and smarter than she'd been at the age, had failed to make her mark in that freshly limed, mini-vanned, Laura Ashley world, when the dishes were piled high and the litter boxes needed changing and her husband was out getting sloshed. How heavy Alana must have felt, too, when she'd failed to light up her mother. I could see how a girl might break under that kind of pressure, might do anything she could to dull her own heat.

I really worked myself up, thinking about these things.

And I don't know what I was planning to say to her, exactly, when I drove to the Coach Light Inn pub the following day, in the late afternoon, or what effect I hoped my words would have. I wanted her to know I understood what a dick I'd been. Maybe I imagined we could be friends again, that we'd have a toast, right then and there, to our shared past, to the comic failures of the Hawthorne Dynasty, to the fact that we'd never ruled anything on the field, that we resembled the soap opera cast more than the Carolingians or the Stuarts or the Romanovs. Maybe I thought I could help her, somehow.

I walked in, took in the smell of stale popcorn and beer, the light like the bottom of a whiskey glass, the tattered curtains and the torn up booths. A girl with long blond hair, pink at the ends, sat at the bar, a cigarette in one hand—this was before the smoking laws—her shoulders curved inward in a way that seemed familiar.

I sat down beside her. There were a couple of men my father's age at the other end of the bar, dressed in auto mechanic uniforms, who stopped talking when they saw me. The bartender put a napkin in front of me but didn't ask me if I wanted anything. I sat there, staring at the television, on which the New York Yankees, my father's team, the team I now hated because of their money, were pummeling the New York Mets again.

"Alana?" I tried.

The girl turned to face me. It was her, alright—same big brown eyes, same wide mouth—but she looked ten years older than me, deep lines framing her mouth and dark circles shadowing her eyes, a certain weariness in her gaze like she'd heard one too many pieces of bad news. Tattoos of birds and cherries and spider webs and the faces of people I didn't recognize bloomed out of the deep V-neck of her tank top, ran up and down her arms, which were well-muscled, as if she'd taken up weight lifting as well as drinking.

"Huh?" Alana said.

"I'm Rachel. The Hawthorne Dynasty, remember? Haha," I said.

Alana took a sip of her drink, which was clear and had a lime in it, a vodka tonic, I would figure out later. "How are things? Do you still live in Hawthorne?" I asked, my voice sounding high and fresh and clean in my ears.

Still, she only stared at me.

"I just, I'm sorry we lost touch the way we did. I know things were hard for you back then. We were all such assholes. We should have told you to keep playing. You were so great. Better than any of us."

Alana squinted at me. "What? What the fuck are you talking about?" Her voice was scratchy and thick. She took another sip of her drink, looked me full in the face, and then let out a deep cackle of a laugh. "Ah, right. Rachel Moskowitz."

A man walked in, tattoos all over his arms like Alana had, and in tight black jeans and a checkered T-shirt. She turned to look at him, and I did too. I couldn't stop staring at his shirt, which hugged his biceps. He was the kind of guy I'd always half-wanted to date, arty, effortlessly cool, a little menacing. He stood beside her, put his hand on her shoulder and squeezed, said, "We've gotta go."

"Get a load of this chick, from my super soccer star days," Alana said, looking me up and down and laughing again. "Look how cute she is."

I was suddenly aware of my flowered vintage dress, purple tights, and patent leather shoes, the clothes of a little girl playing dress-up.

"We've got to go," the man said again. "Set-up's in thirty minutes, show's at eight, Taconic's a shit show."

"Jesus, Mary, can I finish my drink?" Alana said, sounding for an instant like her mother. Then she pounded the rest of her vodka tonic, dropped some cash on the bar, stood up, and stretched her arms behind her back. She was taller than I remembered in her platform boots. She smelled of smoke and a complicated perfume I couldn't identify, a combination of sage and lavender and men's cologne.

She cracked her knuckles, smiled hard at me, and followed the man out the door, out into the bright afternoon, out into a life I knew nothing about and could not imagine.

I stared at the bartender. "Can I have what she had?" I asked.

He poured me my first vodka tonic, which was strong and sour and which I did not finish, leaving a minute later, slipping into my parents' Honda Civic, eager, all of a sudden, for vacation to be over, to get back to college, to the life I still figured could only keep getting better, to the self that could only become more knowing. I rolled down my windows, turned up my new riot grrl CD, drove through the hilly streets of Hawthorne, back to my leafy neighborhood, back to the house I would not admit I still thought of as home, where clean laundry and clean floors and a good meal and a made bed were waiting for me, the house set up on the hill, far from the street, the house that did look, from the bottom of our driveway, like a kind of toy castle, a place where the restless daughters of kings wiled away their adolescence, fretted over their ball gowns, questioned their gilded mirrors, glared at the plastic bars on their unlocked windows, slept fitfully in their tiny, pink-walled rooms.

Grayhound

He meant it as a nice gesture. It was summer and his wife seemed more depressed than usual, their oldest, their girl, gone off to college early. And the breed made a kind of biographical sense. When was the last time she'd put on her track shoes? He imagined woman and dog coursing the trails of FDR Park in the blue-black mornings, her coming home flushed, downing a glass of orange juice, making them bacon and eggs. She'd laugh at his jokes. They'd make love. She'd finally get better.

He did all the legwork, had the yard fenced, took the boys to Caldor for fake rabbits, a fishing rod for a pole lure, a chainlink crate like the kind she would have lived in back at the track. He said, "Name her." His wife refused, went back to her crime novel. Before he could press her, the kids said "Roadie, like the Road Runner, beep, beep," and it stuck.

But all through August the dog didn't take, flitted through the house at night, ghost gray, pissing in clean laundry baskets, nosing the walls for cracks. Days she kept to her crate, to her bleached white bones. His wife kept to her old clogs, to her sea of dandelions in the back yard, pulled the hairy bodies up with soft grunts.

"Take it easy," he told her.

"Who else will pull them?" she asked.

She'd get like this before a low period, cleaning like crazy, pacing the rooms with a bottle of lemon cleaning solution in her hand, then bringing up old fights: the time he forgot about her at his work Christmas party two years ago, left her alone all night to make awkward small talk with the lawyers.

"You never think about me," she'd conclude, pointing the cleaning solution at him.

Sometimes he'd fight back. Say something like, "All I do is think about you and this damn funk you're in." Or, "If you'd go to the gym now and then, get out of your head, you'd feel better." Or, "You know they make pills for this, Rosalyn. You should get yourself some."

This only made it worse. She'd call him a money-grubber like his father, and probably a cheater too. He'd accuse her of throwing herself a pity party, tell her that her childhood in Queens with her gambler-father wasn't as bad as she liked to claim, that everything was always about her, that she didn't love the kids enough.

These days he tried to be more conciliatory. He'd done some reading, understood it was an illness. "I don't like seeing you this way. What can we do to make it better?" he'd ask.

"I don't know. I need to see someone, I guess," she'd say, and hug him.

But then she wouldn't. Instead, she'd vacuum all the rugs or plant new bulbs in her garden or pull weeds until her shoulder burned and her runner's knees ached so badly she could barely stand. Nights she'd take a long, steaming bath, down four Omega-3s, then come to bed with ice packs, cold, wet fists thrust between them. Downstairs, Roadie would howl.

"You better walk her," she'd tell him. "I never asked for this."

He decided he'd show her how to love a hound. "Come outside, just for a minute," he told her one night after dinner.

"Run her," he instructed the boys, a camcorder balanced on his shoulder. "Let's see what she can do." The dog opened up, whisked through the burnt grass in quick circles and it was beautiful, though after awhile she seemed to limp a little, to wince when her feet touched ground.

"Give her a rest," his wife said, moving between him and the dog. "You're hurting her."

Then she was coating her golden capsules of Omega 3 in peanut butter, feeding them to Roadie with a spoon, baking homemade dog treats using the Christmas cookie cutters, calling, "Here, girla, girla." At dinner she talked osteo-arthritis, the damages of racing. On the couch in the evenings, reading her meditation book, she traced the curves of Roadie's ribs, gently, with her fingertips, as if she were a violin. "My sweet girla."

Yet when the dog's hips went three years, three therapists, four medications, and two gym memberships later, he was the one who dreamed of those big eyes in that thin, skull face, who woke weeping, who stood in the middle of the kitchen in the middle of the night eating a bacony Christmas tree, wondering if he'd run her too hard, wondering what else he'd done wrong, wondering if the gray would hound, would haunt them forever.

Jews in Sports

Whenhen they cut me from the Hawthorne under-nine boys basketball team, for my temper and lack of height, my father gave me an illustrated children's encyclopedia entitled *Jews in Sports*.

"Make sure you check out Koufax, Benny Bass, and Jack Rubin," he said.

"Yeah, thanks," I said, holding the volume loosely in my hands. When he left my bedroom, I flipped through the drawings quickly, then chucked the book into the mess of dirty clothes and video game cartridges on my floor.

I was a fidgety, restless heathen of a kid, in those years. After school I would eat a Dorito-and-Easy Cheese sandwich, then wrestle our dog, a sweet, overweight golden retriever, until he barked and tried to bite me. After dinner I liked to strip down to my boxers and run laps around the house, singing House of Pain, *Jump around, jump around, jump up, jump up and get down,* pissing off my older sister, who was bookish and lonely.

At temple, when I couldn't sit still during the Rabbi's sermon, my father would take me by the hand and lead me outside, to the car for our gloves, and then to the adjacent softball field for a catch. We'd throw back and forth until I'd worn myself out, until I could barely feel my right shoulder.

I relished any activity that involved constant movement, contact, a ball. In the fall I played left wing for the Hawthorne under-nine boys soccer team. I wasn't great—larger, more athletic boys would push me off the ball, beat me to the fifty fifties—but I wasn't bad, either. I had my moments of snarly brilliance. My Maradona was fast and tight. My Cruyffs left the beefy farm kids from LaGrange and Dover sitting back on their heels.

"You didn't score, but you should know, you still dominated," my father would say afterwards, offering me a bag of sliced oranges.

In the winter I barreled up and down the Hawthorne Community Cultural Center gym, at guard. When we started to lose, or when the taller, broad-shouldered boys on my team eventually stopped passing to me, I kept the ball too long, threw elbows, cursed, put my head down. It was like my skin was on fire, covered in red jellyfish, and I had to do something to release that heat, shake things up. I'd throw an ugly, deliberate air ball or punt the ball into the stands, or stalk off the court kicking at any water bottles or chairs in my path.

The refs—tired, volunteer fathers in New Balance sneakers—called me, "Ari the terrible."

"You gonna keep your cool today, Ari the terrible?" they might say during warm-ups, laughing nervously, chucking me over the shoulder.

I'd push away from them, throw up a hook shot, thinking *shut the fuck up*.

"Relax," my father would say to me on the bench, when he saw the frustration building in me. He'd put his hands on my shoulders and squeeze. "You're doing fine son. Relax."

"Leave me alone," I'd say, ripping his hands off of me.

Of course I sensed I'd never be a good enough athlete for the pros, or even for college ball. I had second string high school varsity written all over my anxious jump shots, my hurtling lay-ups, my weak rebounding. Still, my father wanted me to have hope.

"You know, when he was a boy, Abe Attell used to get beat up every day," he'd say, referring to the 1920's featherweight cham-pion, the Jewish Hammer, pictured in *Jews in Sports* administering a right hook to some anonymous, blond-haired schmuck.

"Sandy Koufax made it onto the Dodgers as a walk-on, and it took him years to hit his stride," my father explained, on the car ride home, after I'd been cut. "You know he refused to pitch a game during the World Series because it was on Yom Kippur?"

"Big whoop," I said, feeling particularly beastly. "I would have pitched on Yom Kippur."

• • •

In a New York suburb populated by Irish and Italian Catholics and Anglo-Saxon Methodists, we were reform Jews. It had to do with my mother being Catholic, and my father not wanting to go to temple three nights a week. "It's like the minor leagues of Judaism," I would tell my non-Jewish friends years later, in col-lege, to get a laugh. "Think: the Binghamton Senators of Judaism. The Binghamton Mets of Judaism."

The temple was a few blocks from our house and shared its space with the local Bucks Lodge. During the oneg, held in the party hall, you could still smell the Miller Light and the cigarettes the Bucks smoked during their meetings.

In the evenings, you could hear them gather. They met every night around eleven o'clock. The lights in the temple/lodge would all go on at once, and then, at exactly eleven, the bell out front would chime eleven times. I'd wake up in my bed, always alarmed, and then I'd imagine a secret society of creatures that were half man, half buck. They'd have painful looking antlers sprout-ing from their bald heads, brown fur creeping up their necks. The chimes would call them together to howl in pain at their desperate, hybrid condition, to stomp the floors with their heavy hoof-feet.

I'd seen a lot of horror movies as I kid. I loved *American Werewolf in London.*

If I couldn't get out of Hebrew school for a soccer game, I'd sit in the musty classroom and look for traces of Buckmen activity: hoof prints pressed into the wood floor, bits of hay, droppings, blood stains from when their antlers broke through the skin. While the rest of the class repeated Hebrew words out loud, enunciated the "ch" of "Baruch" and "Melech," which I always found vaguely embarrassing, I drew fierce, menacing Buckmen in my notebook, created a Buckmen's language, half English words, half grunts.

Sometimes our Rabbi would walk in and catch me at it. "And what are you doing there, little monkey?" he'd say, smiling widely, his voice filling the small room like he was giving one of his sermons about the state of Israel. His face was old and wrinkled and greasy, like he'd bathed in Vaseline. He would come close to me, put his hand on my shoulder, then pinch my ear, hard. "What a strange little monkey."

I have few other, vivid memories of my Jewish education. One was the time Adam Fisher—a quiet kid with acne and corduroy pants that he wore too high—farted during the shower scene in *Schindler's List.* Our teacher kicked Adam out, saying he wasn't taking the film seriously. This was ridiculous, because Adam was the only kid who ever did the Hebrew school homework. I had hated him for his dedication. Once, at regular school, I led the other boys in giving him a wedgie, made fun of his fish-patterned boxers.

"Think before you act, Ari," my father said, when Adam's mother called my mother that night.

At eight, I hadn't minded Adam, or Hebrew School, that much. I liked the brutal, Old Testament stories, the hangings and burning bushes. For the annual Purim Carnival costume contest,

I had wanted to go as Haman. Specifically, I wanted to be *monster*-Haman, to wear the devil horns and tail and fangs left over from my Halloween costume, to add facial scars and green face paint. What was the point of being Haman, the guy who plotted to kill all the Jews in ancient Persia, if you couldn't be scary?

"It doesn't match up with the iconography, buddy boy," said my father, who taught high school history and cared about details. "It would scare the younger kids, and it would be incorrect."

"Why can't you just let *me* do it?" I said, swinging an imaginary baseball bat, not looking at him.

"If you want to win, you should try to get it right, son. That's all I'm saying. You should take some pride in it."

I responded to this argument reasonably, by running up to my room and kicking a hole in my bedroom door, then slamming it so hard it came loose from its hinge. My memory of doing this is vague: there was that familiar heat moving through my arms, into my wrists, into my hands, that sense that the house, that my father's voice, was a thorny net flung over me.

"You do what you want," my father shouted from the living room. "I'm done with you. I'm done."

An hour later, my father came to me with a can of Coke, a box of Triscuits, and a spray can of Easy Cheese. We settled on a Torah costume, took the box the big screen TV had come in and painted it in the unfinished basement, blue and silver and gold. My father let me decide how to do the scrolls, let me write some of the Hebrew letters across the front, the few I could remember. He didn't make me redo sections that weren't to his satisfaction. When it got late, he left me to finish the project on my own.

"This is for you, son," he said, more to himself than to me, and walked slowly up the basement stairs, away from me, closing the door gently behind him.

• • •

In the year before his heart attack, when I was twenty-five and newly married and living in the city, my father told me about his own father, who had died before I was born. The old man had worked as the vice president of A&S, cheated on my grandmother, rarely did anything with my father.

"He was cold. A real shit head. He never should have had children," my father said. "Though I guess I'm lucky he did."

On the weekends my grandfather golfed at the Port Washington Country Club with the vice presidents of other Manhattan department stores. During the week he came home late and disappeared into his workroom, where he carved Old Testament scenes into clay and ivory pipes. He displayed the pipes in the parlor on special mahogany shelves, or donated them to the temple bazaar.

Only once, when my father was eight, did my grandfather suggest a collaborative activity, a father-son rubber-band propeller airplane race they were holding at Port Washington High.

My father was excited. "He'd never taught me golf, or carving. I thought, here's one thing. I thought if I did a good job, he might teach me more."

Then it became clear that my grandfather had no intention of letting my father anywhere near the plane before the competition. He created it the way he made his pipes, hunched over a cluttered workroom table, a single halogen lamp burning, paintbrushes of various sizes lined up, the door shut. When my father came in and asked to help, he was shooed away.

"By the time we got to the high school, I hated that damn plane. I wanted to crush it in my hands," my father said. "You're not the only one in this family with a temper."

As my father hooked the plane on its string—they raced them strung across the gymnasium—his hands shook with anger. When the rubber band broke and the plane stopped dead, half way across the gym, he laughed out loud, so loud that the other fathers turned and stared at him, and my grandfather dragged him away by the elbow, hard, threw him into his Lincoln town car, drove him home without retrieving the beautiful, broken plane.

"*Good riddance* was what I was thinking," my father said. "I've never been so happy to see a thing fail."

I was proud of my Torah costume, though I only wore it for the opening minutes of the carnival, long enough to win second place and a jar of jelly beans. It was heavy on my shoulders, itchy somehow. I ditched it recklessly, left it in a corner next to the food table to play box ball in the parking lot. While I was gone, someone left a dirty plate on the top, and someone else spilled grape juice down the front, smearing the gold lettering. In a few days it made its way to the end of our driveway, along with the broken door, ready for the pick up. It hurts me now to think of it there in the cool, March rain, a sacred thing turning back to ordinary, the colors blurring and running down the gray street.

It reminds me of the day the temple/lodge was defaced. It was a raw, rainy morning in November, a Saturday. I was fourteen, freshly Bar Mitzvahed and free, I thought, of Judaism and all its rituals. I remember being angry at being woken up early, on a day when I liked to sleep in.

"You'll get over it," said my father, and something in his voice made me stop arguing and pull on a pair of jeans from my floor.

We rode without speaking, the rain pelting the windshield in big, heavy drops. I held in my lap the yellow raincoat my father had given me to wear, which I'd refused to put on. Mara Hoffman, the only Jewish cheerleader, might be there.

"What the hell happened?" I asked at last.

"There's been some graffiti. Don't say 'hell'," my father said.

When we drove up to the building there was no Mara Hoffman, but there were twenty or so other people in raggedy looking clothes, trying to wash away the swastikas spray-painted on the walls of the building. Dipping car wash sponges into buckets, pressing their hands against the brick, the people looked tired and small, not so much removing the red, white and blue paint as blurring it, turning the swastikas to faded fireworks. There were some Bucks wearing their Sears jeans, their VA baseball caps, and the kind of cheap ponchos they sell at gas stations. There was Adam Fisher in his ill-fitting pants and a windbreaker, his face pale.

My father cut the motor. Full of shame, I put on my raincoat, pulled the hood down low over my face, followed him toward the volunteers. I was a boy who had never learned Hebrew, who had read the Torah transliterated, who had taken any chance to mock this place and the people who loved it. I was terrified that any one of them, Jews or Bucks, would suddenly know me for the asshole I was, recognize my ugly kind in their midst, call me out.

But if they sensed my shame, both groups were too busy and miserable to say anything. And so I applied myself hardcore to scrubbing, like they were paying me for it, like my dinner depended on it. I scrubbed until my arms burned, until my back ached, until my hands went stiff with cold and my fingers pruned and I could barely grasp the sponge.

"Take it easy, son," my father said.

"Fucking idiots," I spat.

"I'm sure they didn't mean anything by it. Probably just some kids being young and dumb."

I hoped he didn't see the heat rise in my face, the guilt in my eyes. I went back to the work, hoping, as we all hope at some point in our lives, that this one, selfless, earnest act would make up for, or even retract, a hundred other, selfish ones, that this would remake me into the kind of son I wanted to be, composed, appreciative, careful with my father's love.

Afterwards, my father and I went to the diner for eggs and bacon, the things he wasn't supposed to eat on his low cholesterol diet, and it felt like it might be so. We gossiped about the bossy, sisterhood women who spoke to the reporters from the *North County*

News. We talked Mets and Jets. I thought: this is a new beginning. I thought: I'll go with him now, every Friday, to services.

And then I didn't. It was three years before I stepped inside the temple again, and it wasn't for prayer or ritual. I was eighteen, had a part-time job at the golf course snack bar and too much time to myself. I drove around in the family mini-van with Tone and Paulie, two guys from the basketball team, cans of light beer balanced in the cup holders. We swam illegally in the reservoir, polluting the county drinking water with our lusty stink, smoked pot, shot off illegal fireworks at the elementary school playground, sucking in the charred, coppery smoke.

One night, we stole my father's good Russian vodka, a half-liter bottle, and drank the whole thing in an hour's time, passing it around in my basement while we played Mortal Kombat on the big screen.

"Think. Think about what you're doing, Ari," my father would have said, when I suggested we make it our mission to discover the nightly machinations of the Bucks Club, to spy on their eleven o'clock ritual.

"We'll have to be stealthy," I said to my friends. "No laughing. No burping. No crying in baseball."

We walked down the middle of the street in a line, the way suburban kids walk anywhere, city or country. Each time a car passed, we would push each other toward the curb, tackle each other onto the grassy lawns, like we were protecting each other in a combat zone.

The back door of the temple/lodge was unlocked. We entered through the kitchen. The sweet-sour-fish smell made my stomach churn.

"You okay, Ar?" Tone asked.

That summer my sister had gone away early for college—they had some kind of ice breaker hiking trip for freshman—and my father had had an affair and moved out, to a small apartment in the next town. I went to see him once a week. Usually he would take me to the sports bar and grill down the road, where they didn't care that I was underage and let us sit at the bar and eat our bacon cheeseburgers and drink Cokes. In my memory the Mets were always playing, always just about to start losing.

Sometimes my father would ask me a question about school, or about my mother. I'd field it monosyllabically. We were not talkative men, at least not with each other, and our sessions felt as uncomfortable as being in temple, repeating words I didn't quite know or understand. Soon I made up excuses why I couldn't see him: a friend's birthday, a summer baseball game, a phantom date.

Standing in the temple kitchen, I remembered making Hamantashen, Haman's ears, with my mother and sister at the counter, at the last Purim carnival, while my father set up a game of Pin-the-Tail-on-the-Donkey for the younger kids, all of us there, separate but held together by the thin mesh of ritual. I remembered the old woman who always stole food from the oneg, stuffed macaroons and hunks of challah into her big, black purse and disappeared.

"Hey, Ariella," one of the guys said, and snapped his finger in my ear.

I shoved the hand away, hard. "What the hell?"

"Hey, hey, hey. Listen."

Upstairs, there was the sound of men singing, something sad and slow.

"Proceed with caution," I said, trying to recover myself. We pushed through the swinging door and into the hallway, up the stairs, past the electronic wheelchair lift. I held them at the door, at the threshold of the main hall. Then we leaned, as far as we dared, into the smoky room.

Grown men, men our father's age and older, stood side by side in a circle, eyes closed, tears streaming down their faces. There were no antlers. No secret symbols. They were wearing worn jeans and faded beer league softball T-shirts. It was hard to make out the words of their song. My head swirled with drink. They stopped, all at once, and bowed their heads.

The guy who must have been their leader, a man in a Jets T-shirt, said in a raspy, smokers' voice:

Tonight we call to those of us who are lost, those Bucks who roam the cold dark alone, who can no longer enter these warm rooms. In this silver hour, this lonely hour, we remember you. We call you home. The great, swelling heart of Buckdom calls you home, now and forever.

Later, I made a joke out of the last bit. I sang "Deep in the heart of Buckdom," to the tune of "Deep in the Heart of Texas," and Tone and Paulie laughed.

In the moment, though, the prayer did not strike me as funny. I remember the unnamable dread I felt when the leader stopped speaking and the bell began ringing, eleven hard, spare strikes. I stood as still as I could, sweating, the sound moving through me, pinning my feet to the floor, pinning me to that lodge, to those men, to my parents asleep in their separate beds, to my grandfather, mean and cold and dead, to death itself.

Then I was vomiting all over the carpet, awful, wretching sounds. The men looked up at me, horrified, confused. The leader turned, his face red, said, "Excuse me, can I help you gentlemen," an edge to his voice, and then my friends were dragging me away, back down the stairs, all of us banging into the walls as we went, knocking down framed photographs of smiling Bucks.

We staggered through the kitchen, back out the door and into the damp night. We ran across the softball field, into the trees and through the quiet streets of Hawthorne toward the edge of town, our feet sickeningly light on the pavement. We ran all the way to the Croton dam. Only there did we stop and put our hands on our knees, our chests heaving, our throats full of bile. The roar of the water and the memory of the bells filled my ears.

• • •

In the morning, I used my golf course snack bar money to buy my father a new bottle of vodka. I suggested that we go to the driving range and hit, a thing he'd taught me how to do after he'd taught himself. When he corrected my swing, or when I hit nothing but air or the putting green, I tried not to lose my temper, to not throw my club into the air.

Afterwards, we went to the diner for eggs and bacon. I thought: soon I will be able to tell my father not to eat all that bacon. I won't care how mad and offended and prickly he gets, that his own son is telling him this, I won't care when he shouts, "I'm an adult, I can make my own choices, thank you very much," like he did with my mother. I'll laugh it off, come up with something firm yet witty and comforting to say, something that will save us both face. And then we'll move on, me with my life, and him with his own long, long life.

• • •

And in the years that followed, I did try hang around his apartment more, even when the woman he'd had the affair with went back to her husband, even when my mother remarried, and his place got increasingly sad and messy, old newspapers piled on the living room floor, his porn left right out on the coffee table, his fridge filled with low calorie versions of the foods he loved: low calorie Oreos, low calorie Triscuits, low calorie ice cream sandwiches with an anorexic looking cow smiling maniacally on the package.

Sometimes I'd even sleep over. We'd rent a bunch of George Carlin, Robin Williams, and The Three Stooges, order a pizza.

"You should know that people don't ever change," my father told me one of these nights, when we'd just finished *Annie Hall*. Both of us were exhausted, drunk with cheese and grease and too many diet Cokes.

"I guess," I said, because I didn't want to go into it, didn't want to believe him. If people couldn't change, than I would not change, would always been irritable, angry, restless and alone, doing freelance reporter work in this hick town. If people couldn't change, then he couldn't change, and his life would remain this lonely. There would be no healing. There would be no new love. There would be, finally, no peace.

"Do you have any lighter movies?" I said. "Do you have any action movies?" I asked. " Or is there a game on? I'm tired of the Stooges. Slapstick gets boring after awhile."

• • •

A year later I started dating Cara and got my first job as a copy editor for *Tennis Magazine*, in Manhattan. I came up to Hawthorne less and less. I wasn't lying when I hung up on my father after five minutes, saying I was busy. It felt like my life was a new car, a red Cadillac, and if I didn't drive it often enough someone would realize that I didn't deserve it, that it wasn't really mine. They would take it back to the shop.

"Not a lot of Jews in tennis," my father said, one of the last times I came to visit him. "It has to do with that waspy, country club culture."

It was June, Father's Day. We'd gone to hit a few golf balls, and I'd noticed that he was more winded than usual, that he didn't say a word about my swing. I figured he was tired. He'd taken his students on a class trip to Washington D.C. the weekend before.

"So what if there aren't any Jewish tennis players?" I told him, suddenly irritated. Why wouldn't he just be happy for me? "I don't think religion is a big part of who a person is, anyway. I'm more an editor than a Jew," I said.

"Oh, yeah. I see what you're saying, son," my father said, standing up from the couch, going into the kitchen for another of his Skinny Cow ice cream sandwiches.

"Want one?"

"No thanks. If I'm going to eat something, I'm going to eat the real thing."

Oh, I was full of grand ideas that year, the way I'd been full of too much physical energy when I was younger. I brandished them without thinking, like a kid with a new toy bb gun, a kid who should know better.

My father sank back into the couch heavily, like his bones had turned to iron. "I'm sorry. I didn't mean to upset you, son."

I turned up the volume on the television, where the Mets were just about to start losing. My father ate his sandwich too quickly, so that it made his head ache.

• • •

It was months after my father's funeral when I found *Jews in Sports* again, in my old room. It was wedged tight between my old yearbooks, those flip books of our former selves. I opened the volume up slowly, afraid, somehow that it would speak, or that spiders would fly from the binding. Instead it was just the old pages, yellowed and musty and good smelling.

The entries were darker and more comprehensive than I remembered, darker than anyone would expect to find in a book written for children. You can learn, for instance, that Abe Attell, the Jewish Hammer, was accused of playing a part in the 1919 World Series fix, and that he died alone in New Paltz, New York, in 1970.

You can learn that Jack Rubin, or "Mad Cap Jackie," the 1930's heavyweight champion who stitched a Jewish star on his trunks, died of a heart attack in the Roosevelt Hotel in Hollywood, far from his family on the East Coast. The doctor had thought he had the flu. When he brightened up a little, when the pain in his chest seemed to subside, Jackie made a crack about how he shouldn't have ordered the Roosevelt's largest steak for dinner. Then he keeled over, turned blue, and said, "Oh God, here I go."

I don't know if my father mistook death for indigestion, or if he thought he was going somewhere else, or believed that God was waiting for him. When it happened I was in the city with Cara, hadn't been home in months.

And in all those years of temple we never talked about the afterlife, or about God, not really. We stood next to each other facing forward, mouthing the words in the book, singing the old songs, my voice quiet, the ancient language as uncomfortable to me as my dress clothes, my father throaty and unashamed, a man who'd grown up Orthodox with a different kind of father, a man who had Holocaust nightmares as a boy, dreamed of the Gestapo taking his family away, a man who could, perhaps, link the prayers, however shortened, however Reform, however minor league, to Russia, to the pogroms his great grandfather escaped, to losing a home forever.

We kept our eyes on the pages, rose up and sat down, thought our separate thoughts, until the start of the sermon, when the stillness and sadness and the heavy maroon carpet and the mahogany beama and the deep, lurching voice of the Rabbi became too much for me to bear. Then I'd wrap my knuckles on the pew in front of me, or curl the blue prayer book ribbon around my fingers, slowly, one by one, turning each finger purple.

My mother would look at my father and he would take my hand, lead me through the black suits and the crushed velvet dresses. Looking back, I imagine him as eager for a break as I was, eager for a way to escape the stern voice of the Rabbi and the many references to eternity, as he stood next to the woman he no longer loved. Or maybe, each time they took out the Torah, he thought of his own father, of all the old man had not given him, mixed up with what he had.

And though this happened in all seasons, in my memory it is always spring when we slip outside the temple, the ground soft with snow melt, the air full of mud and new grass. We take off our jackets, walk onto the field, not caring about the damage we'll do to the ankles of our dress pants, or to our good shoes. We throw back and forth, back and forth, the darkness and stillness and sadness lifting off our bodies, until we are laughing, until he is saying, "swing batta, batta, batta," even though I'm not batting, and "What a wise guy," like Curley from the Three Stooges, when I throw too hard. The temple fades into the back ground, the Cantor's solemn voice distant as the whir of the Taconic weaving to the city, and then it is just us, not speaking, the smack of the ball in our gloves a private, unsanctioned pleasure.

What must the people have thought of us those Saturdays, driving by on Route 202 on their way to football and baseball and ballet practices? Did we appear to be two delinquents playing hooky, an impatient man and boy mucking around in their formalwear? Did our flushed cheeks, our sweat-glazed brows mark us as men or as beasts, as damned or as blessed, or as both at once, forever, amen?

Autumn Begins in Hawthorne, New York

after James Wright

In this town it is us girls who scrabble for grace come September, who chase a soccer ball on the ragged FDR Park Field, our lungs burning, the forest around us still summer green, the sidelines long gone ghostly with weather. It is us girls who, at age eight, that year of lanyards and D.J. Tanner and hand clapping games, learn to shield and head and fake while our fathers watch, camcorders balanced on soft shoulders, office shirts tucked into khakis, Diet Cokes set on the ground beside them.

At ten, our cheap cleats falling apart, the soles separating from the imitation leather, our fathers tell us it is time to get serious. They do not like our current coach, an eighteen-year-old boy from the Parks and Rec Department who reeks of pot and does not remember our names and shouts for us to *boot it*. They did not grow up with soccer, grew up in the city playing stickball, but they can recognize a slacker when they see one. They can recognize a job half-done. They want us to know our game *in depth*. They don Adidas warm-up suits and silver whistles, peer into handbooks with titles like *Confident Coaching: The Ultimate Guide to Soccer Tactics*, and *Coaching Ophelia: The Baffled Parents' Guide to Coaching Girls*, and *From Corner Kicks to the Corner Office: Girls, Soccer, and Self-Esteem.* They gift us with red, girl-sized cleats made of real leather, with expensive soccer balls from the Adidas outlet in Monroe, with shin guards that they dip into pots of boiling water, mold to our shins.

They name our teams after big cats that do not live in Hawthorne: the Jaguars, the Tigers, the Cheetahs. Or they name us after animals that do not exist, that never existed: the Gryphons, the Chimaeras, the Phoenixes.

"What is a gryphon, a chimaera, a phoenix?" we ask our fathers.

They describe a creature with the body of a lion and the head and wings of an eagle, strong and wise, guarder of treasure, protector of the gods, blazoned on a thousand heraldic crests, a creature with the body of a lion and the tail of snake, breathing fire through the mountains of Lycia, terrifying the Titans, an immortal bird rising from its burning nest, its gold and red feathers on fire.

"Cool," we say, though we are scared. Can we ever be as fierce, as powerful, as mythic, as our fathers imagine us?

"You'll do fine," our fathers say, and squeeze our shoulders, give us tennis balls to kick against the pink walls of our rooms, to teach us what they call "control."

At night, while we are asleep, they study the handbooks, learn all the positions, watch Premier League games on ESPN 2. They purge the kitchen cabinets of Grasshopper cookies and Doritos, restrict our diets to whole grain bread and peanut butter sandwiches, apples, roast chicken without the skin. In the after dinner hour, while our mothers do the dishes, they call us out into the backyard, show us how to pass with the insides of our feet, how to shoot with our insteps, how to juggle the ball up on our thighs. They say *thatta girl.* They say *now we're cooking.*

They laugh when the ball bounces off their own shins, careens across the grass and disappears into the pachysandra. They say, "It's harder than it looks."

Our fathers are trying. Our fathers are teachers, home contractors, and insurance men. Our fathers want to be more loving than their own fathers, who ran department stores and law firms and medical practices, who were as impossibly elegant and distant as the Manhattan skyline, which we can see from the top of Turkey Mountain if we squint. When we sprain our ankles, our fathers call the athletic trainer at the local college, purchase ice packs from Sports Authority, prop our legs up on pillows, demand that we follow what they call R.I.C.E. (rest, ice, compression, elevation).

Our fathers break our hearts.

And still, and of course, we despise them. We hate how, when we are losing, they follow the ref up and down the sidelines, yelling obscenities, their city accents coming out. We hate the elaborate playbooks they create, in which we are blurred stick figures pulling offsides traps, swarming the goal, moving upfield in shifting triangles. We hate how they lose their tempers when we miss our pre-ordained runs, their faces turning red, their silver whistles cutting through the dead, suburban afternoons. We hate the classic rock they play when we're warming up for a game, how they can't resist air guitaring to Queen. We hate the jokey yet authoritative tone they take at practice when explaining a new drill, a combination of Robert DeNiro and Seinfeld. We hate how they lead us in suicides, yipping for us to *look alive, girlies. You gonna let this old man beat you? Fattah boom battah!*

We even hate how they compliment us, how they say *stellar effort* in a slightly British accent they must have picked up from the announcer on ESPN 2.

On the phone with each other, on Friday nights, we do imitations of our fathers, loud enough for them to hear us: *This new game is called hot potato. The ball is the hot potato. Get it while it's hot! Wakka wakka wakka. This game is called sharks and minnows. Shark attack! Stellar effort, girls, really. Absolutely stellar.*

Fourteen, our forest singed gold, our field all divots and crabgrass, we imagine our own line of guidebooks for the daughters of coaches: *A Girl's Guide to Coach-Fathers Who Tell Bad Jokes; A Girl's Guide to Coach-Fathers Who Wear Too-Short Shorts; A Girl's Guide to Coach-Father's Who Bench You for a Missed Shot; A Girl's Guide to Coach-Fathers Who Call Hawthorne a Hick Town and Refuse to Eat in Its Restaurants; A Girl's Guide to Coach-Fathers Who Get Depressed On Sundays, Who Disappear into Their Bedrooms With Boxes of Entenmann's Donuts and a Law and Order Marathon On; A Girl's Guide to Coach-Fathers who May be Having an Affair; A Girl's Guide to Coach-Fathers who Take Long Drives after Dinner in their Honda Accords, Who Talk of Moving Back to the City, Who are Realizing, Year by Year, Game by Game, That This is Not the Life they Wanted, Not at All.*

At fifteen we miss practices to go to Friendly's with our first boyfriends. Or we show up late full of chicken fingers, our hands shining with grease, our sprints slowed. Or we show up with newly pierced ears, wearing velvet chokers and vanilla-scented lotions we buy at the Body Shop in the Hawthorne Mall. The forest flushes with October. The air smells like burning wood.

"Get serious, or go home," our fathers tell us, glaring at the earrings, blowing their silver whistles, the signal for us to circle up and stretch our hamstrings.

We glare back at them, stalk away, glad to be free of their eyes, which are blue like ours, sharp as pins, glad to be free of the itchy nets their voices have become.

Yet it is hard to stay still at home. Our houses are cold and big as barns. Our mothers are cleaning the newly re-finished wood floors, their graying hair pulled back in scrunchies, the chickens they'll bake for dinner defrosting on the counter like giant, drained hearts.

"Why are you always cleaning?" we ask.

"You're tracking mud in with those cleats," they say, spraying our pocked footprints with lemon water.

"This is like living in an Ikea showroom," we say, sounding like a combination of Robert DeNiro and Seinfield.

And we are too young to understand the shape of our mothers' anger, to know how the cracks our fathers make about our mothers' stretch pants, their stiff way of dancing, their inability to enjoy Woody Allen movies, build up like the cholesterol they take Lipitor to try and escape. We don't know how cleaning can be a prayer for calm, a prayer for love, how cleaning can hunch a woman, can become its own, desperate muscle memory. We think of ourselves as stronger, more athletic, more sure of ourselves than our mothers ever were. We think our scissors, our crosses, our grapefruit-sized calves, our headers, our fakes, our seven-minute miles, will save us from becoming them.

We cannot imagine that there will come a moment, ten years from now in another state, riding in a car with a boy, going someplace he has chosen for us to go—a restaurant, a record store, a Wal-Mart—when we will feel our shoulders curl inward, our eyes dull, our statements flipped into questions nettled with hidden anger, our mothers moving through us like ghosts. We cannot imagine the fear and sadness that will work through us after that moment, the way it will spread around our hearts like rust until we leave that boy, leave the love we feel we have recklessly lost ourselves in.

At fifteen we only know that watching our mothers wipe the cleat mud, their scratched Bonnie Raitt records cranked up, their mouths thin lines, we crave our game, crave that witty grace. We take off our necklaces and earrings, tighten our laces, head back to our fathers, to our field, that tattered, crabgrass map where we have jobs—wing, center mid, stopper, sweeper—where we can swagger and cut and preen, where we are praised for our touch, our wall passes, our Maradonas, our give-and-goes, where we feel, for a few hours every day, almost invincibly beautiful.

And when November comes, and the weather turns, and a fine drizzle falls over our field and our weak ankles ache, our fathers ask for our bare feet, wrap our joints in pre-wrap, then thick athletic tape. "Is it too tight?" they want to know.

"It's fine," we say, springing, feeling solid on our feet again.

And we are almost sad when, at sixteen, the last leaves fallen, our field a sea of red and gold, our fathers say they've had enough and take off their silver whistles, leave us to the Hawthorne High School varsity coach. He is a tall, stern man in his seventies, a lapsed Catholic and former football coach who calls the wings linemen and bellows at us to *Think about what you're doing, crimmony Christ almighty, god in heaven, you're running around like chickens with your heads cut off.*

Our new field is kept carefully manicured, the lines freshly limed, the nets neon orange, the whole thing penned in silver chainlink. There are boys who show up to watch us, who lean over the fence calling our names. We learn to roll our Umbro shorts at the waist the way other girls roll their skirts, to let our hair grow long, so that our ponytails pour down our backs, catch the wind when we sprint. During warm-ups we stretch our hard-to-reach muscles slow. Soon we will kneel before toilets, vomit pizza, ice cream, bowls of pasta, anything we think might ruin us for this other game, this other blazoning we crave.

And we will blame Hawthorne, blame soccer, blame our fathers and our mothers. We will move to states in different time zones, with trees whose leaves do not change come fall, with winter nights hot and thick as New York summer. There we will try to love the curves of our bodies in sundresses and A-line skirts. We will try to crack our own good and bad jokes, strawberry beer on our tongues. We will mostly get the jobs we want, spend our days sitting at oak desks, looking up now and then to watch the pigeons wheel through the skies of our distant cities, landing now and then on the rooftops of brick buildings. We will fall in and out and in love again. We will see ourselves flitting in and out of the visions we imagine men have of us. We will try not to.

And we will not think of soccer often, our bodies newly conditioned to dance the two-step at zydeco clubs, to pace classrooms and board rooms in heeled boots, to thread crowded dive bars. Only now and then, when a colleague mentions their child's bantam game, will we remember those long hours honing our one-touch passes, our Cruyffs, and our step-overs, with our fathers.

And now and then we will almost miss it, those years when we were Jaguars or Phoenixes, Cheetahs or Gryphons, Tigers or Chimaeras, when we weaved across the dying grass of Hawthorne in polyester jerseys, the smoldering leaves always already falling around us, those years when we moved in packs, wild and wary, wise and unwise, playing for the flawed, lonely, anxious, driven men who loved us, and who we wanted, despite our feathered, beaked, clawed, selves, our fierce, restless, rising, inexorable selves, to love back.

Calling All Soloflex Men

If you remember anything about me, you remember my before. It's the best part of the infomercial, the moment when you can see another man's unkempt awkwardness, his weak places, his cluttered, unseemly, fat life before he went into the gray room, before the Roman Chair Sit-Up, before the Dorsy Bar Pull Down, before the infamous Vertical Hanging Sit-Up, which *burns as many calories as a hundred yard dash*, if you believe our infomercial MC, former Mr. Universe, and Soloflex inventor, Ray LeBoeuf.

Years ago, I'd watch the befores late at night, when I couldn't sleep. I wasn't overweight then, just a little soft in the belly, a little heavy in the face, from eating our kids' snack foods. I'd been a baseball player in high school, still had the muscled arms and legs, vestiges of the body the Soloflex men were striving for. Two days a week I coached our daughter's soccer team, skipped fifteen six-year-olds around the field, chased down their errant balls, showed them how to pass with the insides of their feet, like they say in the parent-coach handbooks. I never lost my breath. I never needed a rest.

I had this insomnia, though. Ever since our first kid was born, I'd wake in the middle of the night thinking I'd forgotten to lock the front door, or pay the electric bill, knowing for sure that we were all about to suffer tremendously and that it was my fault. Wide awake, I'd head to the basement, plunk down on the couch, and watch Ray LeBoeuf and his machine. Sometimes my wife would join me. We'd share a bag of Cheetos or a sleeve of Grasshopper cookies and speculate about the rotund insurance exec from Scarsdale doing the YMCA at his son's bar mitzvah, his suit straining around his stomach, or the video game addict from Michigan in spandex shorts and a giant *Night of the Living Dead* T-shirt, walking an ancient treadmill, or the ad man from the Bronx cheering at a Knicks game, a beer clutched in one fat hand, his thick hair slicked to the side.

Sometimes we'd agree the person looked better in their before. Happier somehow. More themselves before the muscles. Take the ad man. Now there was a guy you could tell loved his plate of spaghetti and meatballs, a guy you could picture telling crude jokes about lingerie ad campaigns at dinner, his fork loaded with noodles and sauce. As a Soloflex man he looked vacant and sinewy, a marionette puppeted by the elastomer weight straps, *engineered and designed by Gates Learjet Company*, or so says Ray LeBoeuf.

Other times we'd laugh at the befores. I'd make a crack, something like, "People should need a special government ID to buy spandex like that. It's a question of public safety." My wife would say, "Be nice." But then she might smile and put her hand on my knee. We might make love. The house was still new then, the basement cool and unfinished, the kids young and long asleep above us.

• • •

When my own before aired, five years later, my wife and kids were kind enough not to laugh or make cracks. It's actually not a bad picture of me. I'm reclining on a lounge chair by a pool in a voluminous Hawaiian shirt, holding a greasy cheeseburger. The sun is shining in my eyes. My cheeks are sunburned. My legs are pale and birdlike, crossed at the ankle. I'm smiling easily at the person taking the picture (my wife? the host of the party?). I look tired, but satisfied.

By then our kids were so good at soccer they'd been placed on these prestigious select teams. The teams had names taken from a famous European soccer league. The Westchester Hotspurs. The Westchester Arsenal. Names that meant nothing to my wife and I, but we trusted the coaches, serious looking men in Adidas track suits who called soccer "futbol," who called the team practices "training sessions," who had our kids sign special forms promising to not play other sports during futbol season.

They lead our children all over the Northeast to compete against other select children in games that were beautiful to watch, nothing like the grape soccer they played when I coached them. Back then they would all bunch around the ball, moving in a shifting clump. Now they were artisans of space, sorcerers of geometry, weaving up and down the field in expanding and contracting triangles, their touches gentle and precise, their faces all futbol professionalism.

We became friends with the other team parents during these years; you have no choice, you spend so much time with these people, sitting on sidelines in Port Washington or Hamden, staying in chain hotels in the Poconos or Virginia Beach. By the end of the first year, there was a team party nearly every weekend. A pre-game party. A post-game party. A post-pre-game party. My before must have been taken at one of those.

They were good parties. Lots of booze. Sometimes dancing on a back deck or a freshly mowed lawn. But they always seemed a bit more pretentious than your typical suburban shindig. There'd be a wheel of brie imported from France instead of cheddar, take-out from Miragio's, the best Italian restaurant in town, instead of homemade ziti, chili made with ground lamb instead of ground beef. The women chucked their sideline jeans and sneakers for

Talbot's dresses and heels. The men donned button-down shirts and shoes from Nordstrom's. Though none of us would have admitted this then, I think we thought of ourselves as a select tribe of parents, Westchester's wise, chosen ones. For look how they prospered, our talented spawn. With each passing season they grew stronger and faster and smarter, streaking across those manicured fields, juggling the ball to each other in the back yard, deepening their own private language.

And yet, with each passing season, we felt a parallel shrinking inward, my wife and I. Our backs stiffened in sideline camp chairs, coffees and diet Cokes and energy drinks perched in the cup holders. We grew fat on post-game fast food, talked select at breakfast and at dinner, barely saw each other on the weekends, each of us pairing off with a different child. When we did connect, it was at a team party, and then we drank. We'd guzzle the craft beer from the inevitable cooler in the yard, and then my wife would disappear into the hosts' kitchen for gossip. I'd flirt with the mother of a boy on my son's team, a woman who'd grown up in Manhattan and made her own jewelry. She wore what she called "Egyptian-style chokers," these thick silver bands, tight at her neck. I'd imagine making love to her, pressing my fingers, very lightly, on those bands.

Before long we fell to arguing at the parties, my wife and I. Little tiffs, but it was ugly. I'd get loose and jokey, make cracks about her bowl haircut or the gift she'd gotten me the Christmas before, a thing called a Depression Lamp that's supposed to *fill your room and your heart with light*, if you believe Dr. Janet Turner, Ph.D. and inventor of the Depression Lamp. My wife would come back at me with something like, "Get your own drunk self home then." Sometimes she'd take the kids, leave me at the party to find my own ride.

Other nights my wife would get quiet after dinner, lingering by the platter of cut vegetables with a beer gone warm in her hand. Then she'd call me to her and turn brooding and accusatory, asking why I never asked her questions about her life, and why I was always talking to that woman, and why didn't I notice when she got quiet, that it meant that she was feeling sad and needed someone to talk to and if I loved her I would know this by now. I'd say something sensitive, like, "I'm not clairvoyant."

When we managed to attend the same child-soccer-game, we stood next to each other on the sidelines without speaking, our eyes trained on the ball. We shouted our kids' names until our voices went horse, then drove home in silence.

The last team party we went to, we didn't fight, but there was this awful tension between us, like the hour before a migraine hits. We were somewhere in Chappaqua. There might have been a pool. It was summer. They were grilling quail. I was secretly gorging myself on the bagel pizzas meant for the kids. Couples were dancing on the back deck, the way my wife and I once did. The Manhattan woman was standing next to me in a black dress fancier than what all the other women were wearing, her choker shining in the fading light. My wife drank more heavily than usual, so that when it was time to leave she was calling our kids by their baby nicknames, shouting, *Get in the car, Tiltawhirl. Right now, Bugaboo.*

We slumped into the Outback, my wife at the wheel, and as she weaved back and forth over the double yellow lines of the Taconic, then exited shakily onto Baldwin Road, the darkest road in Hawthorne, I made a crack, something gently teasing, like, "Are you trying to kill us all?"

Soon after that, she drove us into a telephone pole.

And I was so tired of our marriage at that point, so drunk and lonely and angry, that as we pitched forward into the airbag clouds, as the windshield bloomed with cracks and the front end made this awful, crunching sound, I was thinking that this was the kicker, that now she'd really done it, that now I had an excuse to leave her. Only the sound of my own kids screaming snapped me out of it. It's a sound that feels like being decapitated by a dull skate blade, in case you've never heard it before.

We pulled them out of the back seat, my wife and I, though they insisted that they were unharmed, that they could do this themselves. We hugged their still-whole bodies. We kissed their arms, grasped their bulging calves and thighs, so shaped by their sport. We took their faces in our hands and shook them.

• • •

The week after the crash, she joined AA and I ordered the Soloflex. Three times a week, twenty minutes a session, the machine would be a way of taking control of things, a way of feeling like my old self again. If she could buy into the whole higher power, twelve-step thing, what was so shameful about a physical fitness regimen? What made that a lesser form of redemption?

"All I need is knowledge, desire, and the right *equipment*," I told my wife, quoting Ray LeBoeuf, trying to make her laugh.

"It's not good for the body, all that repetition. You'll lose your range of motion," she said. She's a physical therapist, so she knows all the small ways you can fuck your body up.

"Maybe you can help me with my range of motion," I told her. Then I did my best Arnold Schwarzenegger impression, which did not make her laugh.

For a while, though, things seemed to get better. She found a sponsor she liked, a woman with Sinead O'Connor hair and her own electrolysis business. I did not make a crack. She went to meetings every night, hiked Turkey Mountain in the afternoons, coming home with her face flushed, smelling of wood smoke. I set my machine up in the basement, went down there every night after dinner. At first my hands burned from the pull bar, and my legs ached from the frontal squats, but then I grew accustomed to the strain. I lost weight, started eating better. At the high school where I taught freshman history, the kids started calling me "The Hulk."

In response I would growl and bug my eyes out and pretend to rip off my shirt. They appreciated this, or at least pretended to.

And even our own kids, who had kept their distance since the accident, warmed up to the parental transformations. They would make good-natured jokes when I'd go down to my Soloflex, like, "Dad's flexing solo tonight! Dad's going to flex his solo!" It is a pretty dirty name, when you think about it. In October they made my wife cards for her ninety-day anniversary, wrote long, thoughtful notes in them that made her cry.

The night of the ceremony, I took us all out to Miragio's, where we ate family style, sharing giant trays of penne vodka and chicken parm. Everyone had more than enough. At the church, when they called my wife up to get her special bracelet or key chain or strength crystal or whatever it was, I felt proud of her, in her blue-green dress, her small shoulders tensed, her voice thin but steady as she thanked me and the kids for what she called "our constant support." I didn't say how this sounded generic, like something she'd read in one of her new motivational guidebooks. I was grateful, happy for her. Cheesy and macho as it sounds, the next morning, during my work out, I felt like the whole house was balanced on my Soloflex, me the steady Atlas holding us up as we turned, gradually, painfully, willfully, into this next part of our lives. The elastomer weight straps slid soundlessly up and down the steel spine of my machine.

A week later I got the call from Ray LeBoeuf about the infomercial. "We hear you're a teacher, a family man, and a Soloflex Man," Ray said, his voice huskier and scratchier than I remembered it from TV. More of a smoker's voice. "We've had too many horny bachelors on the infomercial lately. We want you."

I was supposed to bring the whole family down to the studio in Manhattan to film. There would be a hefty compensation, "enough for a back yard pool," said Ray, as if he knew that this was how I would convince the kids to go on camera.

And so off we went, on a Saturday morning, my wife in a new dress, my kids in their soccer uniforms: Ray wanted to film us kicking the ball together in Central Park, though we hadn't done that in years; they were way too good for me now.

It wasn't a bad day and Ray LeBoeuf isn't a bad guy. He didn't lord his Mr. Universe success over us, or go on about his muscles like those frat guys we all knew in college. After the filming, he took us out for burgers at this spiffy joint on Madison Avenue, the kind of place with oak paneling behind the bar and Tiffany's lamps and a life-sized painting of some championship racehorse on the wall. He didn't lecture me about his physical fitness regimen, or the value of positive thinking, or the need to have goals. In jeans and a flannel shirt, his face still orange with bodybuilder tanning lotion, he told us about the day he was exhibited at the Whitney Museum, along with Arnold Schwarzenegger and Mr. America.

"It was horrible. They called it, 'Articulate Muscle: The Male Body and Art,' or some crap like that," Ray said, downing his double whiskey in one swig, biting into his burger. He'd ordered it "fresh kill rare," and blood from the meat dripped onto his thick fingers. "They had us posing on these rotating, white platforms, in this gallery room with white walls. There was this panel of experts, real academic types, all in sweaters, talking about whether men should lift or not, and how we mold our bodies like clay, how we're artists of physique, yad-ah, yad-ah. I felt like one of those stuffed animals they got in the Natural History Museum."

He ordered another double whiskey, ran his fingers through his handlebar mustache. Up close, you could see the lines around his eyes and mouth, the bulging awkwardness of his body in the jeans and shirt. "I felt sick up there on that platform. They didn't even have posing music."

When my wife went to the bathroom, and my kids left to browse the sneaker shop next door to the restaurant, Ray talked about his two ex-wives. "Lifting is like sex but it ain't the same," he said wistfully. "Lifting keeps a guy steady. I probably would have burned my second wife's house down, if it wasn't for lifting."

"Maybe it isn't half bad, tearing your life down now and then," I put in. I was getting drunk on rum and Cokes, on the thick amber light. My life back in the suburbs, with its select teams, its lonely machine, suddenly seemed far away.

"What the hell are you talking about?" Ray LeBoeuf said. He slapped me on the shoulder, which hurt. "You got it good. Don't fuck that shit up."

"Okay, okay, geez," I said.

Ray's mouth twitched a little, then settled into a hard smile. "Long as we're clear. I'm not trying to be your role model or any shit," he said.

Even so, it was a good night. I was sad when Ray called for the check, when we piled back into the new Outback and headed towards Hawthorne's thick quiet.

• • •

We must have had other good nights after that, my wife and I, but I have trouble remembering them. Come winter she started going to double AA meetings, then having dinner with her sponsor afterwards. It was a particularly bad winter and she'd go out even in heavy snow, even in an ice storm, wearing the Shalimar perfume I'd gotten her for her birthday, saying how the new Outback had four-wheel-drive and why was I such a worrier. She'd come home after I'd gone to bed and gush about this or that recovery story her sponsor had told her, or this or that vegan meal her sponsor had cooked her.

"You know, sometimes I wish we could just share a glass of wine again," I said to her one night, when she was on her way out to a meeting in Armonk in the freezing rain.

"I miss the old you, sometimes," I said.

"You just don't get it, do you?" she spat, and slammed out the door.

I began to spend more time in the basement. I worked on my machine every day in the dark mornings before school, in the gray afternoons after work, sometimes even at night, after dinner. There are these small windows down here, near the tops of the walls, looking out on the yard like the portholes of a ship. Back in the summer they'd been filled half with my wife's irises, half with sky. In winter I lifted and pulled down and upright rowed and watched them fill with snow and cloud, until it was hard to distinguish one from the other, until the world was a solid block of gray, until it seemed like this was the only world I had ever lived in, until only the elastomer weight straps seemed to keep me from disappearing into it, or becoming filled with it, a man made of cement.

Sometimes I'd close my eyes while I lifted and imagine my machine was a boat and I was rowing away from this hick suburb toward the city, toward a different kind of life, one where people talked art and politics instead of youth sports, where people went to impromptu midnight movie showings on week nights, where I could show off this new body on a real dance floor with a live jazz band playing in the background, where the Manhattan woman was my wife. I'd get lost in these fantasies and lose track of time, of my repetitions, of the rhythms of the house above me.

When I came up, I was irritable, even mean. I'd see my kids eating fried peanut butter sandwiches with bananas for breakfast, a thing I'd taught them how to make when they were young, and I'd say something like, "You know that's how Elvis got heart disease, eating things like that. Do you want to die of a heart attack like Elvis?" It got to the point where, when I came up, my wife would think of an errand to run and my kids would go outside to juggle their soccer ball. I would slug back a protein shake and descend the basement stairs again, full of dread and gratitude for my own, secret submarine.

It got to the point where I'd sneak the portable phone into the basement and call the Manhattan woman, just to vent. She was very sympathetic over the phone. "I understand, I understand exactly," she said. "Let me tell you about my marriage," she said, her voice smooth and polished as her silver chokers, wrapping around me, bracing me.

And here is what Ray LeBoeuf knows, what any lifting man knows, but won't tell you: every human transformation has its hidden fractures, its loose ends. We can all point with our eyes closed to the places on our bodies that remain outside the reach of the elastomer weight straps, or the treadmill runs, or the grapefruit lunches. At night, turning in our beds, newly strong or newly sober, we breath in and out and try not to jostle the hunger or the desire or the anger or the lack that is not banished, is not transmuted, is simply shifted to another, less obvious place inside us.

Months passed, maybe years, while I lifted. My job called the house and then my job stopped calling. My wife left meals at the top of the stairs. Sometimes she opened the door and shouted that I should come up and talk to her, that I was sure to injure myself irreparably this way. "I know what I'm doing," I shouted back, until she stopped coming to the door.

For awhile the kids would come down and watch the Yankees while I lifted, yelling out the scores to me. I'd try to participate, but it had gotten harder to speak through the exercise, which I couldn't seem to stop doing. I couldn't catch my breath long enough to ask them to help me unclench my hands from the metal. Eventually they stopped coming down here, and I don't blame them, I really wasn't much use.

One time the Manhattan woman snuck down to see me in my gray room. There were the occasional sounds of my wife and kids above us, shutting doors, turning on faucets. She said it reminded her of some place she was supposed to be. Her hands on my hands on the pull bar, she said, "It feels like a tomb down here. We're buried."

"Not such a bad way to be buried," I said, leaning in to kiss her choker.

She never came again. Which I can understand. I'm not much use to anyone down here.

These days the sounds in the floors above me have grown distant, impersonal. Someone in high heels walking across the kitchen floor. My wife? My daughter going to a dance? Someone playing a patriotic song on the clarinet. My son? Someone thundering up the stairs and down again, having forgotten something? I couldn't tell you.

If they leave the basement door open, I'll get scraps of conversation. They talk about their days and their successes. My daughter is doing well in honors history. I miss talking to her about her classes. My son has his first girlfriend, a dancer two years older. I wonder what questions he has about love, if he'll ever come down and ask me, and what I would manage to say.

"We're on an austerity budget," my wife announced one day. She said she wanted to move the family to a condo in White Plains. She said she wanted the kids to get part-time jobs. She said, "He'll find his way out of there, when he's ready." I did fifty reps a minute for ten minutes, this made me so angry. Not the part about leaving me—I could understand that—the part about the kids working. They should be focused on their schooling, on their select teams.

Of course, I should just leave. Unclench my hands from the pull bar. Rise up on two strong legs. Thing is, I've forgotten what I'm supposed to do up there. I have vague memories of the old Soloflex infomercials: flag football games, shirtless days at the beach, women in wedding dresses to lift by the waist into your arms and carry up to bed. What am I to make of these images? My running shoes are un-scuffed by the craggy world outside the portholes. My before feels as distant as the other Soloflex men, an ugly, uncouth, ungainly ghost who will not be summoned, will not be called back to this gray room, to this cold frame.

Though there are mornings, when the light in the portholes changes from gray to silver, when I'm lifting so easily, so steadily, my arms could become wings, when the iron and rubber that surrounds me feels sacred. Those mornings I almost hunker up the stairs and bellow, as I push through the hallway, out the front door, up into the gray air, shedding the house like dead skin, *I love you, I love you, I love you. Goodbye forever.*

Girlhunt, Spring 1999

Our mothers give us hiding clothes and cowbells for our sixteenth birthdays. They tell us not to be afraid. This is the suburbs. The streets end in cul-de-sacs. The woods are long rid of bears. The porch lights have motion sensors and the fields are caged in chainlink and reserved for organized sports. If the boy is too rough, if we don't like who finds us, if we feel lost in the dark, we are supposed to ring the bells.

We love you, our mothers tell us, and shut their doors.

We understand. Our mothers have a lot on their minds. It is the spring of stunted divorces, the basements full of cheater beds—moth-balled blankets thrown over ratty couches—the back porches echoing infidelities late into the night, strained, shifting bird calls. We listen in our trees, terrified, intrigued. We are getting an education. One day, we are moving to the city.

We see you out there, listening, our mothers shout into the dark. It is early March, the ground covered in mealy snow, our mothers in pastel nightgowns, faded vacation-town-sweatshirts and winter boots. Their voices are calm lakes filled with sharks.

You can't stay up there forever. What are you so afraid of?

And one by one, in the cold, muddy maw of the night, we slide down rough bark, streak into the thinned woods fast as hares. In our black skirts, T-shirts, and ski masks, we look like a search party for a kidnapped kid who is already dead. We sing our favorite songs, braid one another's hair, compliment and criticize each other's skirts. *Too short, too long, too frilly, just right, whisking the tops of your knees.* We wait for the boys, for our girl-hunt, to begin.

Growing up, you hear stories. Like how some girls hide stu-pidly behind saplings and end up found and taken right away. Or how your weird great aunt was the best climber, the best hider, so good that people said she didn't want to be found. Now she's the hunched crab apple on your grandparents' lawn. You hear of a running girl from Poughkeepsie who turned into a towering oak, the rooted altar of a cop named Tim, her name engraved on all his guns. Or how your own father used the joke strategy on your mother, left jokes like crumbs on the ground so that your mother laughed herself out of a tangle of sweetbriar. Waiting in the woods, kicking at the dead leaves, you try to picture your stiff, sad, angry mother laughing. You try to picture your father want-ing her to.

"Hey," the boys say, emerging from the other side of the woods in their tight pack. They look nervous, swinging imaginary baseball bats, looking down at their sports cleats, already clumped with leaves and mud. They start their count to one-hundred, and for an instant you feel sorry for them, wandering the dark on their own while all you have to do is wait.

You think of your crush, counting with his brown eyes shut, his hands balled at his sides. Track runner, rail of a boy, his name rolls off your tongue like cold milk, and at first you want him to find you, find you, find you crouched inside your mother's favor-ite azalea, where she posed you each spring in your ballet cos-tume. You want him to push aside the gushy, pink blooms, pull you roughly to him, so that you come loose in a cloud of wilted flowers. You are that young, that naïve.

When at last he finds you, he is dumber than you remember him being. No matter. It is good to be found. "Oh," he says when he sees you, and unthreads you from the spindly branches in a way that breaks your heart a little.

In other ways, he is not careful. And neither are you. The kisses draw blood. Your skirt bunches awkwardly around your thighs. The ground is hard. It is cold. A new hollowness shoots through you. Your hand goes to your cowbell and rests there. *What are you so afraid of?*

When he is done he turns you over, tucks your arms and legs under you, as if he's trying to fit you into a too-small pan in a too-small oven. He folds you back into the azalea. "Thank you," he says. You grip the bell tighter. "Yes," you say when he finds you here again, then again, then again.

• • •

Morning and the sky is a washed out blue. The snow is gone. You are woven into your azalea, trying to stay hidden. There is the brief clang of a cowbell somewhere out in the woods, then silence, then laughter. All over town girls are ripped from sweetbriar, hooked and reeled from beneath porches, netted and lifted from itchy seas of pachysandra. They walk into the houses with their boys, tired, swaying on their feet. The girl-hunt is ending. Your mother is on the front lawn, saying, *This nice young man is looking for you. I don't know who you think you are. Come out of there.*

And you don't emerge, you don't shake a branch, you don't call his cold milk name when he calls yours. You know you should, it is expected, but your body won't follow. The words rise and fall back down your throat. Azalea blooms press against your skin. The hand on your cowbell tightens, moves back and forth. The rusty, guttural clang seems to come from deep inside you, the only thing you will ever be capable of saying, *find me, find me, find me,* rattling you, ungluing you, though you don't know who you are calling to. Dumb, inarticulate rescue call.

You think of the novel everyone is reading, the one about the kidnapped Southern girl. The rapist kills her, buries her out in her family's cornfield, and one day the family dog comes home with her big toe in his mouth. You wish for that kind of death, the wise, unimpeachable death of the kidnapped girl. Or you'd take the brave leaving of the runaways, the girls of the YA novels. Or the survivalist girl's resourcefulness. The hard face she points at her loneliness. Wanapalei. *Island of the Blue Dolphins.*

But you are not brave, loneliness breaks you easy, and this is the suburbs. We are not lost. We are not rescued. We are not left. We don't disappear. We only come home, one by one, stronger or weaker, night after night, on our own. And so you open and shut your azalea eyes, unfurl your stick limbs, think of a joke to make your mother laugh—you love it when she laughs—something about how you're working on a new line of camo themed accessories for girls. Make promises to yourself, resolutions like unlit sparklers in your pockets, your heart a briary thicket of anger. *One day I am moving.* You have no idea that again and again, wherever you are, you will have to fight your way out of this hiding. You smile your mother's hard smile, run a hand through the leathery leaves of your hair, and step back into the broken world.

The Body in Space

They were sending her father to space. They were sending him in one month. The matter was non-negotiable. The war was going badly. There were no jobs. The government letter said in so many words—though not enough words for Rachel's mother—that the people needed a thing to look forward to, that only space travel could offer the glossy, new-toy pride the country needed *at this current, sensitive juncture in our history.*

The letter also said they liked her father's story, or what they called his *undeniably American past.* His own father had been a Russian Jewish immigrant, had made his living as a junker in the Bronx, combing the fetid back alleys for rusted car parts and discarded appliances, his hands going numb on the cold metal in winter.

You are a man who has risen.

Rachel's father had been to the state university, had a house and job at SUNY Purchase teaching mathematics, a son at Tufts majoring in physics, a rail-thin wife with a delicate nose and bright blue chips for eyes. He had Rachel: seventeen, artistic, a soccer player, still a virgin (the government had its sources).

You'll have the honor of being the first professor in space. Imagine what your father would have said.

The government did not know that Rachel's grandfather had been a cold, mercurial man, given to casual, lasting acts of cruelty. He had died before Rachel was born, but her father had told of how once, when he had crashed his bike going over a jump made of a bent car hood, tearing the skin on his knee almost to the bone, the old man had slapped his face, plucked a needle and thread from his mother's sewing box and ordered him to fix up the wound himself, that would teach him to be reckless. Eventually his mother had taken him to the hospital, where they had undone, then redone his mawkish stitches, had cleansed the infection. Her father still had the scar, the thick, grinning mouth of it running straight across the kneecap, visible when he wore shorts, visible in the evenings of Rachel's girlhood, when he would take her in the backyard in the after-dinner-hour and pass a soccer ball to her across the dampening grass.

Those nights seemed long ago now, part of an intimate language they no longer spoke. She thought of him as an unfunny comedian with too much air time, holding her breath when he spoke to her, her chest burning with an anger she could not name except to say it had to do with his long absences in the evenings, with her mother's eyes in the mornings, bloodshot, rimmed with accusation.

We also view your twenty-year marriage as a model of strength and coherency in these uncertain times.

Her mother had quickly placed the government letter in a drawer where they kept the bills and stray paper clips, saying it must be a joke, a prank from a former student who'd less-than-enjoyed her father's "space math" unit.

"Must be," said her father, resuming his red pen and his stack of long division tests.

But later that night he read it to himself and then to Rachel, who sat at the kitchen table with her history book.

You'll join the proud coalition of real Americans entering space: a single, working mother of four from Iowa, a soybean farmer from

Nebraska, and our very own Olympic gymnastics champion, Katie Crug—you know, the one who vaulted with the sprained ankle. Inspirations, all. We'll be in touch.

"I wouldn't really want to go, even if it was real," said her father, his voice full of longing. "I bet there's no pastrami in space."

• • •

Then NASA called two days later, wanting to come for dinner. "You already have my support. Our support. We're all in," her father had told them, his voice rising, while Rachel listened on the stairs. In the kitchen her mother carved a roast chicken. Their dog, an overweight lab, panted for scraps.

"My son's in college. It's not a great time for a visit."

"Okay, sure, come meet The Family. Dinner will be fine."

"No, I'm not nervous. She'll love this."

"Space then," said her mother when he hung up the phone, her voice turning in on itself like dead leaves. "Good for you."

They'd met too young, Rachel's mother had told her once. On her second glass of wine her mother became chatty, her pale, freckled hands stuttering over the stem of the glass, her voice breaking now and then.

"We met and married and started with kids right away, without any time for ourselves. It was what people did. I still love him, of course. It's just hard sometimes. Don't marry till you're thirty. It's a rule. Promise me."

"I'm never marrying," Rachel said, and her mother had looked up at her suddenly, as if not recognizing her, as if she thought she'd been talking to somebody else.

• • •

On Tuesday a man and woman from NASA arrived. They were wearing matching khakis and polo shirts with bright silver moon landing logos on the pockets. They were careful not say Challenger, to talk around the word gently like a crevice or a wound.

"The space program has come a long way since the eighties," they said. "NASA will double, no triple check everything before lift-off. Statistically the trip is safer than a drive down the Taconic. Really."

"There are plenty of other teachers who would love to go to space," said Rachel's mother, setting down her fork and knife. Sober, she was a quietly assertive woman, cheerful but firm, a figure skater smiling through a difficult spin. "You see that this man still has a child in the house."

"Hasn't he always dreamed of going?" the representatives argued, Rachel's father nodding along. "Hasn't he gone to the space camp for teachers in Gulfport?"

"Yes. Yes, that's true," said Rachel's mother, the authority seeping from her voice.

Rachel's father took a long gulp of beer. The representatives asked for seconds of the purposefully cheap meal Rachel's mother had prepared for them: chicken tenders from frozen, Rice-A-Roni, and canned green beans.

"It's good to have a real American meal," they said. They took more than their share. They chewed funny, like they were trying to show how much they liked the food.

"This conversation isn't really necessary," Rachel's father said finally. He forked the last soggy green bean on his plate. "We're all excited. I know Eric is excited. You're excited aren't you, Rachel?"

"Of course," Rachel said. The prospect still seemed like a fantastic game to her. She said, "Do we get a lifetime supply of space ice cream?"

As a younger girl this was the most impressive aspect of space travel to her, once she discovered a person couldn't run the marbled rings of Jupiter. She no longer cared for the chalky substance, but she knew her father liked it when she acted like a younger girl. It put him at ease, reminded him of the years when they knew each other better.

"All the space cream you want!" said her father, laughing, standing up, waving his hands across the table as if he could make the ice cream magically appear

"Of course, of course. Chocolate?" said one of the representatives, making a note on a legal pad.

"She's cute. Watch out for that one," the other one said, winking at her father.

Her mother served a sour lemon tart for desert. The NASA officials ate it in gigantic bites and smiled hard, drops of yellow curd sticking to their teeth. They slid a neat pile of paper work across the table to her father and Rachel was asked to leave the room. She slipped out of the house into the foggy April night and settled into the pine-smelling cool of the minivan.

· · ·

When the van was new, when they were children, they had not thought of it as one. Rachel and Eric had liked to play in it. Sometimes they pretended it was a city apartment, like the kind her father used to say he wanted for weekends away with their mother. The front seats were the parlor, the middle seat their bedroom, the back seat a balcony looking out over Manhattan. They imagined New York life to be like a James Bond movie, the height of sophistication and swag. They reclined in the two rows, sipping their juice boxes like faux martinis, picking at their bags of fruit snacks like they were caviar. They talked about going "downtown" and what they would do there, about leaving, "this suburb full of hicks," as her father sometimes called it.

Months later, when her father went to space camp for teachers and began the 5th grade space math unit, the van became Rachel and Eric's spaceship. Shaped like an egg, painted a pale, emerald green with the word "Quest" on the side in silver letters, it lent itself better to this fantasy. They would get in the bucket seats, Eric pressing the brake and gas pedals, then announcing to Rachel, "Please prepare for lift-off. We are now headed for Mars."

It was understood that as the older sibling, as the male, as the one more skilled at mathematics, he would always be captain.

"Passing through the atmosphere," he would announce, and they would vault themselves between the two seats, bumping elbows in an imagined microgravity, until they got dizzy or Rachel accidentally elbowed Eric in the eye. Then he would say peevishly, glaring at her, "We are now touching down on Mars. Please prepare for landing. All crew members restrain your selves."

Landing they would explore the forest behind the house as if it were Mars, collecting chunks of granite and broken beer bottles, which they called "Mars rocks," taking them back into the mini-van for inspection. Rachel would write down Eric's observations in a composition book. "Definite signs of water. Some green substance, possibly life."

Of course, the space van quickly became shoddy, became theirs, became the thing itself. Mud and grass from soccer cleats caked the floors. The air took on the smell of the fast food dinners her father ate on late night drives home from what he said were work meetings.

One day, while he and Rachel drove to a July soccer game in LaGrange, the back window shattered, all at once, completely. Her father said a rock must have flown up from the road. A confetti of glass covered the whole back row for days.

Now Rachel had inherited the van. It felt lonely without her family in it, like driving around a restaurant that had just closed for business. There were tiny pieces of window glass between the back row seats, grinning like a promise of future disaster. Still, it was amazing to have wheels. She drove the van to school and to practices and games. She drove it when the house made her stiff with the anger she could not name. She drove it to pick up Chris Watson, who she liked to fool around with in the back row.

She was not sure if she loved him. There was the textbook tone he took with her sometimes: when he was helping her revise one of her history essays or correcting her grammar midsentence. Sometimes when they had fooled around she felt homesick, like she was traveling far away from everything she knew. She would watch her reflection in the dark windows kissing him, a girl with a too-tight pony tale, comically serious. Where were they going? Where was she? What would her father say?

But she liked the curve of his spine, the narrow vulnerability of his hips, his lacrosse player's body. She abandoned her one girlfriend. She lost ten pounds, eating sour grapefruit after school. He was the first boy she had ever kissed.

"My father's going to space," Rachel said now, her throat sore. They were parked in the county bike trail lot, their usual spot. It was down a dirt road in the middle of the woods. As they talked, the last of the day's runners and bikers sped by, their red faces clenched with effort and pain.

"No kidding," said Chris Watson. "No kidding. That's incredible. Actually I already heard about it in the paper. They published the list of Real Americans. Will you get to go in the ship before it takes off? Can I go too?"

"They're usually pretty strict about who goes on the ship."

"How do *you* know? You don't sound happy." He pointed to the sickle moon, which looked pasted onto the clear, dark sky. "Look. Your dad will be up there. Do you even know the constellations?" His finger left a smudge on the windshield.

"I know the damn constellations," she said, though all she could remember from grade school was the Big Dipper. Empirical knowledge would not stick in her mind. The quadratic formula, the Pythagorean theorem, the parts of the human cell, all of these she had mastered and then forgotten. Other things, like the song her father sang to her when they road their bikes on this trail, back when she was six and it had just opened, she knew she would remember forever. The song rang in her now.

Wah-oooooh, werewolves of London.

"I know you know," he said, and took her hand. "I'm sorry. This must be hard for you. My father's too drunk all the time to be in space, but if he were, I'd be nervous." The bike trail had gone dark. The lot was empty. He kissed her hard, all teeth. His body moved over and around hers, and then they were swimming toward the back row. His hands spread across her muscled thighs. The windows filled with darkness.

"I love these soccer girl legs," he whispered, as he always did, not knowing that she was trying to slim them. She wanted to be as light as she could, to be floating over him, a mermaid girl. His fingers worked the buttons of her blouse, one by one, fast, like he was shucking oysters. The car filled with the smells of salt and sweat. His hands up and around her breasts, beneath her waist band, heat spreading into her face, until the homesickness seeped into her gut and she held the damp hands still.

• • •

Her father's transformation was fast and severe. It seemed like whole parts of him were being sliced with a chopping knife. Every day after school he went to a NASA training center in Manhattan, where they had him on special machines and eating special foods to build bone mass, muscle mass, and to increase the size of his heart.

"A person ages faster in microgravity," he said one night, sitting on the edge of Rachel's bed while she worked geometry proofs.

It was two weeks until he would leave for space.

"The heart doesn't have to work as hard to move the blood. The muscles and bones don't need to be as strong. In space the body declines. Sort of like being a couch potato. Is that a new sweater?"

He touched her arm, very briefly. She looked at him. The new muscles in his arms bulged at the seams of his work shirt. Lighter, stronger, he flew through the house, appearing beside Rachel when she hadn't heard him coming. It was unnerving.

She looked at him, a man preparing to enter a country she would never enter. She wanted to ask him if he was scared, if he thought about dying. What were his regrets? She wanted to ask him about the woman, the meetings, the other part of his life she knew must exist. She imagined his ship catching fire, then fading, a beautiful, hot coal thrown into the dark. She could make him not go, she knew. But he seemed so happy now, standing up and snapping his fingers. "It's not new," she told him.

He stood in her doorway, the hallway a dark tunnel behind him. "You know, I'll be able to contact you there. This is WDAD, coming to you from space."

When she was a young girl, and he tucked her into bed, he had pretended he was speaking to her from his own radio station. "This is WDAD saying good night," he would say, his voice screwed up to sound like a sportscaster's.

She smiled at him, said, "Cool. That'd be great." He looked at her for a moment, then he was gone. A moment later she heard his voice somewhere else in the house, calling the dog for her last walk of the day.

• • •

In the remaining two weeks, Rachel's mother seemed to warm to the idea of her father in space. Glad to see him at last *taking good care of himself*, she cast off her sullenness and dedicated the house's décor to space travel. A Build-a-Bear was decorated in an astronaut suit and placed in the front foyer. Posters of the moon hung in the living room like great cratery eyes. In the basement, where her father read the NASA recommended books about space travel, she stuck glow-in-the-dark stars to the walls, like the kind Rachel and Eric had had as children, Eric's in all the constellations, Rachel's in shapes she chose: a pie, her name, a bicycle like the one she rode.

You don't even know the constellations.

The refrigerator was covered with pictures the children of Hawthorne had drawn for her father, wishing him luck, expressing their bubbly admiration. His cartoon image smiled ecstatically, floating among stars, standing on the moon beside a giant American flag, waving a giant space hand at the earth, a flawed, blue-green marble behind him.

• • •

At the Coalition of Real Americans picnic, one week before the launch, Rachel, Eric and her mother made small talk with the other real Americans. They were gathered on the White House Lawn. A table was spread with lukewarm, Thanksgiving-type food. Lakes of cooling butter lay in piles of mashed potatoes. There was an oily looking green bean casserole, a giant, half-carved turkey. The grass of the lawn glowed an eerie, neon green, as if the government had dyed it for the occasion.

"I'm so excited," said the mother of four, a tired-looking woman with frizzy hair in an ill-fitting suit. Her hyperactive four-year-old twins kept putting their hands in all the food, and soon she had to turn away to reprimand them.

The farmer wore overalls and dirtied boots. "They said to look rustic," he said, shaking his head. "I didn't know everyone else would dress normal." Then he criticized the flavor of the vegetables. "Unnatural fertilizers, that's what that tastes like." Then he was off to have his picture taken holding a shovel someone had brought for him.

Then there was the gymnast, who was only a year older than Rachel. In a baby doll dress she cranked first one leg, then the other, back behind her back, each foot touching her head, as if she was trying to break herself in two.

"Agility training," she laughed, when she caught Rachel and Eric staring. From somewhere a camera flashed, and then a cadre of reporters enveloped her short, pale body.

"I bet she doesn't menstruate. All muscle, no tits," Eric whispered to Rachel.

"That's none of your business," Rachel said, scanning the small gathering for her father. He stood next to the turkey carcass, talking to someone on his phone. He looked angry.

"Damn parents won't let me do my job," he said when Rachel approached, swiftly tucking the phone into his pocket. "I'm sorry sweetheart. Where's your mother?"

They found her mother talking to the gymnast. The reporters had moved on the mother of four, whose six-year-old girl was in her ballet tutu and was demonstrating her glisandes.

"Such a darling," they were saying.

"It's just *amazing*. You're such a lovely *creature*," Rachel's mother said to the gymnast. "I could *never* move like that. You know men really go for that kind of thing." She glanced at Rachel's father. "Men really like a woman who's flexible. Just make sure you keep it up. They don't like it if you go slack."

· · ·

Her mother's acquiescence lasted until exactly one night before her father was to go to space. The family was gathered for a parting dinner. They ate filet mignon, garlic mashed potatoes and buttered rolls, all her father's favorites. When all the dirty plates were cleared her mother stood in the kitchen, hand on hip, telling him not to go. "I feel like this is a death row meal," she said.

Rachel and Eric sat on the stairs listening.

"Oh come off it Kit," her father said. "If it was you, you'd go. You're jealous. You're stuck in your own little world and you can't see anyone else's. Its how you've always been, with me, with the kids."

"I wouldn't go with a daughter still to raise. You could have failed one of the fitness exams on purpose. Invented a vision problem. You had a choice here. You're already there. You're already gone. You know what? Fuck you. Go to space right now. Leave. You heard me."

Yes, leave, Rachel thought, hating herself for thinking it. *We're all tired of the in-between, of all this waiting.*

Her mother cursed again. There was the slamming of a door, the sound of her father's car engine turning, the screech of tires on wet pavement. Outside, it was raining.

"This is why I never come home," said Eric, sulking up to his room and shutting the door. There was some exam that he'd been studying for since he got home. She wouldn't understand it, he had told her. She heard the flick of his lamp go on, the heavy thud of a textbook thrown open on the table.

• • •

She snuck out of the house into the minivan and then she and Chris Watson sat in the bucket seats, light leaching from the sky, waiting for the bike trail to empty.

"You nervous tonight?" Chris Watson asked.

On the bike trail a man her father's age ran by. He wore no shirt and his large belly trembled with each stride. A woman in bright green spandex and roller blades quickly overtook him, her arms swinging by her side, her motions fluid and aggressive.

"Why should I be? It's just like a trip down the Taconic."

While Chris Watson talked to her about the size of the universe, about the physics of the trip, Rachel remembered when the bike trail had first opened. The pavement had been so smooth it was like riding your bike on water. Whole families traveled to it on Saturdays, packing lunches to eat on the bridge that crossed the Hudson, babies strapped onto bike seats, dogs well leashed. It seemed her family had ridden as a pack then, speaking to each other on their bikes, warning each other of bumps or patches of wet leaves. Or maybe that was just what Rachel wanted to believe of them. Maybe they had always been tacitly racing each other, maybe they had always left one another behind, maybe they, maybe *she*, had always been looking for some kind of advantage, some way out.

"Let me know what you need," said Chris Watson. "I love you."

He was not a bad person. She could be comfortable here. What was the worst that could happen? A lie small as a splinter, shiny as the key to a mysterious castle, slipped from her mouth. "I love you, too."

She pulled him closer and they swam out of their bucket seats and through the darkening van. She felt that air had become water, that she had scales, fins, gills. The sky clouded. It began to rain, great sheets of water pouring down the windows so that the trees blurred. When another car pulled into the lot they saw only vague headlights like falling stars, like dying suns, and they continued their swimming. She watched their reflections in the windows for a moment, two fish-birds moving through deep space, then closed her eyes.

And even if she had gazed through those rainy windows, through the night's thick fog, the black Honda Accord on the far side of the lot would have looked anonymous. Like the van, it had no distinguishing external features, no bumper stickers or dents or window ornaments. Rachel's father had taken meticulous care of it. She would not have seen her father's tense face in the driver's side window. She would not have seen the face of the woman in the passenger seat, her long, dark hair or her chapped lips. She could not have heard the woman say that yes, this was it, this was the *last time*, she was sorry, there was a house of people who loved her too much. She could not have sensed her father's large, healthy heart filling with sadness and regret, through all that rain. They would have looked only like two other teenagers, two dark heads coming together, two bodies swimming backwards inside another family's spaceship, the doors and windows sealed against the elements, praying for safety, going somewhere else.

Egg Toss, August 1989

In my memory my sister's ninth birthday is always almost over. The pre-made burger patties have been grilled, the supermarket cake cut, the glut of white frosting smeared on paper plates. The three aunts up from the city have smoked their cigarettes, have told the stories of the dead grandparents, of weekend childhood abandonment for Temple Bazaars, Atlantic City. The dance to Debbie Gibson's "Electric Youth" has been invented and performed. The games of TV tag have been played, the show names—*Wonder Years*, *Who's the Boss?*, *Growing Pains*—screamed into the hot afternoon. Our father has unfurled the Slip n' Slide. We have coursed the lemony strip on our stomachs, the girls in pink bathing suits, me in too-big lacrosse shorts I think make me look tough. "Ari, pull your pants up," our mother shouts. Our father announces the last game, says, "Pairs, please, ladies and gentlemen." The grass, high and thick with summer, sticks to our legs.

And it would be a lie to say that we were happier then than we are now. I can see how the aunts sit facing each other, curled away from my father, their baby brother, who they always forget to call. I can see how our mother fishes the cooler for the last beer, her hand coming up full and numb, how she drinks it too fast, pats her newly permed hair which our father has repeatedly made fun of. I can see how our father's shoulders sag as he walks into the house for the pink carton, our ringmaster, our tired stand-up comedian who we think of as tireless, who is thinking, *How many has she had?* or *Does she have the car keys?* or *When are all these people leaving?*, not knowing yet that, in a year's time, he will fall in love with someone else and be the one leaving.

And I can see how, standing in the yard, my sister has her arms crossed over the chest of her bathing suit, looks down at her thick, soccer girl thighs, which she will whittle to spindles at sixteen for her first boyfriend. In another moment I will throw an egg to her, too hard. The yoke will spill over her small hands and she will cry, will run into her room, into the hard, blue agate of her sadness, and I will not know how to follow her. I still don't.

In another moment, a warm wind will blow the paper plates across the lawn, send them flying into the pachysandra like a flock of startled birds. Our parents will chase them down with black garbage bags, angrily, not looking at each other. I know the argument that comes later, the way their accusations—*Why didn't you? Why couldn't you? Where were you?*—will crack the house open. In the morning crows will stab at the yard's slick places, the eggshells highway-cross-white against black beaks. There will be a rotten smell.

For the moment though, in my memory, my lying, longing memory, there are only the rich smells of charcoal and wet grass. The aunts' laughter spirals up into the darkening trees. The pairs move closer together. My father places the egg in my cupped hands, says, "careful." It is exquisitely cold, a tiny space ship, a miniature planet. My sister looks at me fiercely, says, "gentle," and I am floating it toward her. It hangs between us in the blue-gold light, round, whole, opaque, blessed, its casing so smooth and so thin.

Night Games

It's just after New Years when their rock hits my window. I stick my head out into a night cold as gunmetal and there they are, the night game girls, piled into a dented station wagon.

"We're springing ya, sweetie," says Connor Smith, their leader I guess. She leans on the hood, stares up at me. In jeans and a black fur coat cut to her hips, her eyes all serious, she looks different from the flirty, mini-skirted girl I know from school. She holds another rock loosely in her hand.

"No thank you. I'm not allowed," I say, though no one has specifically disallowed me. No one's mother would like what they do. They sneak out of their parents' houses in the middle of the night, drive to some hidden lake at the edge of town that no one's deemed safe for skating, play what they call hockey with their brothers' and fathers' nasty old pads and skates and sticks. Afterwards they drink a fifth of whiskey. At school they have their own table in the cafeteria, where they eat from greasy bags of fast food and laugh louder than everyone else. They cut class and smoke pot behind the science building. Some of them wear their hair cropped short like boys.

My older brother Derek calls them "the lesbo table."

I don't care what they are. My problem is they're trying to recruit me. "You must want to fuck some girls up, all that's happened to you," one of them whispered to me in the bathroom before Christmas break, while I was fixing my French braid. She wore a frilly polka dot dress and boots and a bike chain choker, like she thought she was some kind of punk Lucille Ball.

And it's not true. I'm not angry, not at my father and not at the girl. People have desires. People make mistakes. What I want is to disappear for the next three years, and then I'm leaving Hawthorne for the best out-of-state college I can find. Justin Mosely understands this. He's my first boyfriend, though we don't believe in labeling each other that way. After school he makes me bagel pizzas, then takes me down to his basement and kisses and touches me beneath his old G.I Joe bedspread until I forget everything but the weight of him and the heat between my legs. He plays tennis and has nice arms. My mother says he treats me well, that I'm lucky to have him.

"Sometime this year, doll," says Connor.

"Yeah, today." I recognize the thin voice of Winnie Friedman, a skinny-legged girl who had the most tentative jumps of anyone back at the rink. In that life I used to scream her from the corners to do my lutzes. Now she sounds ready for a fight.

"I said 'no thanks.'" But I haven't closed the window yet. In the next room my mother listens to Joni Mitchell, this one sad song about skating down a river, set on repeat. It's so stuffy in here. The night streams through the window, icy and unknown. I'm sticking one leg out slowly, like some kind of idiot burglar.

"Jeans and a T-shirt, doll. You can't skate in your fuzzy wuzzies," says Connor.

"Forget it," I say, stepping back into the warmth. What was I thinking? Derek is parked somewhere in his Celica, the Bat Mobile, drinking Milwaukee's Best with his other underage friends. My mother has stopped coaching at the rink and cooking and cleaning. In the mornings I leave an egg sandwich for her on the counter. Sometimes when I come home from school it's gone, usually it's still there, flies buzzing around it.

We live off what they call child support, but I'm the one holding us up.

I slam shut the window. The frame shudders. The station wagon burns rubber down our driveway and I'm relieved to hear it go, I am.

• • •

My father made it all the way to fourth place at Nationals before he gave up. He used to tell me he could've gone for gold, could've perfected his quadruple axel, but he wanted to have a family. He wanted to have me. This version of his life used to make me feel loved and grateful to him.

He took well to teaching, walked into this dinky suburban rink north of New York City in his black leather jacket and jeans, his curly hair slicked back, and suddenly girls were practicing five days a week, girls were driving down to Queens for five-hundred-dollar custom skates, girls cried on the ice, girls quit, girls developed eating disorders, girls started to win. He was firm without being mean, exacting without losing his temper. He could even tell a girl when it was time to hang it up, when it wasn't worth her parents' money.

He met my mother in those early years, when she was seventeen and pretty and talented and his student. *People didn't care about those things as much then*, my mother used to say when they were still in love, when I was in elementary school. *Of course we waited until I was nineteen, to do it.*

When she was nineteen she got pregnant with Derek, and then a year later she had me. Derek didn't care about skating but I was a rink rat, my spins so fast they made other girls shiver, my double axel the cleanest in Westchester County. I won in Darien and Katonah and Greenwich, towns so Waspy you have to wear J. Crew to get served at the restaurants. I kept my fingers laced and my back straight, the way my father taught me.

I miss it sometimes, but only because I did it for so long. The truth is at the end I was getting tired of it. A week before a competition I'd lose my appetite. I'd tell my mother I wanted to eat in my room while I did my honors math homework—a good lie, I'm a good student—then I'd flush the food down the toilet. When the competition came, I'd have trouble getting psyched up for the jumps. My spins slowed. You can only fake your love of something so long. I was glad for the excuse to quit, when the trouble came.

The girl was my babysitter a few times, when I was twelve and she was fifteen. The newspaper liked that part. Her name was Christine. She was a nice skater to watch, languorous and graceful, with long, thick legs and blond hair she wore in a loose ponytail over her shoulder. My father was pessimistic about her professional prospects. *Too heavy, too bovine to be great,* he told me once, though I guess he found other things to like about her.

I liked her as my babysitter. I've always been uncomfortable around girls my age. I'm overly serious, people say. Christine made me feel light and savvy. She would bring over her mother's sixties etiquette books, put on a grunge band she liked, and we'd make fun of the dating advice. *If a boy asks you to a movie, say you need to check your calendar, then call him back. If it's a horror movie or a sex movie, you're busy. Beige on the first date says: I'm not sure about you.*

"I get along better with older girls," I liked to tell Derek.

My mother liked her too. We were glad when her parents sued. Glad when they had him fired and tried to send him to jail (Christine claimed she was seventeen when it started, so no dice).

We were glad when my father moved out of our house to a small apartment across town. A year later Derek and I were allowed to meet with him in public places. We did it once or twice. We sat in the uncomfortable chairs at the Starbucks, him drinking a coffee with some kind of booze in it, us with cocoas, the girl Christine hovering in the air between us wearing her abortion hospital gown, ghostly, angry, unspeakable. He asked me about school and skating, which dried up fast because I'd quit by then. He asked Derek about his lacrosse. I could tell he was really trying because he never talked sports with Derek. It didn't make much difference though. We were all glad when the allotted hour was up.

This past summer, around my fifteenth birthday, my mother told me he was moving to the Midwest where the whole thing could be forgotten. "He's gone out to the corn," she said vaguely, like the Midwest was a prison colony, the new Australia. I nodded, as if she'd just told me about the Nets moving to Brooklyn. Good for him.

Of course I miss him. I'm not some kind of ice queen, like they always have in movies about figure skaters. I miss watching old Burt Reynolds movies with him, I miss the way he would make me repeat my jumps until my landings were all neat checkmarks, I miss getting burgers with him after practice. "Stellar job today, Jess," he'd say if I'd skated well, and I would lock those words inside me, hold them in my hands during the long school day when I felt so old and steady and alone.

• • •

They're back a week later with a larger rock. It hits like a bird in full flight, almost shatters glass. I open the window tentatively, feeling like I'm in a horrible cross between a romantic comedy and a stalker movie

"You only got a couple more months to show us your stuff," Connor says. In the garage light her red hair shines wine red. She tosses another rock several feet in the air, catches it in her open palm, her gaze never leaving mine.

"I don't think so," I say, my voice sounding flimsy as a pair of rentals.

Derek is out with his new girlfriend in the Bat Mobile, probably impregnating her. My mother is in her bedroom with a man she introduced at dinner as Smitty, an old high school boyfriend. I can hear Blondie playing, the squeak of the bedsprings. Like Derek said before he went out, "It's good she's fucking dad out of her system," but it's skin scrawling bad being here.

And there's this itchy heat in my arms and legs, my pajamas are heavy on my skin, and next thing I know I'm throwing on jeans, slipping through and into it, into the cold, onto the roof, shimmying down the gutter and jumping onto the frozen ground. My legs, still muscled, are strong beneath me.

"Impressive," says Connor, cracking a grin.

Then we're barreling off in the station wagon, the night air rushing around us, mixing with the smells of vanilla body oil and Connor's pine air freshener, away from the sleepy houses, past the town limits, the woods thickening, the darkness deepening. She drives too fast on these curvy roads. They're tightly packed in here, don't seem to care if their legs overlap, if they knock into each other, if one girl has to sit on another's lap, which can't be safe or comfortable. I'm wedged between Winnie Friedman and the door. I press my cheek against the cold glass, breathe in and out.

Not wanting to, I'm thinking about my father, how in the early mornings before school he would take me to the high freestyle session. I'd sleep in my skating clothes, wake up and stumble into his car. His coffee would steam the air between us. Passing all the dark houses, Led Zeppelin howling on the stereo, I felt like we were on a secret mission the rest of Hawthorne was too ordinary to partake of.

"Ready Jaguar," he would say when we pulled into the gravely rink parking lot. He called me that for my speed and the composure I used to have in competitions. "A real predator, my girl," he would say, and I would smile though I didn't believe

I was one. "Inscrutable," a judge once wrote on my scorecard. I didn't know what the word meant then but I liked how it sounded, like a surface that can't be scratched, like a girl who never falls apart.

Connor turns down a dirt road and stops at the shore of what she calls Gerdie's Lake. "Named after my grandmother. She was a tough bitch. Put up with my grandfather's alcoholic bullshit for ten years and still hiked the Adirondacks every winter in her snow shoes."

It's more like a pond but it's beautiful, still and smooth and silver in the light of our high beams, surrounded in cattails. There is another car in the lot, another group of girls already putting on their gear.

"Hey you Briarcliff fucks!" Connor calls to them, so that they turn around and in unison give her the finger.

"Our archenemies," she explains to me. "Think they're hot shit because of their Metro North stop and Mariah Carey has a summer house in their town. Also they're jealous. *I'm* the one who found the lake. We're the ones started all this."

She hands me a stick, a set of shoulder pads, elbow pads, a pair of bulky gloves and an old pair of hockey skates. Everything smells like mildew and sweat and feet. I struggle to put it all on, watching the other girls to see how they do it, hoping I don't get ringworm. When it's on I stand and wobble back and forth, a flawed Transformer toy. How does a person move in this?

Then they are out there, skating fast circles to warm up. It's like no skating I've ever seen before. They move pucks back and forth fast, shoulders hunched, edges grinding, flecks of figure skating grace showing here and there in an elegant crossover, in a too-frilly turn, in a T-stop.

Connor links her arm around mine, pulls me into it. There is so much room in these skates. When I lean forward I fall hard on my knees.

"Jesus Christ, Cutting Edge. I expected more out of you. Keep your stick on the ice. Loosen up. Don't lean on the stick like that, like you're a god damn tripod."

Connor bangs her stick on the ice three times and the girls split into teams. The game flows around me, too intricate to enter. I stay on the fringes, trying not to get in the way, and watch. They say Connor played with boys before she hit puberty. The mothers of the boys on the team didn't like her kind, called her names in the rink women's bathroom where she had to change. One day she punched one of them in the face, and that was the end of her official hockey career.

Her game is mirthful and angry and fierce. She checks girls into the cold, damp snow, elbows them beneath their pads, taunts them as they stick handle. *What you got? What you got? What you got, doll face?* She is a girl-creature wreaking havoc on the world, a scorned woman taking a fiery revenge. My feet itch, there's that strange new heat again. What it would be like to move like that, move with her? How do I keep my legs from shaking?

"Come on, Nancy Kerrigan," she says, circling me, "move it."

"I like to move it, move it," Winnie Friedman sings, glaring at me.

And suddenly I'm Little Red Riding Hood surrounded by wolves. I'm a cardiganed good girl fallen in with a bad crowd. I'm an ingénue, a thing I hate being. I want out. I want home.

"This ice is like a crater," I say and hunker away from them, take off the miserable pads, wait in the cold car for my body to stop shaking, for it to end, for the night game girls to float off the lake and drink whiskey from Connor's flask and talk whatever petty gossip they talk and then drive me home, where I'm sure Derek's passed out in the garage, about to choke on his own vomit.

• • •

In the morning my mother calls me into her room. I get ready for her to cry into my shoulders, or give me a new warning about men. I expect her to still be in bed, her hair greasy and matted. Instead she's on the floor doing yoga stretches. Her collarbones stick out, her cheeks are sunken, her legs are so thin her leggings sag, but her hair is shiny and clean. Her eyes are bright.

"Where were you last night?" she asks.

"Some crazy people made me go out. I don't know why I went. How was *your* night?"

She let's out a quick, fluttery laugh, comes out of her downward dog and flops down on the bed. "It's good for you to hang out with your friends more. That boy can't be everything for you."

"I have plenty of friends."

She pats the bed and I sit down stiffly beside her.

"I'm going back to teach next week. I can't stand this sitting around anymore. I thought you should know."

"That'll be good for you," I say.

Her hand moves through my hair, like I'm a little girl who just missed one of her competition jumps. She was always the sensitive coach, my father the unyielding critic. Good cop, bad cop, people would joke.

"My Jessica, always so concerned for me," she says now, the edge of some new anger in her voice. "It would be good for you to let yourself go a little now and then. Sow your oats. I'm worried about you."

I push her hand out of my hair, stare at the old podium pictures on her dresser: my mother at fifteen and sixteen and seventeen, her hair done up in a tight bun, gold medals yoked around her neck, her expression sassy and bored, as if she'd rather be out somewhere else causing trouble with all the friends she must have had. "We can't all do yoga and let things go to hell. Someone has to keep it together," I hear myself shouting, my face growing hot.

My mother stands up, rolls her neck until it cracks, as if she's about to do more yoga. When she looks at me again, her lips are set in a hard line. "Look. I'm sorry I haven't been myself these last few months. This last year. But I'm not going to be the reason you deprive yourself. You make your own choices in this life."

It reminds me of the dumb arguments she used to have with my father. He'd yell at her for not wanting to join him at the rink bar on Fridays. "It's the weekend," he'd whine.

Usually she'd put down the mystery novel she was reading, spritz Shalimar perfume on her wrists, slip into the red dress he bought her when she was twenty and disappear into his Honda. Other times she'd say, "It's your life, hon," and he'd stay home and drink whiskey until he was unconscious. I used to get angry at her those nights. Why couldn't she love him the way he needed?

Now I'm thinking it was more complicated than that but it doesn't matter anymore. He's gone. It was their business. There is a numbness in my throat, as if I've swallowed gauze. My mouth buckles.

My mother sits back down next to me, puts her arm around me. "Why don't we have a girls' night this Friday? We could rent movies, eat junk food."

Her voice is under my clothes, taking me apart. "I don't know. I've got some oats to sow. Got to get my hoe ready, you know what I mean," I say, forcing a laugh, getting out of there fast.

• • •

A rock, a window, a flush of cold air. The next night Connor shows me how to make a cut, how to shoot, how to pass, how to hook a girl around her ankle, how to crash the goal. *Like this, like this, no, like this.*

"Thank you, teach," I joke but she doesn't laugh. When it comes to this, she's all business.

Afterwards, I catch my breath while the Hawthorne girls stand around the car and sip whiskey. I don't ask for any; no one offers me some. They talk about how four years ago the game had been a joke between a few of them, how some of them had even tried to play in the old white boots that never fit right. They tell how one night they challenged the boys to a game at the rink. They lost but Connor took out their best player, causing a full ice fight that resulted in three girls and Jason Smith going home with black eyes and a town investigation of Gerdie's Lake, to determine its location.

"That boy can't play for shit, but he does some other things well, you know what I mean," an older girl says, and the others laugh. I'm shocked that they talk about sex that way. I kind of like it. I catch myself laughing.

"Your parents know about any of this?" I venture.

"It's a secret lake for a reason," the Lucille Ball girl with her arm around Connor says, and begins the story of Marissa Russo, who was part of the game until her mother and father found out about it. They tried to get the town to put a fence around the lake, but no adult could find it and no girl would give it up, so they decided to home school Marissa, to protect her from "those hooligan girls." They bought a pair of Doberman Pinschers, kept them mean and underfed. They painted the glass of Marissa's bedroom window white so their darling wouldn't get any ideas. Before the paint dried she used her fingernail to write her initials. You can see it if you drive by; one large M, one slanted R. She must miss us. I miss her. What's she do in there all day? God damn it.

They pass the whiskey around. No one says anything for a solid minute. There is just the wind moving through the trees, the darkness, the cold night.

Connor tells how years ago, a wolf crept into the woods while she was practicing, sat waiting for her at the edge. He was huge and hungry-looking with big teeth, come down from the

Adirondacks. What Connor did was shoot him square on the forehead with the puck. It knocked him dead. She threw the carcass over her shoulder, lugged it home, and in the morning her grandmother, who is from upstate and knows how to butcher beasts, gutted him, skinned him, and made the fur coat she wears today.

"Bull *shit*, Connor. That fake-ass pelt's from Deb in the mall and you know it," someone says, and I laugh though I want to believe. Connor seems strong enough to kill any threatening thing.

Blue light shifts between the trees and then it's time to duck back into the car, time to head home, time for each girl to maneuver her own, secret re-entry. I think I could listen to these stories all night. They fill a girl up. They let a girl forget herself, and remember herself at the same time. I wonder how I'll tell them about good cop and bad cop. The lake is a blank page. For the first time in my life, I hate the daylight.

• • •

Lately I keep my window open and wait for them. There's no need to sneak, but I like it better this way. It has to do with the new meanness that unlocks in me out here, the different kind of girl pushing at my skin, rising in my bones. I cut to the goal like a hunting thing, I check Winnie Friedman onto her bony ass during warm-ups, I swear when I mess up and when I score, streams of profanity I thought only belonged to my brother, *shit fuck shit, fucking A, what the shit, mother fucker.*

I go to the game the night after a blizzard, when we have to spend the first hour shoveling wet snow from the surface.

"Looks like someone's got the game bug," Connor says, smiling at me.

"Nothing else to do in this town, except eat disco fries at the diner and become uninteresting."

She shakes her head, "Listen to the newbie, a regular comedian," and easy as pie I'm blushing.

Some nights Briarcliff doesn't show and it's just us, playing each other. I like this best. You get more time with the puck. You get to really dig into each other. Those nights I develop a keen hatred for Winnie Friedman. She clings to you when she's guarding you, grabbing at your jacket. If you foul her she yaps like a small dog. She compliments my shots in that dog voice, calls me by my last name instead of my first as if she's my coach. She's always licking at her chapped lips, her mouth surrounded by a ring of red as if she's just eaten a plate of chicken wings.

The nights there's no game I steal my mother's car and practice alone. The trees, coated with ice from the latest storm, clatter above me like fingernails rapping a desk. I stare into the forest around me, feel the dark enter me, a drink I'm gulping too fast.

During the school days I limp through the hallways, exhausted, dark shadows under my eyes. In the afternoons I tell Justin I'm too tired to hang out. I've gotten bored with our long groping sessions. They feel like swimming in mud.

"Maybe you should date one of them, you're with them every night," he says the fourth time I blow him off.

"You don't know anything about me. It's not about that," I tell him.

I break up with him the next afternoon, while we're watching *The Big Lebowski*. I stand on the driveway and watch him sit in his car and cry, then drive away.

"You're looking like a zombie hulk these days," my mother says when I come inside. She's making dinner from scratch for the first time in a year. A chicken roasts in the oven. A huge pot of potatoes boils. "Those arms and legs. Those bags under your eyes. And you could have been gentler with that boy, after all he did for you. I saw how you just treated him."

"Since when are you spying on me? It's not your business."

She's right though. I didn't cry at all. I can already sense how fast I'll forget him. What is wrong with me, feeling nothing for my first boyfriend?

"Sit down, please. You're driving me crazy pacing like that." She purses her lips, looks at me like I'm a stranger she happened to have birthed fifteen years ago. "You thinking of going back to the rink soon? Might be good to have some structure again?"

This breaks my heart a little. She must miss being a figure skating mother, sewing all my dresses and helping me pick music. Competition days our house would become a bird-girl salon, the living room floor littered with stray feathers and sequins, the air stinking of hairspray and clouded with rouge.

"I won't be back there. I've found something else," I tell her, looking down at my hands.

She only shrugs, turns back to the stove and deftly lifts the boiling pot, pours it into a strainer balanced on the sink. "Doesn't that seem like a lifetime ago? The stress, the gossip, the driving, the money, the outfits. It's much better just coaching beginners."

I don't know what to say. I'm oddly offended. Was it her life as my mother that didn't matter, or her marriage, or my skating, or all of it? She must have been thinking things I couldn't imagine while she sewed those sequins.

"Of course I would never take any of it back," she says, her face red and glowing with steam, smiling hard at me, this cranked, painful smile. I can barely look at her, this coach, this ex-wife, this former champion, this strange woman, my mother.

• • •

It's February and Winnie asks me to come with her into the trees while the girls drink whiskey. She wants to show me something. Her face moves in close to mine so I can smell her peach lip-gloss. I smile at her, this new, cruel power coursing through me. Even if I liked girls I wouldn't be interested in

Winnie. I kiss her because I can, because I want to see what it's like.

It's nice. Easy. Afterward I say, "I don't want anything serious." I have no idea where I get these lines from, but the words roll off my tongue as if I've always had them in me.

"Oh, me neither," she says, walking back out of the woods, and I can hear the lie in that, an unmistakable hollowness.

It happens again the next night, like it's no big deal. I like the kissing, I like how she feels under her sweatshirt, warm and smooth and damp in all that cold.

One night she hands me a quartz stone pendant strung on a black leather chord. It is the most beautiful necklace I've ever been given and I know I shouldn't keep it.

At school the next day, when she tries to sit with me at lunch, I refuse to look at her. "I'm busy, can't you see," I say. Then I turn and hand her back the necklace in front of everyone.

Before she can start crying in front of me, I make for the girl's bathroom, the roar of the cafeteria chatter in my ears. I feel more like myself and entirely unrecognizable. My backpack is light on my shoulders, a fresh piece of cinnamon gum stings my tongue.

• • •

That night, there's no Winnie at the night game, and no Briarcliff. And Connor's gunning for me. "That was a dick move, with Winnie. We don't treat each other like that here, little girl. We have enough enemies," she hisses before we start.

A few minutes later I'm on a breakaway and she hooks me with her stick, sending me flying up into the dark, then down hard on the ice. When I land my left knee bends backward at an angle I know it shouldn't.

I'm lying still. She's asking me questions. Can you move it? Can you bend it? Her voice is blurred and worried and far away. I can't answer. I look out into the trees and for a second I imagine my father there watching. He's wearing his old leather jacket and jeans, but his skin is scaly like an alligator's, his eyes are two black marbles. "Nice work. Just great," he says. "Time to hang it up." Then he yawns and disappears again into the dark.

Are you okay? Can you bend it? Can you straighten it all the way?

I don't know I'm crying until Connor and another girl are hauling me across Gerdie's Lake by my shoulders, saying, "There girl, there girl, you're okay, it's probably just a sprain."

I cling to their voices, two solid ropes. They lay me on the snow bank and my face comes apart, my sobs huge and ugly and stupid, the cries of a ruined animal cast off to some icy moon.

Connor hands me the whiskey. "I'm sorry. I didn't mean to get you that bad."

"I'm sure it's just a sprain," I manage to get out. I take a long sip of whiskey, the liquid burning down my throat. I take another, then another, until my whole body feels warm and loose, until I'm feeling no pain, until I'm standing up, getting back on the ice, singing it to myself, singing just a sprain, just a sprain, just a sprain, I won't have to go back inside, I won't have to close up my window.

"Easy there," says Connor, and then she's holding back my hair while I puke into the snow.

• • •

I was good once and I've let myself go to seed, the mothers at the rink will tell you. It's on account of the trauma I have suffered, they'll say. *Of course she'd lose her taste for discipline, of course she'd be susceptible to . . .*

Let me tell you. It's almost spring, the wind balmy, the ice gone mealy with warmth. We play longer and nastier and with more fear, bruises blooming on our arms and legs, until the sky lightens and there's a groan from deep within the ice and Connor says "Enough."

Afterwards we sit and drink and the stink of our gear and our sweat rises around us. I breathe it in. It feels good to be a woman with a smell.

On the way home I chew cinnamon gum to hide the whiskey. I kiss my mother goodnight, lie awake willing more cold air down from Canada. The rhythms of the game rock through my body like ocean currents. I turn in bed, wanting more dark, more game, more drink, more of things I can't name yet. I turn and think of Marissa, how at night maybe she looks out through the M R at slivers of night, scraps of stars, missing those gushes of winter air. I think of Derek and all the times he came home drunk and stumbling and I shook my head at him, flushed with pride, thinking not being bad is the same thing as being good.

I think of Christine. What was it like those nights my father drove her home from our house, his hot hand on her knee? Did she shudder with the awful awakening of it? Did she secretly love the moment when it all came out, when her mother looked at her and for the first time knew her for what she'd done? Was there a brief spark of relief, a tremor of joy, before the pain began?

How Mary Lou Retton Took Over Our Lives in the Summer of 1994

It was the summer of the Barcelona Olympics and my sister was in love with the gymnasts, the girls. Feverishly. Devotedly. Jealously.

"I would give up all my Christopher Pike and my left kidney, to be that good," Anna told me one night, the two of us hunkered on the couch with a bowl of fake-butter popcorn, Tatiana Gutsu swooping in and out of the uneven bars and releasing in a triple somersault.

We'd both quit our lessons at Gymnastics City the year before, when our mother, a high school art teacher, moved out to an artist's loft in Peekskill, and our father lost his job at IBM.

"I'll never be an Olympian anyway," Anna told our parents, when they offered to take out a bank loan.

And she was right. She was too nervous to be a gymnast, biting her nails on the car rides to lessons, looking down at her feet during her tumbling passes. Her coach, a stern Romanian who used to coach with Bela Karolyi, was always losing his patience with her, shouting, "If you're going to half-do-it, just go home and eat bonbons." Afterwards Anna would buy a Yoo-hoo from the soda machine and slump onto one of the spectator benches, more relieved to be done than impassioned.

Still, she watched the gymnasts with such longing. "I would give up my cashmere cardigan and my VHS of *The Thing* and kill a kitten, to be that good," she said.

"Me too," I agreed, though I've always been more of a ground kind of girl, a hiker, a bowler, a walker of the neighborhood dogs, thick-waisted and thick-limbed like the Russian women on our father's side of the family. I'd only ever done gymnastics because Anna did. It gave me an excuse to be around my sister.

In those years, Anna was the kind of older sister who makes a plan with you—Let's hike Turkey Mountain and look for abandoned cars, Let's rent horror movies and make a frozen pizza—and then cancels at the last minute, if a popular girl invites her to the Danbury mall. The kind who breaks your heart now and then but who you love anyway because she's prettier and funnier and better at school than you, because she can stand up to your mother's rages with ten times more verve than you, because her love, when she directs it at you, lifts you out of your body, out of your parents' sad house, out of your dinky suburb with its lizard-eyed popular girls, their T-shirts saying where they each lost their virginity: *In the car, At FDR park, Under the football bleachers.*

All that summer, during the days, my sister and I stayed in our separate rooms. While our father kept busy with triathlon training, and our mother painted for the first time since before Anna was born, I played the SIMS and Anna disappeared into her tea-stained journals, her poetry, her incense, her Stephen King, her door locked.

At night though, we'd settle on the couch together, turn on the television, find our heroines. There was Kim Zmeskal with her fiery double-backs, her body whipping across the blue mats like a weapon thrown. There was Shannon Miller with her lanky grace, her languorous double pikes. There were the girls from the Eastern Bloc countries, the pixies with that bluesy sadness in their eyes and those names like expensive lace: Svetlana Boguinskaya, Rozalia Galiyeva, and Tatiana Gutsu, the favorite, Odessa's painted bird.

"I would give anything," Anna said, a third time that night, like an unwise girl in a fairy tale.

"To move like this," I said, and performed a clumsy candle-stick, farting and banging my foot on the entertainment center, making my sister cringe and laugh. It wasn't such a bad night. It wasn't such a bad ritual.

• • •

The next day, Mary Lou Retton came to us. It was early evening, that blue-gray hour after dinner and before Olympic coverage when we never knew what to do with ourselves. We were sitting on backyard swings we'd long outgrown, sucking those blue ices that come in long, plastic tubes, when there was a rustling in the woods behind our house.

I thought: deer. Then I thought of our mother's lettuce, which the deer would always ravish, and how our mother didn't live with us anymore. Then I was getting all weepy about a stupid deer, about some stupid lettuce I hadn't even liked to eat.

"Look," said Anna, pointing to the edge of the yard.

A girl in an American flag-patterned leotard and white sneakers stepped through the pachysandra and bleeding hearts, a gold medal slung around her neck. She walked slowly and delib-erately toward us, like she owned the place.

"Hey gals," she said, standing before us, one hand on her hip, the other hand running through her pixie hair cut.

She looked just like the gymnast we'd loved as younger girls, with our Mary Lou Retton posters, our Mary Lou Retton leo-tards, our Mary Lou dolls. Same cheery smile. Same compact, muscled, pixie body, as if, all these years, she'd been kept in a vault.

"Who are you?" I asked, suddenly frightened.

"Come on. You know who I am," said the girl, handing me the gold medal. It was cold, like it had been stored in a refrigerator. And it was heavy. It felt real. "I just felt like a little vacation. Sometimes a girl needs a break from her routine, you know? I've always loved New York State." Without missing a beat, she lifted herself onto the rusted swing set bar and spun slowly and smoothly around it, as if she'd turned the air to wet clay.

Anna hopped off her swing. "It's a pleasure. I'm Anna Klausner," she said, biting her lower lip, which was blue from the ice.

"I know who you are, sweetie," said the girl we now both believed to be Mary Lou Retton. She snatched her medal back from me and looked at my sister, turned those big brown eyes on Anna's bowed head. "It's a shame you're not in the sport anymore."

"We ran out of money," said Anna, as if she expected the Olympian would know her story.

"You should have taken an after-school job, or extra babysitting," said Mary Lou Retton. "You'll never get what you want in this world if you don't work for it."

"I guess that's true. I could have gotten that money," Anna said, her voice shaking. I slid off my swing and stood next to my sister.

The Olympian smiled hard at us. "Why don't you show us a cartwheel, Anna girl? I haven't seen a good, basic cartwheel in *forever*."

Anna took out her pony tail, pulled her frizzy hair into a bun so tight her eyebrows arched, then launched into the most energetic cartwheel I'd ever seen her do, springing into the humid air, her *Night of the Living Dead* T-shirt slipping up to show her bra.

"Beautiful," Mary Lou Retton cooed. "Now you, Patty," she said, pointing at me, at my stomach, as if to press the doughy layer of fat there.

And then I was doing it, a muddled, labored rotation. When I took lessons, the coaches hadn't bothered to get frustrated with me.

"Not bad," said Mary Lou, when I landed heavily on the grass in a sit-squat. "Next time try taking more of a running start."

"Like *this*," said Anna. She backed up to the edge of the woods and sprinted full force toward us, cartwheeling so hard I feared she'd fling herself against the side of the house, split her skull open and then when our father came home from his bike ride I'd have to explain how my sister killed herself trying to impress Mary Lou Retton.

Instead she landed neatly again, her face red, a smile spreading across it. The Olympian clapped and laughed, this high-pitched, girlish laugh even though, if she was real, she must have been in her late twenties by then. Then her voice turned somber as she said she had to go home, there was dinner to make, her husband didn't like it when she was gone. She walked back into the woods and disappeared at the threshold, seeming to become part of the heavy July trees.

• • •

"Don't tell," my sister said in bed that night. She'd invited me into her room for a sleepover, for the first time in years. It was nice. There was the smell of her sandalwood incense, the glow of the neon stars she'd stuck to the ceiling. There were her gymnastics trophies—third place, fourth place, fifth place—lined up on a high shelf, beside her old Halloween masks: a sneering vampire bat head, a glowering Ronald Reagan head, a pirate fish head.

"The whole town will show up and mob her if we tell, and then she'll go away. Maybe, after a little while, if she allows it, we can invite some friends over to meet her," Anna said.

I didn't remind her that I was shy and awkward and didn't have any friends, or that her friends, the popular girls, usually left her out or stood her up, promising to meet her at the Hawthorne Diner and then not showing. I didn't ask her why a star athlete would want to visit two lonely girls in a Northern suburb, two girls who couldn't even afford lessons at Gymnastics City.

"I won't tell," I said.

"I can't believe Mary Lou Retton complimented my cart-wheel. What the shit," my sister said, and let out a long, deep laugh.

Our father knocked on the door and told us he had triathlon training at five a.m. and could we please show some respect.

"Dad needs to get laid," Anna said when he closed our door, and then we were laughing together, two sisters with inside jokes and a secret, the cool night air streaming through the window.

• • •

The next night we sat on the swings again, with our blue ices. Again the Olympian came to us, in the same patriotic leotard and sneakers.

"Let's try something more adventurous tonight, chickies," she said, looking at Anna. "The trick with the back handspring is to not *think* about what you're doing. Forget what you had for dinner. Forget yourself. Take *flight*."

My sister stood, put her hands up, tried to arch backwards and fell onto the scorched grass. "Shit fuck shit mother fucker," she said, cursing in the beautifully fluent way she had then, and might still have now. It's hard to say. We don't talk much, me in Alaska, her in New York, two sisters a whole country and several time zones apart. We try to make time. We do what we can. My mother says she is happy.

"Watch your language," said Mary Lou Retton that still, summer evening, kindly but firmly. Then she was helping my sister up, putting her arms behind her back and guiding her through it again, then again, complimenting her, encouraging her, saying, *That's it, almost, you're so close, once more*, until Anna was doing it on her own, until Anna and Mary Lou Retton were high-fiving and smiling at each other, the woods thick with evening.

"If only I could go back in time and make you a champion," the Olympian told my sister.

"Eh, I'm done with all that," Anna said, but she looked happier than I'd seen her in months, this new heat shining in her eyes.

• • •

The Olympian came to us every night for a week after that, while our father took advantage of the cool dusk to do his last long bike ride. Each time she came we would rise quick from our swings, ready to do anything to impress her. At first she didn't ask much: hand springs and flips from Anna, back walkovers and round-offs from me.

"Great job!" she would tell me, no matter how poorly I performed.

It wasn't unpleasant. When I walked the neighbor's unruly mastiff, I loved the new strength in my arms, the steadiness in my legs. I imagined it seeping into all the rest of me, so that soon I wouldn't fear the sound of my own voice at school, soon I would be sharp tongued and knowing and lithe like my sister.

And suddenly Anna was in a good mood all the time. In the mornings, after breakfast, she'd ask me to hike with her through the forest behind our house. It wasn't much of one, ringed in other houses, thinned each year by backyard pools and patios. When I got older I would need more wilderness, would leave Hawthorne for the Appalachian Trail, for the Green Mountains, for, at last, Alaska.

But that summer, walking with my sister in the brash haze of late morning, our backyard acre of trees seemed newly exotic, capable of sustaining a compelling mystery. Nestled in the dead leaves we found unspooled mix tapes, broken radios, a pregnancy test in a plastic bag. It looked like a thermometer, two cheerful pink lines across its calm, white eye.

"Someone's in the shit," said my sister, explaining.

We found beers left by the neighborhood teenagers, breathed the yeasty smell of the last dregs, held the amber bottles up to the light.

"On their planet, these are required for love rituals," my sister said, in her alien robot investigator voice.

We found condom wrappers, labeled "with spermicide," which sounded like "homicide," as if sex were a crime you committed. Was it always? Only sometimes? We shrugged our shoulders, two sister-anthropologists. I thought: it isn't so bad having an Olympian in your life.

• • •

Then, the second week into our friendship with Mary Lou Retton, the Olympian's mood shifted. She would show up with dark shadows under her eyes, an oversized vacation T-shirt thrown over her leotard, her hair frizzy.

"There's no sleeping in that house," she said one night, leaning against the swingset bar, hip cocked, her eyeliner smeared around her eyes. "It's too quiet. It's quiet as a coffin in there. I don't know how he sleeps. Sometimes at dinner I stare at him while he eats, to see if he'll notice. I want him to ask me a question, or tell a joke, anything. I stare at the bald spot on his head. He never looks up."

"You could try listening to the radio, to sleep," Anna suggested.

"Please get warmed up, ladies," the Olympian said, and glared at us while we stretched, pulling our arms behind our heads, lowering ourselves into splits. "Get up," she would snap suddenly, then demand increasingly intricate flights from my sister, double pikes and double flips, passes that should only ever be done on mats.

"I'll try," my sister would say, her old hesitation coming back.

"If you risk nothing, you gain nothing. You think I'm fooling around?" Mary Lou would answer, her brown eyes never blinking.

My sister would take a deep breath and attempt whatever it was, biting her lip, grunting, catapulting her increasingly thin body across the dry grass with such abandon I could barely watch. *I would give anything.*

And with each new maneuver, each new muscle memory, my sister herself changed, the heat in her eyes seeping away, leaving a dull, searching gaze, as if she were constantly squinting at herself in a fogged mirror. There was a cold edge to her voice when she said, at dinner, *Patty, cool it with the tater tots. We've got practice soon.* Prudish, inspirational phrases worked their way into her language, pushing out her old curses and nerdy jokes and John Carpenter references.

"Follow your dreams," she told me in the woods one morning. We'd come upon a burnt-out firepit surrounded by empty beer bottles and a smashed guitar. My sister used a stick to extract a pair of pale pink women's underwear from the ashes. Her face went blank and then twitched, reminding me of those scenes in *The Thing* when the monster takes over its next researcher victim.

"Respect your body, Patty. Only you control your destiny," Anna said.

"And only you can prevent forest fires," I said, trying to make her laugh.

She only looked up into the trees and sighed, as if searching for the Olympian's secret portal, a way of following her, of rising up into that blue-green.

The next Saturday our mother noticed it too. We were eating lunch at the Indian restaurant near her artist's loft. Our mother took a second helping of saag paneer, saying, "I know there's a gallon of butter and cream in here but this is just so, damn, good."

Anna set down her fork. "Maybe you should stop eating so much. Success comes through small victories just like this."

"Who are you, Richard Simmons?" said our mother, laughing, taking a huge bite of the saag paneer anyway.

In our house she'd always been tense, her shoulders hunched like a linebacker's while she cleaned at eleven o'clock at night, our father shouting from the bedroom, "I refuse to participate in this insanity," our mother, answering, her voice muffled by the storm of vacuum cleaner static, "How can anyone think straight in here? How can anyone do anything worth a damn?"

Now she seemed like a more vivid version of herself, dressed in red cowboy boots and faded jeans streaked with paint, silver bangles sliding up and down her arms as she served herself more chicken curry and joked, "You sound like a self-help book, my Anna girl. Eat-up, please. I don't like how thin you're getting."

"You're the one who should think long and hard about who you are," Anna told our mother, pushing her untouched plate of curry across the table.

Our mother stared at Anna's plate, and then at Anna. She pushed Anna's plate back toward her. "How dare you," she said, the anger she used to carry around our house like a boiling pot rising into her face.

"Look mom, just relax. I'm sorry, okay?" Anna said.

"I'm trying to make things better. I'm trying my best for you girls. I don't know what else you want me to do. Where is this coming from, Patty?"

Our mother pointed her hurricane eyes at me, the easier of her two daughters to crack.

"Oh, we've just been watching a lot of gymnastics," I said, and then prattled on about my summer reading assignment and how the curry made me think of India and what it would be like to go there, until our mother looked bored and asked for the check and Anna was smiling at me, our secret crackling in the air between us.

• • •

In late August she winced with each landing, her body wracked by minor damages: a twisted ankle that swelled like a plum, a bruised shoulder, a sprained hip-flexor that hobbled her walk.

"Take a break. Ice it tonight," I told my sister as we cleared our dinner plates, the sky gray and heavy, the air thunderstorm quiet. "She'll understand."

"I'm fine," Anna said, and put on the red leotard she'd bought at Caldor, swallowed a handful of ibuprofen from our parents' medicine cabinet, and grabbed our ices, the only thing I ever saw her eat anymore.

On the swings she stared at the pachysandra and bleeding hearts, the place where the Olympian always emerged, told me that she was saving herself for marriage, that I should do the same.

"I don't think anyone wants to do it with me. I'm a fat girl in a small town," I said, getting annoyed, thinking this must have come from the Olympian. In our basement *Encyclopedia Britannica*, I'd read that Mary Lou was a religious conservative, had campaigned with Reagan in '84 after winning her medal.

"Be serious, Patty," my sister said, shaking the last drops of sugary blue water into her mouth, spilling some on her leotard.

I wondered how much longer the Olympian would stick around. Was she some kind of demon, like in Anna's Christopher Pike? Did she want to steal my sister away to Texas, where, according to the *Britannica*, she lived with her real-estate developer husband?

Yet when Mary Lou Retton came to us that night, she looked too tired to perform any kind of supernatural abduction. Her shoulders sagged, her fingers were pruned. She smelled like lemon-scented cleaning solution. In a jean skirt and plain black tank top, her pixie hair gelled and combed to one side, her face thinner and lined, her skin the unearthly orange of fake tan, she looked like she'd aged ten years overnight.

"Can we give it a rest tonight, girls?" she said, falling heavily into my sister's swing, pulling a pack of Camel Lights from the tiny red purse slung over her shoulder.

"Of course," said my sister.

The Olympian lit her cigarette, inhaled and exhaled deeply into the still night. Then she talked about how much she missed her family in West Virginia, how she and the Texas husband barely spoke in their big, Texas house.

"Don't get me wrong, I'm happy," she said, kicking at the worn ground beneath her feet. "You take certain risks. You choose your life. Our house has intercoms in every room. You don't need to shout or even climb the stairs to reach each other, if you wanted to reach each other. Can you believe it? Intercoms!"

And it occurred to me how little we actually knew about Mary Lou Retton, or Kim Zmeskal, or Shannon Miller, or Tatiana Gutsu, or any of them, these brave bird-girls we so admired. They were hollow to us as dolls, distant as the moon.

Anna didn't seem to notice, though. She smiled as our heroine droned on, rose and arched into a bridge, her ribs visible through the fabric of her leotard, like things you could cut yourself on.

And all at once I longed to escape with her back into the house, to put on *Children of the Corn* or *Pet Cemetery*, something gory and simple and cheap, bring my sister back to the strange, inward girl she had been before the Olympian came to us, even if that girl hadn't liked me very much.

"Let's go," I said, grabbing her by her tiny wrist, feeling the bird bones there.

"Get off me," said Anna, ripping out of my grasp.

Then she was inviting Mary Lou Retton to Sunday Dinner. She said it just like that, *Sunday Dinner*, as if our family was the type to have such a cozy ritual. She promised roast chicken and mashed potatoes. She promised our mother and father would be there.

"I guess that would be fun. I'll bring Monopoly," said Mary Lou Retton, sounding non-plussed. Then she slipped off her swing and walked slowly away from us, towards the woods.

"See you Sunday night," Anna said to her back.

"We'll have the chicken ready!" my sister shouted into the trees.

"I don't think this is a good idea," I told her that night. We were in her room for what would be our last sleepover, though I didn't know that yet. The air was stuffy, the windows clamped shut, the pink curtains drawn to form a kind of cocoon. On the high shelf the trophy girls glinted in the moonlight, faceless and impeccable, bodies cranked at impossible angles. The Halloween masks were gone.

"Don't pull any of your pouting at the dinner. Don't ruin this for me," Anna said, springing from the bed to the floor, to do splits.

I stared at the faded Mary Lou Retton poster on the wall, which she'd kept up all these years. The photographer had caught the Olympian just after landing, her arms raised like wings, the hard muscles in her stomach straining beneath the stars and stripes of her leotard. Her eyes were open too wide, her lips clenched in the same sickening smile my sister now favored. I shivered, looked away.

"She's going to bring over Monopoly. When was the last time we all played board games together? It's going to be *fun*," Anna said, stretching her legs farther and farther apart.

And yes, it did sound nice, this vision of our family interacting civilly, competing jovially, the money fake and colorful. I could see how Mary Lou Retton had succeeded as an inspirational speaker, post-Olympics. Who, suffocating in their own life, wouldn't be tempted to believe that really we all desire the same things, that happiness is just a matter of pushing through the bad nights, tamping down the errant dreams, of trying, just a little harder, to hold a certain version of yourself together.

"I'll try, but no promises," I told my sister, who seemed not to hear me, reaching her hands to her toes, pressing her face into her knee.

•••

It was easier than I'd thought to arrange "Sunday Dinner." Our mother needed to pick up some art supplies she'd left in the basement and our father wanted to ask her about the mortgage.

"And you know, I was married to your mother for fifteen years. I can sit across the table from her for one hour, for god sakes," said our father, filling his water bottle at the kitchen sink Saturday morning, pulling his foot back to his butt to stretch a bulging, tri-athlete quad.

The cooking took all the next day. We peeled two pounds of Idaho potatoes, gutted and cleaned the massive chicken Anna had picked, stuffed its pale body with fresh thyme, lemon and garlic. We washed and trimmed a pound of string beans, set them to roast with olive oil and sea salt, shucked five ears of Maryland sweet corn, peeled apples for a pie.

And it felt good to do these things. Since our parents' separation, we'd eaten mostly take-out, or things from frozen, or meals out of cans. Now our father laughed when he saw us squinting at the yellowed copy of the *Joy of Cooking* that had been a wedding gift.

"You girls are really going all-out," he said, as I wove the pale strips of pie dough into a lattice.

I nodded, proud of us, of the smell of roasting chicken filling all the rooms of our house.

•••

At six o'clock, neither our mother nor Mary Lou Retton had arrived.

At six-thirty, our mother pulled up in her Outback. "You girls have gone all Julia Child on me. What's the big occasion?" she said, pushing past us into the dining room we only ever used for holidays. Anna had set out the good porcelain.

"We just wanted to have a nice Sunday dinner, for once," my sister said, her voice high and tense.

At six forty-five, Mary Lou Retton still had not arrived. "Why don't we play a game of Boggle?" Anna asked.

"I'm *hungry*," said our mother, taking the lids off the casserole dishes.

"After the news is over," said Anna, putting all the lids back on.

And so we sat uncomfortably on the couch, watching the anchor talk about how to exercise during a heat wave. *Drink lots of water. Wear light colored clothing. Work out in the evenings, or in the early mornings, when the sun is at its weakest.*

At seven o'clock, our mother said, "If I don't eat now, I'm going to eat my hand."

Our father said, "Eating too late will disrupt my training schedule."

And then we were all serving ourselves, and Anna was explaining how the extra place setting was for someone who still might come, a guest she wanted them to meet and treat respectfully.

"We look forward to meeting your friend," said our father.

"You know, we're always here for you, honey. We accept you for whoever you are," said our mother.

"I'm not a *lesbian*," my sister said, spitting out the word in a way that made me shudder, though I didn't yet know that I was one, that in seven years I would fall in love in the Green Mountains, with a woman in my college hiking group, my legs strong beneath me, my voice steady, identifying trees by their leaves, animals by their tracks, at last saying her name.

"Let's eat," said our father, digging into his mashed potatoes.

"Amen," said our mother.

And it was a mostly nice dinner. Our parents proclaimed how good everything was, how we should take this show on the road, their two daughter-gourmands. They made small talk with each other, like two people on a first date, our father nervous and restrained, our mother loose and wise cracking. He told her about a news story he'd seen on the Hudson River revival, how they were making real progress with the PCPs. She asked him if being a triathlete meant he got super powers, warned him to be careful, if he lost more weight he'd float up into the air on that bike of his, wind up halfway to the moon, stranded with only a Power Bar. This made him laugh. And you could see how opposites would have attracted, once, a long time ago.

Then our mother asked our father if he'd been checking the classified ads, for jobs.

"I told you not to bring that up in front of the girls," he said, his face shuttering closed. "Have you shown any of those paintings in a gallery yet?"

"No." Our mother took a long sip of her wine.

"See. How do you like it?"

"That's not what I meant. I'm just concerned about you. And since you asked, my work is going well."

"Oh, so it's your *work* now. That's great, Roxanne. Don't let me keep you from your work. Don't let your *daughters* keep you from your work."

"You don't know what you're talking about," said our mother, stabbing at her last string bean with her fork. "You don't know what it's like to want something elusive, that you can't program into a computer."

Our father sighed, heavy and long, and the whole house seemed to sigh with him. Outside the light faded, the forest turning to dark shadows against the sky.

"I'm sorry girls," our father said. "Look at me, ruining this great dinner you both made."

"Yes, yes, thank you, Anna and Patty," said our mother, wiping the wine from her lips with her napkin.

"If you're done, I'd like to leave now," said Anna.

"Of course. We'll do the dishes. You girls go. Go and relax," our parents said.

And I could hear the relief in their voices, that the dinner was ending, that soon she could drive off into the still night, back into the new life she was building, that soon he could hop on his bike, let the long, flat county path work through him. What had we been thinking? What had Anna been thinking?

"Let's go," my sister said to me, clutching two ices, pulling me toward the back door.

We sat silently on our backyard swings, the ices going warm and limp in our hands. Our mother came out and kissed us good-bye. Our father came out and biked away. We heard the teenagers in the forest, the hiss of their beers opening, the rough strum of their guitar, the sound of their voices, still reckless with summer, joining together in something by Jimmy Buffett.

And Mary Lou Retton did not come, and did not come, and did not come.

"Why don't we go look for her?" Anna said, her voice young-Olympian perky.

"No thank you," I answered. My chest hurt and my stomach ached from all the rich food. An itchy heat spread over my skin. I scratched the mosquito bite on my leg to bleeding.

"Come on, Patty. I bet we could find her up there in the trees. I bet she's waiting for us. Please," Anna said, turning to face me, her eyes tearing up.

And I could understand my sister's anguish at getting stood-up by the Olympian, her disappointment that, after all her desperate leaps, all her painful splits, she was still herself, still stuck in her body, still stuck in her loneliness, still stuck here on the ground. I understood but I was tired.

"I don't feel like it," I said.

"Patty, what's wrong with you?" She stood in front of me, her hands on her hips, her leotard faded and sweat stained from so many washings. "What the hell?" she said, glaring at me, so that I sensed what was coming, that soon we'd go back to our separate rooms, our separate fears and obsessions and dreams, two girls marking time in the box we called our home.

"Come on," she said, and grabbed me by the arm.

I ripped easily out of her weak grasp. She looked at me for a second, as if she didn't recognize me, then shook her head and stalked off into the pachysandra and bleeding hearts. I watched her thin body disappear into the darkening trees. A moment later I saw a scrap of red rising into the green, heard her scrabbling up the dried-out pine from which, in ten minutes, she'd fall, breaking her leg, the weak bone shattering like hard candy smashed in its wrapper.

And I did not follow her into those flimsy limbs, did not call her back to me. I rotated my neck until it cracked, then hoisted myself onto the swingset bar, hung by my legs for a penny drop, the last and most dangerous move Mary Lou Retton had tried to teach me. The idea was simple: swing by your legs, then release so your body whips upright and you land on your feet. The yard should whirl out of focus for one exhilarating instant, then return to normalcy, you standing in it, a sorceress of gravity. All well and good for people like Anna and Mary Lou Retton. I had never been able to let go, always imagined falling, my neck breaking. I would hang there until my sister sighed, tolerant and resigned to my awkwardness, and then put her hands beneath my stomach, delivered me to the ground like the flawed, fearful animal I could not help being. In this she was not unkind.

Now I rocked my torso back and forth unafraid, my whole body thrumming, my arms and legs full of the strength new anger gives. The bar, still warm from the day's heat, pressed the backs of my knees. Blood rushed around my head and my eyes blurred, the house and the forest sliding in and out of my vision. I closed my eyes, rocked faster, let loose and careened out into the soft dark. It would be a long time before I touched ground again, far away from my sister.

Love Song for Ellipticals
After Divorce

At first I thought you vaguely sinister, with your hulking frame, your insect arms, your face flashing neon data. Lined up with your kind at the Hawthorne Club Fit, you could have been a member of an alien army in a sci-fi, post-apocalyptic movie, sent to the suburbs to trap me in your giant pedals, drain my life force, brainwash me, or perform insidious research on my species. "Human woman, eighteen, healthy, enjoys disco fries, sometimes too much, sporadic drinker, lonely, but hopeful," you'd relay back to the mother ship.

This was during that restless, plush summer before college when I worked part-time in an ice cream truck, slept with a boy I didn't love in the back of his family's Taurus, feared pregnancy. I came to you to forget the symptoms, mounted you quickly, my body still boasting what I considered real world athleticism: high school soccer games, hikes up Turkey Mountain, illegal reservoir swimming. I'd just take you for a spin. This wasn't permanent. Your pedals swung easily beneath my weight. You gave me none of the keen ache I was after. Like running in whipped cream. The gym equivalent of bumper bowling. I did not bother with resistance, left you for the hard, flat surface of a treadmill, your plainer, more serious cousin.

At twenty-five, bleary with new love, beer soaked, I found you again. We did it quick and dirty, perched above a university gymnasium where young girls learned to cheerlead. I was an artist, not an athlete, I had decided. He was a writer in black Converse sneakers, hated sports of any kind, had declared at a young age that athletic acts were ugly, unattractive, undignified. I wore kids' cowboy boots with cartoon horses printed on the insides, a white cotton sundress patterned with yellow flowers. *Exactly*, I told him, married him, hung up my cleats. I did not want muscles. I did not want endurance. I only wanted you to sculpt my thighs for him to push apart, to give me that flushed high, then that cool calm to last me through the fetid, Louisiana afternoons. You purred like an expensive vacuum cleaner. I did not think myself weaker or stronger. I did not think about strength at all.

In Los Angeles it is easy to forget you live in a desert. There are so many palm trees. All this transplanted green. Those first months I would get nauseous in the middle of the morning, two cups of coffee in. He'd make me down glasses of water. He was kind. It got worse anyway. At the end we lived off frozen pizza, frozen dumplings, ramen noodles swirling in salt. Leaving him, I thought I'd turn myself into a pillar. I thought I deserved it. Some days I still do.

At the Hollywood YMCA, I find you in front of the obligatory mural of old Hollywood, the same one they have at the grocery store and at the bank. Marilyn Monroe. Charlie Chaplin. Godzilla. Familiar ghosts in their familiar guises, as if gathered for a family reunion at which there will be moderate drinking and a few arguments, political and personal, but no full-fledged fights because we're too old for that now, aren't we? I am hazy with lack of sleep. I don't know what I want from you. I am in tattered sneakers not meant for running, have not stepped onto a field or run a lap or swum a lake in years. I bring you ruined knees, brittled ankles, cigarette lungs. My balance comes slow. You don't mind. It is like always. You ask me the usual questions, make your secret adjustments, take us metaphorical walking and hiking and running and stair climbing, measure the beat of my heart.

I have heard them call you grim reaper, mad scientist, anesthesiologist, and fake psychic healer, your habitat a kind of addictive mirror. Compared to gritty games of pick-up touch football, to volleyball spiking, to bike riding on craggy trails, to the aerial feints and calibrated lunges of basketball players, they say you're a limp-wristed ghost. Lately, my nights stretching out like the line at the DMV, the people I love scattered across this multi-terrain country, this too-big country, I wonder, what is so wrong with being held this way? Where is the evil in the way you cradle my rusted joints, guide my muscles through these gentle, repetitive motions, let me choose how easy or how hard I want it. Where is the sin in this brief illusion of control, in knowing, quantitatively, how long I've been going and how long I've got to go?

And if, after kicking a soccer ball or dancing, I feel a soreness in my abdomen, the place on my body you never touch, does that make your imprints on my arms and legs less real, the muscle memory of pedaling less true? When you tell me I'm through, after thirty minutes of moving my feet in circles, of new music moving through me, of not crying, not crying, I take out my ear buds and wipe sweat from your body, wipe you down. Twenty-first century horse. Ungainly robot. Familiar song. I'll always come back to you. And as always, I will be more and less myself.

Reverse Trampoline Fail

Each snowflake stirs before
lifting into the sky as I

learn you won't be dead.

—*Matt Rasmussen, "Reverse Suicide"*

June and Ellen says it's time to get rid of the trampoline. She wants to put a rock garden in the corner of the yard where the trampoline sits. She's worried drunk teenagers will sneak in and jump on it in the middle of the night, the way Josh and his friends would do after basketball games or jam band concerts at the Chance, careening into each other, singing rambling, toothless songs about lost childhood and lost love, spilling Bud Light on the black mat.

One broken neck, Ellen says, and we'll have a lawsuit on our hands.

"This weekend," I promise, and go back to alphabetizing my movie collection.

It is Friday morning, three hours before lunch. Two years ago, I lost my programmer job at IBM and Josh graduated from high school, enlisted in the army. One year ago, he died in Iraq, on that hill outside Fallujah. You can look him up on the Faces of the Fallen website. He was twenty when he went but we sent in his high school senior portrait. He looks more like himself in his gray thrift-store suit, his red, Pee-Wee bow tie, his hair pulled back in a pony tale, one eyebrow arched like John Belushi.

He always loved movies. These days, I'm remaking our basement into a home theatre, plasma screen, plush, leather sectional we can't afford, mini-fridge stocked with Bud Light, framed posters of his favorites: *Breakfast Club, Back to the Future, Pee-Wee's Great Adventure, Ferris Bueller.*

I'm not an idiot. Displacement, I know a therapist would say, though misplacement feels more right, like I can't find the script I'm supposed to read from, can't find my lines for this kind of story.

"Just stay home another year. Consider your options," I told Josh that summer before he left. "We'll make it nice for you and your friends. You can entertain."

"There's nothing in Poughkeepsie," he said, staring at his hands. "They pay for your college and I don't want to go into debt. Matt and Paulie are going."

"Fine. Do whatever you want. It's your life," I said and closed my office door, went back to watching porn and searching for a job that no longer exists.

I was tired of fighting him. It seemed we'd had the same argument for years, for every math and science class he'd ever taken, every part-time job he'd ever gotten and then quit, me yelling at him to stay focused, to take some pride in his actions.

During the day, I'm sure there's no way I could have gotten through to him.

At night, though, when I'm lying awake, I travel back into that moment, my son whole and in front of me. I say, "You're not cut out for war, you dipshit." I say, "You're too jumpy, too twitchy, too skittish. You couldn't even sit still in math class."

I say, "Remember how you were going to start a band? I know I made fun of you, of the music, but you're solid on that guitar."

Josh looks up at me. "You really think so?" he says, and his eyes gleam with hope the way eyes only gleam with hope in the movies.

Then I'm the one who can't sit still. I roll out of bed and stalk through our dark house, make myself fat summer sausage and cheese sandwiches, pour myself a giant glass of Coke, sink into my office, into my ergonomic chair. I google movie trivia: who slept with who, which directors were pricks, which sets were cursed, which actors died young. My fingers swell with salt. My body grows heavy and stiff.

I google trampoline injuries, discover frightening statistics, warnings from the American Academy of Pediatrics, X-rays of ruined spines, shattered knees, dramatic open wounds, a foot ripped away to reveal the wet, white of an ankle bone, an ulna poking through the purple skin of an arm, a young man in Utah paralyzed from the neck down after a badly timed flip at Hang Time Trampoline Fun Park. My shorts pull tight around my waist. My legs lose circulation. At some point the air-conditioning shuts off—Ellen's out of work too—and the house turns hot and still. It is late August when she opens the door.

"Please, take that piece of crap away," she says, "or I'll find someone else who will."

She's in the same dirty robe she wore when the soldiers rang the bell. Out the window, the sky is a harsh blue, the sun desert bright, all our grass burned brown.

"When it cools down some," I say and she sighs like an open grave.

It is nightfall when I make it outside. The trampoline squats next to the driveway, a deflated basketball underneath. In middle school, Josh and his friends would drag it in front of the hoop, turn on Jock Jams and perform slam dunks, film themselves imitating Ewing and Starks and Jordan, their faces full of rage and fear. I have these movies stored on a shelf in the home theatre, labeled "On Fire: Volume 1, Volume 2, Volume 3."

We did not worry about them getting hurt back then. They were athletic boys, sprung up even when they landed funny, even when their legs fell through the space between the trampoline springs, even when they missed the hoop completely, banged hard against the pole and fell to the ground.

"Fail!" the other boys would shout, then stand around laughing at the recovering party until he got up.

Once, they sent one of these crashes in to *America's Funniest Home Videos*. They'd seen the montages of trampoline fails, the Vermont boys flipping up into the branches of pine trees, the Connecticut boys in lacrosse shorts and tournament T-shirts, careening into privacy hedges or adjacent swimming pools, the thick-limbed Midwestern boys spinning into blue skies, disappearing into high, summer corn, the fat boys in bathing suits, falling through the mesh, the groups of wrestling boys, shirtless, aggressive, breaking the metal supports, collapsing the whole apparatus.

Ours is still in pretty good shape, though the springs are heavily rusted. I drop my toolbox, haul my old, heavy body onto the mat, stand. All the neighbors' houses are dark, quiet with easy sleep. All of Josh's friends are alive and happy, I am sure of it, sitting on new couches eating warm popcorn, watching movies about moody teenagers struggling with detention, with cutting class. When the credits roll, they rise to play easy games of pick-up basketball, their joints intact, bone linking elegantly to bone, hearts snug in the cavities of their chests, their lungs perfect balloons stretching, collapsing, stretching.

And I am bouncing up into the thick, summer air, a grease fire in my gut, my breath a torn, ragged flag, my arms ready to be twisted from their sockets, my neck weak, aching for the release of the snap, my eyes clamped shut against the full moon and the dead land. In my head a movie is playing, my son's trampoline fail in reverse. The camera pans out and his body unfurls from the hard ground, floats into the air beside me, lands on the forgiving mat.

Tampax Pearl Active Soccer Girl

The ball is a pearl is a moon I am always about to kick across the depthless, blue field of the box. My body is cut from a Lite-Brite screen, my face blurred, gold bulbs. I'm your Title IX Tinkerbelle, your feminine hygiene mascot. I have perfect form, arms wide for balance, shooting leg extended back. Beware bitches. This is not about protection.

This is not your mother's Tampax. Gone are the hoisted, wedding-dressed Tampax girls, the cheerleading Tampax girls, the aerobics Tampax girls, Courtney Cox in her white leotard and pastel headband. Gone are the bikinied Tampax girls running blond beaches, the girls your mother watched on TV in her parents' brick row house in Port Washington, Long Island, your mother who loved swimming, who butterflied the Atlantic until her father said "Enough. You'll damage yourself. Don't you want to have children?"

Gone is your mother.

Of course, I am not really the girl on the Tampax Pearl Active box. I am a scuffed, corporeal girl, a former varsity striker with wrecked knees and too many exes, a sculptor with too many unfinished projects. My medium is paper. Come by my apartment any day and you can see the scraps scattered around my living room, the makings of elaborate royal crowns and neon ranch houses gathering dust in the corners, my X-acto knives and knitting needles spilled like pick-up sticks. At night I take pain pills, those pale blue pearls, drink tumblers of bourbon, slip into a blue-gold haze. I think about the exes and who didn't love whom enough. I think about my mother, who died this past winter, her salty heart stilled. I think about my father, who I speak to on Sundays at three. We talk about the English premier league, how our team, the Tottenham Hotspurs, needs to ditch the 5-4-1 formation, they can't play defense for shit. We talk about the latest detective show. We never talk long.

Tampax Pearl Active Soccer Girl, did you ever have a coach-father? Did he come home from the used car dealership each night and teach you this wry, witty game, this game his own father refused him, spitting, "What use? What use?" Did he teach you to pass and shoot and trap? Did he teach your best friend Debbie Costello too? When you turned ten, did he form you a team, the best team in the state? Did you play under hot, gold lights?

When, at fourteen, you came home from a boy-girl party at Debbie Costello's, your face flushed, one Doc Marten untied, did your coach-father decide it was time to fight what he called your "feminine impulses"? Did he tell you about girls, how they never want anything enough? Did he make you want it enough? Did he punish your bad traps with duck walks that ripped your thighs? Did he blow his steel whistle on you, freeze scrimmages to scream your mistakes, to scream your teammates mistakes, until you all played with a kind of stutter, your passes pre-emptive apologies scuttling out of bounds?

Did he threaten to bench you, to cut you, to take your cleats and your pearl moon ball that was really his and to turn off all the Lite-Brite bulbs inside you?

Did he take the same tone with your mother? When the depression came, and then the depression weight, did he say "Get more active"? Did he say, "That stationary biking isn't working. Run one mile every morning"?

Sometimes I'd run with her. She never looked good, always in the same gray sweatpants, the same faded Disneyland T-shirt. We'd get a quarter mile from the house, outside my father's gaze, and then she'd slow to a walk. "You're in such good shape," she'd say. Then she'd try to tell me things about her girlhood, about swimming, about the time she'd tried track instead, made it all the way through the grueling pre-season only to have her father say, "Absolutely not. What man would want a muscle mole?"

I'd run ahead of her then, anger sparking my joints. She'd filled my closet with Sears florals, wrangled me with strands of her mother's dulled Akoyas. She'd placed a box of bulky pads in the bathroom and whispered, "This ought to last you awhile." She'd said, *Honey that temper of yours, it's really not attractive.*

Tampax Pearl Active girl, have you ever blacked out during a game, the ninety minutes a blur of rage and fear and red and yellow cards? Did your father tell you you'd played like a bitch? Like a whore? Did he say he was mistaken, he thought you were someone else, a different kind of girl, a golden girl, a magic girl, a girl who was not a girl at all?

At the Hawthorne Diner, eating cheese fries with Debbie Costello, did you admit how you sometimes dreamed of quitting, how sometimes the game felt like a too-small aquarium? Did part of you hate the moon that is the pearl that is the ball? One afternoon in Pelham, a week out of ACL rehab, did you ruin your left knee for good, nothing left for the surgeon to graft? Did relief and dread move through you in waves? Did your whole body flicker and go dark?

Did you find a nacre-walled apartment far away, build your paper sculptures, your fragile, neon crowns with their globes and arches, your houses light enough to fly as kites? Did you love a series of men who seemed to rewire you, to turn you magic and golden again? When you inevitably flickered, when the sculptures wouldn't cohere, when you lost patience with knives and glue, did you turn on them? Did you disappear into your blue pills, into your gold bottles? Did you speak to yourself, in a steel whistle voice?

• • •

Get more active, he told your mother, as in I love you, be more healthy, as in I hate you, be a different kind of woman, as in be thin in Laura Ashley like the other sideline mothers, as in clean the house for team dinners, as in cook lasagna for thirty-two, as in your Joni Mitchell records can wait, as in that out-of-town workshop on graphic design can wait, as in that photography business you want to start can wait, as in bury your desire deep in the backyard, a coiled snake of battered pearls, as in sneak fast food on the way home from work, as in hide your anger deep in your bones, in your struggling, salty heart.

"I heard about your mother," Debbie Costello says on my voice mail. "I know it's been awhile. I just wanted to say I'm sorry. I hope you're okay."

I call her back and it's awkward at first—So you live in L.A. now? How's life?—but we can still laugh at the old stories, our mothers taking us to that head shop in Mount Kisco called "Nowhere," our mothers shaking their heads at our tie-dye, at our hemp, at the sandalwood incense we weren't allowed to burn inside, our mothers blasting Cher and Joni Mitchell in their Outbacks, singing loud and off-key, our mothers in Esprit stretch pants. We can remember our mothers.

And what if the Tampax Pearl Active Soccer Girls walked off their boxes? What if they found their own scraggly, rutted field, found each other? What if there was no one to blow a steel whistle on them? What if it was possible to move through one's mistakes? What if a girl could shrug her shoulders and imagine her next fake, her next risky cut?

I hang up the phone and for a moment I can see them, their stiff, Lite-Brite bodies flickering, dulling, going dark, brightening, dulling, cracking, girls half-light and half-opaque. They do not move with much grace, not anymore. Their vision is blurred with pain pills, their bodies heavy with alcohol and grease, their lungs cigarette-gray. Their joints ache from years of playing too soon on a tear or a break because to rest was to be weak was to be a girl.

I can see my mother in a blue bathing suit at Jones Beach. While I raise castles with my father, she butterflies the Atlantic, swims against the undertow, a steady and rhythmic crawl, her dark hair rising and falling through waves. Her body cuts a determined line. She emerges half an hour later, freckled skin beaded with light.

I can see my father, fourteen years old, a year before my grandfather throws out his ball and turns my father's body dim, my father juggling a soccer ball in a used car dealership lot on hot, July afternoon, the ball flowing from his feet to his thighs to his head and back again. Above him, gold fringe pennants glint.

And I am standing in the clouded aquarium of my apartment, one eye a bright gold bulb, the other gray. There is no one coming over to make the walls shine. There is no one coming over to paint the walls gray. There is no one to light me up or burn me out or correct all my flawed scraps. In my closet, there is a box of Pearl Active Tampax tampons, which are of course like any other Tampax tampons. And in this new stillness, just for a moment, I can feel it deep in my chest, warped with sweat and oil and chemicals, almost unrecognizable, the ball that is the pearl that is the moon that is my mother's that is my father's that is mine.

Notes

"Autumn Begins in Hawthorne New York" was inspired in part by James Wright's "Autumn Begins in Martin's Ferry, Ohio," which appears in his book *The Branch Will Not Break* (Wesleyan University Press).

The epigraph from "Reverse Trampoline Fail" comes from Matt Rasmussen's poem "Reverse Suicide," which appears in his book *Black Aperture* (LSU Press).

CPSIA information can be obtained
at www.ICGtesting.com
Printed in the USA
LVOW12s2157210917
549604LV00001B/5/P

The Power *of*
FORGIVENESS

A Guide to Healing and Wholeness

Emily J. Hooks

To Zach

For teaching me the meaning of life:
To love without reservation.

Acknowledgments

This book would not exist without the help of some extraordinary people. First and foremost, I would like to thank the folks at KN Literary Arts, and especially my editor, Nirmala Nataraj. Nirmala's otherworldly capacity to take my words and help craft them into something understandable and enjoyable to read cannot be overstated. I would be sitting in the corner of my office, buried under a pile of crumpled pages without her guidance and hard work. I'd like to thank Tyffany Hermann, who asked one simple question that changed everything. Tyffany ignited in me my purpose; you are one of my angels. Thank you to Frank Salas, my business mentor and friend, for insisting I stop trying to figure it all out and just start writing.

Special thanks to my parents, Bill and Shirley Hooks for supporting me on this long and winding journey. And, to my son, Zach. You have been a beacon in the darkness since the day you blessed me and the world with your presence. Thank you for being you.

"It takes not time nor money nor the sweat of [the] brow to change the world: it takes only love. A forgiven world is whole, and in its wholeness one with you. It is here, in wholeness, that peace abides and heaven is. It is from wholeness that heaven waits for you."
— *A Course of Love*

Contents

Acknowledgments... v

Introduction ix

Part One: Let's Untangle a Few Ideas

1. What Forgiveness Is, and What It Is Not...................1

2. Why Bother Forgiving? 15

Part Two: Practicing Forgiveness

3. The Forgiveness Academy Competencies and Process..... 27

4. Self-Forgiveness and Forgiving God of the Universe 59

Part Three: A Deep Dive Into Concepts
For Mastering Forgiveness

5. Staying Open to Life with Non-Judgment................ 73

6. Expanding Awareness with Empathy 83

7. Self-Empowerment and Spiritual Warriorship 93

8. The Healing Power of Self-Love........................ 101

Conclusion..113

Resources 119

Introduction

Who ever can see through fear
will always be safe.
— Tao Te Ching

This book is about forgiveness as a healing practice. You will learn everything you need to know to use the power of forgiveness to become the most empowered expression of who you were meant to be.

This is not a book about the philosophical or theological concept of forgiveness; there are many great resources about forgiveness as an idea.

This book is not about the relationship between forgiveness and justice, although we will discuss the impact of forgiveness in the world.

This book is also not about what you should or should not do. The only "should" in this book is this: Honor yourself. I cannot know what that looks like for you. What I *do* know is that forgiveness is an act of self-empowerment. It is an act of self-love.

Finally, this book is not a social treatise. It is geared toward the individual. Forgiveness is an inside job with no requirements from another human being. There are extraordinary implications for a world filled with people who practice forgiveness, which we touch upon in later chapters, but before we can change the world, we must shift the individual paradigm that currently chooses punishment, blame, and suffering over wholeness and peace.

The sole objective of this book is to facilitate access to personal healing; whether you view this as a spiritual, emotional, or psychological evolution does not matter. The process is the same, and only the way it is framed changes. Where the message seems inaccessible because of the language used, I encourage you to reframe the words in a way that makes the most sense to you.

To give some perspective, I would like to briefly share the foundational beliefs that inform my journey. I believe each of us is an aspect of the divine. We are all part of a larger consciousness—not merely connected, but rather, an integral part of it.

"You are not a drop in the ocean. You are the entire ocean in a drop." — Rumi

I believe we choose to learn the lessons we are here to learn before we are born. That does not mean we write a contract saying we will endure sexual abuse or the genocide of our community. It means we agree to contribute in specific ways to the advancement of our collective human consciousness. The details emerge here in this life.

I believe when we harm others, it is because we ourselves are suffering. I believe non-suffering is possible, and all suffering has purpose. Its purpose is to compel our evolution toward a united and peaceful human condition. Suffering herein refers to any form of disharmony that reveals itself in us. From the subtlest impacts of non-forgiveness, like being aware of how our aloof or indifferent disposition impacts the well-being of others, to deeply impactful manifestations, such as chronic depression or aggression, all suffering is, at its root, the same.

I believe many of our most heartbreaking human experiences happen over and over because we fail to heal. We fail to honor our contribution and share our lessons. We fail to forgive. We seek vengeance in the name of justice and wonder why the world gets more vengeful. But forgiveness and justice are not mutually exclusive; they are partners in healing us and the world in which we live.

I believe time is an illusion. For this reason, the past and future are also illusions. Everything that ever *was* is happening *now*, because time is a figment of our limited human capacity to perceive all that is.

I believe we access our capacity to heal when we practice nonresistance. When we drop our defenses and let go of the idea that things should have turned out differently and give ourselves fully to what *is*, we access the only point at which true change takes place.

Finally, I believe the healing force in the universe is love. If we wish to frame that force in a way that anchors it in something we can visualize, we could call that pure force most closely correlated to love "God." God is the experience of absolute love.

All healing takes place in the present moment and in the heart. Those are the only two conditions we need to heal: being present and feeling love. As I see through fear, I see the truth of who you are: a perfect expression of your divinity. Or, for those of us who resist the idea of our divinity, let us say it this way: The whole you is the perfect expression of you, because within it, nothing is left out. The whole you is made richer by the integration of every single one of your experiences.

I know with certainty that your contribution to the world is as important as anyone else's. You have the power to change the world. And you have your experiences to thank for that. Now, if only we could facilitate our liberation from the pain of the experiences that seem to have caused us harm so we could encounter the world around us unencumbered by our attachment to the past.

Forgiveness creates healing and permanent change by freeing us from our perceptions of the past, from the idea it should have been better, or different. When we forgive, we heal at the most fundamental level, evolving toward a greater understanding of the meaning of life and our purpose in the larger context of living on this planet. My mission is to share the power of forgiveness with the world, and to empower us all to realize our true strength in the absence of both fear and the illusion of victimhood.

∽

There is a hard truth about forgiveness. We come to realize, with practice, we are responsible for our own experiences.

I acknowledge that when we consider childhood abuse or the unjust death of a loved one, this idea is challenging. I encourage you to keep an open mind. You do not need to believe you are responsible for what has happened, but as you heal, this will likely be what emerges. Embrace it.

The forgiveness journey is about empowering ourselves to materialize into a new consciousness. Approach the more difficult concepts in this book from the perspective of possibility. When you encounter resistance to an idea, simply imagine the possibility that it is true. You do not necessarily have to change your beliefs to fully experience this process. Rather, just sit with an idea that bothers you and contemplate it as truth. Ask yourself what it feels like in your body, in your heart. Do you have a glimpse of peace? Is suffering momentarily alleviated? These responses in your body and heart direct you to a point of power. I am not here to tell you what is true for you or what to believe. For the most part, it does not matter. However, I know that if you embrace the ideas in this book with an open heart and mind, you will heal.

∽

You are not the person you were yesterday, let alone a year ago or ten years ago. This is true at a fundamental level. Our cells die, and new ones are generated every day. Our bodies change and evolve. Given this fact, why is it we carry psychological injury forward with us through time? I believe it is because, in part, we choose to. We allow our experiences to inform the person we are today—which makes sense, right? I mean, if we did not do this, we would make the same sub-optimal choices again and again, and we would repeatedly find ourselves in situations we do not want to be in. Thus, we learn to adapt and incorporate aspects of our personalities based on what has happened in the past. But what we have *not* learned is to evaluate how these choices serve us throughout our lives.

We need to take the time to look closely at our beliefs, the resulting behaviors, and how they contribute to suffering. If we find they do not serve us, we must let them go.

The healing power of love emerges when we do something we have been taught not to do: Experience our pain. Although many of us may vividly re-live the details of our experiences through internal self-talk or in how we relate to the world, we rarely take the time to fully be with or feel our pain. Rather, we replace our feelings with stories and use judgment to separate us from our suffering.

We honor ourselves when we feel the hurt we hold on to in our bodies. Throughout our lives, we learn to resist emotional discomfort. An integral part of the forgiveness process (and all healing) is allowing ourselves to experience our pain in safe, healing ways so we can finally let it go. Self-love and non-judgment facilitate this release.

∽

We start in Part I by talking about what forgiveness is, what it is not, and why we should engage in this powerful but often painful process. *Do not skip this.* It may sound basic, but it is an essential foundation for our journey together. We have many false ideas about what forgiveness is, all of which have the potential to create unnecessary resistance. Chapters 1 and 2 untangle these ideas so we can clearly focus on the work at hand.

Part II of the book begins with Chapter 3, which takes us through a framework to facilitate forgiveness. The structure is designed to strengthen the competencies we need to fully forgive: clarity, telling the story, emotional awareness, empathy, non-judgment, and, of course, forgiveness itself. Chapter 4 is about self-forgiveness and forgiving the universe or God.

Part III, comprising Chapters 5 through 8, discusses concepts related to forgiveness that deepen our understanding of the healing practice. We close by talking about the impact of personal forgiveness on the world around us, including the implications for justice.

∽

I would like to close by sharing my personal story of forgiveness, which was the seed for the Forgiveness Academy™. This is my journey through great suffering to healing and the realization there is nothing to forgive.

In October 2002, I rolled out of bed in a darkened room with only the light from under the bedroom door seeping in. I heard voices on the other side of the door and moved quietly toward the sound to listen. As I tiptoed past a large mirror hung over an old oak dresser, I noticed something drawn on my back like a large, intricate tattoo.

My mind flashed to a memory of the man I had called my partner for the past year, straddling my legs and drawing on my back with a magic marker. As I turned to look over my shoulder, I saw the words "Treat me like a Queen" sketched across the width of my tiny, frail frame. In the other room, the voices grew louder, shifting my attention from the inexplicable words I was reading on my own body as if I were reading them on an advertisement for an animal shelter adoption program. On the other side of the door, I heard the man I loved say, "How much will you give me for her?"

An unfamiliar voice on the other side of the door responded, "Nothing. She's not worth it."

I speak about this moment metaphorically as an awakening that spurred a change the many heartbreaking events leading up to it did not. At that moment, I saw my life from afar. At the time, I realized I was going to die, having only lived a tragic life. My family was going to bury me, and the only thing they would have to say was how sad my life had been. At that moment, a compassion for self I had never felt emerged. The darkness pulled back, and an awareness of my torment peeked through. Then and there, I resolved to survive. I resolved to liberate myself from suffering and live a life filled with the joy and gratitude that broke free in me that day.

Today, I no longer see my life up to that point as tragic. But how did I get to that place? What choices had I made that led to such a moment in time where I was no longer human but merchandise with no power and no value?

To tell that story, I have to go further back in time, when my forgiveness journey truly began: April 10, 1979.

My father called my mother and asked if I could come to Boston to spend the Easter holiday with him. Despite the request being out of the ordinary, my mother agreed. My father flew to Texas and picked me up the next day. Five days later, he left a message for my mother telling her she would never see me again, and that if she tried to find us, he would tell me she was dead.

I do not remember leaving the country, and I did not know I had been abducted. My father told me my family did not want me, and that my mother was too busy to call. I spent the next three and a half years living with various family members, with the head matron of one of the schools I attended, and with my father. Eventually, I attended boarding school on the Welsh border. Altogether, I lived in at least six places and attended four schools I can recall. I had no idea he was hiding me or why I was moved so often. He told me it was to find the best schools, and that education was the most important thing in life.

Ironically, in some ways, he was right about this. Being educated and understanding how to solve complex problems would eventually contribute to saving my life.

In March of 1982, after changes in federal law creating protections for victims of parental abductions, the District Attorney's office in my hometown filed felony kidnapping charges against my father. An investigator for the county, Roy Davis, was quoted in the press after my return saying he'd had a hunch I was in England. Davis had written a letter to the Department of State, who contacted the U.S. Embassy in London asking for help.

On my eleventh birthday, the Embassy had called Davis and informed him I was living in the country. My mother, aunt, and a private detective flew to England in early July that year and found my exact location by reading every page of a phone book, scouring it for a phone number she had gotten from my father. Because there were no custody agreements filed in England, they were forced to kidnap me back. My mother and the detective, James, arrived at my best friend's house in the late evening of July 4. She picked me up and whispered, "Do you want to go with me?" in my ear. For the second time in my short twelve years, I left the life I knew with the clothes on my back.

These events had a significant impact on my family. I came home to a very different life. My half-sister had moved across the country to live with her father and his family. My mother was deeply affected by the years of struggle and emotional torment my father and his family had put her through. Many years later, I came to recognize I spent the next ten-plus years in a sort of daze. I started using drugs at an early age, dropped out of high school, and moved to California when I was eighteen, only to return to Texas nine months later. This relocation started a trend of staying on the move that would carry throughout my adult life.

In November 1990, I gave birth to my son. This initiated a period of learning how to trust and love, and allowing myself to have fun. Despite my youth and complete unpreparedness, I was a natural mother, and we were easy companions.

I worked multiple jobs while attending college during the first seven years of his life. I found comfort and security in school, particularly in studying science, which gave me access to tangible and knowable facts and methods. Through my studies, I could escape the chaos in my mind and heart. But the relative harmony did not last.

As graduation approached, the fear of not knowing what I was going to do next, of not having a job, and not having a plan threw me off the balance beam I had been teetering on since Zach was born. I also felt lost, as a mother, for the first time. Zach was becoming a little boy of the age I had been when I was abducted. Not only did I know nothing about boys, I knew nothing about how a seven-year-old might experience life under normal circumstances. These changes stirred in me a sort of paralyzing terror, and I began to self-destruct.

I turned to the coping mechanisms I had learned earlier in life. In 1998, I embarked on a four-year journey through hell. I started using cocaine and methamphetamines intravenously in late 1998. The following year, I lost everything, including custody of my son to my mother and stepfather, who were willing and able to take care of him. I lived in a car, traveling back and forth across the state, sleeping in lit parking lots, hidden under trees and praying for safety on the warm nights when I had to keep the windows cracked to let the breeze through. I met many interesting characters during this period, souls I will always cherish for teaching me the meaning of true empathy.

As human beings, we like to draw lines in the sand between us and them. "I am empathetic but I would never . . ." One of the gifts of this time was my discovery that those lines are illusions. All of the hurtful things we do are cut from the same fabric: suffering and responding to suffering.

∽

In 1999 and 2000, after losing custody of my son, I made two attempts to end my life. On a sunny day in late 1999, I calmly blew out the pilot light on the stove and turned up the gas. I lay down and went to sleep. I dreamt I was watching from above as my mother and son entered the room and found my lifeless body. I watched as my mother tried to protect the young life I had created from more anguish.

People caught in an addictive pattern make a strange rationalization others seldom understand. Because we are so far from ourselves during these times, we believe the people we love are better off without us. We believe we are protecting them by not being in their lives. But as I watched my mother and son's agony unfold in my dream, I realized this was not true. Despite the hatred I had for myself, I knew I was loved, and I mattered.

On August 10, 2000, I tried one more time to end my life. I was very ill from abusing drugs, and not functioning in life by this point. I drove to a private spot on the Paluxy River and tried again. This time, as I lay on the dry limestone riverbed, I saw the clichéd white light quickly moving from the horizon toward me. As it approached me and my body began to dissipate into the light, something happened. I do not remember "who" it was, but I had a conversation with someone. As the being faded, I "saw" everything that ever was and ever would be. I knew why everything was the way it was, and for an ephemeral moment, I experienced no suffering. My heart filled with love, and I regained consciousness with a violent jolt.

It would be romantic to tell you everything changed that day. It did not. I scrambled for a pen to write down what had happened, could not find one, panicked, called my drug dealer, and got high. I had not yet experienced the dark night—when all meaning is questioned—but I believe this moment laid the foundation for my eventual healing.

This is the reason I know there is divinity in everyone. I know all fear is an illusion. I do not always come from this place of remembering, but it is the foundation of my faith in purpose. My prayer is that you can share in this knowing and choose to not suffer.

∽

Something strange and ironic happened as a result of my failed suicide attempts. Rather than being imbued with a deep sense of purpose and gratitude, I felt helpless in my suffering. I felt I had failed at yet another endeavor in life. I continued to try to end my life by placing myself in extraordinarily dangerous situations. I resolved to make the most of the life I was living by getting tougher and meaner. The meaner I became, the more my intuition beseeched me to yield, to soften. I spent the next two years continuing to act out of my suffering, causing unfathomable pain for those around me and those who loved me.

In 2001 and early 2002, I experienced a "dark night of the soul": a crisis of faith in which one feels utterly abandoned by God and life. During this time, life became meaningless, hopeless. I had no sense of what was true and what was an illusion. I often regressed into a state of repeating, "Everything is as it should be" over and over again as the only anchor I could find, but I did not believe the words, nor did I understand what they truly meant. I experienced love as suffering. My spiritual and psychological pain was the only thing I could see or feel.

In late 2002, my unwitting wish to no longer suffer almost came true. In the early evening of a fall day, I stood in the RV my grandfather had purchased to keep me off the streets and argued passionately with the man I had been dating. The scene turned to slow motion in my mind when I said the words, "You're so f***ing stupid!" A rage I had never seen in another human being arose from him. His violence, which very nearly killed me, created another shift that shook me from the trance in which I had been living. This was the beginning of the end. A few weeks later, I woke up and read the words scrolled across my back.

That moment of grace was fourteen years ago. Everything began changing in my life within a short period of time. I left the city I was living in, got a job and a place to live. Zach came home to live with me. I started studying spiritual and religious texts. I studied the well-known recovery books and practices. I implemented the concepts consistent with my core beliefs of non-resistance and our inherent divine nature.

To help with the mental and physical pain of the transition, I made rules to live by. I resolved to always do what I said I was going to do, even if it was only an agreement with myself. This helped calm the mental disarray manifested in subtle but highly disruptive ways, like getting in my car to go somewhere and then just driving around aimlessly for hours, failing to meet simple obligations.

Much of our suffering is rooted in an obsession with thinking about the self. Service to others allows us to break this cycle and focus on others with kindness. I quieted my mind by volunteering and being of service. I started being gentler with myself and the world around me. Slowly, the darkness began to pull back, and I remembered what I had learned. I knew I was and had always been exactly where I was supposed to be. What I came to understand is this: I was choosing the life I had.

Everything is as it should be, because it can't be any other way. We choose our lives based on our fundamental beliefs about ourselves and the world around us. Our lives manifest from the words and feelings we share and experience as a result of those beliefs. The wonderful news is, we can also use our words and our feelings to change our beliefs. You see, the language we use can empower or disempower us. It is a creative force in and of itself. Keep this in mind as you move through this journey. The words you use change everything.

I remembered fear is an illusion, despite how real it seems. I focused on building a life reflecting a new understanding of the self, not as a powerless victim, but as a divine being with the freedom to make new choices.

But the clouds did not magically part to let the sun stream through. My realizations did not yield great joy; in fact, life was harder than anything I had endured up to that point because, in the parlance of AA, I was living life on life's terms, with all its challenges and all its discomforts. I was staying present to the suffering I had sustained and created in the world around me and in those I loved the most. I learned the meaning of integrity and took full responsibility for my experiences. I began to systematically forgive everyone who had ever caused me harm, including myself.

I came to see the relationship between resistance and suffering, which is something we will talk about in Chapter 5. All suffering is resistance. The first step in healing is awareness followed by simply accepting what is through non-resistance. We have to start from where we are. When we yield, we ground ourselves firmly in the space of now.

When we anchor ourselves in the present, we relinquish our ideas about the past, as well as our grip on what the future should look like. The present opens up possibilities, allowing us to step into newness and the unknown. I find great comfort and power in not knowing, being free from the chains of certainty. Does that mean I always get it right? No, absolutely not. Far from it. But thank God for that! How dull would it be to have it all figured out? Viewing the world with curiosity and a willingness to see what is truest in any given moment brings me a peace that figuring it all out never could.

Now, I wake up grateful almost every day. I know there is nothing to forgive, because every moment leading up to this one has made me who I am today: a perfect expression of my own divinity. A perfect expression of Emily-ness in the world. I am as responsible as every other living soul for the evolution of human consciousness. I am here to do my part.

My hope is this story of healing and forgiveness will inspire you to embark on your own journey of self-discovery. All you need to begin is willingness. The more open you are, the better. The tools to move forward are outlined in the following pages.

Your experiences need not define you. You are exactly who you were meant to be, because it brought you to this moment in time. The question you need to ask is: *Who do I want to be next week, next month, and next year?* If the answer is someone who is freer, someone more present, someone unfettered by your experiences, then you are in the right place. I look forward to taking this journey with you.

PART ONE

Let's Untangle a Few Ideas

Chapter One

What Forgiveness Is, and What It Is Not

True forgiveness is when you can say,
"Thank you for that experience."
— Oprah Winfrey

Joshua yearned to be home. He watched the tide wash up the shoreline and rush back out to the horizon, day after day, from the small open window of his prison cell. As the months passed and his loneliness and despair grew, Joshua wished he could speak to the man who had wrongly accused him. He needed the man to regret his decision to consign Joshua to a life of unending pain and torment. Night after endless night, he imagined speaking to the man, begging, bargaining for release and remorse. He staggered between passionate anger and pleading, cajoling the man to show mercy and confess his error.

Joshua's faith gradually crumbled into meaninglessness. He loathed God for his misery, for taking away his freedom and allowing his pain to continue. But, as the years drifted by, Joshua tired. His mind began to quiet. With the silence of non-judgment, his heart softened. For the first time, he could see life here in this tiny stone room was his life. He began to look upon the walls, the floor and the ocean nearby through a gaze of wonder rather than despair. What had he missed?

One early morning, as the sun rose, Joshua conjured an image of the man in his mind's eye. Where before, all he could see was the man

1

responsible for his suffering, now he could see something he hadn't before: Joshua was not the only one suffering. Joshua's heart expanded as he came to the realization that the prison he endured was not his alone. Just as our suffering is intimately tied to another's, so is our joy. So is our acceptance. As Joshua gazed out at the wide and placid ocean, he could feel how its waves lapped at the shore without discrimination. Teeming with life energy, the ocean was there for all to behold and enjoy if only they could see.

With a full heart and eyes transformed by his new awareness, Joshua went to the door of his cell, only to find it was not locked. It never had been.

Just as Joshua realized, absolute forgiveness is possible. It is a gift we can give ourselves. It does not take away the fact that we may have suffered or endured pain in the past. It does not excuse the actions of those who may have hurt us nor does it excuse the things we have done that caused harm. It enables us to see everything that led to this moment is in perfect alignment. We can finally accept what was, what is, and what might come to be. When we do this, we become free. We become free regardless of our circumstances, whether in an actual jail cell or a psychological prison we have created.

With absolute forgiveness, we recognize, indeed, there really is not anything to forgive. We recognize both other people's transgressions and our own mistakes transform from a cacophony of seemingly random, even violent, inputs into a symphony whose overture is the *present moment*. What emerges from this shift is gratitude for all of our experiences and an awareness of our personal power that lets us believe we have the freedom to make new choices.

Absolute forgiveness is a state in which we perceive, beyond doubt, there is *nothing to forgive*. When we are filled with love and gratitude for everything that has led to this moment, we have an instinctive understanding that there are no mistakes. We develop a deep self-compassion and a limitless sense of love. We come to see that, had we not had the experiences that impacted us (even leaving scars in their wake), we would not be who we are today.

When we come to truly know we are exactly who we were born to be, we surrender our hold on all past resentments. Gratitude for all our experiences emerges. The healing power of forgiveness enables us to come to a deeper awareness of our true nature. In fact, the belief we are anything less than whole because of something that "happened to" us in the past falls away.

∽

I realize to those who are now suffering from the wounds of the past, the concept that there is nothing to forgive sounds absurd. My aspiration is that you will feel a ray of hope that warms you to the possibility of being so free from the bonds of the past, your perception of them as wounds will transform. It is wholly possible to begin to see your painful experiences as building blocks that will lead you to manifest your highest truth and your deepest peace.

However, we do not need to get to the point of absolute forgiveness to experience the joy and compassion only accessible through forgiveness. You can come to realize greater peace, power, clarity, energy, and ease without ever coming to believe there is nothing to forgive.

Throughout the process of forgiveness, you have the capacity to experience shifts that will bring you closer to clarity and neutrality. You will be able to look at your past clearly without being imprisoned by it.

∽

Let's look at another definition of forgiveness that embodies the essence of the experience as we move through this wondrous healing process together:

Forgiveness is a process of self-actualization in which we choose to move through hurt feelings such as shame, anger, and resentment in favor of self-compassion, self-love, and empathy.

Simply put, self-actualization (a term originally introduced by Kurt Goldstein) is the realization of one's potential. Forgiveness contributes to our actualization because it liberates us from the past. Living to one's potential implies the growth of latent qualities or abilities, the development of our full selves. However, we cannot do this if we are in a state of withholding forgiveness, either for ourselves or others. When we choose not to forgive, whether we consciously know it or not, we are inhibiting our growth and our potential. Our energy is consumed by regret, resentment, or righteous indignation. While these reactions may seem perfectly justified, they never allow us to move beyond a confining perception of the past.

The only moment we can create new possibilities is the *present moment*. Right now. We cannot create in the future. We cannot create in the past. If we are tied to the past via perceived psychological or spiritual injury, we are giving away our power to manifest. Forgiveness breaks those ties and allows us to live boldly in the present moment.

∽

The first component of forgiveness is **self-compassion**. This is an experience of deep connection and understanding of the self in the absence of judgment. It requires awareness and acceptance of how we feel: emotionally, spiritually, and physically. This awareness allows us to offer kindness and love to ourselves, particularly in moments of difficulty. Instead of ignoring our pain or numbing it, we move toward it with fascinated curiosity and the desire to see which of our needs may be going unmet. Because we are all indelibly connected, this compassion for self naturally manifests as an expression of gentleness and acceptance toward others.

Self-love is unconditional love of the *whole* self. It is not a theory or idea, but a perceptible feeling we experience, just like the love we have for a child, partner, parent, or best friend. It is an experience of love not only for the parts of ourselves we adore but for the parts we perceive as being "the dark side" of us. When we bring these aspects of self into the light, their power is transformed. They become a part of the whole.

Interestingly and unfortunately, we are most often not taught to love ourselves. In fact, we are frequently taught to judge and ridicule ourselves into acting the way the world prefers. By succumbing to this control, we believe we will gain other people's approval. The good news is, learning to experience love and honor ourselves is not actually hard; it merely requires our willingness and a little practice.

The final component of forgiveness, **empathy**, refers to being able to relate to another's feelings and experiences totally. It enables us to walk the proverbial mile in someone else's shoes and to accept that, indeed, we might have made the same choices they have made had we lived their life.

Empathy is a feeling of innate connection with all that is. It keeps us from creating caricatures of "right" and "wrong" out of the people in our lives. We discover a sense of unity with someone or something outside ourselves, most often another human being. The remarkable thing about empathy is it elicits compassion for our shared human experience. As it makes the possibility of forgiveness concrete, it expands our perspectives about ourselves, others, and life itself.

Forgiveness is a process.

Quite simply, it is a series of actions taken toward a specific and intended outcome.

Think of it like a breath.

There is the in-breath—a time in which we expand, grow, and heal—and the out-breath—a time for creating and contributing to the world, and of integrating what we have learned so we can show up in a new way in our lives. But there is also the space in between. Imagine this to be the moment of realization. A shift occurs during the pause between the in-breath and the out-breath. This moment might include feeling our suffering as we have never felt it before, or we might see the subtlest sign of humanity where it had once been obscured. The forgiveness process is designed to initiate these moments when perception shifts.

When my healing journey began, I felt deep sadness for my life. Up until that moment, I resisted the pain of my experiences because I falsely believed I would be overcome with a despair I could not handle. This did not happen. Instead, a profound experience of self-compassion and self-love I had not known up until that very moment transpired.

In the process of forgiveness, we begin by acknowledging the shift in our awareness, usually a realization of previously unrecognized suffering. We take energy in from the world around us as we heal. Gradually, our perception changes as a result of this expansion, and we are able to give back to the world through newfound presence. From here, we start over—not necessarily with forgiveness, but with growth, expansion, and often, healing. As our point of view continues to evolve and as we unshackle ourselves from the armor of our old identity, we grow and continue to discover new aspects of who we are.

Forgiveness happens during the in-breath and ends with the pause, which is when our perception transforms. This can happen many times during your forgiveness journey, always building on the revelations that came before. On the other hand, it can take only one shift to transform your entire understanding of the world. Only one moment of regarding the person who caused you harm with a compassionate heart can change everything.

The forgiveness process is about releasing hurt feelings in exchange for compassion and empathy. Love is the ultimate actor in the process. As Jesus said, love heals all wounds. The Buddha similarly said love has the power to transform suffering.

Have you ever wondered why kissing a child's boo-boo stops her from crying? It is because she feels your love. The child is healed by your expression of love and caring. All healing emanates from love, but the unique challenge is teaching ourselves to experience self-love rather than love from an external source.

∽

Forgiveness is a choice.

How many times have you heard someone say, "I *want* to forgive, but I *can't*." Well, that is not true. You *can*. It's just that you are choosing not to.

You can choose to forgive, and you can choose not to forgive. Both are valid options. In fact, not forgiving appears to be the favored option in the world today.

In the process of forgiveness, we are *choosing* to move through our hurt in order to make space for compassion and empathy. Compassion and empathy are the outcomes of the healing process. They can also be tools we use to reach the point of allowing for forgiveness.

Not wanting to feel unity with or compassion for someone or something who has hurt you is understandable. But if you do not want to empathize with the person or people who have hurt you, you are choosing *not* to forgive. I know this is a hard pill to swallow, but it is true, nonetheless. A harder pill to swallow is the fact that you are hurting yourself by not forgiving.

Often, when we make a choice to forgive, it is because we have hit a breaking point where we realize our suffering is too great a burden to carry. Forgiveness often begins when awareness of our own suffering becomes more acute than our indignation or desire to be right.

We may not want to admit this to ourselves, but our suffering is worsened when we withhold forgiveness. Our energy is squandered on resentment, bitterness, and the belief that things should have been different. Our very life energy is wasted on a sense of righteousness that does not serve us.

∽

Forgiveness is an internal job.

In truth, we do not need anything from anyone to heal. There are no exceptions to this. If you feel you need something you do not have from someone—such as an apology or acknowledgment of remorse, as Joshua experienced in the opening story of this chapter—to move forward, you are *choosing* not to heal. There is great power in this truth. You can choose to forgive wholly with no input from another.

That said, if you have a willing participant who is able to contribute to your healing and offer you something to help facilitate your journey, this can be a powerful tool. Healing is about connection with other human beings. Allowing space for contribution can be additive to the process.

Forgiveness is a discipline that, with practice, will become an integral part of who you are. Just like working out, the more you do it, the easier it becomes.

Today, when I encounter a traumatic event in the world, my automatic response is to see the suffering of the person who appears to be doing harm. I do not even have to look for it. As soon as this connection is made, forgiveness takes place. Of course, in the case of personal situations, recognizing a perpetrator's suffering can be more challenging. But the more we allow compassion and unity to rule, the more quickly we heal and move forward.

∽

Finally, *forgiveness is the relinquishment of judgment.* (We will talk about this in detail in Chapters 3 and 5.) There is no space in the process for judgment, because healing takes place in the heart, not the head.

In the absence of judgment, we also yield to the idea we do not know the absolute truth of what happened. Not knowing creates space for possibility. This corresponds to the pause in the metaphorical breath of forgiveness. In the space between healing and contributing to the world/integrating our experiences, we stop the activity of knowing, and open to growth. The place where we end up on the other side of the in-breath may be wildly different from where we began.

As you relinquish judgment, you need not decide to let go of knowing, but this is eventually where you will end up.

∽

It is important to understand what forgiveness is *not*, because these misunderstandings about forgiveness are our primary source of resistance to the process. Make a star next to each bulleted item that rings true for you, and when you find yourself struggling with the process, come back to the list and ask yourself if you are experiencing opposition because you are falsely envisioning one of these to be true.

Forgiveness is not:

- Condoning unfair or unacceptable behavior
- A lack of justice, or letting someone off the hook
- A sign of weakness
- Just moving on or pretending it didn't happen
- Forgetting
- Trust and reconciliation
- A negotiation
- Inherently religious

Society expects us *not* to forgive. It seems the world has fallen into a collective trance that believes if we heal, we are condoning our perpetrator's harmful actions or we are indifferent to justice.

However, forgiveness is not letting someone off the hook or justifying what happened as being acceptable in any way. It is not condoning unacceptable behavior. If it caused harm, it is not okay— period. In fact, forgiveness is an act of self-empowerment. This is because, as we learn to love and accept ourselves as we are, we intuitively create boundaries to reflect this love. We can make bolder, better choices. It is self-empowering because, as we free ourselves from the mental filters we have put in place to protect ourselves, we can see the world more clearly. This clarity empowers us to respond to the world more accurately and to express our passions with integrity.

One of the reasons we fear injustice as a consequence of forgiveness is that forgiveness necessarily leads us to the unknown. Our prior wishes transform as we evolve in the process. We cannot know who we will be until we get there, and we fear if we heal, we will not have the motivation to seek justice. This fear is legitimate, but is easily allayed. This is an issue of character that can be solved by choosing now who you will be. You can say to yourself, "I will seek true justice when it becomes clear," with the knowledge your definition of justice might change.

In fact, it will. Your understanding of justice will change from vengeance to fairness and compassion—which is what true justice is about. Vengeance perpetuates violence and disharmony. When you do forgiveness work, you have the power to break the cycle, because you liberate yourself from the filters of the past and are able to see the world as it is in the present moment. With a compassionate heart, you are free to focus on restoration for all.

Another common misunderstanding is that forgiveness is a sign of weakness. This could not be more false; in fact, turning the other cheek requires enormous strength. Gandhi said, "The weak can never forgive. Forgiveness is the attribute of the strong."

Forgiveness is not easy; it requires courage and emotional tenacity. In an unforgiving world, forgiveness demands we take a stand to prioritize our peace and healing. Essentially, forgiveness enables us to take back our power and refuse to let anger or false beliefs keep us from having the lives we want and were meant to have. Forgiveness also allows us to be in the driver's seat of our own life because it is a refusal to allow other people's actions to alter us or diminish our true essence ultimately.

To address another common concern about forgiveness, it is not pretending something harmful did not take place. On the contrary; through the process, we become even more present and aware of how our experiences impacted and continue to impact us. We learn to honor what happened, and how it left its mark.

Accordingly, forgiveness is not about simply moving on and forgetting. This is what many of us are taught forgiveness is. "Don't let them get the best of you." "Don't let them see you cry." Forgiveness gets a bad rap for this. We believe there is no true power in forgiveness because we think we are already doing it and it is not helping. But forgiveness requires active participation and a willingness to fully feel our pain, not to harden ourselves against it. It also requires active empathy, not numbness or indifference.

Some of us want to forget; others do not; forgiveness cannot help with this. It may be, as our attachment to past events fades, the memory also fades—but it will always be a part of who you are. This is the beauty in the process. We learn to love our whole selves and become grateful for the things we might now prefer not to remember. For those who fear forgetting will increase the risk of history repeating itself, Dr. Robert D. Enright says, "Forgiveness will not produce amnesia." Indeed, it will not.

Forgiveness is not explicitly about trust or reconciliation. We may rightly never trust someone who has caused us harm, and likewise we may not wish to have a relationship with them, but we can still forgive. One obvious exception to this is in the case of self-forgiveness. We rebuild trust of the self by creating rules to live by and developing a strong foundation of integrity.

The Buddha made a distinction between forgiveness and reconciliation that is helpful to note. He rightly said reconciliation is much more difficult than forgiveness and is not always possible. However, forgiveness is *always* possible. Forgiveness does not imply reconciliation will or should take place. If someone has hurt you and has not acknowledged or changed their behavior, reconciliation is not favorable.

Because forgiveness is an inside job, it does not require negotiation with anything outside of ourselves. Although there is bound to be collective or communal benefit, we embolden ourselves when we recognize the other person has nothing to do with the process and need not be an active participant in our own healing. Pay close attention to any subtle inclination you are subconsciously engaging in to get something from another person, God, or the universe. This will always create obstacles to healing. Be motivated by your liberation and self-love and success is guaranteed.

Finally, forgiveness is neither a moral obligation nor an inherently religious decision. It is a choice. Leveraging faith is a great way to increase our trust in the process, but it is not a requirement. The challenge with approaching forgiveness as a moral obligation is that when we feel we *must* forgive, we are often compelled to go through the motions of saying "I forgive you" and then attempting to move on. When we force the situation in this way, we are not honoring our experiences and how we truly feel. Approaching forgiveness as a religious decision can inhibit the process of feeling our pain and coming to a profound awareness of its power to transform us for the better.

The journey you are about to undertake toward a full expression of who you are—who you were always meant to be—will be challenging. It will require releasing some, or all, of your past ideas about forgiveness, even if you think you have already done the heavy lifting. There may be moments when your steadfastness is diminished by the trials of letting go of being right or allowing yourself to empathize. This requires a clear understanding and faith that the result will be worth the effort. It requires a determination to transform your very idea of who you are, and what you are capable of.

Chapter Two

Why Bother Forgiving?

The wound is the place where the Light enters you.

— Rumi

Sam's fists clenched as she thought about the argument with her boss. Her heart raced as the scene played through her mind like a movie.

"How could he have been so cold? What a jerk!" Her mind looped with vivid detail over and over again, as her body continued to tense. With irritation, she imagined the picture of his family placed so casually on her boss's desk. "As if he actually cared about them! All he cares about is making money at any cost." she thought contemptuously.

Walking down the hallway to the doctor's office, Sam began to feel lightheaded. Her chest tightened, and she could not breathe. She quickened her pace and entered the waiting room. Immediately, she rushed to the reception desk to get help.

"Your blood pressure is 150 over 80," the doctor told her. "That is very high for a woman your age. And your heart rate is 120. I'm not at all surprised you're feeling a little lightheaded. What's going on?"

Sam looked around the room and thought of her husband and daughter. The bright lights and wallpapered walls felt stark, cold. They contrasted with the light-filled kitchen table they had gathered around together that morning, arguing over the best flavor of jam. Sam's body loosened as she drew in a deep breath. Her mind flashed back to the fight with her boss, David. Once again, she recalled the picture on his desk. This time she could see the love in his eyes as he held his twin boys. She could imagine another possibility for him.

Sam glanced at the doctor. "Nothing really—just stressed about work, I guess," she responded.

The doctor was stern as he looked at Sam. "You can't let it get to you that much—it'll kill you, you know?"

There are as many reasons to forgive as there are stars in the sky. We may wish to be free from the burden of our experiences, or we may want to create aspects of the life we want that are limited by our current ideas about the past. It may be as simple as just wanting to be happier.

As we explore the many reasons we are motivated to forgive, I encourage you to take the opportunity to dream your highest dream for how you wish to experience life. What vision lights a fire in you? "I want to be free from worry," or, "I want to be fully present in every precious moment." In the next chapter, you will have the opportunity to write your reasons down. Start now, if you are inspired.

For many of us, our first inclination is driven by how we can help others. Maybe we want to be more present for our spouse or partner, or less angry or reactive toward our children. Maybe we want to have a bolder voice at work. Perhaps we want to fight for a cause related to things that have happened to us, but find it too painful to be involved.

For many years, the source of my inspiration has been providing security and a loving foundation for my son and his future family. As you explore what prepares you for the in-breath of healing, listen to your heart. Feel how your body responds to your intentions. If you feel lighter, have less tension in your body, and sense the expansive presence of love in your heart, this is a powerful place to start.

Let me caution here, however – we need to be aware of the purity of our intentions. It is easy to trick ourselves into believing we have good intentions when we are actually attempting to subtly negotiate with others or with God. This is important, because, as we move through the process, our focus will start to shift from the internal work of healing to the external, as we watch for clues of success from those around us. This is a sure recipe for failure, because it is the integrity of our intentions that spurs authentic change.

For example, you might start with the intention of "making life happier at home," which is certainly a valid starting point. However, it could be what you feel underneath the idea is, "If I stop being angry, my wife will sleep with me more often."

Ask yourself this question to check the nature of your real motivation: Does my reason for forgiving create outcomes to support the individual aspirations of everyone involved? This question gives us access to whether or not we want to control other people's outcomes and behaviors, which is not the purpose of forgiveness. Determining the purity of our intentions can be tricky, but at the end of the day, let the heart be your gauge.

∽

We all know what it looks like when we need to forgive somebody— even if we have not consciously decided we are going to. Just like Sam, we run the film of what happened through our minds over and over, filling in details and becoming brasher, wittier, and *righter* with each iteration. Then, we snap out of it and get even angrier because the other person is taking so much of our attention, energy, and focus. The cycle repeats itself with even more intensity and indignation.

What we may not realize, however, is the impact holding onto resentment and anger has on our physical, emotional, and spiritual health. The longer we hold onto our resentments, the more potential they have to negatively impact our well-being. Fortunately, as we address these impacts by engaging in the healing process of forgiveness, the benefits will show up mightily in our lives.

The benefits of forgiveness are obvious to most of us. We instinctively know releasing the past and connecting to the present moment frees us from old baggage. It makes us feel more alive and engaged. It makes us more available for our friends, our families, ourselves, and the full truth of who we are.

However, our opposition to forgiveness can become a habit that is difficult to shake. Perhaps we show up in our lives as angry, aggressive, or resigned. Perhaps we use our wounds as a rationalization for our prejudice (for example, "I know all women are manipulative because my first wife lied and then left me"). Our explanations for why life is the way it is may seem perfectly justified; after all, our experiences speak for themselves, right?

Wrong.

When we choose not to forgive, we take on a very limited view of our lives, who we are, what happened, and what will be. This limited view becomes the basis of our reality. We fall prey to confirmation bias, which is the tendency to interpret everything around us as validation of our own existing beliefs or theories. In other words, if you believe all women are bad, you will automatically collect evidence to prove this belief. You have already decided how the world is going to show up for you, and how you will show up for the world.

Many of us create our reality based on what we most fear. Forgiveness is a process that helps us let go of our preconceived ideas and fears. Think of these attachments to the past like enchanted eye glasses we use to see the world in a protective or even defensive way. We are trying to protect ourselves, and in the process, we obscure our ability to clearly see what is happening in the world around us. Removing these filters frees us from destructive patterns and cycles, as well as recurring outcomes that do not serve us.

Too many people only forgive at the eleventh hour of their lives, after years of allowing their sense of pain and personal injury to call the shots. They get to a breaking point, where the agony of holding onto their suffering (and reaping the same results, over and over) outweighs the pain they endure. Forgiveness can be a potent and beautiful choice we make at any point, but we need not wait until we are overwhelmed by regrets or hit by a crisis. No matter what, we can *always* choose forgiveness—for ourselves, for our children, or for the sake of breaking limiting patterns that may have carried through for generations.

You can choose forgiveness simply because it offers you a sense of peace and fulfillment *right now*.

Below are some of the many benefits of choosing forgiveness. In reading each entry, consider how you are withholding forgiveness, from either yourself or others, and think of how this is impacting your quality of life.

Many of the benefits will not surprise you, but one of the things I find astonishing is that so many of us choose not to forgive, even when we are fully aware of how dramatically forgiveness can transform our lives.

Breaking the cycle of dysfunction in a family and modeling a new way of being for our children or other family members. Our children learn how to navigate life from us. If we choose to harbor resentment and hold on to anger or shame by blaming others or not taking responsibility for our experiences in life, they will do likewise. On the other hand, if we choose to cultivate compassion and empathy for the world around us and stand fully accountable for our lives, they learn that they, too, can experience life with tenderness and curiosity. They learn they have power over their lives. This creates a sense of security and empowerment the alternatives cannot.

Learning to trust ourselves. When we approach life with the multitude of filters we put on to protect ourselves from harm, we make it impossible to see the world clearly. When we misinterpret what is happening around us, we find it more challenging to make the best choices. This teaches us we cannot be trusted to navigate life effectively. We begin to believe we are so fundamentally different or flawed, we must rely on external input to survive. When we forgive, the filters are removed. Suddenly, we see the world with clear eyes. We learn to trust ourselves, as we begin to respond in ways that help us achieve the outcomes we desire. This shift changes many aspects of our lives, including transforming our relationships with others, because we no longer feel the need to defend. We cultivate more intimate, trusting relationships, and become more present. We find the empowerment we have always sought.

Experiencing more compassion for ourselves and others. This change quite literally transforms the world in which we live. With compassion comes an experience of connection we may have never felt. This is the source of our ability to feel we are contributing to the world in meaningful ways.

Expanding our outlook on life by responding to both challenges and rewards with optimism and a positive attitude. Suddenly we see the universe as a friendly, supportive force for our betterment and evolution. We begin reinforcing our understanding of our inherent value. We innately begin to experience more joy in our lives.

Physiological Benefits*

- Lowered cortisol levels, leading to better stress responses

- Lower blood pressure

- Stronger immune system responses

- More energy and focus

- Improved heart health

*Sources: Johns Hopkins University & The Mayo Clinic

Our opposition to forgiveness, despite our full awareness of its benefits, emerges from our lack of understanding: of ourselves, of the nature of forgiveness, and of reality itself. We may have tried to forgive, doing what we knew to do, only to feel the same painful feelings of shame or resentment we had hoped to overcome.

Others of us may have experienced what seemed like a moment of grace, in which forgiveness was magically granted, but there was no real understanding about how we got to that moment in time— meaning we do not know how to *willingly* choose forgiveness. We may also be resigned to not even try because the concept of forgiveness seems too abstruse or inaccessible, something only saints or superheroes would be capable of.

These conclusions point to a lack of understanding. We know now that forgiveness is choice. It is a discipline we can develop with practice that becomes a virtue as we move through the process. Forgiveness is knowable and achievable, and is accessible to anyone willing to do the work.

Another notable point of resistance to forgiving ourselves and others is the realization that in order to heal, we must experience our pain. By definition, this is not a pleasant experience. Much like developing the muscles we need to play any competitive sport, there is discomfort. But we endure because we understand the payoff. My hope is the rewards are becoming clear to you.

We may also think that if we allow ourselves to be fully present to the suffering we have sustained, we will not be okay. We believe we will fall into despair if we embrace our pain and learn to honor it. The reason for this is because, as we experience moments of suffering, we inadvertently begin to analyze them. We shift what is happening in the heart to our thinking mind. It is our thoughts about how we feel that cause us to fall apart, not the feelings themselves. We tell ourselves it is wrong or dangerous to feel our suffering. This is a learned response to the fear associated with suffering, but this fear is an obstruction between us and a higher truth. The truth is, in allowing ourselves to process our pain, we heal it. In the absence of judgment, our anger, resentment, sadness, and shame are transformed into love.

The final category of reasons we resist forgiving is the hard, but oh-so-real and important aspect of human nature we may prefer not to see: We do not forgive because we get something out of not forgiving.

Perhaps being a victim has become a part of your identity. It is not unusual, when sustaining injury, to recognize our best coping mechanism in the moment is submission. This is especially true in ongoing relationships in which there is an abusive power dynamic. What we learn from these experiences is how to covertly use power to get what we want. When we play the victim, we do not believe we can directly access what we want, so we choose to instead manipulate power out of those around us. But this is not an authentic expression of who you are. Ever.

Sometimes, withholding forgiveness gives us a reason to hold on to anger, which helps us get what we want. Anger is probably the most common symptom of non-forgiveness. We realize using these negative feelings to get what we want from others is easier than using negotiation or compromise. This may be true for a period in our lives, but our anger eventually leads to poor health and unhealthy relationships. As we embark on our healing journey, we need to be willing to let go of anger.

Finally, we might have learned we get attention from our story. This attention gives us a superficial sense of value to sustain us for some time but, inevitably, suffering will arise because we are relying on external forces, such as someone else's attention or sympathy, to give us value. We have not yet offered ourselves the healing of self-love and self-compassion, which encourage us to distinguish between the story of what happened to us and who we truly are.

∽

The "how to's" of forgiveness are covered in great detail in the next chapter, but for now, know you can develop the discipline of forgiveness even before you master the process and use it in your daily life. In keeping the benefits of forgiveness in mind, we create space in our psyches to tolerate our pain. We can, and must, choose to allow it to surface to move forward.

∽

I am not here to tell you *should* forgive. I don't know that. What I know is that I do not want you to suffer. What I know is that the world is healed when you are healed—and I care deeply about both.

I want you to feel joy and compassion, and to be free from the bonds of the past. When you experience this, you will be the most empowered version of yourself imaginable—I am unequivocally sure of this. You will be more capable of standing up for yourself and seeking true justice. You will experience more love and peace, and a greater capacity to create the life you want.

PART TWO

Practicing Forgiveness

Chapter Three

The Forgiveness Academy Competencies and Process

To find the path...to peace, you will have to
meet your pain and speak its name.
— *Mpho Tutu*

The approach to forgiveness set forth here is designed to create clarity and build the capabilities we need to forgive. This framework is based, in part, on my experience learning to fully forgive all of the people in my life (and meeting challenges along the way). It is also founded in practiced psychological and spiritual techniques we can use to honor our progress, such as journaling, ritual, and celebration. The forgiveness process itself, presented in Competency 5, is based on proven methods to facilitate personal growth. Think of the competencies as training drills designed to create the perspective, agility, and strength you need to forgive.

In part, the framework is meant to increase our awareness of our strengths and weaknesses. Some may possess greater skill in some areas, which will serve you well. That said, we should acknowledge that, if we truly possessed these strengths, we would likely already have mastered forgiveness. Pay close attention to the areas you feel the surest about your skills. Often, these are where the work is needed and the reason we may have gotten stuck in the process up to now.

The competencies empower and remind us that forgiveness does not have to be something that "just happens;" rather, with time, attention, and energy, we can play an active and significant role in nurturing our ability to heal. A well-known Chinese proverb says luck is when opportunity meets preparation. The competencies prepare us for the opportunity of grace or revelation, which so often play a part in forgiveness. As you build the skills described by the framework, you create the strength of a warrior to experience absolute forgiveness.

Start by creating a forgiveness journal with space for the exercises and the steps in the forgiveness process. You can also download a template on the Forgiveness Academy™ website (http://emilyjhooks. com/forgiveness-academy-exercises-meditations/).

The Forgiveness Academy™ Competencies

C1. Understand your story.

C2. Create awareness of where you hold psychological pain in the body.

C3. Cultivate empathy.

C4. Learn to release judgment and resistance.

C5. Forgive using the eight-step Forgiveness Academy™ Process.

Competency 1: Understand Your Story

We all have a story. Some of us know it well; others will only now begin to explore what it means to have a narrative that informs our healing. Either way, it is requisite to be aware that, as we evolve, our story will change, too. We will begin to see it with more compassionate eyes.

This first competency prepares us to view the idea of story in a new way. It creates space for us to observe how our story changes. If you know your story intimately, this strength will create non-attachment to a narrative, which may very well define and limit how you show up in the world. As our hearts soften, we need to be willing to show up as the new, improved version of ourselves.

Most forgiveness processes are based on sharing our personal narrative with others. For example, the peace and reconciliation process born out of the end of apartheid is based on the idea that being heard is an inherently healing activity. Such organizations as The Forgiveness Project, the film *Risking Light*, and Project Forgive are platforms created by compassionate leaders designed to give voice to extraordinary examples of forgiveness.

Sharing our story not only heals us, it also creates the opportunity for others to heal. It creates a connection nothing other than the vulnerability required to share creates.

Our "story," as it relates to forgiveness, begins with the action or actions of another that caused harm; this could be you or someone else. It might be a dramatic event, like rape or someone taking the life of a loved one, or it may be something more generalized, such as growing up in a hostile or unfit environment. As you think about your story, I encourage you to reflect on specific events, because we forgive the actions of others, not their character. Character is treated with compassion, which will become a part of who you are through the forgiveness process. When we anchor forgiveness in actions, finding empathy (which we discuss in Competency 3 and Chapter 6) becomes easier. In fact, the whole process becomes easier.

For example, if you think you want to forgive your mother for "being a bad mother," allow specific incidences to come into your mind and write them down. This is the story. It does not have to be a cohesive narrative, but you want to articulate it in a way that highlights *what* you or other people have done.

You have the story. It is what you perceive to have caused you harm. It is the action prompting you to evaluate the person you are today as other than who you were meant to be. Because this perspective causes suffering, there is a need to forgive.

Often, when we reach the point in our lives where we become aware of our need to forgive, we have told the story many times, either to ourselves or to others. As we do this, we begin to flesh the story out to create an account that makes sense and validates our perceived impact. We vividly recollect details and remember exactly what was said. We know precisely how we felt, and why we felt this way.

When you think about your last trip to the grocery store, do you remember how you felt on aisle 8? Probably not. Why? Because that is not how the human brain works for most of us. We rarely even recall traumatic events frame by frame. But as we tell the story of what happened, it becomes more real to us.

This is a flawed sense of reality; things never happened the way we remember them. Have you ever talked about old times with family or friends, maybe at the dining-room table during a holiday, and said something like, "Oh my God, do you remember that time Thomas picked up that kitten and . . .?" Maybe your sister replied, "That wasn't Tommy, that was Alex!" You probably sat there amazed at how crazy it was she remembered it all wrong!

We tend to rely on our own memories when we are referring to important moments in our lives. The more "vivid" the memory, the more accurate it seems to be. But what are the chances everyone else's memory is so flawed, and yours is rock solid? Memory is an unreliable narrator of the truth. We furnish it with an illusory power.

It may be you are very familiar with your story. You know exactly what happened and the impact it has had on your life. Or do you? Not really, but this is a gift.

Before we forgive, we must distinguish "what happened" from the story we are telling about what happened and the impact we perceive in our lives. Distinguishing what happened from the story is important, because when we think our story is interchangeable with what happened, we feel powerless—and, indeed, *are* powerless—to effect change. After all, we cannot change the past. The story, however, is happening *now*, and the only moment we have power or choose to change is *now*.

I know this will be hard for some to hear. We may have been denied the right to our story for many years. Being denied our story can cause us to grasp it so tightly, it begins to define us. I was told I was wrong for many years, so I understand how painful not having a right to your story is.

I am not denying you the right to your story, nor am I asking you to deny one bit of it. Something happened. You *were* impacted. But we need to accept the narrative is only an imprint, an interpretation of those events. This is essential to forgiveness, because as we change the way we see the story will change, so hold the story gently. As you evolve, allow it to evolve with you. If you do not, you will be choosing your story over your healing.

You are more than your story. We have a tendency to define ourselves by the stories we tell. We begin to incorporate aspects of the story into our identities. This is the "illusion of victimhood." It could equally be the "illusion of being a perpetrator." We may have been victimized or victimized someone else in the past, and we should absolutely respect that this is what we experienced. However, you are not a victim, nor are you a perpetrator. You are a *whole person*. You are not defined by the hardest moments in life, unless you choose to be.

If we allow ourselves to open to not knowing with certainty what happened, we will begin to see the story differently. I am not suggesting we make things up. This is an organic process that takes place as our compassion and empathy grow. We see our story, our lives, with more love and understanding. Suddenly, what we once thought to be a tragedy is a blessing in disguise.

Your awareness of the mutable nature of storytelling offers you a power you may not have experienced when you were spinning your wheels in the mud of your seemingly precise memory. Separating your story from what happened brings you back to the present moment, which, as you know, is where all healing takes place.

Do you see the power of letting go of telling yourself you absolutely *know* what happened? Again, I am not suggesting you make up new stories about what happened. The point of power here is in the *not knowing*. We become free to consider that we have the power to choose our attachment to the story. When we recognize the difference between what happened and the story, we start to unravel the attachment. We become open to new possibilities and interpretations. As our hearts heal, this happens naturally.

In addition to differentiating what happened from the story, we next need to consider the perceived impact. The impact is what changed in you, and in your life, because of what happened. This is a compelling distinction to make, for two reasons. First, as we heal, we become more present to the impact by allowing ourselves to feel the pain. This is important because it provides the opportunity for us to take responsibility for how we respond to life. The impact is happening now, so we can choose to acknowledge and embrace it when we see the difference between what happened and how we might have been affected.

It is possible the impacts of past experiences may never fully go away. But what happens in forgiveness is a release of the hurt feelings around the impact. Instead of either suppressing or succumbing to those feelings, we learn to honor them. And we take responsibility for them.

Let me offer an example here. I recently found myself present to what I perceived as the impact of my father's choices when I was young. I was experiencing anger after many years of absolute peace with our relationship. This manifested during a hike in the woods. I was struggling at the time with the end of a long-term relationship. Suddenly, I thought to myself, "What an a**hole," when I thought about my father. I had traced the thread from my suffering today all the way back to 1979 and was angry with him.

But, because I was aware of the difference between the perceived impact (i.e., I used to blame him for all my problems) and what my father did in one isolated period of my past, I was able to empower myself to be accountable for how I felt. From there, I could effect change. In blaming him, I was powerless.

When we experience self-love, we are able to appreciate the impact someone or something had on us, and embrace it. But, as is human nature, we are not always present to an experience of love. When we judge our experiences in life as flawed—in my case, believing I would have deeper, longer-lasting intimate relationships if my father had not kidnapped me—we blame. When we choose blame, we give our power away to the ghost of "what happened."

To a certain extent, we can never truly understand the impact of what happened to us. We have ideas about the impact, but we cannot trace the thread with certainty. Still, it is helpful to take time to identify the impacts of our experiences, so when we experience suffering and find ourselves blaming, we can remind ourselves we are exactly who we were always meant to be and that we alone are in charge of our lives.

Another reason we want to consider the impact is when something like what I describe above happens, when we find ourselves upset at someone we thought we had forgiven, we tend to tell ourselves we have not made any progress. We go to, "I thought I did all that work already! Things are never going to change." Knowing the connection you make between what happened in the past and your life today, you can give yourself credit. Forgiveness does not take away all the impact. It releases us from believing we are powerless, and from the blame and anger we feel about the past.

The empowered response to suffering is to see the reason it upsets us, in the moment. It may be as simple as the fact that it makes us feel sad, and that is okay. It is human nature to experience sadness. We do not have to create a connection between our suffering and "what happened" in the past, which takes away our power. If we are aware of the relationship between what happened and the impact it had on us, we can choose self-compassion in the present moment rather than a sense of being victimized all over again. This way, we will be more prepared to go back and forgive when the impact presents itself.

Exercise:
Identify the Story, What Happened, and Its Impact

1. Take some time to write down, uncensored, your story about what happened. If you are not clear on what the story is, start by thinking about why you feel you need to forgive. This is the impact. As you contemplate the impact, what memories come to mind? Use this as a starting point and just begin writing. It may take a few days of journaling to get clear on what the story is, but you will get there.

2. Re-read the story, and as you go through it, circle what you consider to be the facts. "On April 10, my father called my mother" is a fact.

3. Underline any word implying judgment or evaluation. "He wanted me to get a better education" is an evaluation. It may be based on what he said, but it is not knowable. If it cannot be known or verified, it is not what happened. It is the story. Any words such as "right" or "wrong," "should" or "shouldn't" are judgments (if you are unclear on this part, read Chapter 6 and come back to the exercise). As you look more closely at what you wrote, can you see it is not what happened? If it were, there would be *no* judgment words in the story. Even in the absence of evaluation, what you wrote is not what happened. Remember, this is a good thing because we have power over the story, but not over what happened.

4. Write down your thoughts about the difference between what happened and the story. Is your attachment to your story loosening a bit? This is exactly what you want. Come back to this step when you feel resistance to seeing the story differently as you evolve.

5. After completing the story, go back and write down ways you can identify the events that impacted you. Try to identify ways in which you perceive your life to be different because of what happened. If you struggle with this now, simply save space in your journal and come back to it if something occurs to you later.

Competency 2:
Create Awareness of Where You Hold Psychological Pain in the Body

Most of us are taught to buck up and move on when something bad happens. We do this by denying our experience of hurt, and thus, our own pain. We disallow our experience because we perceive it may be disruptive to fully experience the pain. In fact, at some points in life, particularly during crisis, it is. So we package it up and send it off to never-feel-again-land.

This ability to repress suffering is a genius coping mechanism. Human beings have an extraordinary capacity to survive at all costs. Sometimes we need to be tough, especially as children or in abusive relationships, to survive. We should congratulate ourselves for our ability to do this—but unfortunately, it is only a temporary fix. Dr. Brené Brown's research indicates we cannot numb selectively. If we choose not to feel certain things, we affect our ability to feel at all. We disconnect from our own capacity for joy and peace.

We can view forgiveness as the final step in any healing process, and when it is time to heal fully, we need to create space to experience our psychological and spiritual pain—which we store in our bodies. Our pain disrupts our bodies' natural equilibrium, which can be quite difficult to bear. Some people cope by dissociating or numbing out from the neck down. However, for this very reason, the body is also our biggest asset. Our bodies are the portals through which we recognize how and where we have collected pain. Instead of distracting ourselves from the reality of our hurt, as we have learned to do, we re-focus our awareness and attention on our body and simply *feel*.

We do this by using somatic awareness exercises and meditation to quiet the mind and increase our understanding of where we experience tension in the body in response to pain. As our awareness grows, we allow the stored pain to dissipate. This activity is the soul of healing.

∽

Building the capacity to safely experience our pain cannot be taught—it must be learned experientially. Let us talk about a couple guidelines you will need as you start the practice of reconnecting with your psychological and spiritual pain.

Create a safe space. Make a time for this practice when you can be alone without interruption. This is important, because you will want to come out of the exercise purposefully so you feel integrated and grounded. The space should be quiet and facilitate an experience of safety and comfort.

Don't judge or evaluate your experience. One of the reasons we resist experiencing our pain is the fear we will not be okay or that we will fall apart. This does not happen when we experience the pain; it happens when we judge it. When we tell ourselves we should not feel a certain way or something is wrong, we shift the experience from our hearts to our heads. This not only stops the healing process, but it also causes us to react adversely to it. If you find yourself thinking about how you feel, gently re-focus on your heart and redirect your mind to observing how you are feeling. Remember that feelings are never wrong, so honor them. They are there to teach you something you need to know.

Let yourself experience the sensations of pain, as well as the sadness, anger, shame, or resentment that will bubble up to the surface behind the physical reactions. We all hold our pain in different parts of the body, but you will likely experience the feelings in your throat, chest, solar plexus, or stomach. It may radiate throughout your body. It may manifest as an agitation or anxious feeling, or it may simply feel like muscular tension. The physical reaction is a learned response to protect us from experiencing the suffering. This protection served its purpose, but it is now time to allow our suffering to manifest so we can release it. When you are ready to let go of the feelings, you can start forgiving the perpetrator or yourself, and replacing the pain with self-love.

One powerful aspect of these exercises is that our awareness builds. As you continue to practice, you will be able to associate physical discomfort with psychological or spiritual suffering. You will be able to release your hurt more readily because you can use your body as a guide to let you know when you are actually unsure or upset about something happening in your life. The entire exercise should last only five to seven minutes. The exercise is quite long, so if you would like me to guide you through the exercise, you can find an audio recording online at: http://emilyjhooks.com/forgiveness-academy-exercises-meditations/.

Exercise:
Emotional Awareness

1. **Get deeply present and quiet the mind.** Close your eyes and pay attention to the breath coming in and out of your body. Feel the coolness of the air as it travels through your nostrils, down your throat, and into your chest and stomach. Feel your belly and chest expand and then contract. Do this for three to five rounds of breath. Now, open your eyes softly and gaze at an object in the room in front of you. It does not matter what you look at; it can be familiar or completely new to you, but I want you to look at it as if you have never seen it before. Have the curiosity of a child as you study its shape, color, and the way the light hits it. Examine the lines and details, and the shadows it casts. Allow your exploration to create more wonder and marvel, even if the object is quite simple. As you do this, begin to notice a calmness in your mind and body. Take note of any sensations you are feeling in your body.

2. **Activate your heart.** Close your eyes again and evoke the image of someone or something (perhaps a pet) you love deeply. This is another who, when thought of, brings you joy and gratitude. Put your hand on your heart and begin to feel the resulting sensation in your chest as you permit yourself to experience deep love for this subject. Allow yourself to feel that love for thirty seconds to two minutes. Then, if you can, let the feeling intensify. Try to visualize the feeling growing, pulsing from your chest out to the edges of your body. If you feel like you might cry, allow it to happen naturally. Stay

present to this feeling of love and the sensations it creates in your body as you move on to the next step. How do your hands and feet feel? Your abdomen and back? Does your face feel more relaxed? Are you smiling? Take note of the sensations or vibrations in your body, by using observational words like "tight," "agitated," "bright," "lighter," and so on, rather than the words we commonly use to describe feelings such as "happy," "anxious," or "depressed." These words imply a knowing or generalization that is not helpful.

3. **Experience the pain.** Now, bring the person you are forgiving into your mind (this works just as well for self-forgiveness, so bring yourself to mind if that is what you are working through). Note how the sensations in your body shift abruptly. If it applies to your situation and you are willing, also bring the transgression into your imagination. Allow yourself to fully feel how this memory and the thoughts it brings up manifest in the body. Where are you experiencing it? Is it in your throat or your stomach? Your solar plexus? Is your breathing restricted? Do you feel physical discomfort in your back or neck? Remember, do not judge any of this. As you see the person or the events in your mind's eye, keep your awareness in the *body*. Observe how your body responds to how you feel.

Now, go back to the love you activated. This may be difficult at first, but use your imagination and allow the feeling of radiating love to happen while you also experience the pain. Do not try to change or manipulate what is happening in your body. Just stay present to it. This should cause an intense emotional reaction, as you allow yourself to feel love *and* your own suffering. You have been holding onto this, hiding it, but now you are honoring it and embracing it in order to release it. Let yourself cry or feel anger, or whatever emotions come up, fully. Remember, the key to allowing the pain to release is to not evaluate it. Do not judge how you feel or question whether or not it is okay. It is okay. No feeling is wrong.

Finally, to create the potential for a shift in how the pain manifests, picture breathing into the area of the body where you feel the pain; imagine it migrating from that area to your heart center. Do not try to change the feeling; just see if you can move the sensation in your body. Can you use your breath to create space? Does that space alleviate any of the physical responses? If not, it is okay. With time, the suffering will give way to comfort.

4. **Ground yourself.** After a few minutes, with your eyes still closed, move your attention to the edges of your body. Notice the ground under your feet and how your feet meet the ground. Feel the support of the chair or bed against your body. What does the pressure feel like? Is it soft? Hard? Notice if you feel cool or warm. Next, expand your awareness to the world around you. What sounds do you hear? What smells are in the air? Take two very deep breaths and let them out with an audible sigh. Let your shoulders drop and open your eyes. Now, take your hands and shake them vigorously. Stand up and wiggle like a wet noodle.

5. As soon as you are done with the last step, **get up and do something you enjoy**. Be silly. Engage in an activity that gives you a sense of levity or joy. You have done the work for now.

After the exercise, practice self-care. Do things that reflect the experience of self-compassion you just cultivated. Take a bath or go for a walk—whatever helps you feel loved and cared for. You will be emotionally raw, if you have done the exercise fully. Continue to refrain from evaluating how you feel. You should feel much lighter and freer from both psychological and physical pain.

Competency 3:
Cultivate Empathy

Empathy is a keen awareness of the feelings and emotions of others. It helps us understand what others are going through as if we ourselves were feeling and experiencing the same thing. It is not sympathy (often thought of as "feeling sorry for" another person), because it allows us to connect equally with another by "feeling with" them. When we do this, we are able to imagine that, had we lived someone else's life, we might have made the same choices they have made.

Empathy is connection at the most fundamental level. Rather than making assumptions about someone else or judging their behaviors and actions, we are able to simply be present and consider life from their perspective. There are few mandates for the forgiveness process, but empathy is absolutely necessary to fully relinquish our judgments. Although it may be difficult at first, we need to experience connection with and empathy for those who have caused us harm, because until we let go of thinking we *know* why they did what they did, and it somehow has to do with us, we will feel resentment. We talk more about this in Chapter 6. For now, know that we can begin to cultivate deep compassion with simple willingness.

I would like to acknowledge this is one of the hardest parts of the process. It is perfectly normal and acceptable to *not* want to release our negative feelings about the person who has hurt us. This is where intention and knowing we are doing this work for our *own* well-being, for our own evolution and ability to contribute to the world around us, comes into play. Remember, forgiveness is a choice. We might have to choose more than once along the way.

Chapter 6 includes a variety of exercises you can use to cultivate empathy. What this will look like depends on the nature of your relationship with the person and your starting place. Whatever the case, as you learn to empathize, you will actively turn toward stories that bring you peace.

Reflecting on my own life, I can either choose to "know" my father wanted to hurt me, which brings me more suffering—or I can ease myself into "not knowing," and with a compassionate heart, remember he acted out of his own injury. When we empathize, we consider what they might have experienced to make the choices they made. From this place of pondering, we can create new, more empowering narratives. When we let go of our conclusions about things that are not knowable, like the motivations or intentions of others, we can move into our hearts, where healing takes place.

Exercise:
Developing Empathy with the One You Need to Forgive

1. Write a story about the perpetrator's life. (If you are working on self-forgiveness, write your story.) The other person's story can be based on facts you know, or you can begin with what you do know or think you know and work backward, creating a *realistic* narrative for how they might have gotten to where they were when the harm was caused. It does not have to be long and detailed, but spend some time imagining their childhood, the day they were born, their family life, the challenges they may have faced, and the fear they may have known. What choices might they have had to make in life?

2. Write down a minimum of fifteen things you have in common with the person. This might not be easy, but it is very powerful. Take the time you need and reflect deeply. I promise, you have many more than fifteen things in common!

3. Write about how this exercise feels in your body and your heart. Do you experience compassion you had not felt before?

Competency 4:
Learn to Release Judgment and Resistance

We grow up learning to judge our environment and the people in it. From a survival point of view, this makes sense. We want to feel safe, so we put everything into boxes and work from there. The challenge with this way of approaching life is that most of our evaluations are not founded in reality. They are based on what we have learned from our primary caregivers and our own biases and assumptions about "the way things are." As we move into the healing journey, it is essential we acknowledge this and create space to see things in the realm of possibility rather than as black and white. We talk in detail about why this is so important in Chapter 5, but, as you begin the forgiveness process, focus on how you can loosen your hold on judgment.

One way we can do this is by approaching our memories and the people in our lives with open-hearted curiosity. Begin by assuming you are safe (if you are not, this is not the time for forgiveness, but rather, time to make very practical changes in your life to create the security you deserve). With this reminder that you are a capable, powerful individual, fully in charge of your life, make the decision to approach your experiences as an explorer. When you find yourself saying, "Oh, I know what's going on," stop and instead, say, "Maybe I don't know what is happening." Simply by considering we actually do not know—and, just as important, we do not need to know—we shift our perspective from one of defense to one of receptivity and openness to the wonders life has to offer.

As we have discussed, one of the required conditions for healing is staying in the present moment. We experience the now when we practice non-resistance. Non-resistance simply means allowing what *is* to be. All change begins from this place of allowing and acknowledging what is, and in the absence of judgment, we find a higher-level under-standing of what is actually happening. We tap into our intuition and strength in a way we cannot when judging and rejecting.

Not resisting what is does not mean we do not actively make choices or exert effort. The effort just comes from a different place. Like a well-trained fighter or athlete, the energy applied is focused solely on what needs to be done, and nothing else. We do not make declarations and run around telling the world what needs to happen. We do not judge or evaluate the situation. We vastly underestimate the amount of energy we expend analyzing things.

Developing a habit of non-judgment and non-resistance not only creates extraordinary power in the forgiveness process, as you will come to see, but is also a powerful way to live. Approaching life with what the Buddhists call a beginner's mind manifests a much different world, one more grounded in possibility and beauty, compared to a world where we know what to expect. Just remember, we always find what we are looking for. If you are looking for something to be wrong, that's exactly what you will find.

Exercise:
Release Judgments

This exercise is based on the work of Byron Katie; see the resources in the Appendix for more information on her work. The objective is to create less attachment to our judgments and to see that what we tell ourselves to be the truth is simply a choice we are making to cling to perceptions that confirm or reinforce the story we have about the other person. We use our verdicts to rationalize our suffering.

1. Think about the person you are forgiving and write down ev-erything you think about them, in free form. Do not censor yourself; just put all the opinions and judgments you have about

them on the page. Pay attention to how this feels in your body and write down your observations after you have purged all the judgments you have. Leave the exercise for at least at day before moving on to the next step.

2. Go back through your list of judgments and rewrite each as the opposite of what you originally wrote. For example, if you wrote, "Sara is so stupid," you could rewrite it as, "Sara is not stupid" or "Sara is smart." After each of these statements, write down three ways in which this alternate statement is true. So, if you started with "Sara is so stupid" and rewrote it as "Sara is smart," write down three pieces of evidence you have that this is true. For example, maybe the fact that she always gets what she wants proves she is smart. Or, maybe she got out of a difficult situation adeptly. Note how it feels to consider other possibilities for what you knew to be true. Do you feel lighter, freer from a fixed narrative you had about them? Add this to your journal.

Competency 5:
Forgive Using the Eight-Step Forgiveness Academy™ Process

Now that you have started to build the muscles you will need to successfully meet the challenges you will face during the forgiveness process, you are in perfect shape to dive in. If you find yourself stuck at a given step, come back to the competencies and consider where the resistance is coming from. If you need more work with empathy or non-judgment, go to those chapters and do the exercises included at the end.

It is best to work the forgiveness process with one person at a time. If you are focused on a specific incidence involving multiple people with perceived equal impact, it is okay to work on them together, but list each person and be specific about what you are forgiving. If you do not know their names, make up identifiers such as "lady in black shirt" or "blonde guy." Be as personal as you can to ground yourself in empathy. We discuss forgiving the self and something bigger, such as God or the universe, in the next chapter.

As you go through the process, it is almost inevitable other opportunities for forgiveness will make themselves known to you, especially ones involving self-forgiveness. Perhaps you remember Uncle Bob made fun of you when you were trying to make something right, or you realize you were a jerk because you thought you knew something, then you came to realize you might not really be sure of your knowledge. Reserve a space in your forgiveness journal for a list of people or offenses you think of along the way. If you are able to proceed with the process for the person you are forgiving without addressing the things that come up, do that. If you find yourself newly focused on someone else, or yourself, pause in the process and start on the person in your awareness. Your intuition and inner guidance will be your greatest assets on this journey.

It is common, when forgiving others, to discover the need to pause and forgive the self along the way. As our awareness of our own accountability (fortified by the competencies) grows, we come to realize we are responsible for much of the suffering we have endured. If this happens, honor yourself by taking the time to forgive yourself. Come back to the original process after you find some resolution and peace.

Finally, note this process is not something you sit down and do in a day or a week. Each step after Step 2 of this process, which you will repeat before doing each subsequent step, may take a day, week, month, or even a year. You will know when it is time to move on. If you are unclear, ask yourself, "Am I experiencing judgment or resistance?" If the answer is yes, go back to the competencies and see what you are doing wrong. If the answer is no, you are working the process. Allow however long it takes.

Step 1:

Get clear.

We start the journey of healing through forgiveness by getting clear about our motivations and intentions. Why are you choosing, at this point in your life, to do this work? Rarely do we want to forgive someone for altruistic reasons. We most often want to be free from suffering or pain that manifests in disruptive ways, or we want something more tangible, like the ability to have more fruitful interactions with the person we are blaming (including ourselves). Maybe we simply feel stuck in a particular area of life and intuitively know forgiveness will give us needed traction.

Whatever the case, get clear about why you are choosing to engage in the process *right now*. You might have one big, obvious motivation, or a handful of improvements or changes you want to see in your life.

You also need to get clear on what *success* looks like. Know you can make a lot of progress in one week, including experiencing less physical pain or discomfort in your body, or feeling calmer and more focused. Allow these successful outcomes to remind you why you are doing the work.

This is an important place to begin your journey, because forgiveness is hard work. You will reach a point when you wonder why you are tolerating the pain that is a natural part of healing. You will want to be reminded of your commitment, and why it is important to you.

1. Write down why you are engaging in this process now. What are your truest, deepest motivations? Do not try to be spiritual or noble as you think about this. If your intentions are truly spiritual, fine—write about it, but also share how the process will make life better for you in practical ways.

2. Write down what success will look like in the short term and in one year. Write down a few qualitatively measurable outcomes for each time period. Use this as an opportunity to think about what you want. What are your expectations for the process? What do you need? Consider them to be milestones to help highlight success and to see where more work or focus is needed (rather than as specific goals implying success or failure). For example, "By next Sunday, I will be less anxious and reactive with my kids." You can measure this by simply taking note of how you feel. "In one year, I won't feel afraid when I walk the dogs."

3. What will it look like when you are finished? Think about the highest intention for self discussed in Chapter 2. Do not try to define a date for this intention; just create space for the possibility and take the steps you need to get there. Write your vision here and put a star next to it. This is what you will come back to when you need more motivation.

4. (Optional) Make an agreement with yourself or someone you trust, to help you stay accountable. Sign a written agreement declaring your commitment to forgive the person no matter what resistance you encounter.

Step 2:
Acknowledge your suffering.

Now that you are clear that on why you are choosing to forgive and what success will look like, reflect on what your experience of suf¬fering has been that has led you to read this book. What are you trying to "fix?" Write about this in your journal. This is distinct from your motivations; focus on what the experience of suffering has felt like. For example, if your motivation is to be less agitated with your partner, has the way you have been interacting with your partner caused you to feel deep sadness or anger?

Next, do the Emotional Awareness exercise in Competency 2 to allow yourself to get *present* to the pain. Using the compassion you feel for another while experiencing your own discomfort, allow yourself to feel deep compassion for your own suffering. Move through the exercise fully before moving on to Step 3. All of the power in the process is grounded in this step because, as we know, all healing takes place in the heart. We begin each new session of work on the steps below by getting present to how we feel. As you move through the steps, your awareness will begin to shift from discomfort to compassion and love.

Step 3:
Write down what you need to forgive the other person for.

Begin with Step 2 to ground yourself in an *experience* of healing. Write down exactly what you need to forgive. Again, focus on actions and choices, not the character of the person. We cannot forgive someone for "being" a certain way. We forgive actions. If you think someone is selfish, you can forgive them for forgetting your eighth birthday when you were a child. Clump actions into groups, if it helps cover everything; if the person is selfish, forgive them for not asking how your day was when they got home every day. You do not have to be specific about everything, but the more specific, the simpler it will be to work the process.

Do not try to be kind as you write. It may present itself as a list, or it may be a story. You will be centered in experiencing your suffering, so if you feel angry or sad, say what you feel. Write until you feel you have identified all the things you need to forgive. (Note: This is a good time to leave extra space in your journal. As things pop into your mind, go back and add them). Take a few days (or as long as you feel you need), to process what you have written, and add to the list as needed. Remember, your job is to honor yourself, so take extra time if you need it. This step may take five minutes, or it may take two weeks. You want to feel like you are clear you have written down what you needed to say.

Step 4:
Share the story with a neutral,
non-judging, respectful witness.

Working from Step 2 above, being centered in how you feel, in your own suffering and self-compassion, the next step in the process is to share your story. We have already created an understanding of the difference between what happened and the story we have about what happened. We are clear on how the impact plays into our perception of forgiveness. Now, it is time to share the story.

Find a trusted confidante, counselor, or coach with whom to share your story. Having a respectful, neutral, and non-judging witness to our story about what happened as it relates to our opportunity for forgiveness opens up space for the healing process, because what the story looks like when it lives solely in us begins to evolve as we share it with others. It begins to lose its grip on us. One of the reasons is that we start to use our other senses to experience the story. We hear our words. Suddenly, the story becomes something more tangible and knowable, less scary, when we bring it out of the shadows.

A *neutral* witness (one who is not connected to the story) is important, because you do not want someone to question the story or your interpretation of the story. This person's job is to listen with a kind heart and help you hold the story up to the light. We also do not want someone who will listen while trying to placate or console us. Empathy is powerful, but sympathy or solace can interfere with our interpretation of the story, or even collude with our current perspective rather than encourage the expansion healing offers.

If you have a trusted friend you plan to share with, take time to share what you need from them. Their job is to listen with an open heart and no judgment. They are serving as a witness to the story. Take as long as you need to feel grounded and centered in love and compassion after sharing the story before moving on.

Write about your experience of sharing the story in your journal. Did you experience any shifts? Do you feel better? Worse? If you are sharing the story for the first time, you may feel sadness you had not been present to before. Allow yourself as much time as you need before moving on to the next step.

Step 5:
Write and say, "I forgive you,
[name of person], for [offense]."

Again, begin with Step 2. Write as many of these statements as you need, using what you wrote in Step 3 as a starting point. If you are willing, add "I love you" to the end of each. Rewrite and re-speak these statements for as long as it takes to experience a shift. A shift may show up as feeling less hurt by the person or simply feeling less burdened by suffering. Start writing the statements and speaking them aloud, even if you do not believe a word of it. I recommend doing this for twenty to forty days; it may be much quicker. If, after forty days, you feel the same, take a break. You are probably experiencing significant resistance you had not previously identified while you were building the competencies. Take a break and practice self-compassion. Then go back and identify if you are stuck in judgment. Are you allowing yourself to experience empathy for the person you are forgiving? Are you refusing to be accountable for your experiences? Come back to the process once you are clear on where the resistance was coming from.

This step seems straightforward enough, but it can actually be the source of opposition. We are putting our competences to the test now. Are we really willing to apply what we have learned? You'll know quickly if you need to go back and get clear again on why the work matters. Realize you are just writing on a piece of paper. When you start the process, you do not have to mean it for it to work. Put pen to paper and speak the words, every day. The magic is in the repetition.

Step 6:
Wish the other person well.

It's time to put the virtues you have learned into action. Every day, for the next thirty days, write down your highest intentions for the person you are forgiving. As you consider what these positive visions for their life might be, do your best to take yourself out of the picture. This is not a list of what you know is best for them. Hopefully, by now, you know you cannot know what is best for another person. This is what you believe they would want, what you believe would bring them joy and peace. It can be fairly general, such as, "I wish my mother perfect health and all of the material things her heart desires." Or it can be very specific. For example, I had a client who prayed for her mother to have cows. She knew having cows would bring her mother joy, so that is one of the things she listed.

If you are a person of faith, these wishes can be prayers. Center yourself in contemplation before you pray, and every day, repeat the vision you have for their comfort and peace.

As you go through this step in the process, in addition to rewriting and speaking or praying your wishes for the person's well-being, write how you are feeling about them in your journal. Take special note of any increases in empathy or connection. Note any softening of your emotions.

If the person has passed on and you believe in the eternal aspect of the soul, wish their soul its highest best. Be as specific or general as you want to be. If you do not believe there is anything beyond this life, this step will not be necessary, because you already essentially posit the perfect outcome for them.

If the person is in your daily life, it is important to practice non-attachment during this time. Holding a vision for someone does not mean we have expectations for the outcome. It simply means we can envision their peace. If you do this in the presence of non-resistance, you may very well see shifts happen for that person. If they do not, do not be concerned. Remember, their journey is theirs. Yours is yours.

This step can take a long time. Do it every day for a month, and if you feel you are not ready to go on to Step 7, take a week off to integrate and relax. Then, pick up where you left off. Make it a habit to visualize what happiness would look like in their life. As you cultivate this way of being, you will deepen your sense of love and compassion for yourself and others.

Step 7:
Forgive the person and release the offense.

Congratulations! You have done an amazing job of pushing through the resistance we all encounter on this journey. You have already experienced some major perceptual changes in how you show up in the world and in the narrative you have about your life. This is the natural consequence of compassion and empathy. You are almost there. It is time to up the ante and fully experience your gratitude.

Write and speak out loud each day, "I love you, [name of person]. I appreciate you. Thank you for being my teacher." If you are not in relationship with them, add, "You can go now." While speaking these mantras each day, visualize the person in front of you. Share an expression of love with them. When you speak the last part, you can visualize them leaving the space in front of you, representing their willingness to release the bond held by non-forgiveness. Do this for as long as it takes; I recommend twenty to forty days, and if you need to take a break, take it. This step can take a long time to fully realize the final shift.

If you have significant resistance to any specific part of this step, such as "Thank you for being my teacher," begin by writing the parts that work for you. As you move through the process over time, add the rest when you can imagine the possibility of it being true. Remember, absolute forgiveness is realizing everything has been for your own good. We can thank those who caused us harm when we come to know this truth.

Step 8:
Ritualize and celebrate your success.

Make memories by conducting rituals and celebrating your success. This may sound silly or trivial, but it is actually quite important. Memories ground us in remembering our growth.

Rituals are symbolic behaviors we perform at various times in our lives—usually, before, during, or after meaningful events. They can occur in a number of ways. They can take place in communal settings or in solitude; they can involve repeated series of actions, or be enacted in totally spontaneous ways.

Rituals are as old as the earliest cultures of humanity. There are many reasons to ritualize our experiences. Rituals help us release emotions; this is one of the reasons funerals are so powerful. We take the time to honor the passing of a loved one, and we create the opportunity to let go of the sadness we feel for the loss.

Rituals also create closure. After we do the work of healing that happens on the in-breath, during the pause, we take time to honor our hard work. A ritual can help us commemorate the moment and close the door on that stage of our evolution. It is an important rite of passage.

Finally, ritual is a significant act of memory-making. This is important, because, if we have an experience causing us to question our progress, we can recall the ritual and remind ourselves of our success.

One example of a powerful ritual is a burning bowl ceremony. You can do this outside at a camp fire or in another safe place. Begin with prayer or getting centered. Create a small fire. You can either burn your journal, or, if you want to continue working on other opportunities for forgiveness, write down what you have forgiven on small pieces of paper. Then, toss them into the fire as a symbol of the transformation you have undergone.

Similar to creating ritual, celebration creates memories to help us anchor into the new, more awakened version of ourselves we have worked so hard to cultivate. This is vital because, as human beings, we make choices based in part on the rewards we get for our work. Unlike ritual, which can include sadness for the loss of what was, healthy revelry feels *good*.

This is a time to cultivate joy by giving ourselves credit for the work we have done. It is also an opportunity to share our success with those we love. Finally, celebration motivates us to keep going on the journey of respecting the full cycle of life.

Throw a forgiveness party or take someone out to a nice dinner. Attend a performance or plan a trip to somewhere you have always wanted to go. Have a forgiveness holiday! The possibilities for creating happy memories are endless. The important thing is that it matters to you and you will always treasure it.

Now that the process is complete, let us close by considering how to manage when hurtful feeling re-emerge. They might not. I almost never feel hurt by those I have forgiven, but it is possible, especially at first. This is when it is important to come back to compassion.

Forgiveness is a process. We can reach a point of absolute forgiveness in which we realize there is, in fact, nothing to forgive because we are exactly who we are supposed to be. This gift is offered by deep compassion and self-love. That said, we can and will experience massive shifts prior to reaching this point. And, even after an experience of absolute forgiveness, during inevitable challenging times, we may only have the knowledge of this truth to hold onto, rather than the experience of it. The key to creating space to regain our ground is to not judge where we are. Honor it. Do not evaluate it. Judgment will likely create attachment, making it harder to move back into the space of having forgiven.

If you find yourself feeling hurtful or disruptive feelings about someone you have forgiven, first get in touch with the empathy, love, and compassion you already cultivated. Use the Heart Activation exercise below to help, then go back to Step 7 and release them again with love.

Exercise:
Heart Activation

1. Sit in a comfortable position in a quiet space where you will not be disturbed for at least ten minutes. Close your eyes and take four deep, cleansing breaths.

2. Allow your shoulders to drop and your body to relax. Now, bring into your mind the image of a person or animal you love. Put your hand on your heart and begin to feel the resulting sensation in your chest as you permit yourself to experience deep love for the subject.

3. Now, bring an image of yourself as a child into your mind. Allow yourself to feel for yourself the same love you have for the other. Do this exercise every day for five minutes to cultivate self-compassion and make having an experience of love "normal."

⌒

The Forgiveness Academy™ Competencies and Process are for *you*, and you alone. Your commitment does not mean you need to reconcile with people who have hurt you, or that you must forget the experiences that impacted you. Rather, forgiveness restores you to your essential state of wholeness and peace. Your peace comes from transforming your story of personal grievance and ending the cycle of blame and shame.

Presence is so important in this process. We often believe our distress comes from something that happened to us in the past—some experience that shaped our fundamental sense of self in the world—but this is not true. The forgiveness process helps us connect to our distress in the moment, and to alleviate our pain by increasing our awareness of what is happening for us right now, as well as how we are choosing to react.

Forgiveness frees us to make powerful choices about how we are going to live our lives. We give up expecting people or situations to be other than what they are. We reclaim our own capacity for creating the love, joy, success, and well-being we want. In giving up our wounded feelings, we discover forgiveness is an exercise in self-empowerment that opens us to our most fundamental nature.

Chapter Four

Self-Forgiveness and Forgiving God or the Universe

See the world as your self.
Have faith in the way things are.
Love the world as your self;
then you can care for all things.
— Tao Te Ching

Jane slowly rolled out of her bunk as sirens pierced the air. Four a.m.
was a tough time for an emergency, and she hoped it wasn't a structure
fire. As she suited up, an image of the boy—barely five years old, calling
out to her—flashed through her mind.

Suddenly, the weight of her gear felt heavier, unmanageable, as she
fell to her knees. Rage filled her body. She resented the boy for dying.
"Why are you haunting me?" she pleaded.

She knew what this meant. She needed a drink, or better yet, a
ten-mile run and then *a drink. Those things would quell the fury in*
her soul—she knew this because she'd been relying on them for over a
decade to fight the impulse to mourn something she could not control,
something now so ancient.

There was nothing she could do now. There was nothing she could
have done then. The boy had been trapped.

The memory became much larger in her mind's eye. Jane had run
across the wooden floor as it collapsed beneath her feet. She was a

rookie, but she knew she would not leave without the boy. As the roof buckled before her eyes, she begged God to help her. She begged God to save the boy. Suddenly he was gone, shrouded in smoke and flames, as if Jane were watching the making of a great, melancholy piece of art. His cries hushed as one of the other firefighters, Phillip, grabbed Jane by the waist. "We have to get out of here. Now! It's going down."

Jane had forgiven Phillip a long time ago. But the boy still came to her. The memory was seared into her forever. How could she possibly forgive herself? Did her resentment for the boy mean she needed to forgive him too? Or God, who had so callously ignored her pleas and let the boy die right before her eyes? She knew neither she nor God deserved mercy.

As she knelt there on the firehouse floor, worn from the weight of her gear and the burden of so many years of struggle, something in her shifted. She saw the boy's torment, but also her own. Her rage and sadness, numbed by adrenaline and alcohol, gave way to something new. Sorrow and compassion flooded her body, and she began to weep. She knew it was time to heal, to let love in.

Self-forgiveness is the hardest work most of us will ever do; it has been for me. The reason for this resides in what we are taught, and the nature of the healing process itself. We are taught to judge ourselves harshly if we want the world to accept our failings.

Society bestows a twisted sort of honor on those of us willing to bear the burden of the offender's cross. We are taught to punish ourselves so we don't forget what we have done. We are indoctrinated to identify with our transgressions so we will never make the same mistakes again. We are taught that being injured or acting as if we are unable to heal means we are truly remorseful for our actions. We are taught that wallowing in our guilt and giving up on ourselves is the only way to prove we are worthy of participating in society.

All this is a false understanding of the truth. We will not get to the truth by playing victim to our own choices in life.

Self-forgiveness is unnecessarily hard, too, because we are told it is best to hide the shameful things we do. What's in the past is in the past, right? What *happened* is most certainly in the past, but *the story* and *the impact* live on inside us, hindering our capacity to contribute fully to the world around us.

Acknowledging the story and its impact presupposes we acknowledge our own value and right to feel. To do this is an act of self-love. We are most often not taught to love ourselves, which, as we know, is integral to forgiveness. Self-love is love of the *whole* self. Unfortunately, instead of learning to honor our whole selves, we are told our value is based on the things we do. If we act right, if we succeed, if we win, we have value. If we fail, we have less value, but we should accept this and still do our best to be "good."

This makes sense from the perspective of our ancestors, who were figuring out the best way to function together as a tribe, but our evolution has moved beyond this limited, controlling way of thinking. Our inability to heal our wounds is now limiting our ability to self-actualize and contribute fully on a global level. In our world, so many of us have failed to acknowledge our individual and collective wounds. When we experience and witness so many bonds broken between people, it becomes easy to objectify, judge, and hurt the ones we believe have hurt us. As we sow the seeds of anger, resentment, and blame, this inevitably extends to our communities. We become people who are shadowboxing with our wounds rather than facing the light of reality.

∽

Perhaps the most substantial reason self-forgiveness is difficult is inherent in the process itself. As we have discussed, in order to process our experiences, we must stay present to our suffering. This discomfort is even more acute when we look at the impact we have had on others. But here is the hard truth, which can also be the very thing motivating us: As long as we hold non-forgiveness for ourselves, we are indirectly telling the people whom we believe we harmed that they are *not okay*, they are broken, they are not who they were born to be.

We are saying to them, "I'm so sorry you're this way. If I hadn't done this to you or allowed that to happen, you would be better."

Is that what you want to tell your spouse, your children, or your best friend? I do not think so. This is not about discounting what we have done or minimizing its impact. When we stay present to our suffering, we exercise self-compassion and empathy for those we have hurt. At the same time, we acknowledge all of our experiences have brought us to this particular point in our lives, and that we are being given the vital opportunity to reclaim our wholeness. When we re-enter our true nature, which is love, we make the choice to identify with our wholeness rather than merely the parts of ourselves that have suffered. But, we are also holding space for those we may have harmed to experience their wholeness.

When we do not forgive ourselves, it becomes part of our identity. Think of times when you have come across people who are so profuse with apologies and regret they almost seem to enjoy their own suffering. Remorse is imperative, but wallowing in it is draining—to both yourself and those around you.

Often, in insisting you are a "terrible, horrible, no-good person," you are acting out a dynamic reinforcing this very perception. Rather than staying present to the harm you may have caused, you are cementing your negative feelings about yourself—and perhaps you are finding a momentary respite from the feelings by gaining attention or consolation from the external world. It might feel validating, but it is inauthentic. What you are really doing is fortifying and sustaining the illusion you are a victim. If you are a bad person, after all, you are probably going to feel powerless to change your situation, thereby undermining your accountability.

We may have been either victimized or caused harm at some point, and we might have felt powerless in the moment. But all the choices we made subsequently are *our* choices. Instead of being martyrs to our unskillful actions, we must gently take responsibility for what we have done.

In the process of self-forgiveness, it becomes very clear we are the primary actors in our lives. We are 100-percent accountable for our experiences. This is the major form of resistance many of us face; if we are truly powerful and capable of determining our reality—which we are—we must take full charge of the impact we have had on the world around us, as well as the world within us.

When we do not forgive ourselves, we cause harm in the world. Because many of us are conditioned to desire a stable sense of self, even if that sense of self is disempowering, we do whatever we can to maintain it—even if it means perpetuating the "I'm a bad person who causes harm" story. If we are attached to the idea we are bad people, we inevitably cause more harm in the world, because this aligns with how we value ourselves.

Self-forgiveness not only honors us; it also honors those around us. As we heal, the world heals.

∽

Self-forgiveness is a process with unique facets. It is not exactly the same as forgiving another person, although the steps outlined in Chapter 3 are easily adapted.

First, let's state the obvious but perhaps not fully realized understanding that we would not feel the need for self-forgiveness if we did not feel remorseful. Remorse is the suffering we must have to begin the self-forgiveness process. During Step 2, it is important to acknowledge your regret.

This guilt may be for specific, easily identifiable actions we have taken or it may be, at this point in our lives, a generalized sense that we are not good people. In order to practice self-forgiveness, we need to break through this generalized feeling and get to the heart of it. As we know, character judgments are treated with compassion; actions are treated with forgiveness.

In addition to considering our remorse in Step 2, we need to look at how empathy works in self-forgiveness. We stated that in order to have empathy, we need to accept we cannot know someone else's true intentions. This is also true for ourselves. We are more complex than we often give ourselves credit for. When I began writing my story for another book, I came to see it was not as easy as, "I did this because...." With thoughtful inquiry, I quickly realized I had made some of my most impactful choices for many, many reasons. Use this inquiry to help you develop more compassion for yourself.

To have self-forgiveness, we must become aware of our true value. We must believe we are truly worthy of forgiveness. Unfortunately, through blame and shame, we often shield ourselves from our most fundamental nature: love.

Blame is the act of assigning responsibility for a wrongdoing. It is a judgment, and while it is important from a social perspective, judgment plays no useful role in healing. We must allow ourselves to let go of blame in order to forgive.

Remorse is deep guilt or regret for something we have done. It is a natural and healthy response to being out of integrity, and as we stated, the starting point for self-forgiveness.

Shame is a painful feeling of humiliation or distress caused by the awareness of causing harm to ourselves or another. Shame is an embedded version of remorse.

When we incorporate our negative experiences into our character, this is a problem. Dr. Brené Brown differentiates shame from guilt or remorse, as a transference from feeling we have *done* something bad to feeling *we are* bad. Shame is tremendously limiting and toxic to hold on to. In forgiveness, we are choosing to move through shame in favor of love, compassion, and empathy.

As long as we hold on to shame, we cannot access our true value as whole beings. In other words, we cannot forgive. In working with shame, the correct initial response is self-compassion and awareness. Mindfully explore the *feelings* behind the generalized sense of shame. Did you *do* something you perceive to have caused harm? As with all forgiveness, self-forgiveness is best practiced for specific rather than general experiences. It is always easier to work with the concrete and definable. In Step 4 of the forgiveness process, you share your shameful story with someone you trust, someone who will remind you that you are not what you have done in the absence of judgment.

With remorse, blame, and shame, it is crucial to return to the competencies described in the forgiveness framework, as they will build our capacity to claim our true value. We can allow our experiences of blame and shame to undercut our process of self-forgiveness, or we can allow them to guide the way.

Offering a gesture of restitution is one other distinctive aspect of self-forgiveness. To fully experience the compassion and healing forgiveness offers, we sometimes need to take corrective action, or make amends. It may be as straightforward as an apology. It might be about changing our behavior in the future, or it could be we need to clean up a mess we have made. To be clear, this is not about giving our power away to the person we hurt. It is about coming into integrity with ourselves by acknowledging our impact and doing what is needed to correct our mistakes.

∽

We all have self-forgiveness work to do. We bump up against each other in life. It is simply a part of life in community. But, let us briefly discuss how you can discover for yourself whether you have self-forgiveness work to do. The easiest way to determine this is to call to mind something you might regret. In truth, many of you will not be able to summon these things on demand; after all, we are taught to suppress disruptive feelings. If this is the case, as your awareness expands using the competencies and meditative practices, take note when something comes up. Work from where you are.

Now, ask a trusted friend, coach, or therapist to listen to the story you have about what happened. As you reflect on or share the story, does it feel real and present? If, as you tell the story, you feel tightness in your stomach, chest, or throat, or you become emotionally overwhelmed, you have work to do.

Even after many years of work, I still have occasional moments of presence to the pain of my choices as a mother. This is always brought on by an initial judgment I have about my son. When I see the highest truth for him—his journey is exactly what it is meant to be—I do not suffer. When I lose this clarity, however, I go back and do the steps in the forgiveness process, because I know my healing is everyone's healing. As intense as it may be, the pain passes with non-judgment.

I allow it to come, and I allow it to go. Within a few minutes, it always does. Then I go back to the steps and remind myself of the highest truth and why it matters. I cultivate self-compassion and self-love.

∞

Without exception, we need to take time in the forgiveness process to forgive ourselves, even if we originally started the work with another person in mind.

Most forgiveness work eventually ends up being self-forgiveness work. There are a couple reasons for this. As we heal, we become more accountable for our experiences. We come to realize we have played the lead role in our narrative. We begin to see the suffering we have endured as our self-compassion and self-love propagate. As we forgive others for harm they seem to have caused in our lives, our compassion and empathy grow, and we come to see the mistakes we ourselves have made along the way as we defended ourselves against the pain we felt.

There was no way out of the suffering but through the pain. I know because I tried everything else. I learned the hard way. I tried numbing, repressing, avoiding, acting out, being hyper-spiritual. I tried it all, and each time, I came back to the same existential suffering. Eventually, I learned to allow the pain when it came. During those times, I treated myself with kind-heartedness and non-judgment, like my own child. Each time, the pain came and went so I could stand back up and do what I needed to do. I did not fall apart, because I did not judge it. I did not tell myself, "This is not okay. You're going to lose your s**t if you don't stop crying." I let it move through me, and as time passed, the pain began to dissolve; my compassion grew. Miraculously, the way I perceived my impact on my son also changed. I began to see more clearly he is also the primary actor in his narrative. I cannot know what lessons are his to learn. When I forgave myself, it was healing in the truest sense of the word for us all.

The process of forgiveness paves the way for a reclamation of our wholeness, including the more disruptive choices we have made, rather than giving us another reason to beat ourselves up with blame or shame. Now, we are ready and empowered to honor our experiences and make choices that better serve us.

 ⌒

In life, experiences can occur that cause us to have deep pain not directly tied to the actions of another. We may suffer from the circumstances we were born into (outside of the actions of our parents), or the death of a loved one. We may suffer for an illness or an unjust outcome. Often, what happens in these instances is we develop a resentment or contempt for God or the universe. It is a generalized anguish we have toward life.

The need to forgive God or the universe is debatable from a philosophical point of view. It may be that, rather than forgive we need to change our beliefs about these things and recognize or accept there is no force "out there" working against us. Do painful, inexplicable things happen? Yes, they do. Will we always be granted understanding about these things? No. Sometimes acceptance of what is, is all that is needed.

Einstein said, "The most important decision we make is whether we believe we live in a friendly or hostile universe." I believe what he meant by this is, when *you* decide, it becomes so. If you believe you live in a friendly universe, you do. Likewise, if you believe you live in a hostile universe, your experience will confirm this belief. You will defend yourself. You will approach your experiences looking for what the world or people are trying to take from you and what you can get. You will walk around feeling the world owes you something you were never given, and that you have been severely wronged. Given the nature of the human condition, what you see is what you will get. The pain we feel when we are angry at the larger forces of the universe is caused by our lack of acceptance of the way things are—or put another way, a lack of self-love. We fail to have compassion for ourselves in these situations, and choose instead to suffer. We choose to be hurt when life, other people, or God fail to live up to our expectations. An honest exploration will always lead us to the same conclusion: We suffer because we *choose* to. We may have preferred the indignation of non-acceptance up to this point, but now we see the full impact and weight of this choice. This creates an opportunity for self-forgiveness, and forgiveness of those larger things we blamed.

There are some challenges in doing this because we rely heavily on empathy to heal. Empathy is allowing ourselves to feel what another person feels. This access to suffering leads to compassion. However, we cannot easily imagine how God or a universal force feels. What can we use to build that connection? How can we release our unwillingness to accept everything that happens in the world is for our good?

The answer to this question may not be what you want to hear: faith. Stay with me here. This faith can be born in religion or it can be derived from something else. It does not matter what faith is bound to: what matters is that we can allow ourselves to have confidence that things happen for a reason. The exquisitely ironic thing about using faith to heal our sense that the world or something bigger has been unfair is the realization that we *had* faith to begin with. Think about it: You cannot simultaneously believe a force outside of you needs to be forgiven or has caused you harm, and *not* believe that this force exists. Take a breath and let that sink in. You gave your power away to something you deemed unjust, so, by definition, you believe on some level that something exists. Now, use your belief to your advantage. With this clarity, you are free to define and relate to this force in a way that facilitates healing. You can choose to embrace a higher truth: The universe wants you to contribute fully as the unique expression of humanity you are—you can absolutely choose to see it as a friendly place.

Because we are all expressions of the divine, as we forgive ourselves, the need to forgive God goes away. Instead of seeking answers to futile questions about why things turned out as they did, we learn to live in the middle of the mystery. We come to accept the complexities of the world we live in, of God, of existence, and we relinquish our need to find satisfactory explanations for the human condition.

There is a remarkable peace that comes about when we are able to let go of the why. We discover we do not need to *know*, because we already *understand*. When we prioritize our healing, we gain a higher understanding of what is happening. We become capable of looking at our life and all our experiences from the 360-degree perspective of our wholeness.

PART 3:

A Deep Dive Into Concepts For Mastering Forgiveness

Chapter Five

Staying Open to Life with Non-Judgment

*A judgment is harmless if you immediately recognize it
as such and don't completely believe in it anymore.*
— *Eckhart Tolle*

We do not need to find meaning in our experiences, only the possibility of meaning, to find peace. When we have a sense that the things that have happened in the past have meaning, the things happening right now are easier to accept.

Up to this point, we have explored the fundamental aspects of forgiveness as a healing practice. We discussed a framework we can use to cultivate the competencies we need to master the art of forgiveness, and looked at how to forgive ourselves and others. Part 3 goes deeper into the ideas of non-judgment and empathy as essential aspects of becoming a forgiving person, and as tools for living a peaceful and empowered life. Each chapter also includes exercises to enable you to continually put the principles into practice so you can develop and deepen the key competencies for forgiveness.

Chapter 7 is dedicated to self-empowerment. As we know, this practice is not just about healing our wounds; it is ultimately about becoming the most empowered and liberated version of who we were meant to be. As we move through forgiveness toward self-actualization, we become free to create the life we truly deserve.

Have you ever heard the expression, "The world is a mirror?" Well, this is absolutely true when it comes to our judgments about others, and the world. We judge to separate ourselves from others. But separation is an illusion. The judgments we have about the external world are always opportunities to see something in ourselves we have denied or pushed into the darkness.

We so often hear stories about people with dogmatic ideologies, only to later hear they themselves are guilty of the very thing they excoriate. (For example, a priest denounces sin and evil only for the world to discover he has been engaging in scandals of his own). Our judgments are born from our own fears and disappointments. We put other people down for harboring qualities we cannot face within ourselves. In the words of Marcus Aurelius, "Whenever you are about to find fault with someone, ask yourself the following question: What fault of mine most nearly resembles the one I am about to criticize?"

Our judgments reveal places where we need to come clean and move past our fear. The fear is an illusion that clouds the higher truth that we are all the same. We are all one. The idea we are somehow better or worse is a myth that hampers our capacity for empathy.

We will talk in more detail about empathy in the next chapter, but for now, I would like to point out the relationship between non-judgment and our capacity to empathize. As we allow ourselves to become more empathetic, our need for judgment lessens. We recognize our common humanity, and this realization is enough to allow us to feel safe. It is enough to make us feel capable of facing whatever life brings us. It is enough to let us meet the moment without the stories that make us feel more secure. We can open up to uncertainty, because we genuinely want the best outcome for everyone involved—this is more important to us than holding onto our pride or preconceived notions.

Developing the capacity to be open-minded is powerful in forgiveness, because as long as we are thinking and judging what happened, we are not allowing ourselves to fully *feel* life transpiring in and around us. This allowing places us firmly within the unfolding of life and gives us access to what we need to heal—our heart. Nonjudgment works to abate the incessant input of the mind so we can feel what is happening in our bodies. When the mind is quiet, we are free to fully experience and move through the pain, and into compassion and love.

To be clear, non-judgment is not the same as not paying attention or observing what is happening. It is not about burying your head in the sand or entering a state of denial; in fact, denial is an indication we are judging our experience as wrong. When we practice non-judgment, which is a wholehearted acceptance of the moment, our capacity to pay attention increases. So does our capacity to do so without shrinking from reality.

Many of us think judgment is the same as discernment. Discernment, however, is about perceiving things as they *are*, while judgment is about the comparisons and assumptions we make when we think things should look a certain way. When we choose non-judgment, we choose purposeful neutrality. This neutrality allows us to stay connected to the truth, and not get swallowed by our feelings in the process. Rather, we learn to ride the wave of what we are experiencing, not to identify with the wave itself.

This is central to the Buddhist principle of equanimity. When we accept our life with the good and the bad, embracing every single part of it, we come closer to a full experience of our lives. In facing our pain, we relinquish judgments; this is because we are owning every part of ourselves and taking responsibility for all of it.

Have you ever asked a child what their favorite flavor of ice cream is, or who their favorite teacher is? Something interesting happens the first few times a child hears this question. They are perplexed. You can see it on their little face. They wonder why you would ask, and question themselves for not knowing the answer. It had not occurred to them to assign value to these things beyond "I love ice cream!" or "School is fun."

This deeply ingrained social habit to assign value seems harmless enough, but is it? What are we teaching young people to do? We are training them to judge and evaluate literally everything in their environment. Why would we do that? My best guess is we are trying to make them like us. We are trying to simplify our own lives by putting them into familiar boxes.

But are they choosing purposefully, or are they just randomly assigning value based on their mood or what they think we want to hear in the moment? Are they deciding art is their favorite subject because, on the day we asked, they had a fun project with glitter and glue? I believe this is exactly what happens.

Throughout our lives, we make arbitrary decisions based on how we feel in the moment, on how we perceive others will feel about us, or on some experience we had in the past that left an indelible imprint. We do not like the guy next door because he always has a scowl on his face, when in fact, the day before he moved in, his mother died. We do not like oranges because we decided they taste funny after eating a funky orange twenty years ago (which was actually a grapefruit). We do not date because we know all the potential partners out there are untrustworthy. We think people of a certain race or social class are all ignorant because we met two or three people from the group who were uninformed. The bias grows with time; we have already formed a seemingly bulletproof belief, and sooner or later, as we know, we always find what we are looking for.

This way of perceiving the world is true insanity in action.

How is this relevant to forgiveness? In the healing process, we evolve, and so does our story. Where we once saw tragedy, we now see purpose and meaning. Where we once assigned blame, with compassion we are now able to see suffering perpetuates suffering in the world.

In order to forgive, we must question our assumptions about what we know to be true. There is a time in life for evaluation, and we certainly need some structure to live within. But there is also a time for looking closely at that structure to see if it still serves us.

This can be challenging, as we have learned to become attached to our assessments of the world. We construct a reality where things are ranked and lined up in tidy rows so we can navigate life in safe, predictable ways. But this is not reality. Life is full of surprises and opportunities to learn new things, as well as grow past our perceived injuries.

Our job on this planet is not to tuck in our heads and plow through like we are running a gauntlet. It is to experience life *fully*. Is it scary? Yes. But remember what the Tao says—here, I paraphrase: When we see through the fear, we see a higher truth. And when we look through the illusion of fear, we are safe.

∽

How does the pathology of judging and ranking everything we encounter show up as we move through life? We take the scariest moments, the ones that catch us off guard, and we create a blueprint for life built around making sure those things do not happen again. The irony is, the more we try to avoid what we fear, the less "safe" we actually are. We begin operating from a map that lets us avoid truly living. We increasingly narrow our capacity to fully experience the world. In the process, we actually end up repeating the very patterns we fear.

An example is a child who has an abusive parent. The child learns to do whatever she can to avoid her parent's anger: She learns to judge anger as bad and believes her job is to remain passive and do her best to not affect those around her. She has determined anger and assertiveness are dangerous and even undesirable.

By the time the child has become an adult, she has "learned" to never assert herself and to tolerate unfair behavior, in order to feel safe. As a result of her adaptation, which she wisely chose in order to survive, she now attracts people who treat her poorly. A pattern is in place. She does not defend herself against mistreatment, and because she tolerates other people's bad behavior, she finds herself in relationships that are eerily similar to what she experienced in her early years.

We must test old patterns and beliefs if we want to be free from our misery. The outcome of clinging to our conclusions about reality is suffering on one level or another, whether it be despondency about the meaning of life, a pattern that does not serve us, chronic sadness, or agitation that may lead to anger and acting out against others. The best outcome to this clinging is acceptance or resignation about what life is "like." Such a perception is make-believe. Life isn't "like" anything. Life is just *life*. As the Taoist saying goes, "The only true measure of life is not to measure it at all, but rather, to simply live it fully."

∽

As we master the art of forgiveness and integrate it into our value system, we naturally have less attachment to outcomes because we have fewer expectations. Although they have purpose, expectations can cause suffering.

The more open we are to life happening as it will, the less we will find the need to forgive. With this kind of surrender, we experience freedom from the see-saw of attraction (which propels us in the direction of pleasure) and aversion (which compels us to run away from pain). Rather, we can simply surrender to the moment, knowing it is all for our highest good. In fact, we are being offered an opportunity to move past our narrow preferences and see into the heart of reality.

It is not that having preferences or expectations is bad; both of these things can serve us and help us hone our ideas about what we want and need. However, when we are free from judgment, we need not base our sense of well-being and happiness on likes or dislikes, praise or blame. We can choose to be aware of every facet of our experience without clinging to it or pushing it away. This facilitates healing in a beautiful way. And it is the true definition of empowerment.

⌒

Let's do a little experiment and see if we can demonstrate how judgments get in the way of healing. Think about a situation in your life where you need to forgive. Now, let your mind go to all the judgments you have about that person and the situation. Spend a few moments letting yourself evaluate the crap out of it. How do you feel? You probably have a lot of tension in your body, maybe in your chest and shoulders or around your solar plexus.

Now, explore further. Behind the tension—which always shields us from feeling something deeper—what else are you feeling? When we judge, not only do we eliminate all the possibilities outside our analysis of the situation; we also experience anxiety, frustration, and disempowerment.

Now, take a few long deep breaths and instead of fixating on what you *think* you know, take one of your judgments and imagine all the alternatives. What if you do not actually know their intentions? What if you have mixed up part of the story? How does it feel? Finally, consider one more option: Maybe you do not know. Maybe you do not need to know. How does not knowing feel in your body? If you are doing this experiment with integrity, what you might discover is a sense of calmness, spaciousness, or peace. Embrace the freedom and relief this brings.

Imagine a world where everything happening is occurring in perfect synchronicity, working in concert to support your evolution. Nothing is happening to you; rather, it is happening for you. Imagine all you need to do to see that world is to suspend your constant and obsessive interpretation of what is happening.

This is the power of non-judgment. When we exercise faith in not knowing and respond to the cues life gives us, suddenly we are part of an orchestra making beautiful music.

Exercise:

Pick a day this week and do the following exercise to raise your awareness of your judgments.

Carry a piece of paper or a journal with you. Beginning first thing in the morning, when you wake up, start taking note of your judgments. Are your first thoughts of the day observations, or are they assessments of right and wrong, good and bad? Is it bad the kids are not up yet or good that it is not raining? Jot down what you notice. Continue this throughout the day and write what you observe. Pay attention to your language. Do you use words like "should" and "shouldn't," "good" and "bad?" Even such phrases as "That was amazing" are value judgments. How many of your most commonly used words assign value?

Before the day is over, you may find the impulse to stop judging so much. It really is easy with awareness and some effort to begin to change the way we relate to our experience of life.

The goal of this exercise is not to pile on more judgment. It is not bad if you, like most, find almost your entire day is spent compulsively evaluating and categorizing everything that happens. The goal is to start building the capacity to *not* judge. The first step in the process is awareness. As your awareness grows, you will be able to choose to stop the insanity and simply experience life as it is happening. You might be surprised by the people you meet along the way who add true value and an opportunity for connection when you choose not to judge what people are like based on the way they look or even what they say the first time you interact.

Chapter Six

Expanding Awareness with Empathy

I do not ask the wounded person how he feels,
I myself become the wounded person.
— *Walt Whitman*

The Dalai Lama says empathy is the first step toward a compassionate heart. Imagine a world filled with people willing to share in the suffering of those who hurt the most: the ones who take from the rest of us in order to defend against their own pain. The ones who start wars and harm children. The ones who have been so emotionally damaged they readily inflict pain on others.

If those who harm felt and knew they were not alone, if they believed they could heal and become a part of something bigger—part of *humanity*—what then? We would succeed in healing the world.

Compassion is the foundation for a new world in which we no longer feel we need to defend against enemies because we finally see the truth of their actions: What others do is not about *us*. When we come to see this truth, our defenses drop and peace emerges.

We cannot hope to heal the world until we recognize that everyone's healing is our own. If we could see our oneness as something concrete rather than an abstract idea, we would see there is no perpetrator who is not also a victim. With the healing of forgiveness, each and every one of us has the capacity to release these labels altogether, and with them, our own suffering.

Empathy is the bridge to compassion, which is the mechanism we use to heal ourselves and the world our children will inhabit. It is connection at the most fundamental human level. It is not sympathy, which is feeling sorry for someone else. Sympathy puts the sympathizer in a place of judgment and evaluation, in a superior position with respect to the person they are relating to. Empathy puts us on the same level, and it is not wholly a mental activity. It is felt in the body.

While we may believe some are more deserving of sympathy than others, empathy, in contrast, is not an evaluative action. There is no one more or less worthy of empathy than anyone else. Empathy is not, in fact, triggered by some person's external "worthiness"; empathy arises from you, and your choice as to whether or not you will allow yourself to connect with another.

⌒

Contrary to popular belief, empathy is not a special gift handed to a select few. Some of us may have grown up in an environment where it was an acknowledged and respected trait, so we cultivated our ability to empathize. Many others have discovered and learned the importance of empathy on their journey in life and incorporated it into their values. And yet others of us do not experience it. We choose not to empathize, because the experience can be painful and disorienting if we are not aware of the nature of empathy.

Empathy entails feeling (or at least imagining we can feel) other people's pain and seeing the extent to which they suffer. Most of us have been taught to avoid pain at all costs, so it is no wonder empathy would be challenging.

Because empathy leads to compassion, exercising it can transform us into different people. This is another reason we deny our capacity to connect. Having compassion can get in the way of lots of things you might enjoy doing or you base your identity on, such as making money off the backs of other people, toying with the opposite sex in order to feel a sense of worth, or reinforcing your false identity as a victim. As far as our preferences are concerned, feeling the feelings of another person can be threatening or inconvenient. But when we begin to understand the implications of not allowing ourselves to heal, our hearts and minds change.

We *all* have the capacity to empathize with those around us. We just need to choose it, then learn how to do it.

∽

I am bothered by people who lie. When I am in my judging mind, I think lying shows a lack of character or the liar is too lazy to say what is inconvenient rather than take the time to speak words that show respect and dignity to both of them and the other person. But if I do not want to be captive to the negative energy generated by lying, I can choose to remind myself it is not about me. I can re-examine this interaction from a place of empathy rather than one of self-defense.

If I open my mind through non-judgment and create space for possibility, I can imagine many reasons why someone might choose to lie. Maybe they grew up in a home where telling the truth meant being attacked or shunned by their family or community. Maybe they fell madly in love with someone early in their life who did not value honesty, and they learned they needed to lie to keep what they wanted. Or, perhaps they simply (wrongly) believe it does not matter because it is commonplace. Showing up in the world in a way that causes harm is a learned behavior. We are not born jerks. We adapt for a reason.

Beginning to empathize, or at least opening to new possibilities about the people we have judged up to this point, is essential because it allows us to take ourselves out of their narrative and fully understand it is *not about us*. Consider a principle outlined in *The Four Agreements*, by Don Miguel Ruiz: "Don't take anything personally." As we practice empathy, we start to see the truth: People do not act out to harm us; they act out to harm themselves. They are reinforcing a false belief they have about themselves and their value in the world. This is *always* true.

How does this consideration—that it is not about you—feel in your body, in your heart? I experience less suffering when I realize someone else's harmful actions were not about me. I also experience this with self-forgiveness, when I open to the possibility that I was acting from the limited perspective of my wounded self. I was not trying to harm those I loved—I was trying to reinforce my ideas about my value, which told me I did not deserve love, peace, and joy.

⌒

Understandably, we are wary of empathy, especially when it comes to the people we view as most different from or most opposed to us. We do not want to empathize with our racist boss, the ex who cheated, or the person who killed our loved one. We certainly do not want to empathize with a parent who engaged in or allowed abuse.

When we take ourselves out of the other person's narrative, when we practice non-judgment and come to the realization that people are not out to get us, the story suddenly looks different, doesn't it? *This* is healing. Allowing ourselves to feel our inherent connection with others happens in the present moment and the heart. The thing we thought unimaginable (being able to connect with "the enemy") turns out to be the essence of our evolution and growth. This is further evidence that everything happens for a reason.

Empathy is not just about imagining being in someone else's shoes, though. It is more intricate than that, because, as we explored in the last chapter, the world around us is a mirror. What shows up in the world around us is a reflection of an aspect of ourselves.

Let's go back and look at the lying example. If I were to honestly examine my aversion to lying, what becomes clear is that I have been a liar. This realization came when I was in a relationship with a person who was not truthful. I knew it was not a coincidence I was yet again having this experience in my life. And, because I cared deeply for him and chose to empathize instead of make him wrong, I was able to see my part; I was able to see that *I* was the liar. I spent many years with my head down, just doing what I needed to do to create security for my family. In the process, I lied about who I was. I was dishonest in the relationship, too. I was not happy, although I pretended I was.

I was the one with the lesson to learn.

This does not mean the person who has harmed you does not also have lessons to learn. Empathizing with another is not the same as excusing their behavior. It may feel like it, but this is a false equivalency. To choose empathy is to recognize our common humanity and our basic interconnectedness, period.

Remember–this book is about *you*, not them. Give them a copy if you have an opinion about the healing work they have to do. But know forgiveness is about seeing why *you* are creating the experiences that show up in *your* life.

I hope you can see the remarkable power of empathy. When we connect, we create space for another person's narrative to be about them, and for ours to be about us. When we assume this accountability, it becomes much easier to understand why other people engage in the behavior they do. This creates a greater capacity for connection. Together, with true connection, we all show up differently—as authentic expressions of our highest selves.

Now that you understand the power of empathy in your journey of transformation, you are probably asking, "How do I do it?" "How do I learn to empathize with the person who has hurt me the most?" There are three ways to approach this. I start with the most challenging, because it is also the most direct way to connect with the person you are forgiving.

Exercise 1:

Depending on your relationship with the person or people you are forgiving, this process can be modified. If you know the person and they are still in your life, start by having a new kind of conversation with them. I want you to engage with them with profound curiosity. Use the tools we learned for non-judgment and approach the dialogue with an attitude of not knowing. Let the interaction unfold naturally; do not force it. Listen intently to what they say, as well as what they do not say. What you talk about is not as important as how you show up. The content may be as simple as asking about their day or plans for the next month or year.

If they are anything like some people in my family, answers to questions you might have will be generalized; this is the person's way of trying to deflect the type of intimacy you are offering. They may resist sharing specific details of their lives. For example, if you ask your father to tell you about his time in the war or what his first wife was like, he may try to avoid answering out of habit or because he thinks his answers will upset you. If this happens, remain neutral. Do not judge them, or they will shut down further. Remain open and consider why they might be doing this. Are they protecting you? Are they ashamed? Is it too hard for them to talk about what you are asking? We cannot know, and that is the point. Keep listening with an open heart.

If you do this and you are not able to reframe the interaction without judgment, do not want to speak with the person you are forgiving, do not know the person, or if they have passed on, you can still develop empathy. Do this by working backward from what you know. Do you have some ideas about who the person is and what their life might have been like? If not, consider this for the first time with a compassionate heart.

Next, ask yourself: "What chain of events might have led them to make the choices they made?" Start constructing a viable narrative about what life might have been like for them up to the time they caused harm. Write this story of what their life, starting in childhood, might have been like. The key is not to be factual, but viable. You want to write a story about what life might have been like to get them where they were when the harm was caused.

For example, I asked myself: *Why would my father abduct and abuse me as a child?* He is no longer with us, so I imagined what his childhood might have been like, what circumstances might have appeared in his life, and what decisions he made that led to that moment in time.

I used what I knew: He was raised in an English orphanage from an early age, away from his parents and eleven brothers and sisters. The possibilities for what it might have been like are endless, but it is not too difficult to fill in a few potential scenarios about what life was like in the absence of people who loved him—he must have felt vulnerable and alone. This narrative about my father is not based on facts; it's based on possibilities that empower me to empathize genuinely with him as a human being, as a child.

What story can you imagine that creates the opportunity to connect with the person you are forgiving? What story brings less tension and discomfort in your body and quiets your mind, if only subtly?

Exercise 2:

The second technique allows us to temporarily step back from the very real challenge of trying to connect with the person we least want to empathize with (you will end up in the water but you do not have to jump off the cliff to get there). Do the exercise above, but work through the narrative with someone you have forgiven or are in the process of forgiving. This can be powerful, because you already have some understanding of why you were able to forgive them. If you have truly forgiven, you have empathized with them on some level. You have chosen compassion over indignation. Write what you think you know to be true about this person. As above, construct a narrative that elicits an emotional connection in an authentic way. Note how you feel. Is your body lighter? Do you feel less tension, more comfort? This is empathy. It is letting go of the illusion of separateness.

Exercise 3:

It may be the techniques above are not accessible because you cannot get a sense of what empathy *feels* like. This is not uncommon. Use the exercise below to develop this ability to empathize.

Take a minute and think about the type of people you like the least—the proverbial "them" you identify in the world. Now, go out and spend time with these people whom you perceive as so different from you. Volunteer at a local jail or prison. There are nonprofit organizations that offer services to inmates. Connect with them. Go to an open AA meeting. Spend some time under the bridge downtown.

If you can easily empathize with people in those groups, have a nice long conversation with your obnoxious neighbor or the CEO of your company. Have the type of conversation outlined above: listen intently and with an open heart. Be curious. Suspend judgment.

Afterward, ask yourself the following questions:

- What about this person surprised me?

- What do I have in common with this person (hint: there are many, many things you have in common)?

- What is their family probably like?

- What do you dislike about the person?

- What is it in you triggering this dislike? Be kind but honest when answering this question. Remember from the last chapter—if you are experiencing any judgments about someone else, you are responding to something that already lives within you, whether you consciously perceive it or not.

Make this activity part of your life. Spend time talking to people presumably unlike you. Listen to everyone with curiosity and an open heart. Consider the challenges and choices that led them to where they are today. Allow yourself to feel compassion and non-judgment for people. You do not need to spend extensive time with them. I am not asking you to like their company. But having compassion is not going to endanger you. Feeling a connection to humanity is life-affirming and life-building. There is no risk in it. You still have the right to the same boundaries you always had.

Empathy is the channel to compassion. Compassion is the key to healing. This is the point in time you need to ask yourself: Do I want to be *right*, or do I want to *grow*? There is no correct answer to the question. There is nothing in this work that says you must forgive someone. It is 100 percent your choice. Play your options out in your mind. What does choosing to be right look like in a month or a year? Probably a lot like today, right? What does electing to connect look like? Use these mental projections to help guide you in deciding which path to take. The good news is, there are only two paths to pick from.

Chapter Seven

Self-Empowerment and Spiritual Warriorship

Look well into thyself; there is a source of strength
which will always spring up if thou wilt always look.
— *Marcus Aurelius, The Meditations*

Forgiveness is an act of self-empowerment. The ultimate objective is to liberate ourselves fully from the limiting experiences of our lives so we are free to show up in the world as the person we know we truly are. This practice is not about healing our wounds; it is a process of self-actualization in which we become uninhibited to create boldly in the absence of the bonds that once held us.

But freedom comes at a cost: full accountability for our experiences. We cannot manifest our deepest desires without realizing we are in charge of our lives. If we forgive the offending party, we reclaim our energy, retrieve our fractured soul fragments, empower ourselves, and enable ourselves to move forward. We are empowered when we do not imprison ourselves in our circumstances, but learn to expand beyond them.

There is a subtle but powerful shift that takes place when we become fully accountable for our experiences. When we stand in this space of accountability and experience compassion, we come to realize we are in control of our own destiny. This is exactly what many of us have tried to avoid, because it is terrifying to know we are the boss.

What if we do not know what to do next? What if we make a mistake? What if we hurt others? These questions stir in us a fear we need to be willing to both stand in and see through. The warrior faces her fear and uses it to push through to something better, something truer. Standing up for ourselves teaches us our value and importance, after all. We are finally teaching ourselves our true divine value.

∽

A couple of things can happen when we begin to narrow our experience of life based on the challenges we face. We either form an unbending worldview that feigns to know everything we need to know in order to survive, or we shrink and attempt to disappear from the experience of living altogether.

The problem with these fear-based constructs is they perpetuate the ways of being we least want to manifest. The illusion of victimhood and the illusion of being the "bad guy" become more and more real as we reinforce these false identities.

Often, when we reach the point in life where our perspective shifts and it is time for the in-breath of life, we begin to see glimpses of *our* role in our own lives. We start to see how the choices we made leading up to this moment in time are grounded in the untrue beliefs we have about who we are. This is not a time for self-condemnation or ridicule. It is not time for more judgment. Rather, with awareness and compassion, we embrace our journey and a full understanding that we, and those around us, are doing the best we can. You made it this far! On a journey wrought with opportunities to fall, you adapted masterfully to reach this point still standing on your own two feet. Congratulations! You survived.

However, we cannot disregard the glimpses of a higher truth the universe is giving. We need to ask ourselves why we should feel responsible for everything. The answer to this question rests in something we already know. We are here to learn our lessons, to contribute to the evolution of human consciousness. Your contribution is not about anyone else; it is about *you*. To move forward—to forgive completely—we must heed the call to be accountable for our experiences.

Being accountable for your experiences does not mean those who have caused you harm are not responsible for their actions. Their journey is theirs. They are just as accountable as you.

∽

Self-empowerment is about feeling your feelings fully and getting in touch with responsibility for your experiences. You are in charge of your life. Up until this point, you may have deferred your power to others, or you may have stood in a rigid interpretation of what you thought you wanted, relentlessly pursuing a static vision at all costs. You may have discounted the cues being offered and missed opportunities for love, adventure, or something unexpected in the name of *knowing* what life was supposed to look like. You may have held firmly to your torment, speciously believing it to be a part of who you are, believing you knew best.

With unshakable awareness of the truth of our suffering and an emerging sense of self-compassion, we are reminded we have done the best we could with the tools we have had up until today. Today, we can begin to choose differently and open to leaning into the gifts life offers with curiosity and love in the absence of obsessive judgment and resistance to *what is*. We embrace our circumstances and choose gently what we want to change. We move toward love and an evolution of life that is so much more than anything we could have imagined.

The idea of embracing what is, is reflected in the Buddhist idea of the spiritual warrior, outlined in detail in the works of the Tibetan teacher Chögyam Trungpa Rinpoche. A spiritual warrior is a person who defeats the universal enemy of self-ignorance through compassion toward all of life. Everything the spiritual warrior does is done to liberate oneself and others from the suffering caused when we close our hearts to reality and all the diverse experiences—love, loss, joy, heartache—it has to offer. A spiritual warrior opens their heart to both the joy and suffering of the world, and allows themselves to be transformed by it. Instead of clinging to the security offered by a fixed identity and unyielding way of being, spiritual warriorship entails being as flexible as bamboo, as fluid as water. As life transforms, we, too, are willing to transform with it.

How do we become spiritual warriors? We must be willing to be accountable for our experience of reality, but with our newfound strength, we also need a compass, which is your heart. Not the Cinderella version we are taught to know, but the one that aches at tragedy and quickens when we connect to the soul of another.

We do this by implementing a set of principles to live by. Not an inflexible rulebook, but rather, guidelines we use to ground the daily decisions we have to make for our highest, greatest benefit. For me, my guidelines change with time, depending on where I need support. Today, my principles include using my words for good, gently paying attention to the world around me, not making choices that cause foreseeable harm for myself or others, and offering what I have to give to those in need when the need presents itself to me. We work with values much like virtues, as sometimes achievable and always knowable. We use them to help us see when we get off course, and compassionately redirect.

Sometimes our desire for comfort compels us toward easy choices, but spiritual warriors understand there is little power in "easy." Making difficult life choices moves us into to a fuller expression of who we really are. In this lies an unfortunate and inevitable reality: There is pain. It is paradoxical, but in order to release our suffering, we must get present to our pain. We must honor it.

∽

We too often try to skip the part of the healing and forgiveness process where we get to feel a deep sense of self-empowerment. In our effort to forgive, we deny our anger and indignation, and try to love our way to wholeness. Love is the answer, but if we do not feel in control of our lives–empowered and accountable–we will eventually move back into feeling like a victim or a perpetrator. When we forgive, we exchange anger with self-compassion. How do we do this? By getting in touch with our feelings. If we do not allow ourselves to feel anger, resentment, or anything else we are experiencing, we cannot heal it.

For some, this is not an issue. They live their lives angry toward the world around them. But often, when we have incorporated victimization into our identity, we repress feelings that will "disrupt" the peace around us. We may watch the world hypervigilantly so we can protect ourselves from the unexpected. We may think we are offering others the gift of our love, but in truth, we are protecting ourselves from our own hurt.

You have become present to your suffering, and you are beginning to heal. Now that you feel self-love and compassion for the impact of your painful experience, what might arise is the anger you would feel if this had happened to someone else. This is where we too often get off track. We think our feelings are bad or unhelpful because we want to forgive. It makes sense, but it is also wrong. Emotions are never incorrect, and judging them further disempowers us. Allow yourself to feel whatever you are feeling. It may be sadness, not anger. You do not have to feel angry, but if you do, it is exactly what you should be feeling.

In order to stay grounded in our power, we need time during the in-breath (usually, at the beginning) to allow for the feelings that naturally emerge when we get present to our suffering. How would you feel if the person you loved the most in life had endured the anguish you have tolerated? I can tell you that if my son were to suffer my burdens, I would be angry. I would want the people who seemed to have caused him harm to pay for their mistakes. It would be my first feeling. And, as we know, we have to start from exactly where we are, so I would honor that.

When my healing journey began, this is exactly what I did. I honored the hatred and contempt I felt for the people I would next forgive—the same ones I would eventually learn to love and thank for teaching me the true meaning of life: to feel a part of the whole, and to love without reservations. I sat with my indignation and reflected on my part in the dramas leading up to that moment. I managed my anger with kickboxing and self-defense classes. I did yoga. I sat in the indignation and studied ways to alleviate my suffering. What I came to see was the compassion I felt on that day in October 2002 was the key to it all. I also came to see my own part in the ensuing dramas.

We want to stay present to the anger and indignation we feel, because when we work with *what is*, we get present to both the hurt and the love we have fostered. With time, love transmutes our pain into compassion. We cannot truly get to compassion until we are willing to own our feelings and stand up for ourselves. This teaches us our value and importance. We are finally standing up for our highest selves. This is the foundation of self-compassion, and it gives us the extraordinary resolve to see our grandest visions for life through to the very end.

There are many things you can do to manage undesirable energy when you are present to it, and to direct it constructively. First, remember to never act out toward others. It will get in the way of your capacity to experience self-love and forgiveness. You can, of course, use prayer and meditation. The power of these tools cannot be overstated. But we also have other ways of working with disruptive feelings when they manifest in the body. The key is to get into your body first—to really feel the energy of these emotions so you can transform them. You can run, kickbox, or dance like a maniac in your living room. You can scream at the top of your lungs into pillows or write a passionate letter telling someone to go away (don't send it!). Or you can go for a long, rigorous hike. The magic is in expending or processing the energy without creating bad karma or causing harm in the world.

⌒

One important aspect of self-empowerment is learning to wisely use the tools we have at our disposal. Self-empowerment does not mean "doing it all on my own." Nor does it mean "I matter more than others." It means you are responsible for the outcomes you experience in life, that is all. The most empowered people in the world understand the significance of leveraging their resources. If you are blessed with a partner who sees your true nature, with family who adore you, with a community that not only supports you but also needs you, allow them all to be a part of your empowerment. We stand stronger together than alone.

If faith is an integral part of your worldview, as it is for me, it is important to acknowledge the role it plays in forgiveness and self-empowerment. For many, there is a point of surrender that happens before we learn to see our part in our lives. It is the same surrender we all feel when we come to see we may, in fact, not have it all figured out. Grounding ourselves in this understanding is, for many, the most powerful tool we have. On the other side of surrender, there is a type of self-empowerment that cannot be reached any other way—a process of breaking down and re-emerging with more clarity and resolve than you could imagine. It is the rebirth spoken about by many of the world's spiritual traditions.

As we learn to love ourselves, our tolerance for suffering decreases. Gradually, those habitual behaviors that perpetuate our suffering become unacceptable. Our strength grows, and an ease in the absence of resistance is born. "I can't believe it, but I just told her no," or, "I just chose to stop..." will replace old, disempowered patterns. We open the hand that grasped the event or insult that caused us suffering, and we simply let it fly away.

Exercise:

Go back to the story of forgiveness you wrote in the forgiveness process, and rewrite it from the perspective of someone you love dearly, perhaps a best friend or one of your children.

As you write, pay attention to how you feel when imagining things that happened to you had happened to them instead.

After you complete rewriting the story, write how you feel thinking about them having endured the same hurtful events.

Recognize that the way you feel for them is how you should feel about yourself and your experiences. If you feel anger or aggression, identify constructive actions you could take to manage your feelings in a way that respects your emotions.

Take action to honor your feelings. Could you write a scorching letter or take a self-defense class? Do what you need to do to get in touch with your emotional experience without causing harm to another.

Chapter Eight

The Healing Power of Self-Love

My Lord told me a joke. And seeing Him laugh has done
more for me than any scripture I will ever read.
— *Meister Eckhart*

To love oneself means to feel the extraordinary, radiating energy in our heart space that we so easily feel for those in our lives for whom we are most grateful. It is the longing that makes us smile and brings us to tears, or the feeling we have when we watch a video or read a story that reflects the beauty of humanity. It is not an *idea* but an emotion eliciting gratitude and joy for living in the very skin you have right now.

Loving oneself begins with acceptance of the person we are in this very moment in time. We embrace our whole self with compassion and move forward on our journey to becoming our highest self.

It sounds straightforward enough: Love your whole self exactly as you are, and the need for forgiveness goes away. But how do we do that? How do we learn to love ourselves unconditionally so we can reach true freedom? We have talked a lot about self-love and self-compassion, and their power in the forgiveness process. In Chapter 3, we discussed the reasons we still need to, at this point in our lives, learn self-love.

Let us now examine ways to foster our experience of love for the self, because as we know, it is the key to absolute forgiveness. We cannot simultaneously have an experience of self-love and believe anything leading up to this moment in time was not for our betterment. It does not mean we would not change things, or that we do not have feelings of regret from time to time; it just means that—grounded here in reality and in the present moment, where all creation starts—we choose gratitude, or we choose to suffer. Gratitude is rooted in believing in ourselves, in actually being able to *see* and experience our inherent worth.

Your choice—gratitude or suffering—begins now, but we will not necessarily reap the rewards right away. This is why we say we need to *cultivate* self-love, because it takes effort. It, too, is a process. Today, there are four things you can do to begin the process:

- Be kind to yourself.
  (even when you are disappointed or sad).

- Allow yourself to *experience* feelings of love
  for yourself exactly the way you are.

- Be accountable for your experiences.

- Start doing the things you need to do
  to be the person you want to be.

You are exactly who you were meant to be in this very moment. Pause for a moment and breathe into that. Know, without a doubt, everything up to now has been in perfect order, offering you all you need to move forward with ease into the forgiving, kinder, freer version of you. Before you start making changes, take time to let that sink in. No matter what the details leading up to today, you are right where you were always meant to be.

As we start making space for change and letting go of critical self-talk and feelings of loveless-ness, we remind ourselves what love feels like. Use the Heart Activation exercise at the end of the forgiveness process, or quite simply, get in touch with feelings of love for another. Then turn your imagination to yourself. Think of yourself as a child: innocent, vulnerable. Think of your tenderness today. It is there, even if you conceal it from yourself and others much of the time. Stay present to the feeling, and go back to it every day. It will spark your motivation to act in ways that remind you of how much you truly care.

With an experience of love present, it is time to look closely and honestly at the person you are. Loving the whole self is not just about loving the attractive parts we share openly with the world and brag about on social media. It is our dark side, too. We all have aspects of ourselves that fall into this category. Our dark side is the part of us obscured from consciousness but still knowable. It is often the parts we judge as bad or hide because we have been indoctrinated into believing we should not be a certain way. Sometimes these aspects of who we are cause us to feel shame, jealousy, greed, aggression, lust, and other emotions with an air of destructiveness. Some examples of the dark side of the self might include being judgmental and thinking unkind thoughts about people, having sexual impulses you do not want to have, possessing prejudice toward certain groups (we all have these, whether we choose to acknowledge them or not), or compulsive behavior, including addictions. It could also be something less onerous, like being impatient or lying to make yourself look better. It is different for everyone, but we all, by definition, have a dark side.

Our human experience is dualistic by nature; we cannot perceive light without darkness. Some prefer to simply deny this and point to the oneness of existence, and I understand the lure of this approach. I know there is a higher truth beyond a world defined by dualism, but there is clarity and peace to be found in holding the paradox too, if only during times of healing. We have a great opportunity to see and appreciate the balance between things, to understand that seemingly opposing qualities have value. We can come to see, in fact, one cannot be perceived without the other. There is no path without the forest or the fence to create edges. Here, living life as you and as me, there is a point in our evolution when the most powerful thing we can do is become aware of all aspects of who we are and bring those parts of ourselves that could cause shame or fear into our experience of love. Love heals. Love transforms.

To love our whole selves, we need to be aware of these darker aspects of the self. If we try to deny or repress them, they will actually have more power and show up in more onerous ways. For example, I am a compulsive person. I can become attached to or hyper-focused on things more readily than the average person. My awareness of this allows me to not only see it when it presents itself but also to leverage it when I can (while writing a book, for instance). In the absence of judgment and in the presence of love, the things we once feared become part of us we can choose to embrace, learn to manage, and in some cases, release.

This activity of embracing the whole self serves important roles in forgiveness. Getting in touch with your dark side matters because we have to experience our feelings to heal them. If these aspects of ourselves cause anger, shame or jealousy, embracing those aspects gives us the opportunity to evolve through them into love and compassion.

The other reason it is imperative is when we bring the parts of ourselves that we judge into the light, we develop a greater capacity to empathize with others. Remember, what we judge in others points to something in us. When we see the connection, the resistance falls away.

We cannot work with harsh judgments, so open your mind to seeing the value of your dark side. Ask yourself: *What do I get out of this aspect of myself that I do not get elsewhere? How does this part of me add value to my life? What about this part of myself does not*

*work? How can I honor my dark side, and if I need to, let it go? How
can I embrace this characteristic with integrity? How can I nurture this
side of me without causing harm?*

∽

Self-love is not narcissism, arrogance, or selfishness. Narcissism
is a clinical term, defined as a pathological obsession with the self.
When someone else is talking about something, the narcissist's first
thought always starts with "I" or "me." There is little or no capacity
(or at least effort) to think of others, much less empathize with them.
Everything is evaluated relative to "I" or "me." Even when trying
to think of others, they will subtly shift the interaction to include
something about themselves. This is not self-love. It is a fixation born
from fear, perhaps based in feeling abandoned or invisible or feeling
the need to fight for one's independence. Rather than the expanding
experience of love, it is a narrowing, low-energy manifestation of
attempted self-preservation. The narcissist adapts to manage their
experience of life, as we all do.

Similarly, arrogance is about being preoccupied with the self. It
is grounded in the ego, which is not where we experience love and
compassion. Narcissism and arrogance are used as defense mechanisms to hide insecurity. Arrogance attempts to obscure those inse-
curities by compensating with bravado and indifference.

Selfishness is an action. It is behaving in ways that do not account
for others' needs. We often learn to be selfish solely from a lack of
perspective. We have failed to learn to consider those around us. We
may have instead learned to compulsively draw attention to ourselves
or take what we can get as a survival instinct.

None of these things are a reflection of self-love. On the contrary,
they inhibit the experience of love, because they do not take place in the
heart and are designed to protect or shield us from connection to others.

If you feel you experience any of these ways of showing up in the world, begin with awareness and self-compassion. Do not judge yourself or you will strike up a battle of wills against a potentially well-honed disposition. Allow yourself to experience (not merely think about) love for who you are today. Then take action by shifting your focus to others' well-being many times each day to start releasing your need to protect yourself from others. As you relax your attachment to the ways of being that limit your ability to act boldly, consider there is an opportunity for forgiveness. You chose these ways for a reason. It may be time to let go of resistance and choose to heal. We *all* have the capacity to make these choices at any time in our lives.

∽

We begin with awareness of the self and an experience of love. We encourage the experience with a daily practice of becoming present to the love and compassion we have for ourselves and others. Next, we need to make some decisions about who we want to be. We now know we are greater than the illusion of victimhood. We know we are not the bad guy. So, who *are* you? And, who do you want to *be*?

For me, as my healing journey began, integrity became the foundation of this inquiry. I experienced suffering when I broke my word with myself and others. When I determined to show up one way and showed up in another, I found it more difficult to practice self-compassion and cultivate love.

There are many practical things we can do to cultivate a sense of self-worth that manifests as love. Start by gathering evidence to combat the unsupportive narratives you have about "how I really am." For example, if your unloving story is you are not good at intimate relationships or you are not good at managing money, *do* things to disprove these beliefs.

The language we use with ourselves and others reflects our beliefs. But, as we have already established, it is also the tool we have to begin transforming those beliefs into viewpoints to support our capacity to love ourselves. Paying particular attention to what we say, what we are declaring to be true, gives us power to start making adjustments.

How can we help deconstruct the stories we have about ourselves that block self-love? Looking at the example of believing you are not good at intimate relationships, you could start by creating a mantra to reframe the story into a believable but empowered truth. For example, "I am doing the things I need to do to be a loving, committed partner." Then, do the things you can to support the new possibility, perhaps allowing yourself to be vulnerable even when it hurts or when you are afraid. Perhaps you begin to engage with people who treat you kindly and see your inherent worth. You decide not to give your energy to those who do not see your true worth. Always be kind to yourself when you make a familiar mistake, and move on quickly. Use the power of language to affirm the person you want to bring into existence.

To have integrity means to be an integrated whole, with all of our words and actions reflecting who we say we are. It is a high bar to set but, as with all great feats, much of the payoff is in the effort, not the end game. Integrity is showing up as the person you know you are, even when it's hard, even when you do not feel like it. This goes back to living by your principles. Life is not about always getting our way and only doing what we want to do. Do what you need to do to grow into the person you *want* to be. Build value in your own eyes in whatever way you need, to reflect your inherent value. Be of service to others. Set big inspiring goals and work toward them. Make new friends with similar values. Participate in a spiritual community, or just be kinder. Ask yourself what is right for you. The possibilities are endless.

The principles and core values we discussed in the last chapter were the tools I used to make the changes I needed when keeping my word was difficult. I created gentle rules to simplify life and stopped doing the things that got in the way of my integrity.

A difficult and painful block to self-love and integrity is the experience of addiction. One of the reasons addictions so profoundly impact our lives, even if we are functioning out in the world, is because they make integrity nearly impossible. We know, even if no one else does, our struggle in our private moments. We know addictions make it difficult for us to keep our word, particularly to ourselves. We will say "no more," only to do it again, and to feel a little less kindness toward ourselves each time. Addiction makes true accountability for our actions arduous, and intimate relationships impossible, because our desires and values flex with our disposition.

We need to break these cycles in order to fully experience self-love. This is not because the activity we are addicted to is inherently bad. Rather, despite our best effort, when caught in such a cycle, we work against ourselves. We block self-love because our addiction erodes our ability to trust ourselves. We feel like we are not fully in charge. We redirect our energy to love, create, and build beautiful lives in community to our compulsive behaviors, leaving little love and compassion for others. We essentially act as though we *only* love that to which we are addicted.

I do not intend to oversimplify the challenges of stepping out of an addictive pattern. I know them well. However, we begin all change, all true relinquishment, the same way. We start with compassionate awareness of our suffering. From this unshakable foundation we make achievable goals and create principles supporting growth. With authentic compassion in play, the suffering will become intolerable and how to move forward with love will make itself known, one step at a time.

Being fully accountable for our experiences in the presence of love creates the self-empowerment we discussed in Chapter 7. Empowerment leads to the strength we need to change, but it also reinforces our experience of self-love, because we know we can count on ourselves and contribute fully with compassion to the world around us. With this awareness love grows because we are beginning to show up in consistent, integrated, and benevolent ways in the world. We are anchoring our sense of self in words and actions that reflect our intentions, thereby creating space for love to grow.

∽

Self-care is an essential component of self-love. The yogic traditions born in the East understood the importance of self-care in building our capacity to be, and stay, present. With time, a yoga practice allows us to take the body out of the picture, so to speak. Often, when we try to get fully grounded in the now, we also become aware of physical discomfort arising from the body. Nurturing vitality and ease in the body frees us from this distraction, creating space for deeper inquiry into what is truly happening in the present moment. Ideally, we want our bodies to be an asset, here to support us on our human journey. For those living with illness or limitation, our body may also be our teacher. This too is exactly as it should be for your evolution through this human experience. Either way, we can honor what is and do our best to create our personal version of well-being.

How we treat our bodies is a reflection of how we feel about ourselves. There is no prescription for the right way to nurture ourselves, because we all have different backgrounds and starting points. For me, yoga is an integral part of wellness—as are meditation, rigorous exercise to help expend unneeded energy, and eating foods that create vitality.

Of course, we are not all yogis or meditators. It does not ultimately matter. Do what you can to nurture comfort and vigor in your body. The less diverted your attention is by the body, the more energy and presence you will have to share with the world. What self-care looks like to you will be unique to who you are. But the measure should always be whether or not it increases your experience of vitality. Does it make you feel more alive?

∽

Finally, perhaps the single most important way to create an experience of self-love is to relax and enjoy life. Lighten up; it really is not as bad as you think it is! Maybe even have a little irreverence along the way. Levity is the most enlightened state we can acquire because we come to see life as quite entertaining with all this running around trying to figure things out, interpreting darn near everything incorrectly, and complicating relationships to feel relevant. We come to see suffering as optional. We can embrace what is and learn to work with it in joyful ways.

With self-love, we come to see we are perfect just the way we are. So loosen up and laugh a little. Life is for you. Celebrate your successes, learn quickly from your failings, and remember the struggle is optional. If life is going to be challenging, we might as well enjoy the ride.

Laughing and having fun are not just sweet ideas, though. There is a reason they are so important—so important I mention them last. When we create space to see the joy and revelry of life, we start to see more clearly that life is actually not a burden. We were not born to carry the heavy cross of suffering to our graves. We were born to embody the true meaning of love and share it with others. Suffering might provide some perspective but beyond that, if you look through the fear, what you see is a world designed and created for your advancement toward no suffering.When we lighten up and allow for lightheartedness, this truth begins to show itself. With time, all things are *for* us. Why do you think the Buddha was always smiling?

Exercise:

1. In a quiet place, close your eyes and imagine someone (or a pet) whom you love dearly. Think of a moment in time when you were overcome with love for the person. Perhaps it was the birth of a child, or your wedding day. Now, with that feeling present in your body, shift your attention to yourself. The *you* who you are right now. Smile. Yes, right now! Smile at the thought of *you*. Say "Thank you."

2. Make a list of no fewer than twenty things you love about yourself. Keep writing if you are inspired.

3. Go back through the list and write down how these things contribute to the world around you. How do you make a difference, just being you?

Conclusion

Alex described herself as a likable woman, funny, with a kind disposition. Her childhood was not fraught with trauma or a lack of love. In fact, she was close with her family. Some might call her happy-go-lucky, taking life as a casual endeavor and an opportunity to see what she could get from people. Yet, as the third decade of her life came to a close, she started to see the impact of her aloof approach to life. She saw how she had been quietly telling herself things would change—she would pursue her dream job and find a partner she really loved—only to fail and then pretend she had not made the covenant. The truth of her failings became more apparent when she met a man she fell unexpectedly in love with. Despite the joy and undeniable gift of love she felt, she withdrew. Both she and her lover were heartbroken.

Alex began looking closely at her life. What was it that made her so cautious and distant from the true essence and passion of life? She began by getting in touch with the suffering she had endured, first as the result of her own deceit, then for feeling as though she had missed out on so many opportunities in life. She mourned missed love and the loss of what might have been. She felt angry at herself and desperately wanted to go back to the escapism she had mastered over the years— for her it was sex and drinking, or just checking out from the world in solitude—but this time, she responded with compassion. More sadness followed as the pieces came together, and she realized the pain she had caused others over the years with her casual indifference. But with a chosen compassion for self over judgment and denial, something started to shift. Memories surfaced she had not recalled for twenty years. She remembered feeling sad and confused at a very early age, wondering why her family was not together. She remembered falling in love the first time, and the heartache that followed. Suddenly, she thought about a day not long after her breakup. She remembered determining to never feel that way again. "How is that possible?" she now wondered. "How could I have let my entire life unfold based on determinations made so long ago, by a naïve girl?" She thought about the boy she loved and wondered where he was. With this came a feeling of connection as she imagined his life, joys, and struggles.

These seemingly unassuming shifts in Alex changed everything. She felt a newfound comfort in the vulnerability she had lost so long ago. She thanked the little girl she once was for protecting her. She knew it was okay to let go now. Love, compassion, and gratitude for her journey transformed the sadness over time. Authentic self-love released the hold of ego-driven self-admiration. She felt calmer, more centered. She saw more beauty in life's intricacy and unexpected gifts.

The circumstances around Alex began to reflect this new manifestation of herself. She took a job that challenged her and asked for help when she needed it. She developed warm relationships with the people she met, and for the first time in twenty-five years, she opened her heart to the possibility of love. She felt grateful to her joys and her struggles for deepening her capacity to love.

All forgiveness begins with the thought, "There is something wrong with me right now." This single decree compels us to find fault in our lives. For a moment, close your eyes and imagine what life would look like if every aspect of what is happening right now—your mind, body, spirit, and everything in the world around you—is the way it is for a reason, and that reason is always for your growth and evolution as a human being (and, if you are so inclined, your soul). You do not have to believe it; just imagine it as a possibility. How do you feel? The subtle shift toward peace *is* healing. It is forgiveness.

I chose the case study at the beginning of this chapter because it is important to recognize the healing journey is not only about those of us who have overcome incomprehensible woes. It is about all of us. We are strange, endearing creatures, having determined along the way to protect ourselves from the very point of living: to love so deeply you feel you might die, only to find the seed of joy living right there in the middle of that death. This seed is also the seed of creation. From this place, all things are possible. Healing and forgiveness liberate us from our deepest fears. And, we can *all* choose love, compassion, and empathy over suffering—if we are willing.

This practice changes us in powerful ways. We stand fully accountable and filled with love, ready to face the challenges life will inevitably offer. As we move through life, we will sometimes fail to respond with forgiveness—most often to the things that catch us off guard (even more than the seemingly bad stuff). Go back when this happens, and start the process again. It becomes much easier with time, in part because you see the payoff and you realize it is absolutely worth the effort.

We do not do hard work like this without reward. The reward is a greater capacity to feel joy and happiness and to love and embrace the whole self, both the dark and the light parts. The reward is feeling you are a part of something bigger. As you begin to integrate forgiveness into your character, it becomes a discipline requiring little or no purposeful thought. When you reach mastery, which we can all do if we choose, forgiveness becomes a virtue.

∽

I want to close by talking about the implications of this work on community, on the world we live in, and the world our children will one day live in. To live in community, we need order; we need to understand what we expect from one another, and what falls outside the realm of acceptability. The role of justice is to reflect the values we have agreed upon and enact fairness in the world.

Justice means to behave justly or fairly in the world. When we succeed in finding it, the result is harmony. Today, in a time fraught with division and disharmony, the kind of introspection that deepens our empathy, compassion, and sense of harmony is sorely needed. In the words of former president George W. Bush, "Too often we judge other groups by their worst examples while judging ourselves by our best intentions, and this has strained our bonds of understanding and common purpose."

Today's justice is actually based in punishment. It must be acknowledged that we are so far from peace because the systems we have constructed were designed to control and repress, not enact justice. We are so lost in our own pain and vigilant determination to not be accountable for our part in the chaos surrounding us, we act out of fear. We push away the suffering parts of ourselves, and in so doing, learn to push many parts of the human experience away—including the most important ones.

How do the threads of justice and fairness holding our social fabric together change in a world where forgiveness is a personal value? With a willingness to look within to see why the world around us looks the way it looks, and firmly grounded in a conscious realization that we are all more similar than different, fairness becomes something less complex. It becomes a measure to put things back in balance. We are human, flawed, messy, crazy, and so, so steeped in ego sometimes. We make mistakes, and sometimes those blunders bump up against social constructs. In a forgiving world, when one of us falters, we would ask such questions as, "What suffering have you endured that would cause you to act against yourself in this manner?", and, "What can we do to help alleviate suffering and bring you back to yourself?", and, "What can I do to help?"

In this new world, you and I play an active role in the process of ensuring justice. As Dr. Martin Luther King Jr., said, "The arc of the moral universe is long, but it bends toward justice." Truly, justice is in our nature. This is a justice which goes beyond contempt and derision, and beyond our need to punish, blame, and make others wrong. Rather than perpetuating the suffering we see today, when we all do our part in healing and releasing the wounds of the past, we create a world filled with people who are willing to stand in their impact and offer back something more. We become willing to love in the face of sadness and see through fear to the highest truth of who we are: We are all one. When you suffer, I suffer. When you love, I love. When you heal, so do I.

Appendix

Resources

Project Forgive, http://www.projectforgive.com/. Dr. Shawne Duperon leads Project Forgive, a 501c3 non-religious organization which provides free resources to advance forgiveness education. They focus on leadership in the workplace and schools, while also promoting understanding between forgiveness and behavioral health. Project Forgive reaches millions in social media and its founder was nominated for a Nobel Peace Prize in 2016.

The Forgiveness Project, www.theforgivenessproject.com. The Forgiveness Project is an award-winning organization collecting and sharing real stories of forgiveness to build understanding, encourage reflection, and enable people to reconcile with pain and trauma and move forward. Through a variety of events and programs, the organization uses storytelling to present alternatives to cycles of conflict, violence, crime, and injustice. Check out their book, *The Forgiveness Project: Stories for a Vengeful Age.* The stories illustrate forgiveness is first and foremost a personal journey as mysterious as love: a visceral process with no set rules or time limits.

Risking Light, **http://www.riskinglight.com/,** is a documentary feature film about five remarkable people from the United States, Cambodia, and Australia who have forgiven the unforgivable. The film explores the complexities and unique emotional journeys of those who dare to move toward forgiveness.

Dr. Brené Brown, www.brenebrown.com. Brown is a researcher whose work on vulnerability, courage, worthiness, and shame have made her a household name. Her 2010 TEDx Houston talk, "The Power of Vulnerability," is one of the top five most viewed TED talks in the world, with over 25 million views. She is the author of three bestselling books: *Rising Strong, Daring Greatly,* and *The Gifts of Imperfection.* Her website includes informative articles, videos, and poster downloads.

Byron Katie, www.thework.com. Byron Katie is a revolutionary teacher, author, and speaker whose work is all about showing people how to stop suffering. Katie's method of self-inquiry is called "The Work," and consists of four questions and "turnarounds" offering a way to experience the opposite of what you believe to be true. In questioning your beliefs, you discover choices beyond suffering. Her six books include the bestselling *Loving What Is, I Need Your Love—Is That True?* and *A Thousand Names for Joy.*

Dr. Robert D. Enright, *Forgiveness Is a Choice: A Step-by-Step Process for Resolving Anger and Restoring Hope.* Dr. Enright is a professor of Educational Psychology at the University of Wisconsin, Madison. His book, *Forgiveness Is a Choice* is one of the most comprehensive non-religious books on forgiveness available.

Chögyam Trungpa Rinpoche, *The Sacred Path of the Warrior.* Credited as the lama who brought Tibetan Buddhism to the West, Trungpa was a Buddhist meditation master, as well as a scholar, teacher, artist, and founder of Shambhala, an international organization based on the idea that enlightened society is not purely mythical—it is realizable by people of all faiths through mindfulness, non-aggression, and a sacred outlook. This book addresses both personal and societal problems by introducing a model of "sacred warrior-ship," which promotes the courage of egoless-ness as a way to move toward what he calls enlightened society.

Somatic Experiencing, http://traumahealing.org/. Somatic Experiencing® is a body-centered approach to the healing of trauma and other stress disorders. It is the life's work of Dr. Peter A. Levine, and it emerges from his clinical study of stress physiology, psychology, ethology, biology, neuroscience, indigenous healing practices, and medical biophysics. Levine is the author of the bestselling book *Waking the Tiger: Healing Trauma*. The SE approach actively addresses wounds of emotional and early developmental attachment trauma. The website includes helpful articles and videos that orient visitors to what it means to get centered in the body while doing healing work.

The Forgiveness Academy™, http://forgivenessacademy.com. The Forgiveness Academy™ was born out of Emily J. Hooks' mission to share the power and purpose of forgiveness as a personal healing practice with the world. The vision of the Academy is to teach individuals, practitioners, and organizations to become forgiving, compassionate entities. We offer one-on-one coaching, workshops, group training, and online courses all designed to help transition the personal paradigm to one of wholeness and integration into the world in which we live.

We would love to connect with you.

Follow the book on Facebook at:
https://www.facebook.com/PowerOfForgivenessBook/

Join our closed Facebook group of loving, conscientious human beings all focused on supporting each other on our journey toward wholeness at:
https://www.facebook.com/groups/ForgivenessAcademy/

Sign up for the Forgiveness Academy newsletter and blog at:
http://emilyjhooks.com/

Follow us on Instagram and Twitter **@forgiveacademy**

Made in the USA
Coppell, TX
26 September 2020

38815727R00085